JILO

A WITCHING SAVANNAH NOVEL

By J.D. Horn

Witching Savannah

The Line
The Source
The Void

Shivaree
Pretty Enough to Catch Her: A Short Story
Phantasma: Stories (contributor)

J.D. HORN

JILO

A WITCHING SAVANNAH NOVEL

Published by 47North, Seattle
www.apub.com

Amazon, the Amazon logo, and 47North are trademarks of Amazon.com, Inc., or its affiliates.

ISBN-13: 9781503953734
ISBN-10: 1503953734

Cover design by Ray Lundgren
Illustrated by Patrick Arrasmith
Family tree illustrations by Franz Vohwinkel

Printed in the United States of America

This one's for Rich. He believed even when I couldn't.

BOOK ONE:
MOTHER MAY WILLS

ONE

Savannah, Georgia—August 1932

"The old woman couldn't a picked a hotter day to get herself buried," Jesse Wills whispered as he wiped his brow. A nervous smile came to his lips. The secrets of living and dying would forever remain a mystery to him, but he knew one thing for certain, and that was if his grandmother were alive to hear him speak of her as "the old woman," she'd be chasing him around this here boneyard with a willow switch. "Sorry there, Nana," he mumbled under his breath, not so sure he shared his wife Betty's Christian certainty as to the final disposition of the human soul. If anyone could figure out how to hold on to a piece of this world after passing, it would be his grandmother, Tuesday Jackson.

She'd been a tough old gal right up to the end, his nana. Barely five foot tall and light enough for a good wind to topple, Nana Tuesday had been tough enough to best Joe Louis in any fight. A fool might have messed with Tuesday Jackson once, but he'd never do it twice. Jesse himself had tried her patience more than that, of course, but he was not just any old fool; he had been her favorite grandbaby.

Now she was gone. Being placed in Laurel Grove South Cemetery's earth, one grave over from where Jesse's daddy lay. Right next to the plot his mama had reserved for herself. It wasn't the old way. Used to be his daddy would lie with his own people, near the grave of his own mother, but his daddy's mama had been buried out on St. Helena Island. And Jesse's mama wanted her husband near, where she could visit him. Besides, the world had changed. At least in some ways.

Jesse's cousins had invited their minister, young Pastor Jones, the preacher at Wildwood Congregational, to officiate a graveside service. Nana had never darkened the church's door in her life, so it didn't seem right dragging her in there now, when she no longer had any say over the matter. No, Nana Tuesday had never been a churchgoing lady. When visiting out on Daufuskie or Hilton Head, she would go to the woods to do her praying, or on the rare occasion, to a Praise House. For the most part, she had preferred to keep her religion between herself and her maker, not seeing it as being anyone else's business.

It did no harm, though, in Jesse's eyes, to let the fiery preacher bring comfort to those members of his family who couldn't reconcile his nana's beliefs and practices with their own faith. Could've been worse, anyway. His cousin Joe had gotten all caught up with Father Divine. Ended up handing over everything he had to the man 'cept the very clothes on his back. No, Pastor Jones was certainly the lesser of those two evils. Still, Jesse began his own private prayer that the young fellow would be fast about burning off the steam he'd built up.

Jesse and his little family hung back on the periphery, ceding the area nearest the grave to his uncles, aunties, and cousins, the combined mass of them forming a swaying and waving mostly white-clad circle around it. He loved his nana, as much if not more than any of them, but there'd been no love lost between his wife and grandmother, and the whole family knew it. Best to keep Betty back where her comments stood a better chance of going unheard or at least unheeded.

"Oh, this heat ain't natural weather," Betty said, fanning herself with one hand and shielding her eyes from the morning glare with the other. Those clear hazel upturned eyes sparkled from her coppery oval face. That face was framed by hair straightened by means of Madam Walker's pomade, then curled into finger waves. She'd stained her lips red; her eyelids wore a powdery blue.

Even after all these years among his people, even after marrying him and bearing him children, the way Betty spoke—so slow and with a slight twang like the inland buckra, the whites—bore witness to the fact that she had never become one of his people. "This here heat is hell openin' its mouth," she continued, "to swallow the old woman's black soul." She looked away from his nana's grave and scanned the cemetery. "I can't see why any good Christian graveyard would take her bones anyhow. I mean, this here place is for burying good God-fearing people, not witches."

"She was no witch," Jesse said, a burst of anger causing his voice to come out low and sharp. "She was my grandmother. My mama's mama." His gaze drifted for a moment to his mother, May Jackson Wills. Her eyes had nearly swollen shut from crying. She bobbed at the knees, then rocked slowly back and forth with her arms drawn up tight around her bosom. "And you will show her the respect she deserves." Jesse couldn't bear to see his mama like this. He was her only child. He wanted to go to her and take her in his arms. Calm the low wailing that sounded from her breaking heart. But he couldn't risk leaving his wife for fear she'd get something stirred up in the few moments he was gone.

The sight of his mother's pain hurt him too deeply, so he focused instead on his wife. " 'Sides, you're a fine one to brag about being a good Christian." He said it to hurt her, to punish her, but he regretted it the next instant. Betty's glance met his for a sharp moment, but then she cast angry eyes down at that hot sandy soil and pursed her full lips into a little-girl pout. The same pout that had helped win his heart in the first place.

He stood there, for the moment transfixed by a sentiment from their younger days. Betty shifted from one foot to the other, as if she were growing weary under the weight of his continued stare. When her eyes flashed up to his, the hard defiant look had smoothed into a calm, knowing smile. She knew him too well. She knew he couldn't give her up, any more than he could give up that dark brown—way too dark to be his—baby girl she'd recently birthed. He looked over to see his two natural daughters, Opal and Poppy, standing near the fence that marked the cemetery's edge. The girls held back, even from him and their mama, without any prompting. They seemed to share his sense that it would be best for them to keep to the periphery of the gathering.

Opal looked like her mother, except for the unfortunate addition of his ears. Poppy was the dead ringer of his mama, who in her youth had been as beautiful as Betty, maybe even more so seeing as how his mama's beauty never relied on any manmade artifice. The little one, squirming in her big sister Opal's arms, didn't resemble any of them. And still, he loved her as surely as he did the ones who bore his likeness.

The sun was heading up in the sky, and the fresh heat it brought was unforgiving. His starched white shirt felt like a plaster cast, what with the sweat that ringed his underarms and banded the back of his shoulders where the garment pulled tight. "You keep Jilo in the shade," he called out, and Opal moved out of the sun, taking shelter beneath the canopy of an ancient live oak.

Betty had it right, of course—he could forgive her infidelity; in truth, he could forgive her for just about anything. He loved that head-strong woman to her core. Besides, she still had the power to make him stop dead in his tracks and stare after her, just like that day he'd first laid eyes on her in Atlanta, outside her daddy's store where he'd worked while putting himself through school. For her part, Betty hadn't shown much interest in him until her daddy out-and-out forbade the court-ship. If they took up together, her daddy had shouted out loud enough for the entire city to hear, she'd be marrying poorer. She'd be marrying darker. She'd be marrying down. Still, take up with each other they did, and one fine morning around twelve years back, Jesse and the then fifteen-year-old Betty eloped, leaving Atlanta behind and settling in Savannah, where Jesse himself had been raised.

"Forty acres and a mule," a cousin of his called out, then laughed, making Jesse realize how far his thoughts had drifted from his nana's burial. The knowing chuckles from those gathered told him he wasn't the only one who wished the preacher would be done with his business. Pastor Jones was still talking, but that wasn't going to stop the rest of them from eulogizing Nana Tuesday in their own way.

Jesse had missed whatever prompted his cousin's comment, but that phrase would always make him think of his nana. "Forty acres and a mule," she'd shout out in those moments when the distant past grew sharper in focus than the everyday world around her. "That's what they promised us, forty acres and a mule." Then she'd laugh, as if she found humor in her own youthful naiveté.

The buckra cursed William Tecumseh Sherman as the Yankee devil who'd burned a swath through the South, torching everything right up to Savannah's back door, then giving the city to his president as a Christmas present. To the newly freed people like Nana Tuesday, Sherman's Special Field Orders, No. 15 must have made him seem like the second coming of Christ himself. Old No. 15 granted the freedmen ownership of a good bit of the South Carolina coast. Other promises granted them the Sea Islands from Seabrook to Cumberland.

Even today, nearly seventy years later, the white folk around here still cursed Sherman for his fiery march, but the promises Sherman made to Jesse's people barely lasted a full trip around the sun. No. 15 was overturned before Lincoln was cold in his grave, and any land that hadn't been purchased outright by the former slaves was returned to the hands of their erstwhile masters. Nana had spent pretty near her whole darned life in Yamacraw, the area just south of the river and west of West Broad Street, but the only land she'd ever owned was the dirt left on her shoes by Yamacraw's dusty lanes.

Now, the rich whites were nibbling away at the Sea Islands, or in some cases trying to swallow them whole like that Coffin fellow did twenty years back with Sapelo. Just stepped in and bought up every inch the black folk there couldn't prove they owned. Even built his mansion over the foundation of the old slave master Spalding's house. Jesse had to wonder if it was possible to build your home on the same foundation without fostering the same ambition in your heart.

The sound of Betty clicking her tongue caught his attention. "Cups and spoons and broken plates," she started in again, shaking her head as she surveyed his family. "These people done brought half the kitchen out here. She getting buried, not setting up house. She ain't got no more use for these things where she done gone."

"It's my people's way."

"Well, y'all people got some mighty funny ways," she said, as if she were a disapproving stranger, not a woman who'd made her home among them for a dozen years.

Jesse's family didn't keep up too much with the old ways, at least not here on the mainland. They seemed to have two separate ways of living, two distinct languages, the one bound to the "sweet" water of the mainland, the other seeming to spring from the salt water that cocooned the islands. In their everyday lives, they were so careful, so intent on avoiding behavior that might draw the white man's attention, or worse, his ire. But they were so much freer on rare visits to Daufuskie or St. Helena, and their speech buzzed with words remembered from tongues spoken clean on the other side of the ocean. Jesse had enjoyed explaining his family's customs to Betty early on in their marriage, but he had realized he would never be able to surmount her contempt for their traditions. Now he repeated the same tired explanation he'd given her many times over the years. "These things were special to Nana. Things she used. Bits and pieces of her life. They're memorials, nothing more. You know that."

"What I know is that it don't matter one whit what people put on your grave if you weren't right with Jesus when you died. It's too late for that old gal now. This here heat is proof enough of where she went. We need to finish putting her in the ground and get on with things."

"Well you just let Jesus be her judge and mind your own self," snapped his auntie Martha, who usually pretended to be deaf when in Betty's presence.

Betty's eyes flashed, and she rocked back and forth in a show of defiance, but she must have realized she'd been pressing her luck. She held her tongue.

"Amen, sister," young Reverend Jones shouted out, picking up on Martha's words, though Jesse felt sure he'd been too deep into his own preaching to have heard Betty's. "That's right, Jesus, He is Sister Tuesday's judge, just as He is the judge of us all." A smirk formed on Betty's lips, and in spite of himself, Jesse couldn't help but return it. Had she been a living spectator to the proceedings, Nana Tuesday would have without a doubt hurled some sharp words at this man of God. While she would have allowed him to call her "Mother Tuesday," as most of the folk, black and white, around here did, such a young man would get a mouthful for treating her like a little sister.

"Thank you, Pastor," Jesse's mama said, placing her hand on his shoulder. Pastor Jones looked at her, Bible still held high, seeming to deliberate whether or not he should shrug her off and carry on. "I do so appreciate you coming out today," May added in a sincere tone. Jesse knew his mama, though, and despite her calm demeanor, he knew she'd heard enough. The preacher had been given more than enough time to speak of wheat and chaff and wise virgins with well-trimmed wicks. The look on her face was the one she used when placating anyone in authority—usually the buckra, but occasionally one of their own. "We need to be getting the babies and the old folk out of the sun before one of them falls ill."

The young man searched her face for a moment, then acquiesced. "Thank you, sister," he said, taking a step back from the head of the grave.

Jesse's mama smiled again at the preacher. "You go on, now," she said, dismissing him in no uncertain terms. "We can handle it from here." Jones lingered for a moment, as if considering whether he should listen, then nodded and walked away from the grave, passing by Jesse and his family on his way to the cemetery gate. He hesitated a moment when he reached Jesse's daughters, who watched the young pastor with listless trepidation. Opal shifted Jilo, balancing the baby on her hip. Jones reached out to pat Poppy's head, but then stopped dead at the sight of Jilo, doll-like in her starched white cap and gown. The pastor pulled his hand back slowly and hurried on toward the gate. Silence fell over the group until he was well beyond the boundary.

"Opal," his mother called. Jesse's eyes darted to his daughter.

"Yes'm." The girl startled and straightened to attention at the sound of her nana's voice.

"You bring your sister on up here," Jesse's mama instructed. "Bring Jilo to me."

Jesse felt Betty tensing beside him. "You stay right where you are, girl," Betty said, wagging her finger at Opal, who seemed nearly split in two by her desire to please both her nana and her mama at the same time. "What you need my Jilo for?" Betty took a few steps forward. Jesse couldn't help but notice that she had moved toward his mother, ready for confrontation, rather than toward her baby, ready to protect.

He knew there was no need to protect Jilo from anything that was going to happen here, so while Betty geared herself up for a shouting matching with his mama, he stepped back and approached the girls. "Let me have her," he said with a nod to Opal. Her face relaxed in gratitude as she handed the baby over.

Jesse took Jilo in both hands and shifted her into the crook of his arm. He leaned his head over to plant a kiss on her round cheek, then reached out and ran his thumb over Opal's cheek as well. Over the sound of their mama's indignant shouting, Jesse winked and said, "Your daddy has the best girls in the whole wide world; you know that, don't you?" A smile curved on Opal's lips, and she blinked once before nodding her response.

"And you, my little flower?" he said, turning toward Poppy, who scurried up to him and hugged his leg. He patted her head. "I love my girls," he said. "All three of them." When Poppy released him and slid back next to Opal, he closed his eyes for a moment before turning to face the scene unfolding behind him.

"And I," Betty said, waving her finger in his mama's face, "am not gonna have my babies take part in any of the old woman's Hoodoo. You hear me?"

"Jilo," his mama replied in her calmest voice, even though the angry set of her mouth and the crease that lined the center of her forehead told Jesse she was anything but relaxed, "is the last born. You want to be good and clear of the *old* woman"–her head rocked in indignation–"then we need to pass Jilo over the coffin."

Jesse had almost reached his mother's side when Betty caught sight of him. She pushed roughly past the mourners who didn't have the sense to part between them like the Red Sea at the wave of Moses's staff. "Gimme the girl."

Jesse took a step backward and placed his hand over the back of Jilo's little capped head. "It's our way."

"It may be your way, but it ain't my way, and she's my child." Betty now stood within spitting distance of him, her chest and shoulders heaving. She flung out her arms, grasping at the linen of Jilo's gown.

There was no way he was relinquishing the girl to those clenched and angry hands. "She's my child, too." For a moment, Betty's face froze. Then her eyes narrowed, and she tilted her head. Her lips parted, readying to speak the truth that his cousins had been whispering behind his back, the truth his gut already knew. The truth that his own heart told him was the greatest lie of all. But then she stopped. Her tongue darted out of her mouth and licked her lips instead.

She gestured with a wide wave of her arm that included him, his mother, the casket, and the baby. "All right, y'all heathens go right on ahead. Y'all do what you need to do." She spun around and stomped off, heading toward the gate.

Opal and Poppy started to take off after her, but their mother swung her hand back, signaling for them to stay put. Jesse could read the worry and confusion on their little faces from a hundred paces. "You come up here with Daddy and Nana," he called to them. They hesitated, keeping an eye on their mother's receding back. "Come on," he said and urged them forward with a wave of his free hand. The two girls joined hands and walked forward with some lingering trepidation.

Jesse's mother positioned herself on the opposite side of the coffin. He shifted Jilo off his shoulder, taking her in both hands. She gurgled with laughter, a bit of drool falling from the side of her mouth. Her black eyes twinkled with such love and intelligence, so much soul. It was like she'd already lived a thousand lives, and held every secret of the universe in her chubby, damp hands. He pulled her in close and placed a kiss on her forehead, then reached her over the casket to his mother.

His mama's calloused, yet gentle, hands brushed his. As he let Jilo drop into her grasp, his ears were met with a loud pop, and his eyes registered a flash of bluish light. Everyone stood there gaping in silent amazement. Jilo squealed happily and reached her chubby arms across the void of his nana's grave toward him, a joyous mystery playing in her eyes.

TWO

It was May who had found her mama, and she had covered her mama's face with a towel before alerting the others, hoping to spare her family from the sight. Her mama hadn't gone easy. Still, there were those, including her sisters, who'd insisted on laying eyes on their mama before they could accept she was truly gone. Their souls now carried the same burden May's did.

The mortician, artist though he was, had not succeeded in erasing the look her mama's passing had left on her face. He had gummed her eyes and sewed her mouth closed, but her features remained a frozen, bloodless gray—her brow raised and creased, her jaw jutting forward, her neck arched in an eternal scream. May and her sisters had agreed it was best to keep the coffin closed to spare the others.

It was the magic that had killed her, May felt sure of that. May didn't know a thing about working magic, but she'd grown up feeling it try to work her. It was always pushing to break through the dam her mama had helped her build up against it. Always looking for holes in her dreams while she was sleeping, whispering seductively while she was awake, promising her quick solutions whenever her problems grew heavy on her shoulders. But no. Her mama had put the fear of the magic in her, and May was bound and determined never to go down the path her mama had traveled.

The night before her death, May's mama had come around in the wee hours and let herself into May's home unannounced, just about scaring her out of her wits. May had roused to find the older woman bent over her, the smell of rum thick on her warm breath. "Don't you forget your promise to your mama," her mother said, her lips pressing against her ear. "When your mama's gone, the magic may come after you good and hard, but you don't let it touch you."

Her mama reached down and placed the palm of her hand along May's jaw. "You hear me?" She released May and lowered herself down to sit on the edge of the mattress.

"Yes, ma'am," May said, pushing herself up on her elbows. "You okay, Mama?"

"Your mama, she's just tired. Worn out." She lay down beside May, and May shifted to make room, wrapping an arm around the frail woman once she was settled. "She's been fighting those devils too long, but she's gonna put an end to it now, one way or the other. Even if it kills her."

May didn't ask who "those devils" were, or just how her mama planned to handle them. Getting Tuesday Jackson to share more than she had a mind to speak had always been an impossible task. A direct question would have been met with silence. May lay there quietly, hoping the rum she smelled on her mother's breath might loosen her tongue, but it didn't. Soon, May drifted off. That morning she awoke, as she always did, well before dawn, only to find her mother had already risen and left the house.

Now that May's mama was gone, May wished she hadn't given herself over to sleep that night. She would never lay eyes on her mama again, at least not on this side of the veil.

May knelt beside the filled grave, laying a piece of a broken cup there. Most of the family had already taken off, heading south to May's house by car or by foot, Jilo's name on all their lips. They'd be talking for years to come, no doubt, about how May's youngest granddaughter seemed to have been kissed by the magic. Jesse himself didn't believe Jilo was his, at least not by blood, so May didn't know what to make of the spark that had passed from the grave to the girl. In this moment, she had neither the time nor the strength to consider its significance. It was only a short walk from the cemetery down Ogeechee Road to the dirt road leading to her house, so even those relatives inclined to take a more leisurely pace had probably found their way to the turnoff. They all knew the way, even though most of them didn't live around here.

Her mama had done her darnedest to convince May and her siblings to get the hell out of Savannah, encouraging them to get as far away as they could. She'd succeeded to some degree with May's brother and sisters, which had left the extended family scattered from Augusta to Jacksonville. "Not far enough," had been her mama's staple reply whenever May complained that her sisters lived too far for regular visits. Her brother, Louis, had made it as far as Macon, but he was gone now, too, buried in a plot half a state away, mixed in with his wife Miriam's people.

May, well, she'd married Reuben, and his job, as well as his inclination, had demanded they stay in Savannah. May glanced over at the empty plot between her husband and her mother, both chilled and comforted by the knowledge that she would one day take her rest there.

But there'd be no rest for her today. Even though many of her kin had come bearing baskets of food to share, she'd have to see to feeding the horde descending on her home before packing them back into their vehicles or pointing them north toward the train station. Family as thick as a swarm of locusts today, and nothing but loneliness to contend with tonight.

The caretaker of the cemetery stood at a distance, leaning on the same rake he would use to scrape the grave clear of the pottery as soon as the last of the family was out of sight. The cemetery belonged to the city, after all, and Savannah had no more room for the family's traditions than her fool of a daughter-in-law did.

May was surprised to see a young white man approach the caretaker. Even from this distance, which made it hard to get a good look at his features, May could see his suit appeared well made, expensive. His light blond hair caught the light. May wondered what interest this buckra could have in an old black woman's funeral, his gaze fixed as it was on the dwindling party. She watched as the caretaker nodded his head again and again, like it was on a loose spring. He seemed anxious to convey his understanding of—or perhaps agreement to—the white man's words. The two conversed for another minute or so, then the white man reached out and patted the caretaker's back. He turned away and headed toward a shiny black car waiting just outside the cemetery gate. As the buckra drew near, another man, dressed in livery, rushed to open the car's back door at the exact moment of his arrival.

"You recognize that fellow?" she asked Jesse with a small nod at the car that was already pulling away. An overtired Poppy began crying and tugging on her father's pant leg.

"No ma'am," Jesse said, holding out the baby for her to take. She accepted Jilo from him and wrapped her in a tight embrace. Jesse knelt to scoop up Poppy. "Probably just someone looking for the entrance of the white section. We should get back to the house now. Folk are there already, I bet."

"Maybe," she said, "but seems to me that a fellow who can afford a car like that would have sent his driver to ask directions, not come on his own. No," she shook her head, feeling a chill run down her spine, "I think that man wanted to get a good look at us, at what we're doing here."

"I recognize him," her sister-in-law Martha said, drawing near and leaning in like she had good gossip to share. "That there is that Maguire boy. He's probably come looking for your mama's help."

It was true, her mama had occasionally met those seeking her assistance at the cemetery's entrance. Still, the young man's presence didn't sit right with her.

"Help for what?" May found her gaze turning back to the caretaker, who shifted uneasily from foot to foot under the weight of her stare.

"It was all in the papers yesterday. His father, big man Maguire, had a bad stroke the same night your mama passed. Looks like he might not be long for this earth either. Reckon the doctors told the boy they can't help his daddy, so he came looking to see if your mama could."

"Well, he came a bit late for Nana's help," Jesse said, hefting Poppy up onto his shoulders.

"That he did," May said, placing her hand behind Jilo's tiny head and hugging the girl close. "That he did."

THREE

Cousins, uncles, and aunties were spread out around Jesse's mama's house and yard. The older folk, those around Nana Tuesday's age, sat crammed tight inside the darkened living room, taking their turns at soughing, snoring, and fanning themselves as one reminiscence after another rose up and got passed around, either prompting smiles or birthing discord depending on the memory and how it was either recalled or misremembered. Family members his mama's age and younger had taken to the out-of-doors, sprawling out on blankets beneath the shade afforded by the tall oaks at the rear edge of the property, praying for a breeze.

Jesse's aunties by blood hovered around the kitchen, getting under his mama's feet, arguing over the cooking. Aunties through marriage, the wives of his father's kin, knew better than to join the fray, choosing instead to watch over the children, both the little sleeping ones like Jilo, and the wild, older ones, who were roughhousing and running around, shrieking with laughter until someone would remind them of the passing they'd come to honor. For a time, the laughter would fall silent, replaced by an unnatural, though blessedly temporary, stillness.

Jesse didn't like the quiet. When it got quiet he could hear his family's whispers.

That his mama owned this place outright stood as a matter of pride for the whole family. Not many folk around Savannah, white or colored, owned their own houses, and this one even had enough land for a vegetable garden. Jesse's daddy had been a cook on one of the Central Railroad's executive cars. He'd worked for years to squirrel away the money for this house, not wanting to marry until he had a home for his wife. That was why he'd married a woman sixteen years his junior. "I was his queen," his mama often said of his daddy, "and this place here," she would add with a tone of solemn pride, "was his castle."

Just a bit south of the cemetery, the house was bounded by a creek and a thick cluster of live oaks and pines, which, to Jesse's childhood imagination, seemed to go on forever. He knew this house and its land would come to him one day, after his own mama died. Now, though, he and his family lived in the city's new projects in Yamacraw, joined hips and shoulders to their neighbors with barely the room to spit between. His mama wanted them here with her, but, much to Jesse's shame, blood between Betty and his mama was bad.

The silent glares of disapproval his mama cast at Betty were proof enough of her disappointment in Jesse's choices. She'd sacrificed to get him into the university so that he could become a lawyer or a doctor. Not the dockworker he'd become to support his young wife. Betty refused to live under his mother's roof, where, to be fair, she had never been made to feel welcome. Instead, she used the dusty and crowded streets of Yamacraw to remind him of his failures without ever having to say a word.

By any right, the front porch should be sagging under the weight of his extended family, but Jesse sat alone on the freshly lacquered white swing, beneath the fading haint-blue overhang. His kin was either avoiding him or giving him breathing space. Maybe it came down to a little bit of both. Jesse didn't really give a good goddamn which it was. He'd chosen this seat for a reason, and that was to keep an eye on the bend of the road in anticipation of Betty's return.

The screen door cried out as Aunt Miriam, his Uncle Louis's widow, came out onto the porch, carrying a plate covered with rice and a shrimp-and-okra gumbo. A thick slice of golden cornbread crowned the feast. "Your mama sent this out to you. She wants you to eat."

Jesse didn't want to eat. His pride was hurting. Still, his stomach rumbled at the scent of ginger, garlic, and bay leaf riding beneath the hot sweetness of cinnamon. Biting his lip to keep it from quivering, he shook his head and waved her away.

Shame was riding him like the hag, drawing the very breath out of him. The other men, the ones old enough to be married, had their plates brought out to them by their wives. Even when she was around, Jesse's wife wasn't the kind to go fetching him anything. But after strutting out of the graveyard, Betty had taken off in a direction that decidedly wasn't homeward. No, she hadn't gone home, and she sure as shooting wasn't here. Nobody said a word, but a knowing look passed from face to face, a silent telegraph conveying a dirty supposition of where Betty was headed: off to a man who decidedly wasn't Jesse.

His aunt Miriam's face fell, making him feel all the worse. Jesse realized she'd been using the opportunity to look after him to fill the gap her husband's death had left in her heart. "I'm sorry," he began to say, but she'd already turned away, the scream of the screen door drowning out his mumbled regrets.

His gaze drifted back to the gray sandy path that passed for a drive. Empty. Dry and dusty. He found himself praying for rain. A good solid downpour that would drive his nattering family with their sly smiles clean off his mama's land. A new flood that would wash down the whole world, rinsing away its sins. And Jesse, the new Noah, could ride out the storm with those he loved, on a tiny floating island built by his own hand. No other men to catch Betty's eye, no other man to fill the spot in her heart or her womanhood, the two parts of her he'd once thought she held sacred for him.

He felt eyes on him. "I cooked this to your nana's tastes." His mama stood before him, grasping the plate he'd refused. Jesse was surprised he hadn't heard her approach. He wondered how many other things happened right under his nose without him noticing. "You'd be showing disrespect not to eat. To your nana and me both." His mama held the plate out to him and waited. "Baby," she said after a moment, her tone comforting. "It's yo' girl everyone talkin' about, not your wife."

Defeated, he took the plate, but lowered his eyes. "And what they're saying is that Jilo isn't my girl." He felt a pang in his heart. "But she is. Even if she isn't, she is."

"Of course she is," she said, "and you send anyone who says otherwise to me. I'll clear things up for them right quick." His lowered gaze came to rest on her hands. She was rubbing the knuckles of her left hand with the fingers of her right. Jesse could tell her arthritis was bothering her; her joints were swollen, and holding the plate had seemed like work for her. Arthritis had flared up in her early, way too early. His nana could have used her magic to ease his mama's suffering, but he knew she had never offered, and his mama had never asked.

"No," Mama continued, "what they saying is 'Old Tuesday' left a bit of her soul with Jilo. They saying Jilo gonna have the power now." She sat down at his side, the old swing complaining about the added burden. "Eat," she said, tilting her chin down and looking at him with one eye opened a tad wider than the other. He knew this look. He'd grown up seeing it creep onto his mama's face right before she lost patience with him.

He took a bite. Then another. It was delicious, but his heart remained heavy. He let the fork rest on the plate. "You think they're right?"

His mama shook her head. "No, that was just Mama kissing the little one good-bye. She was telling us she was proud we were honoring her in the old way, but she took whatever magic she had with her." She reached out and lifted his chin, turning his face toward her. "You and I both know she didn't want her magic to live on past her. That's why she never showed me any of it. That's why she never let us rely on it. She didn't want none of that for us."

"Some folk are saying she sold her soul to have it. That she's down with the devil now," he said, regretting his words the second he uttered them. Not only did he not want to bring his mama further pain, he knew she'd know "those folk" were none other than his own wife.

"Then I feel mighty sorry for Old Mr. Scratch," she said, surprising him with a laugh, " 'cause if she is, he's dancing to her tune now." She ran her hand down the back of his head, like she used to do to comfort him when he was still just a boy. Her smile flattened. "The good Lord," she said, her voice dropping lower, growing softer. "He sees into our hearts. I don't know. Maybe Mama did sell her soul for her magic, but if she did, she did it for good reason. I got every faith He's gonna redeem my mama in the end."

She reached over to his plate to retrieve the fork, which she handed to him. "Eat. I ain't leaving till that plate is clean, and I'm going to blame you for any foolishness your aunties get up to in there while I'm gone." She winked at him, a smile spreading across her face, and he took the fork from her calloused fingers and dug in.

"Good boy."

The front door banged open. "May," Miriam called out over the plaintive cry of the screen door's hinges, "we calling all the children in out of the trees." She was trembling as she came to a stop in front of them.

"Why, what's wrong?" Jesse's mama asked, pushing up from the swing.

"The older ones," Miriam said. "They wandered too far out back, all the way to the clearing."

"They shouldn't be going back there." Mama shook her head, reaching down and bracing her lower back. "My land ends just beyond the tree line. I done told you all a thousand and one times not to wander too far back. That's buckra land beyond the trees. Those young ones are gonna get themselves shot for trespassing."

"We done called them in," said Jesse's cousin Charles, joining the conversation as he came around the side of the house, steering his two boys along with him, one hand on the shoulder of each. He maneuvered them toward the porch steps, but stopped short. The younger boy seemed scared half to death, his eyes wide and moist, his wiry frame shaking. "This one," Charles said, giving Toby, the taller of the two, a shake, "he's the one who found him, then the dummy called his little brother over to see him, too."

"Found who?" Jesse asked, standing and resting his plate on the swing.

"The dead boy," Charles said, seeming surprised that word hadn't yet reached the front porch. A swarm of relatives started to circle around the house. Those with cars began to pile their children inside; those without toted their baskets and dragged their little ones along with them, only pausing to give a quick wave of farewell.

"You found a dead boy?" Mama asked the boys.

"Yeah," Charles answered for his sons. "I done seen the body, too. Lying there buck naked." His forehead wrinkled. "Them who did it slit him clean open from his throat all the way down to his privates." Charles's lips puckered, then he turned and spat.

"It's Rosie's boy," Toby said, tugging against his daddy's grasp. Rosie was a white woman who lived out on the edge of the colored area. She made her living selling corn liquor and the spot between her legs.

Boys and girls had been disappearing around this part of town for as long as Jesse could remember. People didn't talk about it. Not out in the open, at least. Most were deemed runaways by the law, but twice before within the span of his memory, boys had turned up butchered in the exact manner Charles was describing. Both of them colored. Rosie's boy was white. The killings of the colored boys never got much official attention. The murder of a white child would, even if the dead boy's mama was the town whore.

Although several years had passed between the murders and disappearances, Jesse didn't doubt that the killer was the same man. Nana Tuesday, she may or may not have known who it was, but she sure knew the reason for the killings, and she had taken precautions to make sure Jesse would never end up like Rosie's boy.

"Boy never was quite right," Aunt Miriam muttered. It was true. Some folk blamed syphilis, others Rosie's heavy drinking, but it was undeniable the boy had been left dull witted and deformed.

"Yeah, but he was still white," Charles said, giving voice to what they were all likely thinking. Either the killer had grown more brazen or more desperate. "He wasn't killed there. Not enough blood for that. Just dumped there."

Jesse's mama took a few steps toward the porch stairs. "Tell me," her voice was low, "did they leave any kind of marks on him?"

Charles nodded. "Lines and squiggles." The school board had just approved yet another school for the white children, but Savannah only had a couple of schools for the colored. These buildings were dilapidated—one of them had even been condemned—and they lacked light and sufficient seats. Even though both schools offered two shifts of classes per day, half of the black children in town never got the chance to attend, and out of those who did, most never got to go further than the second or third grade. Charles had enrolled his boys, but Jesse wasn't sure Charles himself had received the same opportunity. He wasn't even sure this cousin from his father's side of the family could read.

His mama must have had a similar thought because she turned to Toby. "You saw the boy twice. What did they look like?"

"Nothing really, just scribbles," Toby said. "Not like words or anything. Just circles and lines and stars, like this . . ." He squatted down and began to draw the shapes he remembered.

"Don't you do that," Jesse's mama snapped before the youngster could get two lines linked together. "Don't you ever draw those markings out. You forget 'em now." The terror in her voice caused Jesse's skin to prickle. Her eyes were round and full of fear, even though Jesse felt sure she had no clearer idea of what the aborted symbol might signify than he did. She was afraid of magic—Nana Tuesday had seen to it that she would be.

His mama had been unfazed by the heat of the day, let alone the even greater heat of the kitchen, but now heavy beads of sweat formed and trickled down her face. She braced herself against a post and looked up at Jesse and Charles. "You make sure everybody knows to shut up about this. Ain't nobody found nothing. Nobody ever went back to that clearing." Her voice rose. "You hear me?"

"Yes, ma'am," Charles responded. "Ain't nobody gonna say anything. You know that." Jesse reckoned his cousin was right. A murdered white child meant somebody was gonna be facing the noose, and there were plenty of black men in the area, himself included, handy enough for the law to lay the blame on.

"You tell them all anyway," she said, the tone of her voice a stern warning.

"Yes ma'am," Charles repeated. Just then, Charles's wife, basket in hand, came around the side of the house and caught up to him. He nodded to her and began pushing his boys across the yard and down the drive.

"Ain't just the law we gotta worry about," his mama said, her gaze shifting between Miriam and Jesse. "Someone's sacrificing to the Red King. There's still a collector in these parts."

The Red King. Jesse had grown up sitting at his nana's feet, hearing stories about the four demon kings, Red and his brothers. She had never spoken of such things outside the family, but the story had grown legs and run around the community as member after member shared it, despite having promised Nana they never would. Maybe that had been her plan all along. If she'd asked them to spread a warning, folk would've laughed the story off as the rantings of an eccentric old woman. But forbid it to be told, and it gets whispered far and wide.

According to Nana, the three elder kings had been around pretty much forever. This very world had spun into being around them, but the youngest had only come to exist after man rose on this earth. All four took their nourishment from whatever spirit essence was left in a person's body after death, but each brother could only feed from a certain type of death.

The Red King gorged himself on the leftover energy of those who died by mishap or were struck down by others, whether the killing was personal or an act of war. The Yellow King took those who fell from disease or famine. The Black King, also called the "Kind King," only took from those who had seen the fullness of life. Seeing as how he fed on folk who were mostly used up, the Black King's pickings were always the slimmest, earning him a third name—the "Beggar King." He was a wispy shade that lingered among the shadows, coming most often while a body slept. The youngest brother, the White King, was also known as the "Mirror King." He always appeared as a warped reflection of those he targeted: faults, mistakes, and problems magnified to such a degree they'd destroy even the most stubborn sliver of hope. The White King held dominion over those who died by their own hand. He was the only one of his brethren who feasted solely on the human spirit.

Three of the demons were greedy, keeping all the spoils to themselves, but when a servant of the Red King honored him through killing, Red would share with the collector, converting a bit of the victim's forfeited life force into black magic for the collector's own use.

Nana Tuesday used to swear that while the brothers had never existed in the normal sense of the word, they were real all the same. This made little sense to Jesse, but Nana had seemed so sure.

His mama swallowed hard, and her eyes flashed, like a burst of lucidity had just helped her make a connection. "Your nana said she was gonna put an end to this, or die trying."

"Looks like she might've done just that," Miriam said. She held both hands up. "Dear sweet Jesus, I don't want to hear no more of this." With that, she turned and fled into the house.

A chill ran down Jesse's spine. He knew now his nana hadn't died from causes that came anywhere near natural. Jesse realized his daughters were nowhere in sight. He knew Jilo would be safe inside, but given the exodus that had just occurred, he wasn't sure anyone would be out back looking after the other two. "I need to find Opal and Poppy," Jesse said, and his mama nodded.

Jesse took the first three steps leading from the porch to the yard, then turned back to face his mama. "You don't believe any of this, do you? About the kings?"

The corners of her mouth pulled down as she considered his question. "I reckon it don't matter whether I believe it or not. Looks like someone does."

FOUR

In the closet of Jesse's boyhood room, on the shelf, pushed all the way back against the wall, sat an old cigar box. Somehow Jesse knew it would still be there even though he hadn't laid a hand on it—had made a point not to touch it—in twenty years. The box was decorated with a drawing of a man wearing a black top hat, a red kerchief, and matching red pants. His shirt, a long-sleeved white tunic of some kind, exposed a crescent of the man's chest.

In his mind's eye, Jesse could picture the box as clearly as he had the day he'd stowed it up there. In a place where it would be safe, and where it would in turn keep *him* safe.

Jesse's mama hadn't been entirely right in thinking Nana Tuesday hadn't passed down any of her magic. Jesse had received this box, and its mystery contents, from his grandmother's own hands. When he was a boy—just turned twelve, as he recalled—she'd called to him softly through his bedroom window one night, coaxing him out into the approaching twilight. Once he was outside, she held her finger up to his lips to signal that he shouldn't talk, then led him away from the house and into the grove of oaks that separated the house from the very field where the dead child now lay.

"He may call himself John," Nana Tuesday had said, pointing to the name inscribed above the picture, "but this is him all right. This here's the Red King. He changes how folk see him, so ain't no two folk ever agree on the shape of his face or the color of his skin, but you can always tell it's him from his tall hat and the fancy way he dress himself. From his shine for tobacco and rum, and from his foul language. These are the ways he shows himself to us." She placed the box in his hands. "I put somethin' in here, somethin' that will protect you from those who serve him, who *worship*"—she stressed the word—"him. You got to take this inside the house yourself. Nana can't do it, else he'll know she workin' against him. And you can't take it through the front door, either. That'll undo the magic. You take it back with you the same way you came out, you understand?"

Though he didn't rightly understand what that meant, he nodded and said, "Yes'm."

"Okay, then," she said. "Now you get back inside, 'fore your mama realize you out here." He turned and took a few quick steps away. "Jesse," his nana called out, causing him to turn back. "Don't you tell your mama about this. You keep it to yo'self."

"Yes'm," he repeated.

She called out to him once more as he was turning away. "And don't you ever try to open it. Nana sealed it for a reason. You keep that box shut and it'll keep you safe. You open it, and it gonna let out somethin' worse than what she trying to protect you from." She paused and gave him a good hard look. "You gonna try to open it?"

"No ma'am," he said.

"Good, then, you get on back inside."

He had no sooner shimmied back through his window than he held the box to his ear and shook it. Though it sounded empty, the heft of it told him there was something inside. He tugged on the lid, but the edge wouldn't even bend up. He set the box on his bed and fetched his prized pocketknife from his nightstand, intent on sticking the blade into the seam his nana had sealed with some kind of glue or wax. But as soon as he set the blade against the seal and pressed, he felt a whack against his fingers like he'd been caught in a mousetrap. A sharp pop sounded in his ears, and he was nearly blinded by a flash of light. He dropped the knife and shook his agonized hand, wanting to cry. He might have done so, too, but he heard the sound of his nana's laughter drifting in through his window.

He rushed to the opening. "Yo' nana knows you better than you know yourself," he heard her say, though she was nowhere in sight. "Now you put that thing away where it won't be a temptation."

That was all the scolding he'd needed to swipe it up from the bed and push it to the back of the closet shelf.

Until today, he'd done a pretty good job of forgetting about the box, but the thought of that simple child lying dead not a quarter mile away pushed it to the forefront of his thoughts. So did his mama's words about the Red King.

He no longer needed to stand on tiptoe to reach the box. He opened the closet door and reached back to where he felt the cool cardboard. He pulled it out into the light, shocked to see how closely the smiling face beneath its elegant top hat matched his memory. Turning the box, he placed the sharp edge of the knife he'd borrowed from the kitchen against the seal. As soon as he pressed the blade down, a sharp pain shot through him, so strong that he dropped the box to the floor. The Red King's smiling face looked up at him, mocking him.

Seemed that the magic still worked, and as soon as the feeling of having his fingers roasted left him, Jesse decided he was mighty glad of that fact.

There had been enough magic in it to protect him as a child. Now he hoped there would be enough to protect all three of his baby girls. The pain eased enough for him to reach down to grab the cigar box, but he pulled back at the last moment, his body remembering all too well the shock it had just experienced. *Damn*, he thought to himself, and made another swipe, this time forcing his hand to pick it up. "Not gonna try to open you," he said out loud. "Just want to take you home." As if the magic protecting the box understood him—a thought that sent a quiver through him—he felt a cooling sensation spread across his injured fingers and hand.

He turned and closed the closet door, then cast a glance around his old room—same bed, same curtains, same battered nightstand, and the drawer that would stick should he try to open it, full of cat's-eye marbles and sundry other boyhood treasures. Everything was still very much in its place—the only thing missing was him. He left the room, heading out to the front porch where he knew his mama was waiting with his daughters.

His mama had returned to the porch swing, Jilo now crying up a storm in her arms. Before going to his room, he'd also sent the squalling child's sisters to join their nana. Poppy sat next to them, and Opal was a few feet away in the yard, running around and kicking a ball one of her cousins must have forgotten. Everyone else had left.

"Little one's hungry," his mama said, jostling the baby in an attempt to calm her. "Cousin Rose, she took from her own child to nurse Jilo this afternoon, but Jilo's hungry again." Her expression hardened, her eyes narrowing and her nose scrunching up toward her brow in disgust. "*That woman* has no right just to run off and leave her baby. I could forgive her for the older . . ."

"I know, Mama," he said. "She needs her mother. I'll take her home . . ."

"What the child needs is a wet nurse. That woman can't handle being a mother. Do you think she can manage to pull her tit out for someone other than her—"

"Mama," his voice came out raised. "My girls are here. They can hear you."

As if in her anger she'd forgotten they were even there, she gave a dazed look to first Poppy and then Opal, who had just begun to climb the steps to the porch. "You're right. I'm sorry. It's been a long day. A long damn day."

He leaned over and kissed her forehead. "I'm sorry I raised my voice to you, Mama."

"No," she said. "You were right to."

Jesse turned and held the cigar box out to Opal. "Here, girl. You take this for me." She scooted closer and he pulled it up and out of her reach. "Do not," he stressed the second word, "try to open it." He lowered it into her waiting hands. Luckily for them all, his girls weren't disobedient like he'd been as a boy.

"What is that?" his mama asked, though Jilo let out an ear-piercing scream that nearly drowned her out. He reached out for his daughter, more than a little relieved when his mama surrendered her to him without a fuss. He'd almost thought she might refuse to send the girl home.

"Nothin', Mama," he said, feeling more than a little guilty. "Just something that reminds me of Nana," he added, hoping it was a large enough nugget of truth to negate the lie.

"She always did like her cigars," his mama said, her expression softening at some happy memory.

He took advantage of the moment. "I gotta get the girls home, Mama," he said again.

"This should be their home . . ."

"I know, Mama," he said, hoping to keep her calm. "Soon. I promise. I'll get all this worked out." Relaxing back onto the swing, his mama began stroking Poppy's hair.

He felt a chill run down between his shoulders. What if he was taking the one thing that had been keeping his mama safe here alone all these years?

If she knew, she would understand. If she knew, she would want the girls to be protected. If she knew, she would want this last bit of the magic her own mama raised her to fear right out of her house.

"You're gonna be okay?" he asked.

" 'Course I'm going to be." She turned to Poppy and smiled. "Your nana is going to be just fine."

Jilo had fallen momentarily silent, but she began wailing in earnest to make up for the respite she'd allowed their eardrums.

"Come on," Jesse said, waving Poppy off the swing. He hated that the girls were going to have to walk so far with dusk giving way to full dark. He'd planned on getting a ride from Cousin Harry and his new wife, Ruby, but they'd taken off in a hurry in the confusion following the discovery of the boy.

"All right, I'm going to get this one to her mama. I love you," he said to his mama, then carried Jilo, still pitching a fit, down the steps, his older girls following on his heels like goslings along the dusty road.

Jesse led the girls up Ogeechee, which bordered the clearing where the boy's body lay exposed to the elements and any animal that chose to get at the meat. The thought made him shudder and break out in gooseflesh. He held Jilo a bit more tightly and sent up a prayer that the child's soul was at peace. He felt a twinge of shame as his eyes touched the cigar box in Opal's arms. A prayer would suffice for the dead, but for the living he was glad to have something that packed a bit more of a punch.

FIVE

A soft kerosene glow filled May's kitchen; other than the occasional flash of heat lightning, the oil lamp on her table served as her sole source of light. The city hadn't yet seen fit to run the power lines to the small community west of Ogeechee, even though May could see the electric glow of Frogtown only spitting distance north. The city kept promising, but their promises weren't worth the breath they used to make them. She wasn't bothered by any of that right now, though. There were other problems weighing on her mind.

"What were you trying to tell me about the little one, Mama?" May sat at her empty table, in her empty house, posing her question to the empty air. Another wave of heat lightning lit up the room with three quick, bright flashes. "She ain't got no magic. She ain't even your blood. Not really. You know that."

May wrapped her hand around a steaming cup of chicory, shuddering at the thought that what was left of Rosie's boy lay not much more than a stone's throw from her property line. It shamed May to think she didn't even know the child's name. It shamed her worse to think Rosie might be wondering where he'd got to. She shook that thought off. From what she knew of Rosie, the woman probably had not even noticed the boy was missing. Still, the mother in May ached for her.

Rosie's boy had been killed for the kind of dark magic some folk thought could be bought from the Red King with blood. Could another magic, her mama's kind of magic, have protected him? Would the boy be home in his own bed right now, rather than rotting out in a field behind her house?

May set aside her cup.

God must have heard the boy's cries. Why hadn't He protected the boy? Seemed like He made a habit of letting good, innocent folk die. May knew the thought was blasphemous, but she couldn't shake it; it was like a small stain on her soul. She prayed for forgiveness and to gain understanding. A roar of distant thunder sounded like an angry response from God Himself, and a sudden gust of wind blew the back door clear open.

May pushed back from the table and rose, but as she reached out to shut the door, a movement near the tree line caught her eye. She stepped over the threshold, onto the upper step, and craned her neck to get a better look. The quickly advancing storm sent out a bright flash of lightning that for one moment brought full light, then in the next plunged the world into darkness, dazzling May's eyes. That split second had given her the impression of an approaching white dog, but there were no dogs like that in the area. She descended the stairs and took a few steps toward the trees, then stopped as hard and as sure as if she had walked into a wall. Her heart began to pound, her pulse throbbing in her neck even though she felt like every drop of her blood had pooled in her legs. The creature she'd thought to be a dog rose up on its hind feet.

It was no dog at all.

There, at the far end of her yard, coming toward her, she saw the pale figure of that poor, butchered boy, shuffling forward with an awkward gait, stumbling, falling, rising again.

"Sweet Jesus," her words straddled profanity and prayer. A sweat broke out all over her body, and though she was desperate to move, to flee, she found herself nailed to the spot. The child's pale naked skin shone nearly blue in the darkness, a fish-belly white in the next flash of lightning, and as the body drew closer, she could see that the wound to the boy's chest and stomach had been sewn together like some kind of rag doll with a thick, dark cord in a zigzag by a rough and cruel hand.

The eyes, too, had been sewn shut, large black Xs securing the lids. Still, the child's corpse carried on, coming straight toward her as sure as if it could see May frozen where she stood. Its arms spread wide, looking like it sought to embrace her. May could see the child's lips moving, even though no sound came out.

In the final moments before dead hands would touch her, her instinct to survive overpowered the terror holding her in place. May lifted one foot and stepped back. Then the other. She turned and began to flee, but something stopped her. Even though her eyes swore to her that it couldn't be true, she was overcome by a feeling of horrible certainty. She stopped and turned to face the monstrous sight that was now only a bit more than an arm's length away.

"Mama?" she asked, and the pale, destroyed body of the child fell to its knees before her. It raised its face toward heaven and lifted its arms in supplication, before lowering its hands to the sides of its head. Its lips opened wide, and May sensed that if it could make a sound, it would be howling.

She trembled as she took a cautious step toward the body. "Mama, is that you?" Without even releasing its hands from its ears, the body began to nod, over and over, swaying side to side as it did. "Who did this to you, Mama? What can I do?" Her questions tumbled out, one on the coattails of the other.

The body released its head, and began banging on its seamed chest with a fist. May froze for a moment, unsure, until her breaking heart overcame the last of her fear. Her mama was somehow trapped in this white boy's ruined body, and she'd do anything to free her from this prison. She'd give her own life if that's what it took.

May knelt before the body. Even though the stench of rotting flesh nearly made her vomit, she took the body into her arms and held it tight. A cry for justice issued from her heart. Who would have—could have—done this to her mama?

"I love you, Mama," she said. "We'll fix this. We will." But even as she said the words, she felt the body go limp in her embrace. The seam that had been made in the boy's chest split open, and shards of the broken pottery they'd left on her mama's grave spilled out and fell to the ground. Her mind flashed back to that young buckra at the cemetery. But no, that made no sense. What need could a wealthy man like that have for dark magic? His kind already ruled the world. And if such a man were responsible for this evil, how could May even dream of justice?

May jerked back, releasing the body of the dead child. The corpse fell on its side, then rolled back. "Mama," she cried, but a sense of calmness descended on her. A spark of golden light rose from the corpse and floated upward, winking once, twice, then disappearing into the night sky. Her mama was free.

A torrent of rain washed over her as the sky above continued to roil with fire. As the storm raged, May dragged the body away from her house, just beyond the tree line. She went back to the shed to fetch Reuben's old shovel, then did her best to give the poor child a good Christian burial.

May never spoke of that night, not to a living soul.

SIX

The sound of an arriving automobile prickled May's sensitive ears and caused the little hairs on the back of her neck to rise. Not only was Sunday the Lord's Day, it was also May's single day off. She'd only just settled into her favorite armchair, the sole thing she'd inherited from her mama. The armrests and headrests were still covered with doilies her mama had tatted. May had spent the morning praising, and she'd hoped to spend the afternoon collecting her own thoughts, maybe even dozing a bit, while hiding from the heat. The car horn blew. She drew a fortifying breath and pushed herself up.

She cast a glance in the mirror and patted back her hair, then used her palms to straighten out the creases in her skirt. *Who the hell would be coming by now?* she wondered, opening the front door and leaning toward the screen. The searing light of the early-afternoon sun bore down hard, squashing the shadows of everything beneath it flat to the earth, then flared up as it reflected off the hood of a shiny new black car. The flash dazzled her eyes. The driver slowed, doing his best to avoid the ruts in the yard.

May felt her jaw tighten. She didn't recognize the car—most folk around here couldn't afford a rusting Tin Lizzie, let alone one of the new chrome barges with round fenders. She crossed her arms tight over her chest and took a wider stance. She bit her lower lip. She didn't recognize the face of the porkpie-hatted dandy driving the car, but she sure as shooting recognized the face of the fool woman sitting beside him, in spite of her dyed-red Myrna Loy hairdo. The car came to a stop, and the driver killed the engine. May pushed through the screeching screen door and went to stand on her front porch, knowing damned well that while the fading haint blue her mama had made her paint the overhang might keep away the boo hags, it wouldn't do diddly to keep out this Jezebel, this murderer.

Her eyes locked with Betty's, but Betty looked away and turned to face the car's backseat. The door behind Mr. Porkpie opened. May's grandbaby Poppy slid out and ran to her, arms outstretched. "Nana Wills," the girl cried, and the love May felt caused her heart to leap in her breast. The car's other back door opened, and Opal climbed out with Jilo in her arms.

Coward, May thought, returning her focus to the woman who used to be her daughter-in-law. *Sending the children first.* Jilo squirmed in her sister's arms, and Opal sat her on her feet, taking the tiny girl's arm as she tottered along. Poppy bounded up the steps, and May knelt and took her in her arms, placing a thousand kisses over the girl's sweet face.

May heard the car's front doors open, and she looked up to see that Porkpie had moved around to the car's rear. He popped the trunk while Betty swung her nylon-covered legs out and found footing. She took a few sauntering steps toward the house, barely covered by a new and way-too-tight crimson dress. "It's good to see you, May," she said, her tone guarded. She held her head back and a bit to the right, looking down her nose at May. Her eyes were challenging, but a smile parted her haughty face.

May had to fight the urge to fly from her porch, across the patchy dry grass, and slap Betty's smile right off her. Seeming to read May's struggle, Betty stopped a good distance back. This woman. *This harlot.* She had begged, coaxed, and harangued Jesse, threatening to leave him unless he moved his family to Charleston. Roosevelt's New Deal money had begun floating into the state through the South Carolina Emergency Relief Administration, and rumor had it there were going to be riches for everyone, white and colored alike. The fool girl had thought Charleston would be an electric-lit land of milk and honey.

Six months after the move, May received the telegraph saying Jesse got himself killed when scaffolding collapsed, sending a rain of bricks down on him. *Your son I stole from you is dead. Stop. Send money to bury him among strangers. Stop.* Of course, those weren't the cable's actual words, but that was how May's heart remembered them. May hadn't been able to stop Jesse from leaving, let alone from getting himself killed, but she had managed to get him brought home. Jesse now rested between his own father and May's mother. The spot she had always believed would be her own resting place.

"May, I want you to meet Walter Williams," Betty said, placing one hand on her hip. Betty seemed proud, like she was showing off a prize pig at the state fair.

May examined the dark, round-faced fellow. A good three inches shorter than Betty, and a good three inches wider, too. *Walter Williams, my eye.* Porkpie, a cardboard suitcase in each hand, sidled up beside Betty. The Depression seemed to have spared Porkpie, seeing as he had both a new car and a spare tire around his waist. He didn't fit May's image of what a gangster should look like, but she couldn't imagine how else a man could come by the cash for a chariot like this these days. He set the cases down and doffed his hat.

"Ma'am," he said, looking at her with a wide smile. His gaze turned instantly back to Betty, and May realized the poor fool was in love.

"What're those for?" May asked, taking a couple of steps forward to the edge of her porch. "This ain't no hotel, and you sure ain't moving in here with that man."

Betty laughed, a careless sound pealing from a careless woman. "Opal," Betty called her daughter, never taking her wary eyes off May.

The spindly girl let go of Jilo, who scooted off to explore, and took hold of the cases. She set them down in front of the porch steps and looked to her grandmother, not seeming to know what to do next.

"Those are for the girls," Betty said. "Walter and I, we going on to Atlanta. The girls wanted to stop off here a bit and visit with their nana, ain't that right, Opal?"

May's eyes fixed on the young girl's face. Opal's worried gaze drifted down, and her lips began to work, but no sound came out. May's heart nearly broke at the sight. "You bring those cases up here then, girl," she said to her oldest grandbaby. Opal's eyes shot up to meet May's, and a hopeful smile spread across her face. *Poor little thing believed I might turn her away*, May thought, an even deeper resentment toward Betty growing in her heart. *What kind of stories has that creature been telling the babies about me?*

"Yes'm," the girl said, her face now radiant. She grabbed the first case with both hands and hauled it up to May's side, then skittered back down and managed the second, which seemed a tad heavier. May would have helped the girl, but she didn't trust herself to be even a single inch closer to Opal's mother.

"What you going to Atlanta for?" May asked, pulling Opal close and laying a protective hand on her head.

"Walter has business there," Betty responded. May scanned the new auto, its scintillating chrome causing spots to rise before her eyes.

"She a beauty, ain't she? She's a Chrysler Airstream." He smiled, oblivious to May's disdain. "Only thing prettier is my lady here." He reached up to place his arm around Betty's shoulder.

"It's too hot, baby." Betty flashed the man a smile, but stepped quickly forward, sliding out from under his embrace.

"That explains why . . . *Walter*"—May very nearly used her interior moniker for the man—"is going. Why are you going?"

Betty reached back and, seeming to forget her earlier avoidance of his touch, took Porkpie's arm. She beamed and flashed May the most sincere smile May had ever seen on her ex-daughter-in-law's face. "Walter here has arranged for me to have an audition with Ty King and His Golden Syncopation Swing."

"An audition?" May crossed her arms.

"Yeah, I'm gonna sing for Mr. King . . ."

"I know what an audition is," May snapped, but her gaze caught hold of Jilo, still toddling around, chasing after a fat bumblebee. To her disbelief, the bee hovered over the child's outstretched hand for a moment and then landed on it. Rather than startling or trying to run away, Jilo pulled her hand closer and stared intently at the insect. May got the oddest feeling that the two were somehow communicating, and the thought made her feel real uneasy. "Opal, honey," she said, "you go fetch Jilo before she gets herself stung, and take your sisters inside."

She scanned Opal's thin face. "You hungry?" she asked. When her grandbaby didn't answer, she called out to Betty, "You feed these girls their lunch yet?"

Betty began to speak, but May answered her own question. "No, 'course you haven't." The scrawny things probably hadn't even had their breakfast. Forcing her anger down, she placed her hand on Opal's back and gave her a gentle nudge. "Go on, get Jilo inside, and Nana will come in and fix you girls something real good. All right?"

Opal nodded and scrambled down the steps. "Jilo," she called out to the littlest one. Jilo spun around, arms held high overhead. "Come on, Nana says it's time to eat." May was relieved to see the bee rise up and take to the air.

Opal bent to try and lift the girl, but Jilo was having none of it. She pulled back from her sister, intent on making the trip under her own steam, but then stopped and took Opal's steadying hand after a half-dozen steps. Nearing the porch, Jilo let go of Opal and crawled up the steps. May looked down at the smiling face creeping up to greet her. May didn't give a pea-picker's damn that the child's face didn't look a thing like her boy's. This was her grandbaby every bit as much as Jilo's older sisters were.

"Go on and take your sisters inside. Nana will get the bags." Opal herded her younger sisters past the screech of the screen door and into the darkening house.

May reached through the still-open screen door and pulled the main door shut. The spring on the screen door groaned and snapped as it closed with a thwack. "Let's just say you do get this 'singing' job," May made sure her disapproval rang through. It wasn't that Betty couldn't sing, for the woman certainly could, but May knew there was a hell of a lot more going on in those Atlanta clubs than singing. "Who's going to look after the girls while you're out all night?"

Betty rolled her eyes, but only a little. "You saw Opal. She's practically a mother to the other girls already. She always looking after them, bathing 'em, feeding them."

Betty's words confirmed May's worst fears. "She don't have much of a choice about that, now does she?"

Betty's face froze at the older woman's words. There was no doubt in May's mind that Betty had finished with being a mother. May and Reuben had hoped for a household full of children, but Jesse was the only one her womb had allowed her to carry. And now the selfish woman who'd robbed her of her only child was shirking the responsibility of her own babies' care, all so she could be this buffoon's fancy woman.

May felt like screaming, but instead bent down and grasped the handles of the suitcases. "Not much more trouble cooking for you two, if you want to come in." It would take all her strength to allow this woman back under her roof, but never let it be said May refused anyone hospitality, even the likes of these two. As expected, Porkpie's eyes lit up.

"Thank you, no," Betty rushed through her response. "We should be getting on. It's best if we get out of these parts and make it into Atlanta before sunset. Ain't that right, Walter?"

As silly as Betty could be, this time May knew she was right. It wouldn't be wise for a black man to be driving his shiny new automobile around these roads after sunset.

"We could stay a few . . ." Porkpie began, but then he caught something on Betty's face, something the glare hid from May's view. "Yes, I reckon it would be best to be getting on. But thank you for your kind offer, ma'am."

"You at least gonna come in and get the girls settled?" May asked.

"No, no," Betty said. "I think they'll do better if we just slip away now." She turned quickly on her heels and strode toward the car.

Porkpie doffed his hat once more. "Mrs. Wills." He scurried to open Betty's door.

"You just remember"—he stopped at the sound of May's voice— "that that woman with you was once Mrs. Wills, too, and she got three girls here who need their mama."

"Go on," Betty commanded Porkpie. He nodded several times in quick succession, whether in response to her or May, May would never know. As soon as Porkpie opened the passenger door, Betty slid into her seat, backside first, and swung her legs up through the opening. Once she was settled, he jogged with a heavy gait around the front of the car to the driver's side and opened his door. "Ma'am," he called out once more, then hopped into the driver's seat and closed the door with loving care behind him.

May hurried down the porch steps, managing to grab ahold of the opening in the passenger side's window just as Porkpie fired up the engine. Betty's eyes flashed, and her lips pursed as she looked out at May.

"When you coming back?" May asked.

"Soon," was all Betty offered. She rolled the window up and patted Porkpie's arm. He shifted the car into drive, leaving May to watch as it jostled away across the roots and ruts of her yard.

SEVEN

It took an hour or so, but May's three granddaughters finally allowed themselves to be calmed, then washed and readied for bed in their daddy's old room. Chatterbox Opal kept parroting her mother, talking about how good life would be once Mama was singing in front of those big bands. Tearful Poppy, accustomed now to electric light, was afraid of the shadows cast by the flame of the kerosene lamp. Angry, squalling Jilo seemed somehow more deeply aware of her mother's betrayal than her older sisters. Finally, though, May had them settled for the night.

May worried she was too old to raise these three, but she couldn't let the fear linger. If she didn't see to their well-being, who the hell else could she count on to do so? She had only just gotten used to being alone in the house, but the thought of trying to carry these girls into womanhood left her feeling something the loss of her loved ones had not.

She felt lonely.

For the first time in her life she understood those folk who would pay good money to sit at rocking tables and listen for voices from beyond the grave. The good Lord knew what she'd pay to feel Reuben's reassuring touch again or see her Jesse's face. She'd gladly hand over her last dime even if all she got from the other side was an echo of her mama's voice telling her to quit her nattering.

Outside, the chat of mockingbirds, sleepless beneath the bright moonlight, tugged her back into a childhood memory, another full moon night such as this one, when she had complained to her mother about the filching habit that had earned the birds their name. "Why they gotta steal the other birds' songs anyway? Why don't they sing their own song instead?"

Her mama had pinched her cheek, forcing her to smile. "They ain't stealing nothing, baby," she had said, winking at May. "They just trying to imagine what it's like to be one of those other birds. Of course they may get the melody wrong in places, but it's love that make them try in the first place. They just trying to see things through others' eyes. Be a lot better world if people did that, too. Now you leave those poor mockingbirds be."

May extinguished the kerosene flame in the living area, its glow giving way to the silver moonlight that reached in through the window to keep her company. Morning would come soon enough, and May would have to be up and out before the moon had left the sky so she could walk the three miles into town where she worked as maid for the Pinnacle Hotel. She daren't be late.

Even though the infusion of Mr. Truman's money had begun to ease the economy's palpitations, May done had three strikes against her. Older Negro woman that she was, she was lucky to have employment of any kind. Management at the hotel made sure she was reminded of that on a near to daily basis. "Yessir," she'd say whenever Mr. Porter rubbed her nose in it. "It's very kind of you to keep me on." She'd smile. Force her eyes not to betray how she really felt. Angry? No, she was past being angry. Weary, that's how she felt. Weary over the fact that these buckra could never look at her and see a woman, a human being, a child of God. An equal.

Then May remembered her sleeping grandbabies. Would they grow up in the same kind of world she'd known, where they would be forced to smile at smug and yammering white faces that constantly reminded them of the natural order of white over black, male over female? Heat prickled across her skin. Ah, yes. There it was, that anger she'd thought she was past.

She settled into her mother's armchair, letting herself think for a spell on the worries of the immediate future. May didn't have an idea what she would do with the girls while she was at work. Opal and Poppy would be old enough for school come fall, but what about the baby? Guilt struck her as she realized she, too, might end up having to saddle Opal with responsibilities beyond what her age should require. Responsibilities that could prevent her from bettering her own lot in life. No. Come fall, she'd have something figured out. She sighed and leaned back in the chair, intending to rest her eyes for a few moments.

A small hand on her forearm startled her awake. "Nana," Opal said in a near whisper, "Jilo. She ain't in bed."

Groggy, May looked down at Opal, and then, as soon as her grandbaby's message registered, scanned the room for any sign of the little one. "Don't worry, she got to be around here somewhere." May pushed herself up, her knees and back complaining as she did. "Where's Poppy?"

Opal's wide and frightened eyes followed her in the darkness. "She's still asleep."

May shuffled to the table where she'd left the lamp. After removing its chimney and twisting up its wick, she struck a match and touched the flame to the fuel-soaked cloth. The light cast wavering shadows around them as she replaced the chimney.

She lifted the lamp and headed down the hall that ran the length of her four-room wood-frame house, stopping to poke her head in through the opening to Jesse's old room, where she could make out Poppy's sleeping shape curled up in the center of the bed. She craned her head around the door frame. "Jilo," she called out in a whisper that she hoped would get the baby's attention without waking her older sister. Poppy didn't stir, but neither did Jilo respond.

May stepped into the room and set the lamp on the nightstand, pushing through the stiffness in her knees to kneel by the bed and search the space beneath it. She had felt certain she would find the child curled up there, sleeping with her tiny fist in her mouth, but there was no sign of her. Up until then, May hadn't felt worried, but now a sense of apprehension crept up on her, twisting up like kudzu through the pit of her stomach and curling around her heart. She bumped into the bed, causing Poppy to stir. " 'S'alright, girl," she said, hoping to keep Poppy from fully waking. "It's just yo' Nana." The girl seemed satisfied enough with her reassurance to go straight back to sleep. May rocked her way back up to her feet and slipped over to the closet.

"I done looked in there," Opal whispered from behind her.

"Well, Nana's gonna look just once more." May tried to keep her tone measured, her movements unhurried. She eased the door open and poked her head inside. The small space was empty except for the fading smell of naphthalene, and a few odds and ends Jesse had left behind. May's skin prickled, a sensation that felt both cold and hot at the same time. Her intuition told her that something was wrong, but she forced herself to keep a cool head, if only to avoid frightening Opal.

She left the closet door ajar and fetched her lamp, this time crossing the hall and going into her own room, the mirror image of the one where she'd left Poppy soughing. Opal followed on her heels, then dropped to the floor to examine the space beneath the bed.

After a moment, Opal looked up and shook her head. "They something wrong with that girl," she said, her words and tone an obvious parroting of a pronouncement May felt sure Betty had made many times.

"There's nothing wrong with that girl. Nothing wrong with Jilo at all." May's blood boiled in her veins, but she kept her voice low and calm. She went to her own closet, opening it wide and using her free hand to push back the few dresses she had, to see if they might be serving as camouflage for her hidden granddaughter. Shaking her head, she turned back toward Opal.

"Jilo," May called out in a sharp voice, her concern for Jilo now overriding her fear of stirring Poppy. There was no response. May grabbed the lamp and headed for the only other room in the house, the kitchen. A smile came to her face. Of course. The girl was probably in there searching for a sweetie of some kind. May hurried down to the end of the hall and over the threshold into the kitchen. Her heart nearly stopped beating. Unlike the front of the house, with its outer screen door that screeched no matter how often May oiled the darned spring, the back exit had no built-in method of announcing the flight of a child.

The back door stood wide open.

Barely pausing to place the lamp on the table, May rushed out the back and scanned the landscape for any movement. "Jilo!" May called out, this time not worried if she waked those waiting for Jesus. "Jilo, girl, where are you?"

"Maybe she gone to the privy?" Opal asked.

"On her own?" May snapped, but when she saw the stricken look in her grandbaby's eyes, she reached back and placed her hand on Opal's shoulder. "Maybe you right. Don't you worry, Nana will find her. You just go and keep an eye on Poppy." She patted the girl, giving her a slight nudge, but Opal didn't budge. "Go on. You do as Nana tells you." She forced a smile, hoping the shadows wouldn't hide it from the girl's sight. "That fool baby sister of yours is just out here playing. You get on inside and get in bed. I'll be in soon."

May ushered Opal over the threshold and pulled the door shut behind her. Then she turned back toward the yard and hurried down the back steps, her fear loosening her joints. "Jilo," she called every few feet. Deciding to start with Opal's idea first, she made a beeline for the outhouse, but it was empty. *Oh dear, sweet Jesus*, she thought as she wondered if she might have neglected to cover the well. She ran around to the far side of the house, not taking a full breath of air until she saw the cover was indeed in place.

She stepped back from the well and began to slowly spin around, training her eyes on every moving shadow. Nothing that her eyes could see in the moon-softened night bore the form of her granddaughter. May regarded the position of the moon. She couldn't have been asleep for more than an hour, maybe an hour and a half, and Jilo was still pretty new to walking, falling back on her buttocks every fifth or sixth step. How far could she have possibly gone on her own?

In that moment, it struck May that Jilo hadn't wandered off. She'd been taken. May felt it with the same cold and fearful certainty with which she'd known her mama's spirit resided in that buckra boy's broken body years ago. Her mouth went dry; her breath came in quick, shallow gasps. But who could have sneaked in without disturbing her? Every floorboard in her house creaked unless you knew exactly where to step. And how could the culprit have removed the baby from the bed without waking her sisters?

"Jilo," she cried out, unable to keep the panic from her voice. May's skin began to prickle, tiny bumps forming along her arms. The air around her seemed to vibrate; it smelled of a lightning strike. She'd felt this before. She tried to resist, but her hands tingled as sparks, so close in color to the turquoise folk called "haint blue," danced along her fingertips. She swallowed hard and willed the magic to dissipate. She'd made promises, to herself, to Jesus, to her mama, promises never to use this magic that always tested her will in her weaker moments.

Not until May was a full-grown woman had her mama explained why she didn't want her to use the magic she herself employed on a daily basis. "I done sold myself to the devil for using that magic, gal." The memory of her mother's voice tickled her ears as surely as if she'd just breathed the words into them. "Don't you do what yo' mama done. You find another way to get along. That old devil can find another horse to ride." The remembered anguish in her mama's voice nearly succeeded in dousing the sparks, but then the thought of her grandbaby getting carried off into the dark fought its way up. May hesitated, but only for a moment.

She'd resisted the magic all her life, ever since she was a girl not much bigger than Jilo. It hadn't been easy; she'd been tested time and again. But she couldn't bear the thought of that baby, *her* baby, out there alone and frightened. A moan escaped her lips as she thought of that collector her mama had failed to stop. "Just a little," she thought. "Just this once." She lifted her hand and let a single spark escape. That spark, so close in color to her porch's overhang, rose into the air, twinkling like a touchable star.

"Show me where she is," May's voice trembled as she addressed the light. "Show me where they took my Jilo."

EIGHT

The spark circled around May, forcing her to turn to keep it in view. Then it bobbed up and down, floating off toward the live oaks and pines that lined the back side of May's property. The light swam lazily in the still-warm night air, moving no more quickly than May's feet could carry her.

The light led her through her backyard and over the unmarked border where her property ended, just past the grove of live oaks where the tall pines began. She did her best to stay clear of the first pine past the oaks to avoid the grave she'd made beneath it for Rosie's boy. The dry grass gave way to a carpet of equally dry needles, the scent of evergreen reaching up to fill May's senses with her every crunching step. The smell tugged at vague memories—the sound of bees buzzing, a tall man wearing a stovepipe hat, harsh words from her mother—unrelated to the present moment, and at this moment unnecessary, perhaps even detrimental.

The haint-blue light flashed, then dimmed, nearly going out, warning May that she needed to stay focused on finding her grandchild, not on the dim ghosts of her past. As soon as she returned her concentration to the bobbing spark, it began to glow with a renewed incandescence. She knew nothing of how to use magic, and her mother had refused to share even the slightest insight, lest May be tempted to claim the dangerous power available to her. Still, she intuited that it was indeed her attention that was keeping the turquoise glint alive, and if she let her mind wander too far from her purpose, it would be extinguished, leaving her alone in the night, with Jilo lost to her, perhaps forever.

"I'm right with you," she addressed the spark, and it reacted to her words with both an increase in speed and brightness. May sharpened her focus until the spark was at its center. Though she did not like the woods, she picked up her pace, trying not to worry about exposed tree roots that might cause her to take a tumble, and allowing herself only the slightest shudder at the thought of the snakes, spiders, and hundreds of other creatures who made their home in this sap-sticky world. She wondered at her mother—the outside, the night; this had been Tuesday Jackson's world. Not so for May.

The spark carried on, heedless of her very human fears, until it reached the edge of a clearing, where it stopped and hovered in place. As May drew near, another scent, a marriage of smoke and tar, began to overtake the sharp spice of the pines. Fear and worry confounded May's ability to estimate the distance she had come. Even though her common sense told her she couldn't be more than a quarter mile from her own property, her sense of direction had deserted her, leaving her without the slightest idea of where her own house lay. It was almost like the natural world beyond her tree line had transformed into a vast and fearsome forest.

May slowed and softened her footfalls. The scent of smoke grew even stronger, and the sound of distant voices, their words indiscernible, reached her ears. Had the light led her to someone's home? The spark moved again, passing just beyond the tree line, then faded away. May crept forward.

She stopped cold the instant she slid beyond the cover of the trees, and her heart very nearly stopped, too. There was a gathering of white-clad figures at the far end of the clearing, and the silver light of the moon was losing its battle with the darting flames licking at the cross standing in the center of the gathering.

May felt her pulse pounding in her neck and her temples. Surely, she'd been betrayed. This—this was where the magic had brought her. She took a cautious step back toward the trees, keeping her eyes fixed on the sight of the burning cross and the linen-draped monsters who paraded around it. She'd move carefully. Quietly. Draw no attention to herself, until she was safely within the cover of the trees. Another step back, and then she heard it. A baby's cry. Jilo. It was impossible that it was her, and yet it was undeniable.

"Oh, Jesus," the words came out as a shorthand prayer, as the world around her started to spin. Her knees buckled, and she collapsed to the earth.

The flames from the cross illuminated a scene she knew would remain forever burned into her vision. One of the men lifted a small and struggling burden over his head as the others burst into a raucous laughter. May had to rise. She had to go to them. Plead with these demons to return the baby to her. Beg them to simply let her and Jilo leave in peace.

But her body seemed frozen to the ground where she knelt.

The child cried out again, and the man who held her began walking toward the flaming cross. The light from that obscene blasphemy illumi-nated the goings-on all too clearly. The man was laying Jilo down on a table. No, May realized, an altar. Another man moved around the altar, blocking May's view. Jilo shrieked, a high, anguished cry that pierced the night. Somehow May found the power to stand, and managed to take a few stumbling steps toward them. She lifted her voice to cry out to them. To call to Jilo. To tell her not to be afraid. Nana was coming. But her voice failed her as surely as if she'd been born mute.

She took another step forward, trying to shake the concrete from her limbs, but a hand descended on her shoulder, stopping her in her tracks. A small gasp escaped her at the touch. The hand released her, and a woman dressed all in black, her head and face obscured by a heavy veil, circled around in front of her. May could only make out the dimmest suggestion of features beneath the thick lace; race and age were inscrutable. The figure was a bit shorter than May herself, but ample, suggesting a healthy and mature woman rather than a waif.

May lifted a trembling hand and pointed in the direction of her granddaughter's keening. She tried to speak, managing only a few unintelligible sounds. The woman held a finger up to the veil, near where May felt the lips should be. She wanted May to keep quiet, that much was clear. May nodded to show she understood. The woman turned and took a few steps toward the distant crowd, the hem of her long and old-fashioned gown trailing behind her. And then she fell away, her body disintegrating before May's startled eyes, and transforming into a swarm of a thousand or more angry yellow jackets.

May watched in disbelief as the swarm advanced on the group. From the outer circle working in, the hooded figures' casual milling about and occasional saluting turned to panicked gyrations and flailing arms. Their laughter and jeers turned to yelps and cowardly screams. The distance was too great for May to make out the individual insects with her naked eye, but she could guess that many had found their way up under the men's robes to sting their bare flesh. The men began throwing off their pointed hoods, tugging the robes up over their heads. Others gave into panic and rushed away from the congregation. May heard car engines revving up, saw headlights coming to life and illuminating the ongoing riot of those who didn't or couldn't move quickly enough.

A pair of beams shot across the field, betraying her presence to anyone who wasn't caught up in the chaos. May fell back into the shelter of darkness, but not before she felt hostile eyes graze her. She'd been too dazzled to notice whose eyes had picked her out from among the shadows. The light had illuminated her face for only an instant, but intuition told May that the person who'd spotted her had, in fact, been watching for her. Jilo had not been stolen at random. Someone had taken her to make sure May would come looking.

As May's eyes recovered from the flash of the headlights, she realized that the swarm was returning toward her, coalescing at first into a dense yet frantic cloud of insects, and then the form of the woman. The creature, whatever she was, drew near, but she seemed to be almost dancing—like the cloud of wasps she had been—rather than walking.

The creature held Jilo in her now humanlike hands. The sight of the child caused May to forget all danger. She broke free of the tree line, hiking up her skirt, and raced toward her granddaughter, only to stop dead as the moonlight attempted to light up the creature's features. Blurred though they were by her heavy veil, May could now see the moon wasn't reflecting off the creature's skin; rather it seemed to be swallowed whole by whatever lay behind her veil. Still, May could feel the creature's eyes piercing the mesh of the veil, searing through it to take her full measure, inside and out.

The veiled apparition rocked Jilo until the toddler cooed with happiness, using such obvious care and gentleness May's heart nearly broke at the sight. Then she transferred the child to May's anxious and trembling hands.

"That will teach those filthy sons of bitches," the creature said. Then she reached up and brushed back her veil, showing May the utter hollowness that lay behind it. The features May had imagined were nothing more than a trick suggested by the veil and her desire to make this creature into something she could someday understand. The emptiness within unwound to envelop the shell that had contained it, until the strange being was no more.

NINE

May was walking north on Ogeechee Road the next morning as the sun's first rays reached her, a warm and comforting caress that brought to mind the sense of serenity that had descended on her when her own hand brushed that of the odd veiled woman the night before. Her touch had felt like that of an old friend, someone May had never known but had missed her entire life.

No. May knew the creature who'd saved Jilo was not a woman at all. She had seen the illusion of her humanity fall away before her own eyes. If anything, she was a demon. One sent to tempt her into using magic, into breaking the vow she'd made so long ago.

Only once before had she been truly tempted by magic. On that long-ago night, she had gone crawling to her mama's door, banging on the wood and begging her mama to come out and do something, *anything* to heal Reuben. The memory still tugged at her.

Her mama had met her at the door. Tried to bring her in. Knelt beside her. Pulled her close to her bosom. But she didn't waver in her refusal.

"No, baby. You don't know what you askin'. You don't know," she said as she tried to rock May in her arms.

May pushed herself up and shoved her mama away. And as her mama stood, May did something she had never thought she could do. She reached out and struck her own mama. But Mama didn't fight back. No. She took May's hand and pressed it to her lips.

"It's all right," she said, tears streaming down her cheeks. "It's all right. But Mama cannot do this thing for you . . . she loves you too much. She loves your Reuben too much."

With that, she gently pushed May back over her threshold, turning her away. "You go on. You get back to your husband."

Her trembling hand pressed between May's shoulders, but as May started to stumble away, her mama's hand reached out and snatched hers, causing her to look back. "You leave what's gonna happen up to God," she said, pointing to the heavens. "You trust God to do what's right for our Reuben, whether it breaks our hearts or not. Magic, it ain't what you think, baby. Least not the kind I got. Don't you ever let it tempt you to force your own will on things."

May had done as her mama told her. She'd gone home to Reuben; she'd listened to the rattling coughs and gasping breaths that would eventually carry him from this world. Years later, she had buried her mama in the earth, too. Then that white boy had been found before the sun could set on her mama's grave. May knew her mama had hastened her own death to try and put an end to whoever or *whatever* had been taking the children. If her mama had succeeded, it would have been almost worthwhile, but it was so hard to bear the knowledge that her mama had died in defeat.

But May didn't have a choice. She had to bear it. Exhausted from her sleepless night, May barely had enough strength left to put one foot before the other. In the years since May had lost Reuben, she'd nearly worn a groove in this road from making the trek between her home and the Pinnacle Hotel morning and night, six days a week. Tired going, even more tired coming back.

May knew her life was a God-given gift, and she tried to be grateful for each day, but lately she'd found herself talking to her departed

Reuben more often, wondering out loud how many more times she'd have to walk this path until she could join him in glory. Well, that reunion would have to wait now. She was burdened by no illusions that Betty would be coming back for those girls.

May trudged down the road toward the cemetery, her heavy steps rousing a black rooster. The bird's invective startled her, causing her to stop short and catch her breath.

"All right, Lester, all right," she addressed the bird. "Whole darned world done heard you now." May shook her head. The thing had shown up around the time of her mama's death, and it almost seemed like a friend by now. Some folk might think she was crazy, but she always greeted the rooster whenever she passed his home. Not doing so today would only add to the sense of strangeness she seemed incapable of shaking.

May might have believed the whole episode was a dream had she managed to close her eyes for even a wink, but no, she'd had no sleep. There was no choice but to accept that she had witnessed the impossible made real. "See you later, Lester," she said, still hoping familiar habits could erase the sense of oddity the night had sown in the pit of her stomach.

Last night, she'd picked her way home from the clearing more by instinct than by landmark, Jilo asleep in her arms as they made their way through the night forest. Once home, she had slipped the baby in bed next to Opal, who—despite her worry—had drifted off to sleep with Poppy cuddled in her arms. May herself never even considered trying to sleep. Instead, she stoked the kitchen stove and boiled up some chicory that went cold without her even lifting cup to lip. Then she spent the night bent over her Bible, though the words seemed to dance on the page, imparting none of their usual wisdom or comfort.

Even now, as she passed beneath the steeple of Tremont Nondenominational House of Prayer, the prayer she yearned to offer up—one that combined a supplication for forgiveness for having used magic and a request for guidance—remained inchoate in her breast. She hated it, but anger against God Almighty simmered in her soul. *Magic* had saved Jilo, not prayer. It terrified her that one of those evil men had managed to slip silently into her home, as if by witchcraft, and steal her grandbaby right out of her bed. A man who could keep his cool as those around him gave in to panic. A man who would arrange the abduction of a tiny child just to lure May out into the night.

May stopped dead in her tracks as another thought struck her. What if those men hadn't taken Jilo? What if it had instead been the creature who'd presented itself as a friend? The creature could have set up the whole adventure to fool May into believing it was acting as her protector.

The questions made her heart heavy, but pondering them made the remainder of her trek to work short. Before she knew it, she had arrived at the rear of Pinnacle. A concrete sidewalk ran behind the hotel, and May stepped onto it carefully so as not to trip where the roots of an ancient oak had pushed up from beneath the pavement and forced it up. Without giving it a thought, she passed by the entrance used by the white staff, heading to the far side of the building to the door labeled "Colored." Humidity and warping caused the door to stick; each day it took a bit more out of May to tug it open and step through it. The door's handle vibrated in her hand as the resistant wood finally yielded to her. She stepped into the side of the kitchen where the sinks would soon be full of dishes from the guests' breakfasts.

But the dishes weren't May's concern, and she had enough work of her own to handle without taking on more. The hotel had sixty-eight rooms and only three maids. May and the two much younger women did the laundry and cleaned the guest rooms, halls, and great rooms. The younger women worked quicker, but May always did the best job—she didn't miss spots or take shortcuts like her companions often did. The longtime guests, the folk who'd been coming here for years, knew to ask for her to service their rooms, and May felt justified in taking a touch of pride in that. Of course, it did nothing to prevent Mr. Porter, her buckra manager, from telling her she'd be out of a job if she didn't step it up.

"Good morning, Mrs. Wills," said Henry Cook, looking up from the wingtips he had been polishing. The small boy shined guests' shoes and ran odd errands for management.

"Good morning, Henry," May said, letting her hand brush the boy's cheek. "How's yo' mama doing? Getting over her ailment, I hope."

"Yes, ma'am," Henry replied, turning back to his work. May could tell from his expression that he wasn't telling the truth. His mama was still poorly. Sighing to herself, May opened the closet where the cleaning implements were stored. She reached up to take her apron from its hook, saying a silent prayer that the youngster's lie might soon be made true.

The thought hit her that perhaps her magic could be the answer to that same prayer.

No.

She shook her head, forcing the temptation from her mind, and slipped on the apron. Once her uniform was neatly in place, she grasped the handles of the zinc mop bucket in her right hand and the mop in her left. The hotel had an elevator for guests, but not for staff. She planned to tote the cleaning supplies up the back stairs to the top floor and work her way down, meeting the other maids on their way up.

But May's hand cramped, forcing her to set the bucket and mop back down. Following its usual course, the aching in her joints came as a sharp jab, then settled into a repeating throb. She closed her eyes and rubbed her swelling knuckles. *It'll pass. It'll pass.* May took a few breaths, willing the pain to subside.

One eye popped open in surprise. It'd never happened before, but this time the ache had eased. Instantly, at the very moment she'd formed the thought. With both eyes open, she stepped away from the closet, and held her hand up beneath the overhead light. There was no swelling. There was no pain.

Physical relief gave way to concern. Maybe she no longer had a choice about using magic. Maybe once the door had been opened, even a crack, it was open for good.

A door on the far side of the kitchen swung open. "May," Mr. Porter snapped without even stepping into the room. "Follow me."

"Something need cleaning, sir?" May asked, starting to bend over to pick up the bucket and mop. Her eyes fixed on the spots of dried calamine lotion that dotted Porter's thin, gray face and bald pate.

"Leave those and come with me," Porter said. May hurried across the kitchen to join him. Rather than hold the weighted door for her, Porter let it swing shut behind him, closing it right in May's face.

May leaned back to escape being struck, then eased the door open enough to slip through. Porter had carried on without her, leaving her to scurry to catch up to him as he crossed the lobby and entered the dining room.

May only rarely ventured into the ornate room, except to sweep its deep red—Venetian red, she had once overheard a guest say—carpet, or to clean up a spill. The entrance was adorned by pillars, similar to those at the Greek church south of the Forsyth, but not quite so busy-looking at the top. She moved between those columns with trepidation.

The hotel was nearly full, and it had gotten late enough in the morning that May had expected to see guests at most of the tables, but other than the two men sitting at the table near the back wall, the room was deserted. May stopped dead in her tracks, a feeling of dread falling on her. Even from across the room, May had no difficulty recognizing Fletcher Maguire, the elder of the two visitors; she'd seen his picture in the *Gazette* more than once. But she recognized him not from his thick head of gray hair, piercing blue eyes, or prominent chin, but from the wooden wheelchair in which he was sitting. May remembered hearing he'd suffered a stroke around the time of her mama's death. Word was, he'd been in that wheelchair ever since.

Despite his advancing age and declining health, Maguire was still one of the most powerful men in Georgia. He could've been governor or senator if he'd wanted, but he wasn't the kind of man who ran for public office; he was the kind of man who chose those who did. May had read enough of the official news and heard enough whispers to know that what Maguire didn't outright own, he damned sure felt no qualms about stealing.

The younger man could only be his son, Sterling. Sterling was a tall fellow, pink and lean, with hair as light as corn silk. She'd only laid eyes on him once before, and then it had been from a distance. Up close, she could see he was a good-looking boy for his type, but something about him was off. *A wolf in sheep's clothing*, the words came to May's mind. Sterling had inherited his father's sharp cold eyes. Something about the way those eyes took her in reminded her of last night, when those bright beams had illuminated her at the edge of the woods. May began to tremble.

Porter, who had been making a beeline toward the occupied table, slowed and looked over his shoulder, his hand fluttering to signal she should come forward. May did as he bade her. "This is her," Porter said.

"Why, yes, indeed it is," the elder Maguire said with a broad smile. "I knew your mama, Tuesday, well, my dear." May forced herself not to react. The day of her mama's funeral, Miriam had suggested the younger Maguire might have come to engage her mama's assistance, but this was the first she'd heard for sure there was a connection between her mama and this man. Maguire reached up and adjusted his wire-frame spectacles. "And you are a picture-perfect copy of her." He let out a laugh, but it came from his chest, not his belly where any good laugh should come from. "Yes, I knew Mother Tuesday well." He paused. "Or as well as I reckon anyone could. As a matter of fact, our two families go way back," he said, shaking his head and casting a satisfied glance at his son before returning his focus to May. "You do know, don't you? My people used to own yours." The words hung there between them.

May's mouth went dry as her lips trembled but failed to find the words. Her entire body shook with the effort. "Pardon me, sir—" her voice came out sounding odd to her own ears, like a voice from a scratchy recording, "—but that was a long time ago."

"Oh, not so long ago, really, May. Not in the grand scheme." His expression softened and his focus fell to an invisible point between them, almost like he was remembering the slave times with a fond heart.

In her own mind's eye, she saw herself grasping a knife and running it across this man's throat in one quick deep slash, sending a shower of his life's blood all over the white tablecloth and Venetian-red carpeting. The image had come unbidden, and she wished she could say it horrified her. But it lingered, and she didn't feel horrified. She turned it around in her mind like she might turn a smooth pebble in her hand before sending it skimming across a pond's surface. No, she felt no horror. What she felt was soiled, corrupted. This man, his words, his actions, his very thoughts, they were an infectious disease, and he was a malevolent carrier who sought to poison all those around him.

May managed to push the image of Maguire's pale corpse from her mind, praying to be cleansed of the taint this man had put on her soul. She forced herself to stifle her rage. Not for the first time, and she knew not for the last one either, but she felt this might possibly be the most trying attempt she'd ever need face. May nodded and lowered her eyes, not daring to let her gaze meet his.

He motioned toward a chair across the table from him. "Sit," he said. "Join me. Would you like some coffee? Shall I have Porter here fetch you a cup?" May's eyes flashed at her boss, who looked as shocked as she felt—and full of quiet rage, besides. Maguire seemed to take note of his resentment. "You know that is the origin of your name, don't you, son? Porter? One might even say you were born to fetch for your betters."

"Oh, no, sir!" May said, astonished. "I could never . . ." She paused, hoping to find a tone that would avoid offending Mr. Maguire, but still placate her boss. "This beautiful room is for gracious white folk such as yourself." She forced the biggest possible smile. "And Mr. Porter," she tossed a quick glance in his direction, "he's my boss, sir. I couldn't let him go fetching anything for me. It wouldn't be fitting. I know my place . . ." Her words died in the air, cut off by a twinge of the same anger she'd felt the night before. Why shouldn't she sit here? Why shouldn't she let that white boy who wasn't half her age and who never did a lick of real work bring her coffee?

She caught herself, but it was too late; Maguire had picked up on her thoughts, had read them in her eyes maybe. A tight smile curled on his lips. "I insist." He motioned again with his hand toward the empty chair. "Sit."

May felt her knees weaken. She certainly could bear sitting down, but somehow she knew this was a trap.

"But Mr. Maguire," Porter began, protesting for her. "We can't have a colored sitting in here. It just isn't done. This is a whites-only establishment." May wondered at the pride she heard in his voice as he made this pronouncement. "Always has been, always will be. I'm afraid I cannot allow it."

"*You*"—Maguire turned the word into a barb—"cannot allow it?" Maguire tilted back in his chair and laughed. This time his laugh came from his belly. "If I say the woman sits, she sits. Afterwards, you can buy a new chair. You can buy a new table. You can burn this whole god-damned hotel to the ground and build it anew. And you can send me the bill, but by God, you'd better never contradict me again. You hear?"

Sterling never said a word—May reflected that perhaps he didn't dare lest his father's vehemence turn on him—but his eyes gleamed with enjoyment over Porter's plight. From Sterling's expression—the way he tilted back his head and looked down his nose at Porter, the tight smile that threatened to morph into a snarl in a second's notice—May could tell Sterling took far more than his fair share of pleasure in the suffering of others. May herself tried never to be cruel, never to hold hatred in her heart. She knew it'd be a moral failing to delight in this man's suffering. Still, it was undeniable that a part of her might have enjoyed watching Porter's already-gray skin blanch a shade or two lighter, enjoyed the sight of his sweat causing the calamine to dampen and run. The thought brought a twinge of guilt, but she knew the suffering headed her way was bound to be much worse than his could be.

"Of course not, Mr. Maguire." Porter wiped at his forehead, smearing the pink lotion and transferring it first to his hand and then to his pant leg when he lowered his arm. "I'd never intentionally contradict you, sir."

"Then go on and get the hell out of here."

Porter began backing out of the room, never taking his eyes off the old man. "Yes, sir, you just let May know if you need anything."

"Porter," Maguire called out, bringing May's boss to a full stop. "I don't want May here working for you anymore. You go on and hire yourself a new girl."

May might never have found the nerve to take a seat on the embroidered chair, had these words not caused her knees to buckle. As it was, she barely managed to land on its cushion rather than the floor.

"But Mr. Maguire, I ain't done nothing wrong, sir. I need my job. I got . . ."

"Yes, yes, I know. You have three children to feed," Maguire said, waving his hands not only to stop her talking, but also to dismiss her thoughts. *How could he know that unless he was the one who ordered those men to take Jilo?*

"Go on, Porter. You aren't needed here," he said, then waited for Porter to make his exit. May could feel the cloud of confused and angry energy that filled Porter leave the room, even though the thick carpet muffled his footfalls.

The moment Porter was gone, Maguire's lips curled up into a sly smile. "It's just us now, May. Family. So please allow me to speak plainly." He waved his finger at her like she was a naughty child. "Old Tuesday, she done told me that you didn't inherit any of her magic. She lied."

TEN

"Oh, yes, your mama done told me a fib, now, didn't she?" Maguire said, a canary-eating cat smile setting up camp on his face. May knew she was the bird, and that even though he was enjoying every second of batting her around, soon tooth and claw would come out. She hesitated, her skin tingling as she contemplated fleeing.

"Look at it, Sterling," Maguire's words pulled her from her calculations. "Isn't it beautiful?" May's eyes followed the men's stares right down to her own hands, her own fingertips that were alive with the same blue-green sparks she'd spent a lifetime trying to extinguish. "This isn't just some old Doc Buzzard hair, spit, and metal shavings buried under your porch. That there is real magic."

Doctor Buzzard. A single name shared by many root doctors, men who with varying degrees of sincerity and skill worked Hoodoo, taking your hard-earned money to put a fix on your enemy or—worse yet—remove the fix your enemy put on you. A lot of the Buzzards were charlatans, plain and simple, but there were a few, a precious few, who really did know how to work magic. These men, the ones who weren't just playacting, mostly didn't mess around with curses and fixes. No, the men with real power spent their time trying to help people.

'Course it wasn't just men. Plenty of women working the Hoodoo, too. The women weren't called "Doctor," though. They were always referred to as "Mother." Folk around Savannah had always assumed May's mother was just another of these root doctors, but deep down May had always known better. Even though Mother Tuesday had refused to share the details of her magic with her daughter, May had always known her mama had tapped into a source of power that the others didn't even know about. May had always known that if she so desired, she could draw from that same well.

"Closer," the older man's voice startled her. "Closer!"

Sterling scrambled to navigate his father's chair nearer to May. In his haste, the younger man bumped into the table, causing his half-full coffee cup to jitter around in its saucer. Maguire's body lurched forward, unprepared for even the slightest jarring. It chilled May's soul to watch as the elder Maguire looked up at his own flesh and blood with complete disdain. "You clumsy oaf. You tip me out, and I will see you horsewhipped. You hear me, boy?" Sterling blanched, his reaction telling May that this was no idle threat. Maguire pushed on the arm of his chair so that he could turn a tad more toward his son. "I asked if you heard me."

"Yes, sir. I heard you," Sterling replied. May nearly felt a twinge of sympathy for this young man. What kind of upbringing must he have had? What daily tortures had he faced at the hands of his own father? Her expression must have betrayed her thoughts, for Sterling seemed to take note of May's softening toward him. His face hardened, forming creases and lines that shouldn't find a home on a face so young. His eyes narrowed with a hatred so complete May shuddered under its weight. She looked away before it could bore any more deeply into her soul.

May felt Maguire's focus return to her. She reached down and wrapped her hands up in the length of her apron, but Maguire snatched up her right hand. She struggled to free herself from his grasp, but even though his lower extremities had failed him, his hands revealed a steely strength. He watched the sparkles with an enraptured glee in his eyes.

"Yes, I knew old Tuesday was lying," he said, turning May's hand over so that he could see the palm. He traced the crease of her hand with his index finger, then leaned forward and attempted to kiss her palm. May's revulsion was so complete that it gave her the added strength she needed to break free. In the same movement, she scooted her chair back a good two feet.

The old man tilted back, his eyes widening for a moment in anger, but then a hearty laugh broke free from him.

"I don't use it." May tried to make the statement sound matter-of-fact. Final. "I promised Mama."

"Well, your mama is longer here. I've been bound to this damn chair since the day Tuesday left this world. She tried to take me with her, but all she managed to do was this." He pulled the blanket covering his legs to one side and slapped his hand angrily against his unusable limbs. "She took my legs." He hesitated. "And she took my power. Now you," his right eye twitched as he spoke, "you're gonna help fix what your mama done broke."

He's the one, May thought. *This is the man my mother died trying to stop.* "I'm sorry, sir. I can't. A vow is a vow, whether she is with us or not. She made me promise not to make the same deal she had made." Even though May knew the other staff must have been ordered to stay away from the dining room, she still cast a nervous glance around before continuing. "My mama said she made a deal with the devil to use her magic. She made me promise I wouldn't do as she done."

Maguire pursed his lips and narrowed his eyes. He leaned forward, his body convulsing, and at first May thought he had developed a coughing jag. When he sat back up, tears of laughter were rolling down his flushed cheeks. "Oh, my dear girl," he said after he managed to catch his breath. "A deal with the devil?" He paused. "If only it were anywhere near that easy."

"No, sir." She shook her head. "No, sir. I want nothing of it. I've never used it. I never will." She focused on the floor, not daring to look him in the eye.

"You used magic last night, May." His words came out in a slow grumble. "I can smell it on you."

May realized her head continued to shake as she spoke. "No, sir. It wasn't me. Whatever you think I did, it wasn't me." May did her best to recompose herself. She forced a smile and smoothed her skirt, preparing to stand and make her exit.

"That's the way with your kind, always lying when the truth would serve you better." He paused, as if giving her a chance to confess, and then boomed out, "I saw you there with my own two eyes," any pretense of civility cast aside. May startled in spite of herself. His face was nearly purple with rage.

May was an honest woman. It pained her to tell a lie, let alone be caught in one, even by a man such as this one. "Only a little. Last night was different. It was the first time. The only time. I was so afraid . . ." May's word died in the air as she wondered again at the Maguires' role in the events of the previous night. The father could never have managed it. The son was graceless. He could never had entered and exited with such stealth. Still, if they hadn't done it themselves, they'd arranged for it to happen. They couldn't have relied on magic, for the haint blue her mama had made her use at every entrance and window would've kept hostile magic from creeping in. No, it could only have been a flesh-and-blood intruder. May wished she knew how they'd worked it, if only to prevent it from happening again. But she dared not even confront them with their crime.

Maguire disregarded her silence. "And still, first time out, you achieved outstanding results."

May's knees went weak, too weak to stand. She drew her arms around herself, folding them over her chest as if to protect her heart. "Yes. I used it last night. Somehow. But I don't know how I did it. I don't know anything about the magic, sir. Mama, she never explained it to me." May thought of the creature who had come to her at the edge of the clearing. She came close to mentioning her, but something told her to hold her tongue. "It just happened, like it's happening now." When she held up her hand, the sparks were still shooting along her fingertips. "I don't know anything about it at all."

"What is the source of your magic?"

"I . . ." May's lips moved, but it took a while for her words to catch up. "I don't know."

Maguire's anger faded as quickly as it had been kindled. "No, maybe you don't," he said and chuckled. He looked over his shoulder at Sterling. "What do you think, boy? You think she's telling us the truth?"

"I am, Mr. Maguire. I swear it. I am sorry for any difficulties between you and my mama, but I'll never be any trouble to you." She forced a smile again, grateful that the tingling in her hands was starting to fade and the tiny sparks were once again disappearing. "You got nothing to worry about from May. Nothing at all."

May's eyes drifted up to the younger man's face. As their eyes met, May searched for even the tiniest spark of humanity. She found only ice. "I believe her," he said.

"Yes, I do as well," Maguire said, turning back to May. "It's a pity, really, that power should be wasted on one such as you. The Beekeeper—you saw her last night, don't pretend you didn't—that's where your mama's—and *your*—power comes from." The name made sense to May, from the creature's heavy veils to the way it broke apart into a thousand stinging wasps. "I've only ever seen the creature twice, but I've felt her presence many times. You could even say I've courted her, but she has never warmed to my overtures. This creature's magic feels infinite. The wonders I could perform if I had access to it . . ." Maguire's voice took on a wistful quality. "Oh, the wonders I *have* performed with what little power I could attain." Images, unclean and full of cruelty, rose up in May's mind. Her hands rose to her eyes, as if they could shield her from those scenes.

Maguire chuckled at her distress and rubbed his hands together in pleasure. "Perhaps, once I have been set to rights, I should make a study of you, but for now I believe it is *I* who will give *you* a little lesson." He looked over his shoulder at the ever-attentive Sterling. "Help me take off my jacket."

Sterling stood behind his father and helped him extricate himself from his suit coat, which the son then folded and draped over his arm. Freed of the jacket, Maguire unbuttoned the sleeve of his starched white shirt and slid it toward his elbow.

A scent like a freshly struck match reached May's nose. Her nostrils flared as she pulled away from the scent. May was shocked to see the elderly man's arm covered by scarred and blackened flesh that ran from his wrist to beyond the point on his elbow where the fabric was bunched up.

"This here," he said twisting his arm so that May could fully take it in, "is your mama's handiwork. A parting gift, if you will, from old Tuesday." May shook her head and tried to avert her eyes. "Look at it," Maguire's words came out in a snarl, "so that you may understand what has been taken from me. You see, some people, are born to magic. It's born right in them. Others, such as yourself and your mother, have magic come to them. Then there are people like me, those who seek magic out. I am . . . I was what some refer to as a 'collector.' " The sleeve slipped down, and his ancient, mottled hand caught it and forced it back up above his elbow. "A long time ago," Maguire said, his voice taking on a singsong quality, as he held out his forearm for her examination, "I did someone very powerful—someone who was born to magic, call him a witch if you will—a very big favor. In return, he put his mark on me. It was nothing more than a single band back then, but over time it grew." He rubbed his hand along the scarred tissue, stopping to tap his index finger on the ruined remains of what must have been some kind of symbol. As he did so, it took on a faint and sickly luminescence, which spread out along a spider's web of increasingly visible traces.

Maguire looked at May and nodded. "Thanks to your mama, there's not much magic left in me at all. She damaged me so these markings no longer work the way they once did," he said as the lines began to take on new shapes. He leaned in toward her conspiratorially, intimately, as if they were lifelong friends. "The energy of every life I took with this hand would become mine to do with as I wished." His smile fell flat in reaction to something he must have read in her eyes. "Oh, May, even you must admit that so many people waste their potential. Rather than letting them continue to shuffle from disappointment to disaster, I relieved their worthless, unhappy souls of their burdens and turned their energy toward something more productive. In a way, it could be argued that I showed these unfortunates great kindness.

"But your mama"—his eyes took on a strange fire—"she didn't see it that way. No. She didn't like how I got my magic, and she sure as hell didn't like what I did with it. I tried reason, but reason is not an arena in which the weaker sex excels." He nodded backward toward Sterling. "Even a young fellow here like Sterling can attest to that. Can't you, boy?"

"Yes, sir," Sterling responded, dropping his answer as mechanically as a jukebox will play a favorite song for a nickel.

"Your mama was an extreme case. So rebellious, she was, but the women in your family always were. No matter how many times you faced the whip"—a smirk rose on his lips—"or the rod." He leered at her, leaving May feeling soiled. His voice changed in the next instant, taking on the patient and benevolent timbre of a Sunday school teacher. "This world, you must understand, was built to work in a certain way, but your mama refused to see it. Refused to see that this world needs to have its masters. We're the ones who carry the weight of the world and maintain order. We protect you.

"This, my girl, is the white man's world. The way it was intended to be. I've spent so many years, more than you can begin to know, dedicating myself to protecting the natural order. Without men like me, there would be chaos. Your mama, she refused to understand, and she did some damage. Now it's up to you to set things right.

"You see, May, even without my magic or my health, I am still a very powerful man. I've been pulling strings in your life you never even knew were there. It took no magic to make your daughter-in-law's dreams come true. Dangle a shiny bauble before her, and I knew she'd drop those precious little grandchildren of yours right into your lap. And I knew the second you sensed one of your girls was in danger, you'd show me that magic you've been hiding, my girl.

"My Klan brethren were ignorant of my true aim, but they were all too happy to participate in the ceremony. Men like that are best kept ignorant. Makes it much easier to turn their hate toward your own purpose. They only ask that you let them believe the pallor of their unwashed skin is all they need to be worthwhile. You know," he said, placing his hand under his chin, "most of the men who fought and died to preserve the institution of slavery never owned a slave. Never would, even if the North had been turned back. I believe those fellows were fighting for the right to feel superior to someone. The fools never realized they shared the same masters you colored did, only we didn't even have to feed them." He nodded his head as he spoke, seemingly in agreement with his own idea.

He lowered his voice and leaned in to take her hand, acting as if there should be a shared sympathy between them. She snatched it from his grasp. The look he gave her was that of an adult weary of dealing with a recalcitrant child. "If Tuesday hadn't lied, if it were true you had no magic, then this would all be settled. Sure, you would have faced some anguish upon waking to learn the child was gone, but her fate would have remained a mystery. Each night, you could have laid your head on your pillow without the burden of involvement. But as with

Eve, your rebellious nature has cost you your right to innocence. Now, I'm afraid the choice falls to you."

Maguire reached back and motioned to Sterling. "The satchel. The satchel," he said again, never looking at his son, merely wagging the fingers on his upturned hand until Sterling delivered the black leather bag. Maguire's knuckles turned white as he set the bag on the plaid blanket covering his lap.

He released the handle and unzipped the bag. "If it hadn't taken so long to track down my old friend here, we would have had this conversation much sooner." He reached his hand into the opening and pulled out an odd-shaped container. May's soul chilled at the mere sight of it. "Alabaster," he said, "very cool to the touch. It belies the fire contained within." May noticed some kind of lettering had been carved onto the bottle. At least she thought they were letters. Might be they were just pictures. One looked like an arrow.

"This type of ancient jar is what lies behind the stories of genies trapped in bottles," Maguire said, lifting it up in a quivering hand. "It does contain a sort of djinn. A demon, if you will. Conjured into this world by none other than Gilles de Rais himself." He returned the jar to the bag. "Sterling," his son's name formed a full, if unspoken, command. Sterling stepped to his father's side and zipped up the case while it still sat on the older man's knees. Then he moved it to the table behind his sire.

"The demon's called Barron, but don't let the sound of his name fool you. He's no more royalty than you are. Just a minor sprite, really, otherwise I never would have managed to trap him in a container such as this one. No, he's no great shakes in the grand scheme, and sadly his dark powers do not include the ability to repair the damage your mother has done to me. But he has plenty enough magic to wreak havoc on your little world." He held up his damaged arm again as if May could possibly have forgotten the sight of it. "Barron has very *particular* tastes. I'm sure you understand, don't you?"

May found herself mute with fascination. Her head turned left and right and back again, but then her eyes found his arm, and she froze in shock. The lines of Maguire's tattoo had settled into a pattern May recognized way too easily. The features of her own grandbabies smiled up at her from three tiny faces. In the next instant, they faded clean away. May bounded to her feet, knocking the heavy, embroidered chair over. She stepped backward around it, never once taking her eyes off the Maguire men.

"There, there," Maguire said. "No need for a scene. No need to offer up any minstrel-style shenanigans. Sterling," he addressed his son, commanding him with a nod of his head. Sterling circled around and righted the fallen chair, then returned to his place behind his father. "So tell me, what's it to be? Are you going to right your mother's wrongs, or shall I set poor, starved Barron loose on those tender little girls?"

"You, you," May stammered a moment before she found her voice, "are out of your goddamned mind?" She spun around, nearly tripping in her haste to leave.

"Think it over, May," Maguire said in a calm, even voice. "Claim the magic that is yours. Undo your mother's misdeeds. Save your grand-daughters. Or run, knowing that Barron will be nipping at your heels the entire way, eager to suck the marrow from your grandchildren's bones."

May froze in her tracks, knowing she'd been defeated. Her best hope, perhaps her only hope, was to accept the power she'd tried so hard to escape. She doubted that Maguire would be sated even if she did manage to heal him. She was going to have to learn how to use the magic, fast, and hope it was enough to protect her family. There was no hope that she might one day best the man; how could she succeed where even her mama had failed? And so she turned back to the pair, the same smug smile pasted on both their faces, and asked, "What do you need me to do?"

ELEVEN

At Fletcher Maguire's bidding, she followed him and his son to the guest elevator, a rarified contraption that May had only cleaned, never ridden. At the sight of the three of them approaching, the operator stepped out of the elevator and held the door open for them. May stationed herself as far as possible from the men, pressing her back into the wooden wall. To her surprise, the young man in the gold-piped maroon uniform and cap did not join them, but rather let the door close behind them. Sterling shifted around his father, taking the utmost care not to jostle him in the tight space, and produced a large and substantial-looking key. After inserting it into a hole in the brass plate, he gave it a turn to the right, released it, and then twisted the control to the left. May felt the elevator begin to descend. She watched as the hand on the dial that showed the floor shifted from 1 to B for basement, then continued to move counterclockwise as the car descended farther than she'd believed a body could go.

The car came to a smooth stop, and a moment later the doors opened. Sterling removed the key and grabbed hold of the handles of his father's wheelchair, easing him over the space between the elevator carriage and the floor. When May didn't move, Sterling looked back at her. "Come," he said.

She stepped out of the car and into a hallway that seemed to run close to the full length of the hotel above. Lights shone down from overhead, but rather than filling the length of the hall, the beams just provided dots of light in the surrounding gloom. The walls, floor, and ceiling appeared to be made of the same concrete—uniformly gray, but polished so that it gave off a sheen in those places where light reached it.

May watched in silence as Sterling inserted that key of his into a panel on the wall and turned it right. The doors of the elevator closed of their own accord, and May heard a hum as cables lifted it up, returning it, she assumed, to the hotel's main floor.

The hall was bereft of any sound other than the squeaking wheels of the elder Maguire's chair along the stone floor, syncopated by the tapping of his son's leather-soled shoes following behind. If May's tread made any noise, it was drowned out by the beating of her heart.

Each spot of light gave way to shadow, and in those dim places in between, May sensed a presence, reaching out from the emptiness of the hall, craving the light she carried in herself, or perhaps only yearning to blot it out. Feeling something brush up against her, she quickened her pace so that she could follow the Maguires in a tighter pack. Then, repulsed by their nearness, she lied to herself, trying to dupe herself into believing there was nothing lurking in the shadows, that she'd disturbed a cobweb and nothing more. She allowed herself to drift back once again, but this time something small and furry ran across her feet, brushing up against her ankle. She felt the tickle of unseen fingers along her forearm. An invisible hand grasped her wrist. She gasped and pulled away, rushing into the next circle of light. Sterling looked back over his shoulder at her. His smile lifted only one side of his mouth, and there was a gleam of dark joy in his eyes. Her fear amused him. She was left in a dance of gooseflesh and queasiness; left to choose between the devils she knew and the ones that traveled unseen.

Sterling stopped his father's chair before a red door dominated by a brass knocker in the shape of a grimacing, bearded face. Though May would be happy to be out of the long hall, she found herself wondering what horrors might lay behind the incongruous door. Sterling grasped the bottom of the beard and knocked three times before reaching down and turning the oversized doorknob.

"You'll want to enter backward, my girl," Maguire called out to her, "or you might not like what you see. I do have a wee bit of magic left to me despite your mama's best efforts." Sterling opened the door wide, then gripped the handles of his father's chair and backed it into the room. She hesitated, not wanting to turn her back on the men, but she didn't see as she rightly had any choice. Grasping hold of the door frame, she stepped backward over the threshold. As soon as she cleared it, she turned to face the interior—it was a large room, bigger even than the hotel's grand ballroom, but still, as far as her eye could tell, a perfectly normal room.

Six square pillars, constructed of the same buffed concrete as the hall, were spaced evenly around the room. The walls were also concrete, but two were covered in murals wrought by a hand that had brought a nearly photographic quality to them. Their coloring was far more natural than any of the painted photographs May had ever seen. One featured a pine forest that looked natural enough to walk into, and the other, a long stretch of beach, buffeted by blue sky overhead and what looked to be miles of white sand stretching off in the distance. A third wall remained blank gray concrete, and the fourth was painted white with what appeared to be the early stages of a sketch of a pasture with tall mountains.

Unlike the sparsely lit hall, this room was as bright as midday. May's eyes drifted upward to find the source of the light, surprised to see that the ceiling overhead appeared to be a blue summer sky. The light itself was projected by a single golden source in the center of the room that, for all the world, May would have sworn was the sun itself. It astounded her to think she had worked at the Pinnacle for years without knowing this subterranean room existed.

May felt the weight of the men's eyes on her. She turned to face them. "What is this place?"

Maguire's face beamed with joy, his eyes widening and a genuine smile rising to his lips. "It's a work in progress, is what it is." He slapped the side of his chair and waved his hand forward, signaling for his son to push him closer to May. "But when it's finished," he said, "it will serve as sanctuary, a refuge . . ." He held up his hand to tell Sterling he should stop. "A shelter." He raised both hands and gestured around the chamber. "When the big boy drops," he said, "and I assure you he will, this will be the place to be."

May shook her head. "I don't understand."

"No," Maguire said, then laughed. "You wouldn't. But take my word for it. There are greater waves washing over this world than anything you or your mama could've ever kicked up. And I intend to ride that wave, May, but I need you to set me right before I can do that."

May felt a chill and pulled her arms around herself. "I done told you, I don't know what you want from me. Even if I had magic . . ."

"Oh, you do, May. You do. That much has been clearly established."

"All right," she said, "but I still don't know how to use it. I don't know how to undo what you say my mama did."

"You don't need to worry about that, my dear. A battery doesn't need to understand a flashlight. It just needs to provide the power." He looked back over his shoulder at his son. "Is everything in order?"

"Yes, sir." Sterling spoke the words without taking his eyes off May.

Maguire still clutched the jar that held the demon. He now lifted it using both of his weak and trembling hands. "We won't be needing this, will we, May?" His eyes twinkled up at her, seemingly pleased by what they read on her face. He looked back at his son. "Return this to safekeeping." Sterling took charge of the container, then wandered off to the far end of the room. May watched as he unlocked a panel in the floor, opened a trapdoor, and replaced the jar in the hollow beneath it. After he closed the door and locked it, he rushed back over to rejoin them.

"Move us into position," Maguire said, waving his arm toward the far corner of the room. Obedient as always, Sterling began pushing his father in the direction of the older man's impatient gesture. May followed a few paces behind, keeping an eye on the door, calculating the speed at which she'd have to flee to reach it before the younger Maguire could catch up to her. May realized her worn-out joints could never carry her quickly enough. As she followed, she cast a glance around this room of illusions, thinking that this unnatural space might be where she breathed her last. She began a prayer for safety, if not for herself, at least for her girls. Even if she managed to do what Maguire wanted, how could she be sure that he wouldn't still come after them?

"I'm a man of my word," Maguire said, like he'd somehow read her mind. "You do as I ask you, and you will see your granddaughters as soon as we're done. So step quickly."

When May joined them near the blank gray wall, her attention was soon drawn downward to a marking carved into the floor that resembled the number eight lying on its side. Each half of the eight was large enough for a body to stand inside. This reclining eight was encircled by a band of red, whether painted or inlayed, May couldn't say. Far from being the outer boundary of the image, the circle served as the center of an eight-pointed star.

"The Star of Regeneration," Maguire said, answering a question May wouldn't have considered asking. She didn't want to understand the star's design or purpose. All she wanted was to put this nightmare behind her. Maguire placed his hands on the wheels of his chair and took control of its movement, wheeling himself into the center of the star.

"You, May, are the battery, and this," he said, motioning to the space on the floor around him, "is the flashlight. Come closer, but don't step into the circle."

May hesitated, testing it before committing by touching her toe against an outer point of the star.

Maguire laughed. "Really, girl, it won't shock you. I keep telling you, it's you who'll supply the current." May took a couple of steps toward him, but stopped well out of his physical reach. "Your mama damaged this body," he began, once again unrolling his sleeve to show his damaged flesh. "She did her best to kill it." His wording, saying "it" rather than "me" struck May as strange, but most things about this horrible man seemed off to her. "Damned near did what she set out to do, too. I'll give credit where credit is due. She took my legs. And she took my power."

He began unbuttoning his shirt, and May's stomach turned as she saw the newly exposed flesh, from collarbone to navel. Just like his arms, it was covered by the burn-scarred patterns of a collector. The markings had spread to his left arm as well, down to his elbow. She trembled, wondering how many lives he'd ended to complete this hellish pattern. "This took a long time to accomplish," he said, catching her eye, "and, yes, many deaths. And your mama took it all from me in a moment."

He held up his arms, and Sterling stepped up to help him remove the garment. He slid back into his chair, smiling at her, giving her the time to take in the full horror of what sat before her. The burned tattoos weren't the worst of it—a mass sat over where his heart should be, woven from layer upon twisted layer of the ugly filigree, veins knotted and woven together. All the filaments that ran over his arms and torso seemed flattened, dead, and they gave off a scent that bore witness to that ruin. May brought her hand over her mouth. Her eyes returned to the center of his chest, drawn by the pulsing of the inky purple tangle there.

Maguire pointed to the movement. "That's it, May, the last of my magic. And it's fading fast." He rocked the wheels of his chair, maneuvering himself into the right side of the figure eight.

May jumped at Sterling's touch. He had come up behind her and grabbed her by the upper arms. Shifting her a good two feet backward with a strong, rough jerk, he said, "We need you here," and shoved her down. She found herself sitting, her legs bent together and splayed out to the side, in the dead center of the design's lowermost triangle. He reached into his pocket and pulled out a small folding knife. After flipping it open, he knelt before her, grabbed her right hand, and made a quick slice in her palm. It hurt like hell, so she drew a quick breath, but that was it. She'd be damned before she gave him the pleasure of seeing her suffer. He placed her bleeding hand over the point where two lines intersected. Then he did the same with her left hand, which he also arranged at a crossing point of two of the star's intersecting lines.

"Stay there," he said, his bright blue eyes boring into her.

Sterling stood and stepped around her to join his father at the center of the circle. Once in position, he stripped off his own shirt and tossed the garment aside, using enough force for it to land beyond the design's boundaries.

"My son will serve to ground your power, helping to focus it and channel it through the star. Really, you have nothing to worry about. He'll be doing the work for you."

May's mouth went dry. She ran her tongue over her lips. "What do I need to do?"

The old man chuckled. "All I need from you is to stop resisting. Let the power you've been fighting flow through you freely." Sterling knelt in the leftmost portion of the figure eight, but he stationed himself close enough to his father that the two could reach out and take hold of each other's hands. "Imagine it, May, it will be so easy. The power wants you, and whether you want to admit it or not, you crave it. Let go of those promises you made your mother, the promises you made yourself. It's time."

Through the tears blurring her vision, May could see the blue-green sparks begin to dance along her fingertips. If she felt she had a single choice left to her in this world, she would have forced herself up from the floor and fled this place as fast as her feet could carry her. Maguire was right that the power did seem to want to fill her, but he was wrong about her wanting it. No, May had never wanted the magic. May wanted security. She craved love and companionship. She dreamed of a happy and peaceful life for her grandchildren. Not this.

"You have to accept the power. You have to invite it in," the elder Maguire said. "Or perhaps you've changed your mind? Should I have Sterling fetch Barron after all? Maybe you'll be more willing to cooperate after he's tasted one of your sweet girls."

May looked up at him, and it was in that precise moment she lost her lifelong battle—not her struggle to resist the power, but her struggle to resist hate. She let the magic surge through her, though her fondest wish was that it would destroy the old man and his son, wiping the Maguire seed from the face of the earth.

She felt heavier, as if gravity had grown stronger, or the floor beneath her had caught hold of her and was trying to pull her down. When she looked down at her hands, she was astounded to see the magic flowing through them—no longer tiny sparks, but liquid blue flames jetting out of her own body and into the design on the floor. The strange fire tore along the path set out by the intersecting lines and engulfed the circle at the center of the star.

"It's working, Father," Sterling said, his eyes wide with joyous amazement.

"Yes," Maguire responded, "it is."

The energy jumped from the circle to the figure eight within it. Sterling began laughing, cheered on by their success, but the laughter abruptly stopped. He began making strangled, whimpering noises, and the look of joy in his eyes turned to one of fear. "It burns. Why does it burn?"

"Because," his father said, "it's fire."

May watched as the flames rushed away from Sterling and turned full force toward his father. For a moment May hoped she'd have her wish, that she would watch this monster burn, but he seemed to welcome the fire. He watched as the flames climbed up his worthless legs, then threw back his head in a triumphant gesture. Rather than consume him, the flames entered him, traveling into the now-writhing marks of the collector.

Sterling reached over with his free hand, trying to pry himself from his father's grasp, but the old man's fingers fixed on the younger man's arm like a steel trap. The collector's marks rose up from Maguire's body, deserting first his left arm, then his torso. The whole design, now a living band of energy, wound its way around his right arm, forming a tight coil. Then it rose up, in a sudden flash of activity, and a head like a serpent's shot out and buried its fangs into Sterling's arm. The younger man began screaming, but May could only feel contempt as she noticed urine puddle on the floor around him.

The head of the marking buried itself into the young man's otherwise unblemished soft pink skin, then writhed its way through his arm. Just below his agonized cries, May could make out the sound of flesh separating from muscle to make way for the mark. It may have taken a mere minute, maybe two, but soon the marking had completely deserted the father's body and insinuated itself fully into the son. The pattern that had once covered Fletcher was now in the same configuration on Sterling. Fletcher's body had been left with nothing but the scars of May's mama's attempts to end him.

Then there was a bright flash of light, one so blinding it caused May to remove her hands from the figure etched into the floor and shield her own eyes. That light, she realized in a breath's length of time, had come from those same hands. For a few moments the world around her was drowned in piercing light, then her right vision slowly came back to her. When it did, she could see in an instant something had changed.

The elder Maguire sat staring down at his wrinkled and spotted hands, his eyes wide in horror. "Father," the old man's voice creaked out as he looked up at Sterling. "What have you done?"

A wide smile broke across Sterling's face. "I thought you agreed it was a shame to let someone waste their potential." The voice belonged to the younger man, but something in his tone spoke of Fletcher Maguire.

"You," May began, not quite sure how to phrase it, "you took your own son."

"Ah, May, don't look at me like that," Sterling said. "A body can only be marked as a collector once. You get one mark, and then you have to tend it, like a garden. Your mama corrupted that body," he nodded to the old man in the wheelchair, "she salted the fields, so to speak. I had no choice but to find new accommodations."

The old man raised his head. "Help me," he called to her. "Help me."

"Now, now," Sterling said, crossing the room to retrieve the shirt that had been cast aside earlier. "Why on earth would she want to do that?" He pulled the shirt on, and began buttoning it, clearly delighted with the nimbleness of his new fingers. May stood, never once taking her eyes off the pair, and stepped away from the diagram.

Once he was dressed, Sterling knelt by the old man's wheelchair and started to button up the shirt that had been his own just moments before.

"*Father,*" the old man pleaded.

Sterling reached back and slapped the old man, the sound of the blow echoing in the large room. "Don't ever call me that again, or I'll have you committed. And it would be a shame for Fletcher Maguire's reputation to be ruined by having him end his days in a madhouse."

Sterling looked up at May. "You're free to go," he said. "You'll find there are stairs at the far end of the hall." He smiled and gave her a wink. "Of course the exit lets out at a different point each time. Let's hope you don't find yourself stranded too far from home."

May had no idea what the man was saying, but she started backing her way toward the door all the same.

"Oh, May," Sterling called. "One more thing." She froze in place. "Now that you have access to all that magic, don't go thinking you're done with me. What's yours belongs to me, girlie, 'cause *you* belong to me." He stood and grabbed the handles of the wheelchair, nearly running as he pushed the old man's body right up to her. "And don't be thinking about trying to run away either, 'cause I got ways to cure you of your drapetomania right quick."

TWELVE

A cloud of dust kicked up around May as she made her way home. She didn't stop, didn't look up to determine its source. She knew it had to be the same police car that had been trailing her for miles. It would come to a stop every quarter of a mile or so, wait for her to pass, then continue to move. It was a message from Maguire. She was being watched, and the whole damned world was on his side. This time the car didn't rev up its engine and speed past. It pulled up alongside her instead.

"You ain't thinkin' 'bout leavin', now are you, Auntie," a voice called out. She glanced up at the deputy who'd spoken to her, but she couldn't risk doing or saying anything that would give them the excuse to put her in the back of that patrol car. Maybe that was Maguire's intent by having them follow her. No doubt, he delighted in the thought of her stewing behind bars, helpless in the knowledge there was nothing she could do to save the girls from the monster he kept in his jar.

"We gonna keep an eye out on you." The officers in the car laughed, then hit the gas, showering her with a cloud of dirt and tiny stones.

May ignored the sting of rocks meeting flesh. She had to focus on the problem at hand. She had to figure out a way to protect the girls.

Martha had promised to look in on the girls while May was at work. May and Martha had never been the closest of sisters-in-law—Reuben had never enjoyed the best of relations with his brother, Martha's husband—but May knew she could count on Martha to keep her word. She was probably with the girls now. And even though Martha couldn't stand the sight of the girls' mama, she wouldn't hold that against them. She'd help May protect them.

How far from home would May have to go to escape Maguire's reach? Perhaps her only hope was to learn how to use the magic she'd now claimed to protect herself and the girls. Problem was she had no idea where to start.

May rounded the corner to discover the patrol car that had been following her sat at the head of the turnoff leading to her home. She lowered her gaze and quickened her pace, but an odd feeling crept over her as she turned wide to avoid going near the patrol car. She looked up.

It struck her at once that the car appeared to be empty, though she could hear the idling of its engine. Fearful that they might be planning an ambush, she scanned the area around the car and picked up her pace, though not fast enough for it to be perceived as running, an act that might cause the policemen to give chase. She had made it only a few yards when a sound, something caught between a dog's pant and the whimper of a frightened child, caused her to look into the tall grass growing around the drainage ditch that lined the road. The unexpected gore made her startle and nearly scream. A cloud of flies was feasting on a sea of blood, already baking dry in the morning sun, on a large stone by the side of the road. One of the officers from the car was writhing on his back in the grass, his belly ripped clean open, his hands frantically trying to restore his insides to his abdomen. May knew he should be screaming, *would* be screaming, but the flies that had failed to find purchase on the stone had packed his mouth full with their wriggling and opalescent bodies.

May barely had time to take three steps back before a scream from a few yards farther down the road wrested her gaze from the bloody scene. Her eyes landed on the man's partner, struggling near a patch of blackberry bushes. Turning in wild gyrations, he was swatting and clawing at something black that rode on his head. As he stumbled closer, May could make out what that blackness was. Lester, the rooster she greeted each dawn, had his claws buried in the man's scalp, and was happily going about pecking out his eyes.

May heard her own voice rise up, ready to give witness to her own terror, but a few strained groans were all it could muster before her mind commanded her to flee. She ran. Not like the old woman she was, with stiff hips and aching knees, but like a frightened deer that has heard the first gunshot and knows that there are hunters in the wood. She carried on, not stopping and not looking back until she arrived at the gray dirt road that led to her house. Then her years caught up with her. Drops of sweat rained from her forehead, even though she felt colder than she'd ever been. Her heart was pounding so fast in her chest she thought this might be the death of her, but the white walls of her small house peeked through the scraggly pines, and their promise of safety urged her on. The adrenaline that had carried her home deserted her completely, leaving her to struggle the short distance to the house, feeling every bit like there were lead weights around her ankles.

She carried on around the bend, one heavy halting step after another, already breathless when she arrived home. Though she thought she'd had all the fright a body could survive in a single day, the sight that welcomed her stopped her dead in her tracks. The Beekeeper, masked by her heavy veil, stood at the center of a miraculous garden that had sprung up since morning. A few hours ago, there had been only spotty grass and dry soil in this place. Now buds were bursting into full bloom, their opening timed for May's arrival.

May drew nearer, and after several moments passed, she realized her feet were no longer touching the ground. A part of her mind told her that she should be terrified of this creature, but its warning voice grew fainter the closer she got. May rubbed her eyes, certain the shock she had just suffered had stopped her heart. She could not be floating. She knew that. And this impossible creature could not have returned. Could not be standing dead center in a miniature miraculous Eden. No. None of this could be real. She opened her eyes, sure the image would have faded.

Still, the Beekeeper remained, and now May recognized the buzzing sound that accompanied her presence. It was matched by a kind of fluttering, shimmering vibration that made it impossible, even beneath the glare of the full sun, to capture a steady image of her.

May glided right up to the edge of the garden, where the intoxicating scent of yellow jessamine, a flower long past its normal blooming season, vied with whiffs of white gardenia and a kaleidoscope of four-o'clocks. Bergamot and honeysuckle beckoned a tiny hummingbird that hovered and bobbed, as if in homage to the Beekeeper, the founder of this feast, before darting around the flowers.

The soles of May's feet lowered to touch the earth. All fear had sloughed off now, and her heart told her to run and throw herself into the Beekeeper's waiting embrace. But before she could move, before she could act on her will, Martha appeared before her, walking clean through the Beekeeper without taking notice of the creature's presence. The flush of the magic fell away, causing the garden to disappear, its miraculous flowers disintegrating to dust, and May's unquestioning trust of this creature seemed to melt away in the same instant.

Martha came to a stop in front of May and grabbed ahold of her wrist, piercing her with her frightened, tear-filled eyes. "There were men come by a while ago." She pointed toward May's house behind her.

"Things are pretty busted up in there. What did you do, anyway?" She dropped May's arm and pushed her way around her. "No. Don't tell me. I don't want to know nothing about it. I'm sorry, May. I truly am. But I can't have any kind of trouble. I can't be a part of this."

"But the girls . . ."

"I'm sorry, but I got children and grandchildren of my own to worry about. I can't go getting mixed up in whatever trouble you've done gotten yourself mired in. I'm sorry," Martha said again, but she didn't look back as she stomped her way toward the drive, her determined pace carrying her quickly away from May's yard and toward the bend in the road.

"Let this drab little sister go home." May jumped at the sound of the voice, and turned to find the Beekeeper once again stood behind her, although the miraculous garden seemed to have disappeared for good. "You don't need her, 'cause you have me."

"I gotta see to my girls," May said, sick at heart for them.

"Don't worry about your babies. They're safe. And we're gonna see to it they stay that way."

"But they must be frightened."

"Frightened? Those babies of yours are a hell of a lot tougher than you think. If I were you, I'd make sure they knew it was me before I stepped foot inside. They're getting ready to flatten the next person through the door." The Beekeeper first chuckled, then pushed the bottom of her veil to the side and spat. "Dry. Dry. Dry. What the hell does a body have to do get a drink around here?"

Something about the sight of this faceless creature spitting in her yard convinced May she must be dreaming. Any moment she would awaken. Begin her day, her *real* day, not this mad fantasy that couldn't possibly be real.

"I can get you some water . . ."

"I do not want water," the creature's tone turned harsh.

"Chicory, then," the words tumbled from her mouth. "I have chicory. I could brew you some."

The Beekeeper lunged forward. "I do not want your damned chicory. Do I look like a whore for your damned chicory? What kind of goddamned house do you keep, that you ain't got even a drop of drink for your friends? Your mother, she knew how to treat a guest."

This was madness. May crumpled, falling to her knees. Dream or no, she'd had enough.

"There, there, my dearie. Not to worry." The Beekeeper waved a gloved hand in the air, and a bottle appeared in it. Her other hand pushed back the bottom of her veil, revealing the same terrible emptiness that had so frightened May the night before. It was a blankness, a void that gave a person's very soul a sense of vertigo, as if there were a danger of toppling into it and falling forever.

The eternal darkness she sensed within the creature caused her mind to flash on the horror at the turnoff. "Did you kill those men?"

"Only the one," the Beekeeper responded. "Needed the other alive to tell the tale." She took another swig. "That bastard used those men to send you a message, so we used them to send him one back."

She wanted to feel bad that a man had died, but she couldn't. May began shaking. She wrapped her arms around her chest to help still the trembling.

"You calm yourself." The woman waved her free hand over the bottle in her other hand. May jolted when she felt the glass in her own hand. "Go on, taste." May began to refuse, but the Beekeeper carried on. "It is very good rum. It has the pepper's fire," she added before returning her focus to the bottle. "No? Your mama and I used to drink until we were both falling down drunk. Falling through each other. Falling through the stars." A wistful delight sounded in her voice.

"I am not my mother," May responded, holding the bottle out to her.

The Beekeeper wiggled her gloved fingers, and the bottle was once again in her clasp. "More's the pity," she said, then brushed back the veil for another swig. As the veil fell back into place, she jumped to a new train of thought. "She can see me, you know, your little one, even though she isn't of your blood." The creature's tone made it sound like she was contemplating the implications. "But the other two. The ones who should be my daughters. Nothing. I stand directly before them . . ." The Beekeeper was suddenly mere inches away, her veiled face an intimate distance from May's, her hand waving before May's eyes. The Beekeeper took a step back, then stood there swaying, ". . .and nothing."

May trembled. "She's my grandbaby. Blood or no." Fear and longing battled in her spirit.

"Well, of course, the heart speaks the truth even when blood itself lies." The Beekeeper fell back, suddenly several yards away. "But the little one. She's claiming the others' magic. Making it hers. This is something that should not be."

This odd being frightened and soothed her in the same instant, but the need to protect her own pushed her toward the side of caution. May squinted, trying to pin the quivering image in place for inspection. "What . . . are you?"

To May's amazement, the veiled creature began sashaying from side to side, her feet lifting and landing in a peculiar kind of dance. "I am what I have always been and what you would make of me." She began to weave a circle around May, brushing up against her, catlike. "Embrace me, and I am the gentlest of mothers. Flee me, and I am the cruelest of predators. Offer me again your da—" She paused playfully on the word, then continued, "—*delightful* chicory, and you will find out for yourself where I land between those two extremes. Your foolish Prohibition has ended, has it not? For all I have to give you, I do not ask for much in return. Your mother certainly had no trouble finding a suitable offering."

"My mama told me never to have any dealings with you."

The creature snorted, her veil puffing out a bit as she did so. She stopped her dancing and took a few heavy old woman steps toward May's house. May was about to chase after her, intent on stopping her before she could reach the children, but the Beekeeper came to a halt and eased down onto the front steps.

"It's true, my friend didn't want us to meet. I promised her that, if possible, I would let you pass through this world without knowing me. That's why I have stayed in the background, keeping a watchful eye over you but never initiating contact," she said, then slipped the bottle up beneath her veil. This time she took a long draw from it. "But that son of a whore . . ." She paused. "Maguire," she offered, raising the bottle in salute. "The worm forced me to break my vow. Just as he forced you to break yours." She leaned back on the steps, propping herself up on her elbows and splaying her legs in the most unladylike fashion possible on the step below.

"But he ain't gonna mess with you now." Pushing herself up a bit, she turned her face to the heavens, as if she were greeting God himself. "He ain't gonna risk it now that he knows I'm still around." The veiled face turned back to May. "You're gonna have to let me teach you the things I taught your mama. And her mama. And her mama before that. Hell, girl, your family and me, we go a long way back." The Beekeeper held her hand out to May. May felt ill at ease; Maguire had made a very similar statement. Did this creature, too, feel it somehow held ownership of her people?

May took a step or two closer and reached out, willing herself to have the bravery to touch this phantom. Her quivering hand fell back to her side. "I'm sorry. I'm afraid."

Focused on her guest, and her own trembling, May hadn't noticed the front door opening. It was the screech of the screen door that alerted her to Jilo's presence. The little one pushed the door outward, and with one chubby fist in her mouth, stumbled out onto the porch. Her eyes filled with delight at the sight of the Beekeeper.

"Jilo," May called, but it was too late. The child had already bounded, arms flung wide open, to where the Beekeeper sat.

The creature reached over and scooped the child up into her embrace. "This one," she said, "she isn't afraid of magic." She chuckled as Jilo reached out with her wet fingers and pulled the veil high. "She ain't afraid of nothing."

THIRTEEN

The Savannah Morning Star
July 13, 1936
Page A1

Local Luminary Leads Delegation to Berlin Olympics

Distinguished Savannah businessman Sterling Maguire (shown center in above photograph) will lead a group of seven Georgia state dignitaries to the Games of the XI Olympiad that are to be held next month in Berlin. "Before his death, my father grew to be a great admirer of the German chancellor," Maguire said. "I share my father's enthusiasm for this dynamic new leader of the German nation. By combining the best thinking of our own American industry with the subversion and removal of the undesirable and decadent elements of society that led to his country's decline, Chancellor Hitler has single-handedly pulled the German people out of the morass they found themselves in following the Great War. As the German people have learned from great Americans like Henry Ford, so is there much we Americans can learn from great Germans like Adolph Hitler." When asked about earlier pressures from certain fringe elements to boycott the Berlin Olympic Games, Mr. Maguire stated, "Consider the source. Why would those who would reject the Messiah Himself be any more kindly inclined toward Chancellor Hitler?" The delegation is scheduled to arrive in Berlin a week prior to the commencement of the games to allow for an official tour of the city and the new 100,000-seat stadium. The highlight of the visit will be an opportunity for the delegation to meet with both the chancellor and Minister Hermann Göring." (Story continues on page A10.)

May took her time cutting the piece from the newspaper, making sure to hold the scissors firmly in hand and to cut precisely along the straight-edge lines she'd drawn as guides. She flipped through the pages to find the article's conclusion, then repeated the process, although that bit didn't really have much to add about Maguire. It went on about some new thing called television that was gonna let people miles away from the games watch them just like they were sitting there. Kind of like radio, the article explained, just with moving pictures, too.

She dabbed a bit of paste on the back of each portion of the article and added it to the scrapbook with the other news pieces she'd collected about the Maguires since the last time she'd laid eyes on them, there in the basement of the Pinnacle. Maguire had kept plenty quiet; he must've received the Beekeeper's message loud and clear. May had been watching for news of him in the papers, and she always had an ear open for any talk on the streets. Kids still went missing, but at least none had turned up butchered like the boy she'd buried out back. All the same, May was taking no chances. Sure, she was using her magic on a regular basis now, for the benefit of others as well as herself, but she wasn't going to accept silence as surrender. May was determined to know her enemy, track his doings, and try to figure out when he might make his next move against her.

"Fletcher Maguire, Industrialist, Humanitarian, Dead at 62" was the first headline to have caught her eye. It had been front-page news only six weeks after she'd helped the father steal his own son's body. The article alluded to the stroke Fletcher had suffered the night of her mama's passing. From the way the elder Maguire's body had looked, May had thought him much older. Maybe it had been a result of her mama's final attempt to rid the world of him, or maybe it was the hate burning in his soul that had aged him so. She wondered how long it would take his foul spirit to burn through the son's young flesh.

Some days after the grand obituary stained the front page, a single paragraph, buried toward the back of the *Star*'s section C—too far back to be of much interest to the whites and not part of section D, which carried most of the colored news—announced that Mrs. Sterling Maguire had traveled to Arizona with the goal of divorcing her estranged husband. Six weeks and one day later, the society page announced Sterling Maguire's engagement to a blonde Birmingham debutante with a foreign-looking last name.

These more personal items glinted like gold among a pile of other mentions about Sterling Maguire fulfilling some civic duty or other, or mentions of the various businesses in which he owned an interest, a lot of them with names as foreign as his new wife's.

May examined the man's fine young features once more before closing the book and sliding it back under her mattress.

FOURTEEN

For the first time in months, really since the first night she'd used magic, May dreamed about her mother. In the dream, she was walking behind her mama—recognizable only by the curve of her shoulders and the way she carried herself—but her mama wouldn't turn back to look at her no matter how she pleaded.

May awoke to a scent of cigar smoke, something she hadn't smelled in her house since her mother's passing. She sat up in bed, suddenly alert, fearful that one of the girls had caught something alight. But no, she realized the next moment, this odor could be nothing other than a foul-smelling cheroot. She figured the scent was nothing more than a remnant of the dream.

Specks of dust danced in the air, and it surprised her to see sun streaming in through the window. She hadn't missed the sunrise more than a few times in her adult life, and perhaps only a few more times than that as a child.

She sure as hell was no longer a child now. Lifting her old carcass out of bed became a bit harder with each passing day. This morning everything hurt. She swung her legs out of bed and rubbed her aching knee, consciously willing relief to it. The Beekeeper had shown her how to channel healing energy from the earth itself into her aching joints, which eased the stiff pressure and allowed her to move as freely as she had twenty or more years ago. The only problem was that the magic's cure was only temporary. She had to connect with the magic again and again, willing it to rise up from the earth into her muscles and bones, "like sap rising in a tree," as the Beekeeper had put it. May worried it was like an opium smoker returning to his pipe, and the more she came to depend on magic, the more of herself she'd lose to it.

It was Maguire who'd done it to her. If magic was a trap, a snare into which Maguire had willingly fallen, he'd dragged May in with him. One trap, two souls. May understood her mama better now. Her mama had done her best to protect her from magic, and May would go to her grave doing the same for her girls. At first she doubted she'd ever be capable, but now she was determined to succeed where her mama had failed. She'd take Maguire down before she drew her last breath.

As her feet made contact with the bare wooden floor, she heard the click of a door and watched as her closet door eased open. A warm and bright amber light spilled into the room, but instead of marrying itself with the natural glow of the sun, it swirled around in it like the sheen of oil on water. The angle at which the door had opened blocked the source of the glow from her sight.

Laughter, rough but jovial, sounded from behind the door. Last year, she would have figured she was dreaming. Today, May knew better. She rose to her feet, hoping she could deal with whatever nonsense had slipped into her home before the girls awoke.

She crept up behind the door, using it to shield herself from sight, planning to peek through the crack to see what awaited her. Just before she reached it, she realized how foolish it was to think whoever or whatever stood on the other side of that door didn't already know she was there, so she stepped into the door frame, clutching the knob as if it could somehow help her maintain one foot in a sane world.

The cramped dark closet she'd always known had given way to a room whose boundaries were larger than those of her entire house, larger, she reckoned, than Savannah itself. The light she'd witnessed shone from a golden chandelier, much grander than anything the Pinnacle had ever boasted. The walls of the grand chamber before her were lined floor to ceiling with mirrors, so the dazzling bulbs, each like a miniature sun, were augmented through reflection. Beneath the chandelier stood a table whose length seemed to run on nearly forever, its far edge disappearing into the horizon, melding into its own reflection.

At the table sat a man—or at least what at first blush appeared to be a man. May was no longer so quick to make assumptions. His back was to her, but he reached up over his head and waved his hand forward, beckoning her.

"Come in, little sister," he called. In the next instant he was on the opposite side of the table, facing her.

The man, jet haired and as handsome as any matinee idol, was dressed in a worn smoking jacket. He sat in his chair reversed, with one arm draped across its back. On the table before him sat a battered top hat with a band dyed a shocking shade of red and a wicked-looking knife with a long curved blade. He lowered his head, gazing at her with a playful, mischievous look in his midnight-blue eyes. His long, elegant fingers held one of the cigars May had smelled. The other was tucked neatly between the lips of the Beekeeper, who hovered near the man, her feet not touching the ground.

"Ah, now the party can begin," the Beekeeper said, chewing the words out from around the cheroot. Her hand held an empty decanter, which she raised as if to toast May's arrival. Regarding it with disappointment, she pushed it away and reached into nothingness to retrieve another dust-covered bottle. "Do come join us, dearie."

May cast her eyes toward where the floor should be, but there was nothing but an endless depth. Stars twinkled within the sea of blackness, so she cast her eyes upward, rationalizing that its surface was so well polished, it reflected the overhead sky. That supposition was quickly dashed when she saw that the stars above did not align with those below. She tested the surface's solidity, tapping it with her toe before trusting it to support her weight. When it didn't fall out from under her, she took another step inside, pulling the door almost closed behind her, unwilling to let go of the knob in case the floor changed its mind and decided to swallow her whole.

"It's only familiarity that makes you so sure the floor beneath you will hold you up. This"—the Beekeeper wiggled her gloved fingers over the yawning chasm beneath her—"is energy." She pointed over May's shoulder to the world that lay beyond the now halfway-open door, "Just as all that is energy. Now stop trying my patience, child. Come."

May did as she was told, releasing the faceted glass knob and taking another step out into a seeming nothingness. The surface beneath her feet felt more solid as her confidence in its solidity grew.

"Yes," the Beekeeper said, reaching out her hand, which May gladly caught hold of. In that instant, the world beneath her gave way, and she, too, was floating. Her grasp tightened on the Beekeeper's glove. "Do not worry, child," the Beekeeper said with a laugh. "This world is just as solid and real as the dream you know beyond the door." She pulled her hand from May's hold, and May realized that while she didn't feel a surface beneath her, she wasn't tumbling through an eternal darkness. The world around her was sufficient to provide her with the support she needed.

How is this possible? May posed the question silently to herself.

"I don't know," the man said, then lifted his cigar to his lips. He took a puff, and as he blew it out, he raised his eyebrows and shrugged. "How is anything possible? It just is. We just are. You just are." He paused. "I have missed our sunrise meetings," he said, his lips pulling into a pout. She would have remembered this man, but before she could ask him what he meant, he stood and pulled her into a tight embrace. His lips brushed against her ear, the sensation causing her heart to leap and fanning a fire she had thought long extinguished.

"Cock-a-doodle-doo," he whispered. Without releasing her, he stepped back, eyeing her from head to toe and back up again.

"Lester?" the name came to her, though she couldn't bring herself to believe this flesh-and-blood man could be the rooster who'd greeted her so many mornings on her way to work.

"As good a name as any," he said. "I've been called many worse." He winked at her, then let her go and returned to his seat next to the Beekeeper. "Come, little sister. Sit. Join us." He motioned with a flourish of his hand toward the chair across from his own.

Without realizing she had even moved, she found herself across from him. He turned to face the Beekeeper. "She is not as dried out as you led me to believe. There is still much life in her."

"I never said otherwise," the Beekeeper shot back. She snatched up the knife from the table and wagged it at her fellow, then picked up the bottle and used the knife to cut back the wax that had been used to seal its cork. "I have only said that she *denies* that life." She worked the cork from the bottle and sent it sailing across the room. "Hold this," she commanded May, passing her the burning cigar. After taking a swig from the bottle, the Beekeeper snatched the cigar back and pressed the bottle into May's open hand. "There. Taste."

May turned the bottle around in her hand, examining it. Curious yet cautious.

"See, my friend," the Beekeeper called to the man, "she crosses the chasm to join us, but she is still terrified of letting herself go. This one is not afraid of dying; she is afraid of life."

These words snapped something inside of May. She had spent her entire damned life being so careful—head down, voice modulated to sound respectful. She gripped the bottle and pressed it to her lips, tipping her head back and drinking till she choked. The white man patted May on the back as she held the bottle out to the applauding Beekeeper.

"So, what do you have to say for yourself, little sister," he asked, as she felt her insides catch fire.

She said the first thing that came to her mind. "Hallelujah."

The Beekeeper and her associate burst out laughing in unison, and despite herself, May joined them. "Hallelujah, indeed," the man said and swiped away the bottle, tipping it to his lips and downing half its contents in a single draft.

"Hey, hey, hey." The Beekeeper swatted him on the back and wrestled the bottle from him. "Not all at once." She brushed aside her veil for another quick taste, then took a seat at the table and set the bottle down in front of her. Humming to herself, she rocked back and forth until her chair was balanced on its two back legs. She turned toward the man. "I'm proud of her, you know. I wanted her as a child, but her mother denied her to me. And she"—the Beekeeper pointed at May without looking at her—"denied herself to me as well. Until that fool servant of the Red King forced her to turn to me. She came to me not out of love for me, but out of fear of the Red King."

"Well," Lester began, his tone conciliatory, "the Red King is a fearsome creature. And little sister, she was just following her mother's wishes." He nodded in May's direction. "She's a good daughter, and you, Great Mother, should appreciate that."

"Yes," the Beekeeper said, though there was still a shred of resentment in her voice. "It has made our work harder, though, and I must prepare her for what is to come." Her veiled face turned toward May. "After all, there are worse things out there than the Red King."

May startled at her words. "What could be worse than the Red King?"

"The outsiders," the Beekeeper said, then turned to Lester as if looking to him for corroboration. "Tell her about the outsiders."

He leaned forward and planted his elbows on the table. "Ah, yes, the outsiders, little sister. You wake quivering from your dreams of the kings, but there are many more fearsome beings in creation." His bright and feverish eyes caught hers and held them. "The outsiders, they're the ones who came here and changed the native animal," he said, the bright light of the chandelier overhead creating a play of shadows that made his handsome face appear masklike. "They made man less like himself, and more like them."

"Let us make man in our image," the Beekeeper pronounced. Tilting the bottle to her lips, she began to sway and dance.

"And they made you wrong," the man said, taking no heed of the veiled one's gyrations. "Too much of this, not enough of that. No, you may fear the Red King, but the Red King, he fears those from beyond.

"Those they invested with magic, the ones you call witches, were the trickiest of all. They rebelled against the outsiders and sent them back beyond the sky, locking them"—he raised an arm and swept it around in a wide circle—"out there." He reached out and snatched the bottle from the Beekeeper's grasp, draining its contents and sending the bottle sailing to the floor. May watched as it slipped beneath the surface, falling into the endless forever. When she looked up, another bottle had appeared in his hand.

"The cleverest of the witches drew a line," the Beekeeper sang out, "locking some things out, but locking some things in."

"Things," May began, "such as yourselves?"

"No, little sister," the man said. "Not like us." His eyes grew round with terror as he leaned in toward her. "Like *them*." He pointed behind her, and she gasped and spun around, only to see her own reflection. Although her spirit dropped at the sight of her own fearful expression, the pair of them burst out laughing.

May turned back to witness the man using his sleeve to wipe away tears of mirth. "No, little sister. The Lady and I, we've been here as long as there has been a here to be."

"The globe, it formed and cooled around us," the Beekeeper said. "Your kind and all those that came before, they crawled from our flesh, they breathed in our spirit. When the outsiders came, they corrupted you, causing you to forget us and serve them. The outsiders planned to strip us of life and steal our magic. So when the witches rebelled, we helped them. Not that they knew . . ."

"Not that they would thank us anyway," Lester added, his tone full of resentment.

"They think they did it all on their own," the Beekeeper said. "And they think they can hold that line of theirs in place on their own."

"But you, little sister, you are asking yourself what this has to do with you." He raised the bottle to his lips, looking over it at her as he took a sip. "Do not deny it. Humans are all the same, only interested in what touches them directly."

"No," she reached over the table and took the bottle from his grasp. "I am wondering what *in the hell* it has to do with me." She turned the bottle up to her own mouth and drank. The couple with her cheered, but as she set the bottle down, the doorway to her own world swung wide open, revealing Jilo on the other side.

FIFTEEN

September 1940

May's ears detected a knock at the door. Knocks came much more often these days, and they came just about any time of day or night. She knew another desperate soul would soon be standing before her. Sometimes men came, but usually her visitors were women—some despairing over a man who'd gone, others over a man who wouldn't be gone. May usually didn't have much patience for the women willing to sell their souls to hold on to a man. She would just give them the taste of juju they'd come for and send them on their way. She had a lot more compassion for the women who needed to escape a man. A steady stream of them had come to see Mother May; they always did their best to hide the bruises, but most didn't succeed.

May hadn't yet been moved to kill a man, but she'd come close to it once when she was visited by a woman too busy trying to hide the marks left on the babe in her arms to worry about the welts on her own skin. No, May hadn't gotten around to killing yet, but thanks to Fletcher Maguire, she had murder in her heart. Someday, sooner or later, May knew she'd share Cain's guilt. She'd make an offering of her own to the Red King, and when that day came, the blood on her hands would belong to the son of a bitch who'd forced her into this life. On those rare nights when sleep found her, it was imagining what it would be like to watch the light expire in Maguire's eyes that lulled her into restfulness.

But May didn't sleep much anymore, thanks to Maguire and the magic he'd forced her to use. This room had once been her bedroom. Now it served as her office, and as much out of pageantry as out of magic, she had painted the entire place—walls, ceiling, and floor—haint blue. She grasped the arms of the chair that had once been her mother's, now rendered that same calming shade of cerulean.

The room's monochrome palette never failed to make an impression on those arriving—many experienced a sense of vertigo, and some even thought May was floating before them.

May. No one called her that anymore. No one. Not even those who used to know her best. Now, everybody called her Mother Wills. "Please, Mother Wills," or "You gotta help me, Mother Wills." There was always somebody coming to beg her to use the power Maguire had forced her to welcome into herself. Word had spread about her, the Negress who had stood up to Fletcher Maguire himself, and about the two lawmen—one ripped clear through and the other left sightless and disfigured. Many thought his blindness was a mercy, considering what had happened to his face.

Everyone thought she had been behind the attacks, but no one, not even the Maguires, would touch her for it. Some saw her as a hero. Others as a devil. But all were willing to place coin in her hand for a taste of her power. At first May felt bad about charging people in need. Her own mama had only accepted the occasional gift, but Maguire had ensured she lost her job, leaving her with no other means to protect or feed the children.

May had always been an honest, hardworking woman. She had been the best maid the Pinnacle Hotel had ever seen, and now she was determined to bring that same pride to the work she did in magic. Word of her skill had spread in no time, and she'd found herself a steady stream of customers. She might never grow rich—folk around her had a lot more troubles than money—but the Beekeeper had taught her enough to ensure she and the girls would never go hungry. She, too, had come to think of this entity as the Beekeeper, though it had been Maguire who had labeled her as such, not the Beekeeper herself. It was strange how Maguire forcing May out of her job was what had helped fulfill the Beekeeper's desire that May should follow in her mother's footsteps.

She heard the springs of the screen door protest as her latest client entered her home. May drew a steeling breath, which she then exhaled in a prayer for patience. The buzzing of a fat bumblebee sounded in response. May saw it appear out of nowhere, pushing through the blue wall as easily as if the wall were the sky it mimicked. This happened from time to time, the unannounced arrival of an emissary from her patron. "Oh," May addressed the hovering insect. "She interested in this one, hey? Got some sweet nectar she wants to taste for herself?"

The bee bobbed in the air, shooting up, then descending in a slow, lazy circle, until it landed on her shoulder. The sound of high heels clacking across her living room pulled her back to the present. A woman. May worked to put on her most imperious look, so that when the caller reached her, she'd perceive May not only as a woman of power, but as a woman whose time should not be wasted. She straightened her spine and grasped the arms of her chair. Clearly not bothered by her movements, the bee adjusted its position only slightly before commencing to preen itself. May shifted her focus to the entrance of her chamber, raising her head proudly to greet her latest visitor. Then the sound of a voice she'd never expected to hear again on this side of glory knocked the wind right out of her.

"Jilo, girl, you get over here. Don't you recognize your own mama?" Betty's words chased Jilo straight into May's chamber. May's other grandbabies experienced vertigo upon entering the room, but it didn't faze Jilo one bit.

"Nana, there's a crazy white woman out there," Jilo said, panic nearly turning her words into a shriek as she ran into the shelter of May's arms. The bee took off, no doubt rising to observe the scene from a better vantage point.

In the next instant, Betty, or at least a faded version of her, appeared in the doorway, shopping bag in hand. She wore a navy-blue dress, a quiet color May would never have expected of her, and even though the day beyond the lowered shades and oscillating fan of May's living room was stifling, there was a fur stole around her shoulders. Betty stopped at the threshold, teetering on her high heels, and grasped the door frame to steady herself.

"What is all this, then?" Betty asked, her words coming out with a practiced accent that said she belonged in the city, not out in the sticks.

May placed her arm around Jilo, squeezing her right shoulder and tugging her closer in the same movement. She understood the girl's confusion. This woman standing before her looked like any of the fancy buckra ladies who paraded themselves around the Pinnacle. Her hair was as long and straight as any white woman's. Its color wasn't the shade with which Betty had been born, but neither was it the obviously out-of-the-bottle red it had been when May had last laid eyes on her former daughter-in-law. It was brown. Chestnut brown. White-woman brown.

Betty's skin no longer held any of its former warm tones. It showed tan, maybe olive, like she was one of those Italians. May felt certain Betty had been bleaching herself, and she doubted the woman had spent more than a minute in the sun in the five years she had been away. May released Jilo, but let her hand slide down the girl's back and grasp ahold of her tiny fingers. She held the girl's hand tight as she pushed herself up and advanced on the prodigal mother.

"What's all this, then?" May parroted her, waving her free hand at Betty.

Betty released her grasp on the frame and took a backward step into the hall. May continued to will her back, away from her special place and into the sitting room. A pout formed on Betty's lips as she took several awkward reverse steps. May's eyes followed Betty's, which were well fixed on Jilo. "She doesn't even recognize her own mama. She doesn't recognize me at all."

May reached behind herself to close the door to her room. "How in the hell do you expect her to? You up and disappeared on her before she could walk a straight line, and now you've come here with no warning, looking like you stepped right out of *Imitation of Life*."

Betty's shoulders went slack and her face turned down. "I just thought she'd know . . . somehow." A sorrowful glint in her hazel eyes very nearly touched May's heart.

Jilo's hand slipped from May's grip, and the child took a few furtive steps forward, stopping just beyond Betty's reach. Betty knelt and set her shopping bag down beside her. Her shoulders pulled back, as if in preparation to open her arms wide for a hug, but instead she turned a little to grasp the bag and set it between herself and her daughter.

Jilo turned back toward May. "Is she really my mama?"

May struggled, but couldn't prevent a tear from falling. She couldn't bring herself to speak, so she answered with a few quick nods, her heart breaking as wonderment filled her grandbaby's eyes.

"Why, yes," Betty answered for her. "I sure am your mama." She reached into the bag. "And I brought you a present, too. You want to see it?"

Jilo cast another glance at May, her wide-open eyes questioning whether it was safe to approach this woman. Again, May signaled with a nod, trying to force a smile to her lips. She wanted Jilo to feel good about who she was, which would be a lot easier if she felt good about her mother. May felt in her bones this was only a visit. Nothing permanent. This could very well be the only chance Jilo ever had to lay eyes on her mama, and May would not take that away from her.

Following her nana's lead, Jilo responded with a nod of her head.

A bright smile formed on Betty's face, but May could still make out the traces of remorse in her eyes. Well, maybe all wasn't lost for the woman after all, May reflected. At least she knew she should feel guilt. "Brought this for you all the way from New York City."

"That where you been all this time?" The question escaped May despite her resolve not to ruin this reunion. She forced her tone to soften. "It's only I thought you were livin' in Atlanta, with that man. Porkpie."

"Porkpie?" Betty's forehead creased in confusion, then a laugh bubbled up from her. "Oh, you mean Walter. Good heavens, no. I ain't . . ." She paused to correct herself. "I haven't seen old Walter in years. I went up north with the band. I met . . . well, I decided to stay on . . ." Her words faded away, but May surmised she'd met another man. The one who'd paid for the fur. And for the dress that barely covered the woman's knees. Betty pulled a rectangular box from the bag, and took off its lid before turning it around. Inside there was a doll with auburn hair and the palest of skin, delicate freckles painted over the bridge of its nose. Its cupid lips stood out, painted a bright Venetian red like that carpet at the Pinnacle.

"See?" Betty said as she tilted the box back and forth. "Her eyes open and close. Asleep." She tilted the box back and the doll's green glass eyes shut. She tilted the doll back to an upright position. "Awake."

She held the doll out to Jilo, but when Jilo approached, she didn't take the box. Instead, she traced her fingers along Betty's hand, seeming to test if it were real, before laying her own small hand over her mother's. Betty's smile froze as she jerked back from her daughter's touch. "Here you are, sweetie," Betty said and pressed the box into Jilo's hands. "The clerk said she's called Flora, but I reckon you can name her anything you'd like."

Betty stood and smoothed her skirt, signaling, May felt, that she was done with Jilo. "Where're my other girls? Where's my Poppy? My Opal?"

JILO

Your girls. May struggled to force her spleen down. "Yo' Opal, she's gone. Took off with a soldier to California, she did." May didn't say that she'd encouraged the girl to leave. Opal's Nate was a fine young man, and he'd see to it that Opal finished her schooling. "Reckon she had more of her mama in her than I figured." May regretted the words as soon as she said them, but the urge to strike out at Betty had been festering for so very long.

May didn't even have the chance to register if her words had struck home. "She's gonna be a nurse," Jilo said, both hands clutching the box that held her gift, her eyes fixed on the doll therein.

A small smile formed on Betty's lips, and her eyes moistened. "That's good. That's very good."

"I'm gonna be a doctor," Jilo said as she carefully removed the doll from its wrapping. "That's better than a nurse."

Betty laughed, a warm laugh that showed she did hold some affection for the child, but the look of disbelief in her wide eyes told May she was about to say something foolish. "Well now, that can't . . ." May nearly used magic to will the fool woman to stop talking, but it wasn't necessary. For the first time in her selfish life, Betty seemed to think about someone other than herself. She flashed her daughter a smile nearly as superficial as the one lacquered on the doll's lips. "And you're going to be a wonderful doctor, sweet girl. You will." As she turned to face Jilo, the stole she wore shifted, revealing a damp spot on her blouse. "Why don't you go practice on your dolly there, so your nana and I can talk?"

"I don't . . ." the girl began.

"Jilo," May said, turning the name into both a command and a warning. Jilo lowered her eyes, and her lips pulled into a pout. For the first time, May was struck by how much Jilo resembled her mother—a warmer, darker copy of the original. "Jilo." This time her tone was softer, a request rather than an order. "Take your pretty girl to your room."

"Yes'm," Jilo said, moving at a reticent pace, casting a lingering glance back at her mother, as if she, too, understood she should freeze this moment in her mind. Then she turned away and began jabbering childish nonsense to the doll, inquiring about her ailments.

May's eyes drifted from the back of Jilo's head to the damp spot on her daughter-in-law's blouse.

Betty tugged the fur so that it was covered. "And Poppy?"

"Poppy?" May said, nearly having forgotten that Betty had asked about her middle child as well. "Poppy. She's good, but I'm afraid our Poppy doesn't have much of a head for learning. At least not the book kind."

"She's pretty, though?" Betty asked.

May could've gotten angry that Betty would see "pretty" as her daughter's best hope. Poppy was no scholar, but she was honest and hardworking. And there was nothing she couldn't do with a needle and thread. Truth of the matter was, though, Poppy was pretty. No, more than that.

"Poppy is a beautiful girl," May said, then quickly added, "on the outside and the inside, too." Betty's fur-draped shoulders relaxed. "She's got herself work as a seamstress. Up in Charlotte," May added, both hating that her granddaughter was so far away and worrying that she wasn't far enough away. She'd never really accepted Maguire's claim that his grasp reached worldwide.

"But she's so young."

"Only a year younger than you were when you married my Jesse," May said, feeling defensive, but her words caused her to reflect on how Betty's getting married too young had been the root of so many of their troubles. She bit her lip, then gave into an urge to provide the woman with a shred of comfort. "Don't you go worrying about Poppy. Girl has a good head on her shoulders. She ain't gonna get herself messed up with some boy. You wait and see, she's gonna make something of herself."

May stopped and took a good look at Betty. Her pasty skin and fancy clothes. Her pretty features and her selfish heart. May wanted to let the past lie in the past, find a way to forgive this woman, both for taking Jesse and for deserting her own daughters. But May soon realized that even though she might someday uncover a font of forgiveness in her heart, today was not the day it would happen. She folded her arms across her chest and took a wider stance.

"All right now, girl," May said. "How 'bout you tell me what you really doin' here?"

Betty moved her lips to speak, but before she could utter a word, May heard a high and piercing shriek coming from her own front porch. Her head jerked toward the sound. A baby's cry—a tad less angry, but still just as desperate—reached her ears. She flashed a look at Betty's crumpling face, then strode to the front door and yanked it open. On the other side of the screen door stood a young black woman, probably around Opal's age, dressed in a dark gray maid's uniform. Her tight lips twitched as her nervous eyes fell on May, but she continued to bounce a small bundle, the source of the shrieking, and pat the baby's back.

May pushed the screen door open, the young woman taking a cautious step back as the door protested.

"May," Betty said, her high heels clacking across the wooden floor as she rushed to catch up to her mother-in-law, grasping the screen door before the resentful spring could pull it closed.

May took in the sight of a shiny maroon sedan with a liveried driver—a white man—stationed at its side, but neither the man nor the scintillating hunk of steel held her attention.

"Turn it around," May commanded the maid. "I want to see it." The young woman hesitated, but then did as she'd been told.

May approached the bundled child, its face contorted by a degree of rage only an infant could muster. A balled-up fist flailed on the end of a chubby arm. May reached out and took the damp hand gently between her own fingers. "Yours?" May said to Betty, even though she knew the answer. The babe's skin was the same warm copper shade as Betty's natural skin tone. The hair on its head—a coppery red, not too very different from that of the doll Betty had brought for Jilo—caught the sun. The child's eyes flashed open. As blue as a bachelor's button. Just as May had suspected.

"Yeah." Betty's defeated voice came from behind May. "She's mine."

"Well it sounds like she's hungry. If I were you, I'd stop nursing that fur you wearin' and feed her instead." May caressed the baby's soft hand, then looked back at Betty, who seemed grateful to shrug off her stole.

Betty held the fur out toward the maid with one hand, and reached out for the child with the other. "Let me see her," Betty said, then the two traded their burdens. Betty crossed to the far end of the porch and took a seat on the bench swing. She waited until the driver turned his back, and then her moment's modesty surrendered to another piercing cry from the child. Betty shifted the baby to her left arm, and undid the buttons of her blouse with her right hand. The child took to the exposed breast, bleached pale as it was.

"I've been working on getting her switched to the bottle. I have plenty of formula, but these things," she shifted so that her bosom jutted a bit forward, "just keep doing what they do." Betty seemed apologetic.

"What's her name?"

"Ah," Betty said, her own face showing the relief of letting go of her milk. "I've just been calling her Baby, but . . ." Her words deserted her as her haunted eyes met May's.

"But you reckon I can name her anything I want." May felt a pain in her heart at the sight of the poor child in this hopeless woman's arms.

"I can't keep her," Betty keened before managing to calm herself. "He won't let me keep her."

"Came out a shade too brown, did she?" May asked. Betty flinched, although May hadn't intended to cause her more pain.

"He says I have to give her up." She leaned back, shifting the child as she did so. "Wants me to turn her over to one of those horrible convents so they can adopt her out." She patted the baby's tight copper curls. "But you and I both know they ain't never gonna adopt her out."

May heard Betty's real voice, her real words, not the practiced Yankee talk she'd been using since she arrived.

"You hopin' he's gonna change his mind, aren't you? Hoping he's gonna marry you."

Betty laughed, a hard bitter laugh, as hot tears fell down her cheeks. "Mickey ain't gonna marry me. He's already married. And he's Catholic." She looked up at May. "I ain't got no hope for nothing. I just can't bear the thought of giving her over to strangers. Never knowing if she's all right."

May closed her eyes and drew a deep breath. When she opened her eyes again, she patted Betty's shoulder. " 'Course she gonna stay with me. I'm her nana, ain't I?"

Betty's eyes widened and a shudder of relief ran through her. "Thank you," she managed before her words turned to throaty sobs.

"Now enough of that nonsense," May said, a harshness rising unbidden to her words. She braced herself, looking for the strength to give this woman one more chance to do right. " 'Course, you could stay, too. Finish raising your girls here with me."

Betty's sobs stopped cold, and her eyes opened in something very near to horror. "Oh, May," she said, her haughty Yankee tone resurrecting itself in just two syllables. "I could never stay on *here*." She cast a disapproving eye over May's entire world. "No, I have to get back home. Back to New York." She leaned a tad forward, as if she were about to share her most cherished secret. "You see, I love him."

May nodded. "All right, then." She turned to the maid. "You fetch the baby's things. Bring them inside." At the squeak of the porch swing, she looked back to see Betty standing, already holding her infant out toward May.

May accepted the child into her arms and pulled her into her bosom, even as the baby's natural mother fumbled with buttons to hide her own exposed breasts. May turned to take the child inside, but Betty's voice stopped her.

"I know I ain't a good mother. Hell, I ain't really any kind of mother at all." She licked her lips, then rushed on as if to prevent May from responding. "I'm not a good woman. I'm selfish. I'm vain. I'm greedy. If there is a bad choice to make, you can bet your last dollar I will make it. But in my sorry life, I have done one thing right." She paused and fixed May with her gaze. "I have left my girls in your care. 'Cause I want them to learn something I could never teach them. I want them to grow up like you."

Betty pushed past May and hurried down the steps of the porch. She ducked into her shiny long car as soon as her driver opened its door.

This time, May had no urge to chase after this foolish woman child. Neither to punish her nor to beg her to stay. May stood firm, watching as the young maid struggled with the baby's belongings as Opal had struggled with those damned cardboard suitcases so many years before. May ran her hand over the back of the now-sleeping child's head, then placed a kiss on her brow. "Don't you worry, little one. Your nana, she loves you."

SIXTEEN

December 1940

"When was Jesus born?" Poppy sang in a low, sweet voice as she pumped water into a sink full of dishes. She'd inherited her mama Betty's talent for singing. May counted it among one of her greatest successes that the girl's voice was all of her mama she seemed to carry in her. *"It was the last month of the year."* Poppy was such a beautiful thing, even in the harsh white of the electric light. For a moment, May missed the soft flicker of her kerosene lamp, but she had to admit she was growing used to these modern conveniences the "Hoodoo" money had brought their way.

Poppy took after her great-grandmother Tuesday, standing barely five feet tall, and with a waist not much thicker than a willow branch. It both pleased and worried May that she'd filled out nicely in those places that men liked to see full.

May had only agreed to let Poppy head up to Charlotte in exchange for the girl's promise to keep her head screwed on tight and her skirt pulled down over her knees. So far, May believed she'd kept her word, although her guardian, a pastor's wife, had written to say her husband wearied of the sound of pebbles ricocheting off the upstairs windows every night. Poppy was fifteen, the same age Betty had been when she became May's daughter-in-law, and with full lips, high cheekbones, and deep brown eyes, she was prettier than most by far. The preacher's missus informed May that her granddaughter had plenty of suitors, but none of them had managed to capture her heart. Yet. It might be December, but May was no fool. A fresh new spring lay just around the corner.

Poppy sensed her grandmother's presence and looked back over her shoulder. "Nana, you want me to get Jilo ready for bed when I finish up with these?"

"Naw, girl." May crossed the room to place a kiss on Poppy's head. "Jilo's big enough to handle herself now, and Binah, she's sleeping—for now, at least." The baby still hadn't taken to sleeping the night through, although that mattered less to May than it once might have. She almost looked forward to the sound of Binah's fretful stirrings. It made the long, sleepless nights less lonely. "You done helped enough around here today. 'Course Jilo might like for you to read her a story from that book you brung her."

Poppy looked up from the soapy water and smiled at her. "No, little miss is gonna want to show off by reading me one of the stories her own self. That girl is smarter than the rest of us put together." The tone of her voice and the smile in her eyes told May Poppy couldn't be prouder of that fact.

"Yeah, you probably right." May leaned her hip against the sink's cold porcelain lip. "It's so good to have you home, even if it is just for a few days."

"I didn't want to miss Christmas . . . and"—her smile faded—"I just had to see her with my own eyes."

May pulled the girl into her arms. She'd mailed a picture of Binah to both Opal and Poppy when she wrote to tell them they had a new sister, but a picture didn't do much to make a body seem real. " 'Course you did."

Poppy relaxed into May's arms. "I sure wish Opal could be here."

May slid her hands to her granddaughter's shoulders and pushed her back a little so they could look at each other. "How about tomorrow we call up the operator and have her put through a call to that sister of yours?"

"All the way in California?"

"All the way in California."

Poppy threw her wet hands around May's waist and squeezed tight enough to take the wind out of her. Pulling the girl close, May squeezed right back and leaned her head forward to breathe in Poppy's scent.

A loud bang on the front door startled Poppy into making a little jump.

"Even on Christmas," May muttered to herself. As she stepped back, she caught the worried look in Poppy's eyes. The magic had never set well with Poppy. She never said so outright, but May knew it was a large part of the reason she'd wanted to get away. Hell, it was a large part of the reason May had let her go.

"I'll get it," Poppy said, ready to spring toward the door.

"No." She held up her hand. "Don't you worry, none, girl. Nana tell 'em to come back another time."

May shuffled out of the kitchen and down the hall. Her steps fell heavier than they had in years past, and it was taking her more time to get around. May figured there was no escaping time, not even with the magic she had at her command. Another rap, followed by a quick and impatient series of bangs, sounded on the door. May stopped dead in her tracks. "I am coming," she yelled in the direction of the knocking, "and if you keep banging away like that, you ain't gonna want to see me when I get there."

She took her time, more than she needed, really, to make it to the door and brush aside the curtain covering the door's window. Once there, she flicked on the switch by the door, causing the exterior over-head light she'd installed that summer to burst to life, revealing the snow-dusted visage of Henry Cook. His sweet innocent face, combined with the wispy flakes of miraculous snow, gave the appearance of a Christmas ornament. Her annoyance faded at the sight of him. She hadn't laid eyes on him since she'd stopped working at the Pinnacle. His face was unchanged, but the rest of him had gone through a growth spurt. The fellow who stood beneath the harsh glare of the porch light was no longer a boy. He was a young man. He wore a woolen flat cap and a threadbare coat way too big even for his newly broadened shoulders.

Healing his poor mama had been her first solo act of magic; she hadn't been at all sure it would work, but she thanked God that this boy still had his mama. A hot wave of guilt flushed through her, knocking back the cold breeze coming in through the door. Was it God she should be thanking for such a thing? Well, hell, if she was damning herself using magic, she would do what she could to make some good come of it.

May opened the door. "Henry, what on earth brings you out on Christmas night? You should be home with your family."

"I'm sorry to disturb you, Mother Wills."

For some reason hearing this young man address her by her working name cut her to the quick. "No, Henry. Don't you call me that. We're old friends, you and I. You call me May, or Mrs. Wills, if you must, but I don't want you calling me Mother, you hear?"

"Yes, ma'am." The words came out wrapped in caution, and he seemed to deliberate before continuing. "Mrs. Wills. You gotta come with me. You gotta help. There's something real bad goin' on."

The screen door gave its usual complaint as she pushed it open enough to signal for Henry to enter. One of these days she'd get around to replacing that damned spring. Henry reached out and took hold of the screen door, pushing it fully open and stepping into the main room, but not far enough for May to close the other door and shut out the cold. He shifted foot to foot, looking like the slightest noise might make him take flight.

"I just passed by Wildwood Church down the road," he said in a rush. "There's a group of white men there, and they got Pastor Jones with 'em." May was taken aback by the name. She hadn't given the young preacher a single thought since her mama's funeral. "They done set the church on fire, and I'm afraid the pastor's gonna get killed if you don't do something."

"All right. I'll be right out." May closed the door after Henry, and turned away.

Poppy stood at the end of the hall, just outside the kitchen door. She dried her hands on her apron, her nervous eyes focused on May. "Everything okay, Nana? Was that Henry?"

"Everything's just fine, my sweet, sweet girl." She paused. "Nana has to go out for a bit. She needs you to watch your sisters for her."

"Of course, Nana." Worry returned to Poppy's eyes, and her smile flattened. "Where you going?"

"Don't you worry about that." May reached out for Poppy's hand, giving it a tight squeeze. "Nana will be home by morning. You just watch Jilo and Binah, and think about what you want to say to Opal when we call her. And don't you worry, you hear?"

"Okay," Poppy said, obedient as always.

"Promise me. No worries." May released Poppy's hand and tapped her nose with her index finger, causing her granddaughter's eyes to light up again with mirth.

"I promise, Nana."

"That's my good girl."

May took a moment to pull her heaviest coat on over the new cardigan Poppy had given her for Christmas, then found her way out to the porch, careful not to let either of the doors slam and wake the babies. Henry's beat-up Model A truck was running, although the engine sputtered enough to sound as if it might give up the ghost at any moment. After helping May into the passenger side, Henry circled the truck and struggled to open his own door, which would only gape partway. The kid squeezed in through the gap, then pulled just as hard, metal grating metal, to get the door closed.

May noticed only one headlight of Henry's Model A seemed to be working, and it veered its gaze up toward the trees. Fine if you were out hunting possum, but not so good if you were trying to see which direction you were headed. May had never attended the Wildwood Church, but she knew it lay five miles or so south, down off Buckhalter Road. She wasn't sure if it was still considered Savannah proper. She also wasn't sure they'd make it in time to do any good. Henry pressed the clutch and shifted into drive, causing the truck to groan and heave before it began its slothful roll forward.

"What do you think this is about?" May asked him.

"I don't know ma'am. Is it ever *about* anything?"

May stared out the side window, watching the familiar territory pass by at an unfamiliar pace. Even lumbering along, it took next to no time for them to reach the bend in the road. They turned south on Ogeechee and kept on for what felt forever, but what was in reality probably no more than a dozen minutes. Henry turned the rattling beast left on to Buckhalter. May didn't know for sure where the church stood, but she could see the glow of the flames and smell the smoke even before they made it half a mile.

"You stop here," she said as they neared the far end of the drive that cut between Wildwood Church's graveyard and the glow in the night sky she could only assume was the burning remains of the church itself. She reached over and patted Henry's forearm without ever taking her eyes off the devil's sparks rising into the air. She pointed toward a tall clump of wax myrtles she hoped would help hide the truck . . . and the boy. Henry obeyed, easing the truck to the side of the road and shifting to park.

"This old girl can be tricky to start," he said. "We should probably leave it running."

May looked into the boy's warm amber eyes. "That's fine. You're gonna stay here anyhow."

"Oh no, ma'am. I can't let you go on your own. Poppy . . ." He stopped talking after the slip of her granddaughter's name, but the look on his face told her all she needed to know. It explained what this young fellow was doing driving around these parts on Christmas night, and why the little miss hadn't take interest in her suitors up in Charlotte. Henry was on his way to court her. May hadn't seen it coming, but if she didn't get him killed out here tonight, this boy might just be a good match for her Poppy.

She turned on him. "You will do as I damned well say, you hear me, boy?" Henry cringed at her severity. Good. Better to have him scared of her than messing around in things too big for him. She reached for the door handle, only to realize there was none.

Henry's face was still frozen, his eyes open wide. "I got to open it from the outside," he said, forcing his own door open a fraction and squeezing out. He came around to her door and tugged it open for her, offering his arm to help her steady herself as she eased her way out of the truck.

She could see how anxious the boy was on her behalf, so she forced a confident smile to her lips. "Don't worry for old May," she said. "You stay right here, and be ready to take off when Jones and I get back." The smile faded as she considered the situation. Truth was, she had no idea what was waiting for her on the far side of the churchyard. "If something should go wrong, though, don't you try to come riding to the rescue. You scat, and you go get Poppy and the girls someplace safe." Even as she said the words, she wondered where that might be. Still, she wagged her index finger in his face. "Promise me."

He hesitated, then blurted out, "I ain't a coward."

May reached out and placed a gentle hand on his cheek. "I know you aren't. A coward would never have come for help. A coward would have turned around and driven home. Promise me you'll see to my girls." She paused and looked deeply into his eyes. "All of them."

He nodded. "I promise."

She turned and started making her way through the graveyard, feeling the full weight of her years. The graveyard hadn't been active in twenty years, but she had known many of the folk buried here. She was no longer a young woman. Hell, tell the truth and shame the devil—she was an old biddy now by anyone's standards. The best part of her life lay behind her.

She was a widow. Her husband and her only son were buried in a cemetery not so very different from this one, just a few miles down the road. She wove through the stones that had been erected for those who could afford a record of their presence in this world, and the hand-marked whitewashed wooden crosses of those whose families were too busy struggling to stay alive to afford more for their dead. The scent of smoke grew stronger and stronger, reminding her that this world was no place for a decent soul. This world belonged to the barbarous. It was a world of war. A world of killing.

She wanted to be brave, but in truth, she'd never asked for any of this magic. She was frightened, and not only of what she was about to face. Deep down, she knew that she was still scared to death of the magic. Every time she felt it pulsing through her, she wondered if she were drawing herself closer to damnation. The good book said, "Suffer not a witch to live." Was that what she was? Something dark and evil? Something the good Lord Himself would turn away from?

Yes, she was frightened and, more than that, she was tired. She would have liked nothing better than to walk away from it all. Leave this here earth to those who were fixing to fight over it. Maybe it wouldn't be the worst thing if it all did end for her here. Though it shamed her to even think it, Poppy could help raise her sisters.

Of course, this night could come to a peaceful conclusion. Maybe in an hour or so, she'd be back home with her babies. But was that really what she wanted? Didn't a part of her hope things would go awry tonight? Wasn't that what had truly pulled her from her home on Christmas night? Certainly she must have considered this confrontation might bring her to her own deliverance.

Even if she survived whatever evil was destroying the church, she could end it herself. Not rely on these fools. Reuben's old razor. It was still packed away at the house. She could turn around. Go home right now and unpack it. One quick slice across her throat was all it would take.

May stopped dead in her tracks. These were not her thoughts. These thoughts were coming from outside of her, playing on her weaknesses. The voice of the White King. Seducing her with the promise of an easy rest. No, she was not going to let his malfeasance take root in her soul. She shook her head. "Not me, you old devil. Your brother might get me. Hell, he's waiting for me just around the corner, but you ain't ever gonna get May."

She crept out of the graveyard to where she could witness the fire's devastation. A group of men milled around in the hellish glow of the flames. She could hear them talking, but their voices were muted by the roar of the fire that was destroying the wood-frame church. Then the steeple tilted and fell, eliciting a powerful roar from those who had set the building alight. She approached them, unnoticed, from behind. Their attention was fixed on their handiwork. They stood there, not wearing the white robes she had expected to see, their faces not hidden by the pointed hoods. No. They stood out there in the open for all the world to see. Proud of themselves. Proud to be performing their civic duty. Jones was on his knees, one hand pressed against a wound on his head, staring up at the destruction with horror in his eyes.

The heat of the blaze beat back the cold of the black night. It would've felt pleasant had the fire not been the flames of hell.

One of the men looked back and noticed her arrival. "Well, who do we have here?" he called out, causing his fellows to turn.

She stretched herself to her full height and swallowed before speaking, praying her voice would not crack. "I've come for the preacher." She strode up to them, trying to look confident, trying to act like she was in charge of the situation. She held out her hand to Jones.

He looked up at her through his one good eye, the other having swollen shut from the abuse these monsters had dealt to him. He waved her back with a bloodied hand. "Go. Go on. Get out of here."

"No, sir," May responded, walking up to him, taking his sticky hand in hers. "I ain't leaving here without you."

The reverberation of a gunshot caused May to jump, despite her determination to appear calm. A fat man with a rifle ambled up toward them, the other men parting to let him through. "Just who the hell do you think you are sticking your black nose in where it don't belong?"

May released the pastor's hand. She would try to solve this peaceably. Find a way to reason with these people. Yes, the church was lost, but it could be rebuilt. They'd hurt Jones, but he would heal. She would heal him. If she could get these men to let them go willingly, she could prevent any more bloodshed. But before she could respond, another spoke for her.

"Good heavens, Bobby. You mean to tell me you don't recognize the great Mother Wills?" Sterling Maguire walked around the fat man and pulled the rifle from his grasp, breaking open the barrel and removing the remaining shell. May gaped in amazement. Sterling pushed the shell into this Bobby's shirt pocket and handed the rifle back to him. "Y'all are done here now. You can go."

Another man stepped forward and pointed down at Jones. "Come on, Mr. Maguire. You promised us a little fun with that one." He pushed past Maguire and grabbed the pastor by the collar.

Maguire turned on this one, and the flames of the disintegrating church could not begin to match the fire in his eyes. "I said y'all are done here. Now go." The man holding Jones seemed to know he'd overstepped. He released Jones without another word of protest.

The other men milled around, grumbling, but they left as they'd been ordered.

As the last of the men made his way beyond the fire's glow, Sterling drew near May. Her eyes forced her to think of this man as the younger Maguire, though she knew for a fact it was the father walking around in the son's skin. Same old hate in a different package. "Long time no see, huh, May?" For reasons May could not begin to imagine, Sterling began to undo his tie. He undid the knot, then pulled it out from under his collar and flung it to the ground. Then his fingers went to his shirt and began unbuttoning.

"Whatever the hell you think you're doin', you better stop it right now," May raised her hands, fingers pointed toward each other as a ball of blue lightning, the largest she'd ever mustered, formed there, ready and waiting to be launched. She guessed it'd burn a hole clean through a normal man, but this servant of the Red King, with his monstrous living tattoos, well, she hoped it would at least buy her enough time to get Jones to Henry's truck and get back to her house.

"My, my, my, how you have grown, my girl," Maguire said. "You've been practicing." He stopped for a moment, but then resumed what he was doing. "I, too, have seen many changes since we last met." He shrugged off his shirt, and May prepared herself for the demonical sight of his markings. But they were gone, and his pasty white skin was now a clear canvas. He drew closer, presenting himself for inspection.

"Who did you kill? What child did you offer to your demon for this?"

Maguire leaned back, clasping his hands before him. "Ah, May, can't you tell the world is changing?" He paused. "No. Not changing. Returning to the normal, rightful order. Sanity is being restored." He released his clasp and shook his head. "Not a single little one was harmed for this miracle, although I would've gladly commissioned a new slaughter of the innocents for it. No, I no longer have any need of the Red King's crumbs. There is magic out there, the likes of which neither you nor I ever imagined. We, you and I, your mother and I." His eyes widened. "Your grandmother and I. And hell, even her mother before that. Honestly, girl," he said with a chuckle, "I've done lost track of how far back we go. Over the years, we have been slinging pebbles at each other with home-crafted slingshots. Our magic has been like the power of steam. But there are those out there with the power of lightning. The power of the very void from which existence sprang. The power . . ."

"The power of devils," Pastor Jones surprised May by speaking.

Maguire stepped forward and used the sole of his foot to push the battered man from his knees, causing him to land on his side. "The power of *gods*," he said, then spat on the minister. Maguire looked at the pastor as if he'd like nothing better than to gut him, but his expression smoothed over in the next instant.

"The old order is returning," he said, turning toward May. "As soon as tomorrow. And when it does, there will be a need for men like me. There are those who recognize that need, and they're the ones who did this for me." He waved his hands before himself. "Old *lines* are being redrawn. Old ways renewed." He took another step closer, and May prepared to aim her shot, but Maguire reached out and placed one hand above and the other below the ball of energy she'd been cradling. He brought his hands together, and though his face contorted in pain, he squeezed the ball tighter and tighter until it collapsed and went dark. May stumbled back, feeling all her energy fail her. When she raised her arms, it was not in attack, but in surrender.

Pastor Jones pushed himself back up to his knees and made a failed attempt to rise to his feet. "Do what you need to do with me, but this woman is innocent. Just let her go."

Sterling went to the preacher's side and squatted down beside him. "Oh, Pastor. Don't fool yourself. No one who knows that kind of power is innocent. And"—he held a hand out to Jones—"don't be so quick to assume this is about you." The pastor slapped away the white man's hand.

"Fine," Sterling said, rising, "have it your way."

A movement some yards away caught May's eye, and her heart fell at the sight of Henry stepping out of the shadows. The last thing she needed was for him to get mixed up in her struggles with Maguire.

"I told you to stay put," she said, anger punctuating each word. Henry came forward and helped the pastor up.

"And I told him to come along," Maguire said. The dance of the wicked flames turned Sterling's lopsided sneer into a demon's mask. "You can get on home now, boy," he said, giving Henry a rough shove. "Your work here's done."

"I'm sorry, Mrs. Wills," Henry called out. "I'm sorry," he said again, even though he was already leading the pastor away from them. "I didn't want to do it, but he said he'd kill my little sister if I didn't get you out here. He said he'd feed her to the devil. He promised he wouldn't hurt you if I did bring you."

"Go on, boy." Sterling said, miming a pistol with his hand and aiming it between Henry's eyes. "I ain't gonna tell you again to move."

"I'm sorry," Henry dared again before turning. May watched the boy and the pastor disappear into the darkened cemetery.

Maguire let loose a deep laugh. "How the boy exaggerates. Not *the* devil. Just *a* devil. My old friend Barron. You remember him, don't you?" He reached for her, moving too quickly for her to avoid his touch. He caught her arm in his grasp, tightening, tightening, until the pain drove May to her knees. "You know, May, it's funny how the world can change in an instant. Not so long ago that demon, that old genie in a bottle of mine, was my most prized possession on this earth. Now, he's completely superfluous to my existence. Just like you and your seed." He knelt before her without ever relinquishing his grip. "So today is his Emancipation Day." He nodded, his eyes opening wide in parody of her own horror. "That's right, May. I just let him go. I let him go right outside your sweet little quarters."

He released her and stood. "Tell me. Just how fast can you run?"

May forced her way to her feet and began struggling across the gravel drive that separated the glowing remains of the church from its cemetery.

"Call to your Beekeeper, woman," Maguire shouted after her. With each step May was doing just that. But she felt nothing. No response. "Call to her." His mania overtook him, and his voice rose in pitch, following her as if he were shouting directly into her ear.

In the dark, in her panic, she tripped over a low stone and landed on the ground, scraping her hands and knees.

Maybe, she wondered for the first time ever, *the White King could be right.*

SEVENTEEN

None of this made any sense at all to Poppy. She and Henry had been writing each other since the day she got to Charlotte, and with each letter he seemed to grow more and more determined to have her hand in marriage. She'd always been in love with him, she figured, only it had taken leaving Savannah for her to realize it. Every time a boy came calling for her in Charlotte, she would find herself thinking "Henry's taller," or "Henry's smarter," or "Henry's more handsome." Maybe "Henry always makes me laugh" was what had finally tilted the scale of her heart, convincing her that she belonged with Henry. That her heart belonged to Henry.

So when she heard his voice by the front door, Poppy had felt sure he'd come to ask Nana for her hand. The last thing she'd expected was for Nana to go off with him. Hug him, maybe. Scream at him, more likely. But instead the two had flown the coop, heading out to who knows where.

It was growing colder. Much colder. After buttoning up her cardigan, she turned her focus to the woodstove. Nana kept a mitt hanging from a hook on the wall, so she slipped the enormous padded glove over her right hand and grabbed the fire poker with her left.

She knelt beside the stove and turned the handle on its side door. The wood beneath had burned to nothing but glowing red coals. She pierced them with the poker, giving everything a good shake until the logs on the top of the pyre fell to the bottom, popping and shooting sparks. Something about the sparks fascinated her. They felt like little eyes peering out from the smoke. She shuddered, then laughed at her own silliness. Working quickly, she leaned the poker against the wall, pushed another split log into the stove, and closed the door before any more smoke could spill out into the room. Coughing, she waved her gloved hand before her face to dissipate the smoke. She stood and returned the mitt to its holder. And then she froze.

Poppy knew she was just letting her nerves run away from her, but she couldn't shake the feeling that someone was watching. She looked over her shoulder and then turned all the way around. She could see she was alone in the room. Her eyes fell on the windows. The curtains had been pulled tight. Certainly no one could be peeping. She made her way to the house's front window and pulled the drape aside, looking in the direction the truck had gone, hoping to see its cockeyed headlights pointing her way, but the overhead light was still on. In the glare, her own reflection and the image of the room behind her was all that she could see. She leaned in, nearly pressing her face to the glass, but the world outside was still hidden by her own features.

Though Poppy had promised her nana she wouldn't worry, she couldn't help it. She recognized this feeling for what it was. There was magic in the air, and it made her queasy. She loved her nana, but she couldn't wait to escape back to Charlotte, where she could just be a simple working girl, a seamstress, not Mother Wills's granddaughter.

She and Henry had made a plan. They were going to marry, and he was going to join her in Charlotte. They'd leave Savannah and its ghosts and magic behind. Lead a normal life. She felt a smile come to her lips. Soon she wasn't going to be a Wills girl at all. She was gonna be Poppy Cook. Mrs. Henry Cook.

She would miss her nana. She would always love her, but a part of her could never forgive her for getting messed up in such dark forces. Poppy worried about her younger sisters. She felt guilty about leaving them trapped in Nana's odd world. Maybe after she and Henry got settled, they could send for Jilo and Binah. But what if she and Henry started having their own children right from the get-go? Would Henry want to take responsibility for a brood?

In the distance she heard a rumble, a sound she recognized as Henry's truck. Her shoulders relaxed, and she only then realized she'd been holding her breath. Poppy pulled open the front door, a lingering sense of disquiet prompting her to leave it gaping wide in spite of the night's chill. She eased the screen door forward so its protest wouldn't wake the little ones. She stepped out onto the porch, drawing her arms around herself to fend off the cold. It took a moment for her eyes to adjust. Here, without the glare of the electric light blinding her, she could make out the approaching truck pulling onto the tracks that ran up to the house. The one headlight seemed permanently aimed at heaven, but the other sputtered to life and lit the ground. Poppy was surprised to find the house surrounded by a dense, low-lying fog. Thick, dirty billows had turned it into a virtual island.

Henry pulled the truck up before her, stopping nearly on top of the bottom step, but he didn't kill the engine. Poppy did not see her nana with him. He banged his shoulder into the driver's door until it popped nearly halfway open.

"Where is Nana?" she asked, her stomach falling into her shoes as she ran down the steps to greet him.

"Don't worry about that now," Henry said, pressing her back with such force she nearly stumbled backward onto the stairs. "Get the girls. We gotta get out of here."

Poppy dug in her heels. "What is wrong? You tell me where Nana is, or I ain't taking another step," she said, although her eyes remained fixed on the fog. It began to glow.

"What . . ." she said, pointing down, but a sound cut her off. A roar, filled with violence and hunger. She grasped Henry's hand. Tried to step backward. To pull Henry and herself up the steps and into the shelter of the house. But by the time she'd begun to move, it was already too late.

Red eyes consumed her. Her mouth opened to scream, but something rushed inside it instead. The pain was so keen, she felt like she was being ripped apart. Skinned alive from the inside out. She was in a dark room. No, she was imprisoned in her own mind. And this thing inside her was suppressing her will, taking her over, striking out at her from within.

"Poppy," Henry called. The familiar sound of his voice pulled her above the wave that had invaded her, and she saw his blood dripping from the points where her hand, transformed into a claw, had pierced his skin. She managed to release him, but in the next instant, like a man drowning, she was back under. Though she could watch what was happening and feel her body move, it was the intruder wearing her, rather than her own will, pulling her along.

"Run," Poppy screamed from deep within to Henry, to her sisters, but the sound never reached her lips. Instead, she heard a gravelly laughter, much deeper than her own voice could ever muster. The invader raised her head and sniffed the wind. *Oh, God*, she thought. *Oh, God*, she prayed. The beast within her was searching for the children's scent. She could smell the sweet scents of Jilo's nighttime bath and Binah's talcum. The saltiness of their flesh that lay underneath. Feel the heat of their pulsing blood. And it made her hungry. Her body mounted the first step, and although she struggled to pull back from the house, the second. She bounded over the last and onto the porch, and her hand reached out to grasp the handle of the screen door. It screamed in protest as she flung it open. Her body began to cross the threshold, but she stood frozen, pressed up against the open air as if it were a brick wall.

The thing inside pushed forward, straining so hard it felt like her skeleton would rip from her flesh. Something overhead caught the thing's eye . . . caught *her* eye. The haint blue of the overhang was glowing, its enchantment preventing the beast from moving her forward. But its hunger drove it like a wild dog. It clawed at the opening, stretching, straining. Whining.

Henry, unknowing, unaware, thinking he was out to protect her, pushed her forward, his force enough to carry the beast inside her past the blue's protection. Poppy screamed in anguish as the beast stumbled into the front room. Once inside, it pulled her body to its feet and turned to look at Henry. When his terrified eyes met with the thing looking out from her eyes, she could tell he realized his mistake. He stood there for another long moment, seemingly frozen. Uncertain of which way to turn. Then he made a dash around her toward the hall.

She realized he was trying to make it to the room the little ones shared so he could protect her little sisters from her. Poppy summoned all her will, tearing at the beast who shared her skin. But it felt so strong. So ancient. Poppy knew she could never defeat it on her own, but she didn't have to beat it. She only had to slow it down.

She steadied herself, preparing to strike out against it. But it snapped her will like a twig and flung her body toward the wall. After grabbing ahold of the iron fire poker, it jumped clear across the room.

Henry turned, raising his arms above his head in an attempt to protect himself. She watched, helpless, as the creature brought the heavy iron down against her love's arms. He shrieked, a piteous, weak sound, as his arms fell broken and bloody by his sides.

The thing inside her was enjoying the sight and smell of Henry's blood. The breaking of his bones. Henry stumbled backward a foot or so down the hall. Pursuing him, the creature raised the rod again and brought it down with a heavy crack against Henry's skull. Henry dropped to his knees. *No. No. No*, she pleaded even as her arm pulled back to deliver the fatal blow.

Poppy wanted to drop the iron, or at least close her eyes, but she was in control of nothing. Sensing her anguish, the beast hesitated so that it could savor it. Soon, though, it had consumed its fill of her pain. The poker began its descent, but it stopped in midair when the beast perceived the form of a small girl in the shadows of the hall, just outside her bedroom door. The poker slid to the floor. Poppy's body crouched and prepared to pounce. Jilo's eyes widened. The poor thing was horrified, but she still didn't scream the way Poppy would have done at that age, at *any* age. Jilo dived back into her room and slammed the door behind her.

Poppy's body tensed and leaped over Henry. She landed on all fours, like an animal, slipping a bit in Henry's blood.

Somehow, Binah had slept up until then, but the noise must have finally roused her, for her powerful voice sang out in an angry wail. The sound excited the monster inside Poppy. It forced her to crouch by the girls' bedroom door and scratch against the wood. Making giddy sounds with her vocal cords, it drew in more deep breaths, savoring the smell of one child's confusion and the other's fear. Saliva began falling from her mouth, and her stomach rumbled.

There had to be some way to stop this. Or at least a way to shut it out. Would she really have to witness this devil devouring her sisters? Dear God, would she have to taste them?

She saw her hand reach up to touch the doorknob. The door had no lock. It provided the girls with no protection.

Binah's crying continued, but it sounded muffled. Then it came to a sudden stop.

Had Jilo stifled her sister's cries in a misguided attempt to hide herself? Or had she realized what was happening, the hopelessness of the situation, and seen to it that Binah wouldn't suffer? Poppy began to turn away in her own mind. Let herself drift. Though she could still feel the beast's impressions, its sick desires, their impact was somewhat lessened if she didn't try to interfere. She watched as the hands that had once been hers turned the doorknob and pushed the door wide open.

Jilo stood near the window, a sheet hanging over the ledge. The beast moved Poppy's body forward, still crawling on hands and knees as it breached the threshold of the room. Her head reared back in a delighted howl as her body carried her nearer and nearer her sister.

The beast turned Poppy's head to scan the room, but there was no sight of Binah. Hope rose up inside Poppy like a blooming vine, but then the curtains of the window behind Jilo billowed inward, causing the beast to raise her nose and sniff the wind that made them dance. It caught Binah's scent. She loped to the window and looked out. The moonlight betrayed a wisp of auburn hair. Jilo had lowered the child out of the window and to the ground, swaddled in the hanging sheet.

Jilo stepped quickly away from the window, as if she were trying to draw its attention away from her baby sister. For the moment, it seemed to work. The beast circled Jilo, bumping into the little girl and pressing her nose right up against her flesh. Poppy wondered how her sister could stop herself from fleeing, as Jilo stood frozen in place. The creature and Poppy experienced the same thought at once. Something about the girl's scent wasn't quite right. Wasn't quite human. Jilo had something more, something different about her. The creature was disgusted by what it smelled on her. So was Poppy. The two conjoined beings both willed a step backward, away from her.

Jilo cast a nervous glance over her shoulder, out the window, reminding the beast of the other morsel awaiting him. This odd one was not right, but the smaller one smelled delicious. The softest, sweetest flesh. The beast carried Poppy over to the open window and pressed her hands against the ledge, preparing to swoop out and carry the child off into the quiet of the pines before tasting her flesh. Down below, poking out through the tangled sheet, Poppy recognized Binah's tiny head. The beast within her smiled, ready to leap through the opening. Ah, but then a sound, the tiniest of cries, came from inside the chifferobe, behind them. The beast stopped, and Poppy felt her head wrench

JILO

to the side. The beast eyed the chifferobe, then began padding quickly toward it.

"No," Jilo screamed, leaping on Poppy and riding her, pulling her hair, scratching, screaming, doing anything she could to stop her. Poppy's arm twisted backward at an impossible angle and struck out, knocking Jilo to the floor. Poppy felt herself lunge across the room and claw open the cupboard's door. Inside lay Binah. Her diaper had been removed. Poppy realized *that* had been the source of the scent; the auburn hair, she realized, belonged to Jilo's favorite doll. For an instant she felt so proud of her little Jilo. Her plan had almost worked. She had almost lured the beast outside, where with any luck Nana's charms would have held it at bay. But her moment of pride was fleeting, for the beast beat her back down and turned to lay hold of its feast.

When she realized the inevitability of what was about to occur, Poppy tried again to step back, to turn away. But the beast that was riding her wouldn't allow it. It somehow held her consciousness in place, forcing her to experience its every action, its every hunger. She watched as her hand reached into the cabinet, lowered itself to lay claim to Binah's tiny wriggling form.

Poppy felt Jilo's hand grasp her shoulder again, the girl unwilling to be defeated. The beast turned, intending to destroy the pesky little bug that was coming between him and the thing he so completely craved. It reached out for Jilo with both hands, intending to snap the child's spindly neck, but then there was a blinding flash of light, and the world around it seemed to freeze. It was now the beast's turn to cry out in anguish, but Poppy couldn't understand why. The flash had left her eyes confused, unable to focus. Then, little by little, they resolved on the image of Jilo standing—no, her feet weren't touching the ground, she was *floating*—before her.

Lights, some white, some blue, burst like fireworks around the room. The earth beneath the house itself began to shake. And the creature began to lose its hold on Poppy. She could feel its power draining away. Jilo had somehow tapped into the demon's energy, and she was burning it up. The creature raged, but when it could not escape the girl's thrall, it tried to make a dash out the window. The moment it rose up on Poppy's legs to make the leap, Jilo turned her head toward the window. It slammed shut. The beast bounded toward the glass, but though it tried to use Poppy's body to leap through the window, the thing was ripped clear out of her instead. The windowpane splintered into a thousand shards.

Jilo slipped back down to her feet and rocked back and forth a few times before falling forward unconscious.

EIGHTEEN

The New York Clarion
December 8, 1942
Page C12

Making Spirits Bright, Singers Entertain the Troops at USO

With crooner John Briggs acting as MC and dozens of beautiful girl singers in the lineup, the tinsel on the tree wasn't the only thing sparkling last night at the USO canteen.

"Those Jerries aren't going to keep our boys from having a good Christmastime. Not if we have anything to say about it . . . and we do," said stunning redheaded, hazel-eyed singer Betty Wills, pictured here with Briggs and several of our adoring servicemen looking on. Her words were met with thunderous applause. Miss Wills, 28, and many of her peers from last night's performance will be taking leave

of our shores soon to spread holiday cheer to our
troops stationed around Europe and Northern Africa.

January 1943

May shook her head several times as she held the newspaper clipping up to the light, doing her damnedest to recognize any familiar part of her former daughter-in-law in the black-and-white—mostly white, May noted—photo that accompanied the text. Sure, it was Betty all right, all hips and curves and victory-roll hair, but if May hadn't known it was her, she could've passed this woman on the street without looking twice.

The article had arrived by itself, with the words "Show my girls their mama" scrawled beneath the photo in a slanting, loopy script May's eyes had been hard-pressed to decipher. May wasn't sure she should let the girls see it.

May grunted as her eyes fell again on "Miss Wills's" age. Twenty-eight years old with a twenty-one-year-old daughter. True, Betty still looked good, May could tell as much from the photo, but the reporter's acceptance of Betty's claim spoke more of his infatuation with his subject than anything else. May wondered just what the newspaper fellow had gotten in return for the write-up.

May's eyes focused again on the newsprint she held. A semicircle of besotted and uniformed white boys gazed adoringly at Betty. Betty, who was about to set sail with them. For all May knew, those boys might all be over in Europe now. Might even be dead.

Her eyes drifted from the photo to scan the text once more. Imagine it. Betty singing over in Europe. Even setting foot on Africa. Opal was in the Orient, working as an army nurse—the army wouldn't let her say where—and for a moment May found herself imagining the two meeting up overseas, Opal a black nurse, Betty a "stunning redheaded, hazel-eyed" white singer. Would the two even recognize each other if they were allowed to congregate in the same hall?

May nearly wadded up the newsprint, but something made her hesitate. Maybe Poppy would want it. She could mail the article to Poppy in Charlotte, but no. It would probably just get returned, unopened, like every other letter May had sent her over the last two years. Poppy blamed May for the horrors that had unfolded on Christmas night two years back. She had left Savannah swearing that she would only speak to her grandmother again if May gave up working magic. It broke May's heart every time she thought of her girl. Lord knows May would like nothing better than to give up the magic. The problem was that the magic didn't seem ready to give *her* up. When May finally made it home that Christmas night, she'd been greeted by the Beekeeper, sitting sprawled out on her front steps. The damned creature hadn't raised a gloved finger to help May's girls. "I wanted to see how the little one would handle herself," she'd said, screeching with laughter as she began to recount the acts of savagery that had just taken place in May's home.

May had ordered the Beekeeper away. Commanded her never to return. But even though the creature had not shown herself since then, her power continued to flow, as unwanted as ever, through May. *Hypocrite*, May thought. A part of her was more than grateful the magic hadn't just dried up. For one thing, she hadn't managed to track down Maguire's demon, and she was grateful she'd have more than her increasingly disregarded prayers to protect her babies. Maybe Jilo had managed to take it out, or maybe it was just playing possum until it was strong enough to strike again. Besides, she couldn't deny she'd grown accustomed to the little luxuries that the "donations" she received for working the magic, which folk mistakenly believed to be Hoodoo, could buy. Perhaps it was too late for her. Maybe she'd sold her soul just like Maguire—only he was better at bargaining.

Maguire. Without missing a beat, that damned buckra had gone from praising Hitler as a great thinker and a noble man to mobilizing his many factories to join the war effort against the German leader. As best she could tell, Maguire had made money from the Jerries before the war by selling them things they were now using to kill our boys. And now he was making even more money by selling our military the things they needed to fight back. It was all a big circle. A snake feeding on itself, and growing fatter from the feeding. May had no doubt regarding where Maguire's true allegiance lay in all of this bloodshed. His only loyalty was to himself. She held a complete record of his weasel words and deeds, at least those reported in the local paper, in the form of the clippings she still collected about him.

Maybe someday, after May had passed, Poppy would find the scrapbook, and these clippings and the notes May made on them would help her begin to understand what May had been up against. Help the girl find a bit of forgiveness in her heart for her old nana.

Poppy blamed May for ruining her relationship with Henry Cook. Henry. He'd up and enlisted *before* the war, probably as much out of desire to put some space between himself and Poppy as to serve his country. Whatever romance had blossomed between the two was now good and dead.

May remained angry as a hornet at Henry for his part in Maguire's plan, but still she said a prayer for his safe return. He should've warned her about what she was walking into that night, but he wasn't a bad boy. Would he and the other black servicemen be allowed to see Betty's show if it passed through where he was stationed?

The colored soldiers here in Savannah weren't allowed to share the whites' facilities. Folk were taking up money to buy a space the black servicemen could use for their own recreation. Those collecting funds for the cause had even stooped to taking money from May. Polite society had no room for "witches." People who used to tolerate her as the daughter of Mother Tuesday had drawn the line once she started working magic herself. Even the folk who'd come to her, pleading for her help, treated her like she was tainted when they caught sight of her outside the house. Magic had cost her Poppy and her reputation. May wondered what she might lose next.

Of course it seemed the man who'd forced her into this life *couldn't* lose. A new thought struck her. Maybe that's what she should do with this article about Betty. Just slip it into the same scrapbook where she kept the clippings about Maguire. Forget she'd ever received it.

She laid the article down on the table and walked away to boil up a bit of chicory. It was an absentminded move, which had become more common for her over the last few years. She turned her back to fill a saucepan with water, not even noticing Jilo had come into the room until she heard her say, "They'd let *her* borrow books from the main library."

May looked back over her shoulder to find Jilo hunched over, her elbows on the table, examining the story without laying a hand on it. "What's that, sweetheart?" May looked deep into the girl's intelligent black eyes, grateful that Jilo's own logical nature had, with some careful and repeated prodding, reenvisioned the demon's attack as a bad dream. Even more grateful for the role Jilo's nature had played in May's efforts to convince the girl there really was no such thing as magic. May would gladly have her granddaughter believe her to be a shyster if it meant she'd never believe in, or be tempted by, magic. The cycle would be broken.

"Mama. She looks enough like a white woman, I bet they'd let her take books out of the main library." May's heart broke from the knowledge that Jilo dreamed of the day she could borrow books from the big library over on Bull Street.

"They got all the books there. Not like at Carnegie." The Carnegie branch over on East Henry Street was the closest library where coloreds were allowed. Those weeks when Jilo was good, when she did her chores without fussing, May would see to it that the girl got to go, whether she walked Jilo there herself or paid one of the black taxi companies to drive her there and bring her home an hour later.

Well, okay. At least that resolved the problem of whether May should share the news article with Jilo. "Yeah," May said, forcing a smile on her face. "They just might, at that." She paused, searching Jilo's face. "You remember your mama?"

"I remember when she came. When she brought Binah to us. But I'd forgotten what she looked like till I saw this." Jilo's eyes rose to meet May's. "I thought she looked more like the doll she brought me. The one I lost."

May felt her lips purse. That doll hadn't been lost. May had found a way to bind Jilo's ability to access magic to this doll, then buried it out in a part of town Jilo would never have need to visit, miles east in a grove cut through by Normandy Street. May set the sauce pot down and crossed the room to her granddaughter. "She's a very pretty lady, your mama. Real good singer, too. See?" She placed a hand between Jilo's shoulders and traced along the photo with the fingers of her other hand. "She's going overseas to entertain the troops. Doing her part in the war effort. You should be real proud of her."

"Binah wouldn't know her," came Jilo's reply.

May circled around and sat in her chair. "Well, no, I reckon she wouldn't . . ."

"But Binah looks a lot more like her than I do."

May felt a bitterness rise up in her. "She's done tried real hard to look more like Binah."

"Binah gets her hair from Mama, doesn't she?"

May failed to repress a chuckle. "No. Binah gets that from her daddy's side. Your mama gets it from Mr. Nestle's side."

"Mr. Nestle? Who's he?" Jilo's innocent eyes made May regret the joke.

"Ah, Nana's just joshing," she said. "Nestle's the fellow who sells the auburn henna your mama uses to change her hair's color. Your mama's real hair looks just like yours." She patted Jilo's hand. "Though you get the rest of your good looks from me." She reached up and pinched Jilo's cheek, provoking a laugh from the girl.

"She must be sad," Jilo said after a moment, the smile falling from her face.

"Why do you say that?" May said, glancing down at the photo. To her eyes, Betty looked happier than she had any right to be.

" 'Cause she's pretending to be someone she's not, and she's got no one to love her. Not for who she really is, at least. She's got no one else to be proud of her. That's why she sent this to us. I don't ever want to be like her. Making believe like I'm something I'm not."

May felt her shoulders relax. "Ain't no need you ever should." She put her hand over the article and slid it toward her. "How about we put this away somewhere safe, till your sister is old enough to read it?"

Jilo nodded.

"That's good. Real good." May leaned back in her seat. "You go on and get your schoolwork done now. Nana's gonna get supper started."

BOOK TWO: JILO

ONE

Atlanta, Georgia—April 1952

"Why does that man insist we get up at the goddamned crack of dawn?" Jilo pulled the pillow over her face to shield herself from the demanding brightness of the overhead light. Her mouth was dry, her tongue wooden, and a headache was forming behind her eyes.

"I don't see what you're complaining about," Mary said, tearing the pillow away. She stood glaring down at Jilo's bed, the merciless light's halo giving her the appearance of a smug angel. "They used to make the girls who lived on campus get up at 4:30 a.m. every day to wash and iron their dresses. You've gotten to laze around until the sinful hour of six." Jilo reached out for the pillow, but Mary snatched it away and tossed it over to her own bed. "And you better not let the pastor or Mrs. Jones hear you taking God's name in vain. They'd kick you right out of this house, or at least take a switch to your backside."

"They might kick me out," Jilo mumbled as she closed her eyes, "but it will be a cold day in hell before that man lays a hand on me." Still, she knew at least part of that statement was true. The pastor and his wife ran a tight and God-fearing household, and she lived under the constant threat of being sent packing. It was a delicate dance. Jilo hated it here. Nothing would make her happier than to leave. After all, there were other boarding houses near campus, nicer ones. And cheaper, too. But Nana worried about the effect the big city would have on Jilo's moral comportment.

Three months before Jilo began classes, Nana had made the trip to Atlanta with her. Nana had given her the choice of either living here in Pastor Jones's virgin vault or heading right back home to Savannah. It wasn't really a choice at all.

Living under the pastor's roof meant spending the greater part of every Sunday with your bottom stuck to one of the hard pews at Pastor Jones's church. It also entailed rising every morning for devotional prayer and Bible study. Jilo had wanted none of that. After all, she couldn't even remember the last time Nana herself had attended church. Pointing that out in a less than respectful tone had not gotten Jilo very far. Her nana knew how badly she wanted an education. Somehow, and she wasn't quite sure how, Jilo had managed to survive nearly three years under the good reverend's supervision.

"He isn't my daddy. He's just the landlord." She could feel sleep, warm and delicious, calling to her. She tried to roll over and answer its bidding, but Mary caught her feet and spun them around and over the side of the bed.

"No," Jilo protested, but Mary had already taken ahold of her hands and was pulling her up.

"You need to get up and get dressed. You cannot be late for morning devotional . . . again. Mrs. Jones will give you another demerit."

Jilo had collected at least thirty of these demerits, when the official rule was that a girl would be kicked out after accumulating three. The pastor and his wife liked to make their threats, but they didn't have the stomach to back them up. "Her damned demerits don't mean a damned thing. Mrs. Jones can take her demerits and stick them up her—"

"You are lucky enough you didn't get caught sneaking in at two a.m. We both are . . ." Mary's voice fell off under the weight of worry. "I could get in trouble for covering for you. Or maybe," Mary continued, her tone turning defiant, "I should just go down and tell Pastor and Mrs. Jones what you been up to. Sneaking out at night and going off to Auburn Avenue. Just what are you getting up to in that Kingfisher Club anyway? You meeting a man there, ain't you? Is it *him*?"

Hell. She certainly was not going there to meet a man. Oh, sure, there were plenty of them buzzing around her, hoping to plant their little stingers, but a man was the last damned thing she needed. At least right now. A man would be fine someday, but she wasn't going to let a pointed pair of trousers stand between her and what she wanted. The only man Jilo had room for in her life right now was her biology teacher and mentor, Professor Ward, the "him" of Mary's inappropriate question.

The country had medical schools now that were graduating women. Black women. Professor Ward had promised her he'd do all he could to see that she was accepted into one of them. *Professor Ward.* She'd learned not to mention his name to Mary anymore, as Mary kept insisting Jilo was infatuated with him. But Mary didn't understand. She was too old-fashioned to believe a man and a woman could share a purely intellectual connection, an appreciation for each other that lay beyond any physical attraction that might exist between them.

It was true that the professor was a handsome and fine-minded man, but their relationship was platonic, built on the mutual respect they shared. Besides, even if there had been a physical element to the attraction, the professor was a married man. Nothing would happen, could happen, between them. Still, he had warned her that she mustn't speak too freely to others of the private discussions they shared; small minds might make something sordid out of their friendship.

It was absurd, really. Her interest in the professor was anything but romantic. The world was changing, and she was going to help it change. Other girls could waste whole trees of paper scrawling their names as

Mrs. This or Mrs. That, but not her. When she sat dreaming, the name she scribed for her future self was Doctor. Dr. Jilo Wills.

Still, a body needed to have a little fun from time to time, so on occasion, Jilo sneaked out to the clubs on Auburn. Hardly a sin, and sure as hell not a crime.

She opened one eye, doing her best to remember how much she loved this girl yapping at her. "Mary Ellen Campbell. You know better than to say 'ain't.' You are an educated woman. You need to speak like one." Pulling her hands free of Mary's grasp, she let her other eye pop open too, her vision still a little blurry from sleep. "And no, I don't go there to meet *any* goddamned man. I go for the music."

"There, at least you're awake now," Mary said, her eyebrows rising as a self-satisfied smile rose to her lips. "Now you better get moving." She wagged her finger in Jilo's face.

"You better pull that thing back unless you want to be left with a bloody stump."

"Mmm," Mary said, dropping her hand to her hip. "You sure are mean when you're hung over. Maybe next time you sneak out, you should do a bit more dancing and a bit less drinking."

Jilo wished she could see her own expression, because whatever came across her face was fierce enough to shut Mary up instantly. Her friend wandered over to the cracked mirror that hung on the wall, her back to Jilo, and began smoothing her hair. "I'm only trying to look out for you," she said, an obvious quaver in her voice.

"Oh damn it," Jilo whispered under her breath. She hadn't even made it all the way out of bed, and she'd already hurt her best friend's feelings. She pushed herself up. "Listen. I'm sorry."

Mary spun back around. "You're always pushing your luck. Trying to see how much you can get away with before you get caught."

"I've been caught plenty of times."

"Yes, and for some reason the rules don't seem to apply to you," Mary said, her voice heating back up, "the way they do for the rest of us."

It was true. The other girls faced swift and certain repercussions when they stepped out of line, but that line did seem a little less straight and narrow when it came to Jilo. Though she wouldn't say so out loud, she figured Nana must have cut a deal with the reverend. Seemed that the papists hadn't completely cornered the market on the selling of indulgences.

Fat tears fell from Mary's eyes, missing her cheeks entirely and dropping to the floor like rain through their leaky roof. "Sooner or later you are gonna go too far. And Pastor Jones is going to kick you out. And your nana, she's gonna make you go home . . ." Her words petered out as her moist eyes widened. "And I'll miss you when you're gone."

She eyed Mary up and down, testing her for sincerity, trying to determine if this was just another ploy to get her to do as she wanted. Jilo pursed her lips and looked down at the floor, doing her best to convey that she was not in the least little bit impressed by Mary's histrionics. Still, it was the damnedest thing, but she could tell Mary really was worried.

"All right. All right." Jilo threw up her hands. "I'll get ready." She went to the chest of drawers and took hold of the bucket where she kept her toiletries—her permitted toiletries, that was. Her blue eye shadow and Venetian-red lipstick were hidden in the false bottom of a hatbox that she kept in the closet.

"I'll make your bed for you," Mary said, suddenly all sunshine.

Mary's sudden transformation fired up the worst in Jilo. She said the one thing that was sure to get her friend going again. "The pastor has no business going on thinking he is morally superior to the rest of humanity anyway. None of this God stuff is true. There is no such thing as God."

Mary's mouth fell wide open, causing Jilo to chuckle at the sight.

"Oh, Jilo. Don't you go saying that," Mary said, once her jaw started working again. "I know you don't believe any such thing. You are simply trying to get a rise out of me, but it ain't gonna work."

"It *isn't* going to work," Jilo said, correcting her friend's speech automatically, out of habit.

"No it isn't," Mary said. It was easy to pin the exact moment when she realized Jilo hadn't taken her point, and was just correcting her grammar again. "You don't believe that. I know you don't."

Jilo wondered at her own mean streak. She had no reason to try and shake her friend up. No other reason beyond that it was too early, she was hung over, and, well, even under the best of circumstances, perkiness just kind of ticked her off.

" 'Course not," she said to mollify her friend. As soon as the smile returned to Mary's face, Jilo looked away. She couldn't risk having their eyes meet, for then Mary would know she was lying. Truth was, having grown up surrounded by her nana's put-on magic, Jilo didn't believe in anything she couldn't see with her own eyes. Oh, sure, she couldn't see things like magnetism, radio waves, and electricity, but there were scientific tests to prove that those things were real. That they existed. As far as Jilo knew, no one had managed to come up with a test that would prove the existence of the bearded old buckra in the sky.

A rap on the door pulled Jilo from her thoughts. "Miss Wills," Mrs. Jones's voice came through the door. "The pastor needs to speak with you. Immediately."

TWO

Mary's eyes locked with Jilo's, and Jilo gave a nod at the door. After crossing the room as silently as a cat, Mary reached for the doorknob like she was afraid it might burn her. She opened the door a sliver, doing her best to block their landlady's view of Jilo. "I'm sorry, Mrs. Jones, ma'am, but Jilo, she isn't quite dressed yet. She's not been feeling too well this morning."

Mrs. Jones's left hand clutched the edge of the door and forced it open, pushing Mary back into the room. The pastor's wife was a plain woman. Although she was decade younger than the good reverend himself, she still looked plenty old enough to be her husband's mother. Her face bore no wrinkles, but her hair was streaked with gray, and she had a weary look that never left her. It was this perpetual exhaustion that aged her more than the gray in her hair.

Jilo crossed her arms over her chest and planted her feet firm. The older woman's puffy red eyes and small tight-lipped frown told her that she'd finally been caught doing something that might be bad enough for them to send her home. Had they noticed her sneaking in?

The reverend's missus approached her, pressing her palms together as if she were about to break out into prayer, but instead she reached out and gently placed her hand over Jilo's temple. Her skin felt rough, weathered by years of scrubbing floors and dishes and the mountains of laundry she did each day for her boarders.

"Jilo, my girl," she said, "you know that the good Lord has never seen fit to bless me with a child. But He has given me you girls. You are my children. My beautiful daughters." She swallowed back a tremolo that had come to her voice. "You girls who live here under our roof. You got that fine college of yours to take care of educating you in the things this world values. But the pastor and I, we gotta look out for your moral education. Your spiritual well-being. We take this charge seriously."

Jilo forced her face to freeze so that it would betray nothing. Not the anger she felt that this uneducated woman, barely a decade her elder, was talking to her as if she were a child. Not the love, which in spite of Jilo's best efforts, she had come to feel for this gentle lady. She bit her tongue.

"We know you are a strong-willed young lady, and we have allowed you far more liberties than any of the others. But this is a holy house," Mrs. Jones said in the face of Jilo's silence. "A *righteous* house." She dropped back to stare at Jilo. "You go on and get dressed now. The pastor is waiting for you in his study." She turned to Mary. "You come on downstairs with me."

"But I . . ."

"I said come," Mrs. Jones cut her off. Evidently she'd had enough of rebellious young women for one morning.

Mary followed Mrs. Jones out of the room, but not before casting one look back at Jilo, her raised eyebrows and rounded eyes begging her friend to kneel before the seat of mercy and plead for forgiveness. Jilo might be more inclined to do that if she were sure exactly which sin they'd discovered.

Jilo grabbed her pail of toiletries and headed to the bathroom she shared with Mary and three other girls. Most mornings it was nothing but elbows and pardons, but today she had the space all to herself. The other girls weren't early risers like Mary, so either they had been told to stay out of Jilo's way this morning, or they'd made that choice for themselves. She set the pail down on a stand next to the sink and took a good look at her own puffy-eyed reflection. "Hell, girl, this might be more serious than you thought," she said out loud as she grabbed hold of her toothbrush and tin of tooth powder. Her eyes drifted down to the pail while she brushed her teeth. Had they found her makeup hidden in the hatbox? Unlikely. The pastor and his wife were straitlaced, but they respected a person's privacy. She couldn't imagine either of them digging through their boarders' personal belongings. Of course, she wouldn't put it past one of the other girls, especially Louise.

Maybe they had spotted her breaking the house's curfew, or someone else—someone she hadn't seen—had witnessed her good times at the Kingfisher Club. But, the more she thought of it, the less likely that seemed. Who in their right mind would implicate themselves by admitting to having seen her? No. It was without a doubt something to do with Louise. Little Miss Goodie Two Shoes was always looking to land one of her housemates in a pot of trouble.

After she finished cleaning her teeth, she washed her face with cold water, not wanting to wait for the hot to come clanking up through the pipes. The frigid touch of the water didn't help the aching behind her eyes one bit, but it did clear a bit of last night's fuzz from her brain.

She dabbed at her face with a hand towel, then attacked her hair with a brush, doing her best to smooth it. She was just about to dive back into her room to dress when she remembered the smoke that had filled the air at the club last night. Neither Mary nor Mrs. Jones had mentioned picking up the scent, but Mary wasn't the most attentive of witnesses, and it wasn't Mrs. Jones's way to mention such things. Whenever she smelled smoke, she'd leave it to her husband to find the fire. It could be used as another strike against her.

"Damn." Jilo dropped her pail back down on the table and dove into an icy shower, soaping herself as best she could with a pat of Camay so tiny one of the other girls had left it behind as having no value.

Sopping wet and teeth chattering, but now fully awake, she dried herself and pulled on her robe. Back in her room, she dressed herself in a gray shirtwaist dress with sleeves that covered her arms past the elbow. Jilo hated the damn thing—Nana had made her buy it—but the pastor had complimented the style as being suitable for a young Christian woman. If it came down to playing the part of a repentant sinner, a good costume would help.

Jilo made her way downstairs, giving a wide berth to the large communal dining room, where she could still hear bits of Paul's Letter to the Corinthians being read aloud. Jilo surmised that the apostle's thoughts on the topic of charity were intended to fortify Mrs. Jones's resolve to remain patient with her. Lord knows, the pastor's wife had quoted the passage often enough to her over the past years. The thought elicited an eye roll, and Jilo barely remembered to adopt a suitably remorseful expression before knocking on the frame of the pastor's door. The door itself stood ajar, the amber light from his desk lamp spilling out into the hall. She stood in the doorway, waiting for the pastor to look up from his studies.

For a moment, she thought he hadn't heard her. He remained bent over a thick concordance, scratching notes on his pad. Finally, he laid down his pen and looked up at her. "Miss Wills." He waved her forward. "Do come in," he said, folding his hands before him on his desk. "Close the door behind you."

After doing the pastor's bidding, Jilo turned to face his beatific stare. He let her stand there for a moment, just long enough for the silence to grow awkward, then pushed back in his chair. "Please, sit," he said, extending his hand toward a chair opposite him. Normally she had to face his private sermons standing; this chair was a new addition to his space. Though its cushion now wore a different fabric, and a back leg had been repaired with a brace created from splints of wood and heavy screws, Jilo recognized it as a poor relation of those that were still used around the dining table.

"Don't worry," he said, watching her eye the repair work. "I mended it myself. It may have been broken once, but now it's stronger than it ever was." She stepped around the chair and lowered herself onto the seat. "Just like the human soul," the reverend added, the smile on his lips showing her he was quite pleased with his own simile.

Jilo crossed her legs at her ankles, just the way the mistress of comportment at the college had shown them all to do on the first day of classes, giving the hem of her skirt a slight tug as she did so. *Smile. Keep quiet.* Jilo had played this game with the pastor more than a few times over the years. Experience had taught her that the biggest mistake she could make would be to assume she knew which infraction she'd been caught committing.

She and the pastor sat face-to-face as the clock on his desk ticked off a full minute. Twice. The entire time, his eyes searched her. The smile fled his lips, replaced by a stern expression meant to intimidate her and wear her down. "All right," he said with a sigh. "I'm sure you can guess why I asked to speak with you."

Jilo had been composing a mental list of reasons, but shook her head. "No, sir." She made her voice come out as sweet as dew on the morning grass, but then the devil himself twisted her tongue. "Are you in need of spiritual guidance?" The words escaped her before her common sense could close the gate.

The pastor jerked his head back as if she had slapped him. "Spiritual guidance, indeed." He puffed out air and tapped his finger on the desk. Ten times. He was obviously counting. He stopped and relaxed his shoulders. "You may not be aware of this," he began, seeming to have decided on another tack, "I'm unsure of how much your grandmother has shared with you, but I once had a church not far from her house." Despite herself, Jilo betrayed her interest by leaning just a bit forward. It was the first she'd heard that the pastor had any connection to her world. She ran through a list of churches in the area, trying to figure out where he'd come from.

"That's right," Jones continued, "your family and I go way back. As a matter of fact, the first time I laid eyes on you"—for a fleeting moment a smile came to his lips—"you were nothing but a tiny bug of a thing." His focus weakened, as if he were reliving the memory, but then his attention snapped back on her like a mousetrap. "Your grandmother did not send you to live in this house by chance. She sought me out, and I believe her reason for doing so was that she knows I am quite familiar with the women of your family. The best are willful and stiff-necked. The worst, weak. Given to sinning and always ready to drag the nearest man down along with them."

Jilo very nearly lost her cool, but sensing a weakness in the man, she instead took a moment to sharpen the stick she was about to jab in a very soft place. "I see you've met my mama." She leaned her elbow against the arm of her chair and rested her chin on her hand, smiling sweetly.

The pastor flushed, but collected himself in the next instant. "Indeed," he said, a sadness filling his voice. He shifted in his seat and leaned over to open a drawer. He reached into the drawer to retrieve an item, then flashed her another, knowing look, before placing it on the desk.

It was a book, the cover of which she instantly recognized, even though it was upside-down from her point of view. He pushed it toward her, never taking his eyes from hers. "*Lady Chatterley's Lover.*" He raised his hand to preempt the question he anticipated. "Before you ask, how this came into my possession is beside the point. I know even you would have better sense than to leave such a work sitting out for any and all to see, so you can believe me when I tell you the girl who brought it to my attention has been heartily reprimanded for going through your personal belongings." He tapped the image on the cover. "This bird appears as if it has already been caught in the fires of hell. My aim is to make certain you don't share this poor misguided creature's fate."

"It isn't a regular bird. It's a phoenix," Jilo said. He shook his head, not understanding. "A phoenix. A mythical bird that renews itself by setting its nest on fire. Through the fire, it is reborn." She reached out to take the book, but he pulled it back. "In this case, the fire is symbolic of passion . . ."

"I have examined this book," the pastor said. "I am well aware of the nature of what it contains. Still, the narrative concerns me less than what I found written here." He opened the book to its frontispiece, then pointed to a name printed on the facing title page. *Lionel Ward.*

Jilo bit her lip, waiting again for the pastor to take the lead. Professor Ward often shared books from his personal collection with her, books he felt would enrich and broaden her mind. Many were banned from the public library, so it would have been hard for her to obtain them on her own.

Jones closed the book and reached over the desk to hand it to her. She accepted it without daring a word.

"I am not a prude, Miss Wills. I believe that our Lord made relations between men and women pleasurable because he wants us to find pleasure in them." He paused, as he often did when giving a sermon, to emphasize the point he was about to make. "But God intended for these relations to take place within the bounds of matrimony."

"I understand, Pastor. It was wrong of me to bring this book into your home. I'll return it to Professor Ward today, right after classes."

Jones raised a single eyebrow. "I'm not sure I'm making my concerns clear. I do appreciate and accept your apology. Strangely enough, I think it may have even been somewhat sincere. But I am less concerned with the imagined sins in this book than I am with the possibility of actual sin between creatures of God." He held his hand out to her, palm up, signaling that she should give the book back to him. "I will return this book to its owner."

Jilo hesitated, but his tone was firm. She placed it in his hand, and he set it on his desk, covering it with a pad of paper, like Adam hiding behind the fig leaf.

"I do not believe this book is appropriate reading for a girl your age. I certainly don't feel it is appropriate for a man to be sharing with a young lady. As your guardian, I will inform this Professor Ward of that fact myself."

Jilo felt herself go hot then cold with embarrassment. "But Professor Ward is a married man," she said, hoping his marital status would somehow convince the reverend of the innocence of the loan.

"That, Miss Wills, is my point exactly."

THREE

October 1952

Jilo found her eyes resting on the red-and-white tin sitting on the desk-top. A lozenge shape bordered the white silhouette of a man on horse-back, a jouster by the look of his proud lance. The picture struck her as out of tune with the name inscribed below it—a word that conjured up images of hot sands and cool oases, not Camelot.

A burning log in the fireplace popped, prompting her to crane her neck in an attempt to glance in the sound's direction. A chill had settled on Atlanta in October's final days, and Lionel had started a small fire in his office's hearth to beat it back.

Once, she'd enjoyed sitting by the fireside in one of the two com-modious leather chairs positioned on either side of the hearth, talking to Lionel about art, books, and the future—the world's in general and hers in particular. Now, her back was resting against a blotter, and something sharp and hard—a letter opener, she reckoned—poked her side. An unpleasant but bearable sensation.

Her attention wandered back to Professor Ward, who stood holding her legs up around his hips. She gasped in a breath of air and quivered. There was a feeling like a sharp pinch as he entered her. An unpleasant but bearable sensation. His eyes, framed by the gold round rims of his glasses, were filled with a faraway and glassy look as he moved inside her.

He loves me, she thought. *He loves me. He loves me.* She repeated the words to herself as he jostled her into a better position, reaching back to wrap her legs around him. She understood that he wanted her to hold them there, so she did.

"I love you," he whispered, his spoken words sounding in chorus with her own internal chant. His tie—the blue one, her favorite—brushed across her stomach as he leaned over her; his hands, a teacher's hands, soft with buffed nails, found her breasts. "I love you." His weight pressed into her, and the metal and wood behind her back conspired together to make her spine and hips ache. His lips only met hers for a moment before he drew back, his fingers pinching into her legs, separating them wider as the pace of his thrusting accelerated, his straining body pressed fully into hers. He moaned once, then again, and let his weight settle onto her as he dropped her legs and left them to dangle over the side of the desk. His chest heaved, causing a button of his shirt to dig into her skin, and then he pulled out of her without another moment's hesitation.

He stooped to rummage through his pants, puddled on the floor around his ankles, and produced a kerchief from the pocket. "Hold this. Down there," he said, forcing it into her hand and positioning it between her legs, without really looking at her. "There's some blood. Don't want it on the rug." As soon as she did as he asked, he shifted his focus to removing the latex sheath that he had pulled from the red-and-white tin.

She pushed herself up on one elbow, watching as he tied a knot into the end of the thing. He tugged up his pants and buttoned them, and without looking at her, strode to the hearth and tossed the condom into the flames. He grasped the poker, using its hooked end to pull a glowing log on top of the latex. Then he returned the poker to its holder, and without speaking, knelt to retrieve her dress from the floor. He laid it next to her on the desk, turning his attention to the rest of her wardrobe. Odd, but he now seemed embarrassed to touch the bra he'd nearly torn off her only minutes before. He picked it up and dropped it on the dress. A few steps away lay her panties. He picked them up using his thumb and index finger. She took them from him, hoping that their hands might meet, but he dropped them into her grasp and returned to the fire, keeping his back toward her as she dressed.

She pulled herself together as quickly as she could manage, although she had trouble locating a shoe that had somehow been kicked under a step stool on the far side of the room. She crossed to him and placed her hand on his forearm. He looked down at her, his eyes cautious. He cleared his throat. "We'll speak of this matter at a later time."

She couldn't find words to respond. She only nodded and went to the door. She hesitated for a moment, hoping he'd call her back. Hoping he'd take her into his arms and speak more words of love.

There was only silence.

FOUR

Jilo didn't know what possessed her, but she found herself walking a mile and a half away from home, toward the red brick walls and stained-glass windows of Five Points Baptist.

It wasn't a desire to confess to her sin. She couldn't bring herself to see what she had done as a sin. She loved Professor Ward. Lionel. She believed he loved her, too. He had told her so. Many times. The first back in June, shortly after the last day of the term, right before he left for a month in New York. His revelation had come as a surprise. An even a greater shock was the realization that her own feelings for Lionel went beyond those of student and mentor.

And she had no intent of claiming him, of flouncing their love in Mrs. Ward's face. Jilo's love for Lionel, and his for her, was a different kind of love. Spiritual. It didn't need the bonds or trappings of traditional marriage to make it holy.

They had spoken of it often. Their love didn't need the approval of society or the God it had fabricated to keep the fearful in check. Their love was modern. Unbound by law and tradition. So it didn't matter that another woman shared Lionel's name, even if he regretted ever forging that bond. His love for Jilo was somehow more real, more pure, free as it was from any claims of ownership.

Lionel had married too young by his own admission, and though he'd made his vows in good faith, he was no longer the young man who'd pledged himself body and soul to his wife. Besides, his wife was a completely different woman than she'd led him to believe. Now, as a mature man, Lionel dreamed of casting off the bondage of conventionality. Fleeing the proper world that had him trapped and heading out into the world of the liberated mind. And yes, he wanted to take Jilo with him. According to him, it was only Mrs. Ward's fragile health that kept him bound to her.

They had danced around the act for months. A touch of the hands. A brush of his lips against hers. She hadn't expected it to happen the way it had, so quickly. But after so many months of holding back, his hands had suddenly been all over her. His need had flared up with a shocking intensity. And while she'd imagined it differently, he seemed to have planned the whole thing from start to finish—his wife was with her sister on a train to Tuskegee, and there had been a supply of prophylactics at hand. He had chosen, she realized, to take advantage of his temporary freedom. She only wished he would have discussed it with her first. Perhaps then the experience wouldn't have felt so—she searched her heart for the right word—*sordid*.

And then there was the way he had acted afterward . . . She'd given him what he wanted. Willingly. But the way his eyes had failed to meet hers after the fact had left her feeling . . . well, if not sinful, soiled. Damaged. Was he disappointed? Had she disappointed him?

After leaving his house, she had set out walking, and something had brought her here, to Five Points Baptist. She nearly turned toward home, but the same thing that had brought her this far tugged at her again. Without precisely meaning to, she climbed up the concrete steps, nearly stumbling in her hurry.

She reached for the door's large brass pull, her hand feeling small and cold as she grasped ahold of it and opened the door. The scent of worn hymnals and an overabundance of furniture polish administered lovingly by the ladies' council nearly overwhelmed her.

Not for the first time, it struck her that the interior of the church somewhat resembled a theater. The pulpit and choir loft shared a raised stage, with a curved apron that Pastor Jones would strut back and forth over when he got himself worked up in his preaching. A set of stairs ran down each side of the stage, and the altar was situated between the rise of the apron and the first row of pews. Jilo walked down the aisle and took a seat in the third row.

The church only had a single stained-glass window, set into its eastern wall. From her schooling, Jilo understood the chemistry behind the glass's rich colors. Nickel or perhaps copper oxide would have been used to create the blues of the sky. Beams of silver nitrate light touched the white cross made of tin oxide and arsenic—strange that something so deadly could create such beauty. Iron and chromium combined for the green grass in which the cross was planted. A white dove hovered above. Across the arms of the cross was draped a cloth, stained brilliant red with selenium and cadmium rather than the messiah's blood.

Still, even though she understood the chemistry behind the vivid colors, whenever the sun lit up the window, its beauty touched her. The pastor would say the sight was touching her soul. But no, she reminded herself, the voice in her head sounding more like Lionel's than her own, it was chemistry that created the hues, and biological chemistry that created her emotional reaction to them.

Normally she prided herself on her ability to see beyond superstition and emotionality, but today, she felt empty and alone. Though she wished she could allow herself to take comfort from patently absurd beliefs, she'd seen too many folk come to her nana out of desperation and a desire for magic. Nana had never come right out and admitted it, but she would always give a knowing smile whenever Jilo asked if any of it were real. No, Jilo didn't want to build her world on superstitions. She cared only for what she could touch. What she could measure.

It didn't matter now anyway. The sun slanted down from the west, no longer imbuing the window with colored light, taking even that small pleasure from her.

The church was mostly silent, but she knew she wasn't alone. A small room sat off to the right of the pulpit. A squeaking sound from within betrayed the pastor's presence.

He kept a room at home for prayer, study, and—as Jilo could well testify—the occasional disciplinary discussion with the young women who lived beneath his roof. The office he kept here was where he wore his public face, tending to his flock and advising them in their times of trouble. Yes, as with all men, there were two sides to Pastor Jones—the public and the private. As much as Jilo resented him at times, she held it to his credit that the side he showed to the public was, if anything, less perfect than the one he showed at home. He saved his best for those closest to him. That grudging respect was tempered by the annoyance she felt toward this man. So why, out of all the places on God's green earth—she paused a moment to ponder her odd choice of words—when she felt her lowest and most confused, had she been drawn to the one place he was certain to be?

The squeak sounded again, and Jilo could make out the rumble of a chair's coasters gliding across a wooden floor. She raised her eyes to look at him the moment he came to the doorway. If his face had shown the slightest surprise at her presence, if he had asked what she was doing there, why she'd come, she would have jumped up and bounded down the aisle. But he said nothing, and his expression struck her as one of quiet relief, the lines on his face smoothing at the sight of her. He came down the steps, and after standing off to the side for a moment, circled around and took a seat on the pew behind her.

"I see you girls as my children, you know. We both do, Sally and I." He rarely referred to his wife by her Christian name, preferring to speak of her as Mrs. Jones, like she was an extension of himself rather than a person in her own right. "I shudder to think of where I'd be without my Sally," he said, almost as if reading her mind. "I could no more do without her than without . . . well, let's just say that without her, I doubt that I would be." A moment of silence passed between them, but it was nothing like the angry awkwardness of the times they'd spent sitting across from each other with locked horns.

"When she found me," he continued, "I was a broken man. I know what it means to be as low as a man can get and still draw breath. The White King," Jilo's ears pricked up at the name, as she used to hear folk whisper about the "kings" from time to time back in Savannah. She had no idea how such an odd bit of superstition could have gotten its start. "He nearly had me. But Mrs. Jones, she found me, and she patched the pieces of this raggedy man back together."

He fell silent, and for a moment, Jilo felt as tempted as Lot's wife to cast a backward glance. "I know you think I am behind the times," he finally said. "A creature of another era. I understand. In your shoes, at your age, well, undoubtedly I would have seen myself in the same light. It's right that the young move us forward. It's necessary. But sometimes that desire to buck the past can be dangerous and reckless. If I seem to hold on to my ideals too tightly, know that it is because I have walked up many a slippery hill. However you see me, remember this when you are appraising my character; I'm not a strong man, but I do care for you. I would like to think that in time, you'll come to see that. I hate that we so often find ourselves facing off like adversaries."

Jilo didn't look back, but she nodded in agreement. This time she wasn't tempted to turn. Speaking face-to-face might break the fragile spell that seemed to hold them in this place of peace, of understanding. "Why didn't you?" she said, then, realizing that her thought had been elliptical, added, "Have children. Of your own, I mean."

His reply came slowly, causing Jilo to fear she'd overstepped, but then he sighed. "We tried to have children, Sally and I, but it wasn't

His will." The pew behind her moaned as he shifted his weight. "I know she blames herself, but I think . . ." He paused. "Well, you'd think I was crazy if I told you what I think." The pew moaned again, this time with greater vehemence. Jilo realized he was standing, and she spun around. Without quite meaning to, she clasped his hand. For a fearful moment their eyes met, but she felt at peace with him, and judging from the way he relaxed back onto the pew, he seemed to feel the same way.

"What do you care what a silly girl like me thinks anyway?"

He smiled and shook his head. "You might be surprised by how much I care." He leaned a bit forward. "And you're not a silly girl. You're an intelligent young woman. A headstrong young woman . . ." he started, but held up his hands and laughed when she pursed her lips and looked down her nose at him. "You are very much like the daughter I imagine I might have had, if I had been so blessed." She returned his smile.

What would her father have thought of this man as her guardian? Nana Wills had certainly approved, so she figured Jesse Wills would've, too. Her thoughts turned dark. What would her father have thought of Lionel? She knew what Nana would think. She'd kill him if she found out what they'd done.

The pastor leaned back and draped his arm over the back of the pew. "I always knew I wanted to preach the word of God. Ever since I was a little boy." He bit his lip and squinted at her. "You see, I knew I had been called . . . chosen, if you will. Many in this world are filled with doubt, but not I, 'cause I know there is something out there. The grace of God has allowed me to see with my own eyes what others perceive through faith." The corners of his mouth twitched up into a nervous smile. "I've seen His angels," he said, "I've been *taken up* by angels. And well, they changed me. I think they did things to prevent me from becoming a father. To ensure I could concentrate on spreading the word."

Jilo blinked with surprise, but bit her tongue.

"See, you do think I'm crazy."

She weighed her words before speaking. "No, I don't think that. I do think that when we're children, we can have dreams that seem very real to us." She laughed. "I once dreamed that my big sister Poppy tried to eat my baby sister. Took days for my nana to convince me it'd only been a dream."

He nodded, a sad expression washing over his face. "Yes, I understand what you say is true, but these visitations, they happened more than once." He lowered his gaze, as if he didn't want to see her response. "Still do from time to time. I see their holy light, and I am taken up"—he raised his hands and waved them in praise—" 'whether in the body, or out of the body, I cannot tell: God knoweth;' Second Corinthians, chapter twelve, verse three," he quoted, his reference to the good book causing his voice to lift and take on the animated quality it had when he was preaching. But then his voice fell flat and came out in a whisper. "They've shown me things, things to come on this earth. Clouds of fire rising up from the earth to the sky. Death and destruction like this world has never known, with only a remnant to survive. "

He leaned forward, clenching the back of her pew, and she felt herself leaning away from him. " 'And I saw when the Lamb opened one of the seals, and I heard, as it were the noise of thunder, one of the four beasts saying, Come and see.' And I did, for they gave me no choice. I turned my head. I sought to avert my gaze. But no matter where I looked, it was the same. Stretched out before me was a desolate wasteland. Everywhere, fire and wind, and the seas burned clean away." His voice trailed off, and his face turned ashen as his eyes looked out into nothingness. "Not even Mrs. Jones knows any of this." His eyes turned toward her, a flicker of some dawning awareness in them.

He shook his head. Pushing against the pew, he rose to his feet. "Please forget I've said any of this." He towered over her, slowly regaining control of himself, and raised his hand to his temple. "I spend too much time contemplating things that are not of this world. Perhaps you're correct. Perhaps I let my imagination carry me away. Just forget my nonsense."

But then his expression changed again, and the wide-eyed fright melted away into a mask of nearly paternal disappointment. His chest rose and fell, and he reached out and placed his hand along her jaw. She felt the urge to look away, but he turned her face up so that her eyes met his. "But another seal has been broken."

FIVE

May 1953

"I'd like to thank you for joining us today, Miss Wills," said the dean of students, Lewis Washington, looking over his spectacles at her like he was considering a slug he'd just uncovered in a prize flowerbed. The wooden smile he forced to his lips came too late to sweeten the tone that underlay his words. He sat facing her, his substantial desk forming an effective barrier between them. The office's other chairs had been pulled into a straight line, stretching out from her left side to the ominously closed door.

These other seats had been filled by Jane Temple, the school registrar, Professor Charles, head professor of chemistry, and Lionel. She forced herself to think of him as Professor Ward lest she make a slip and an untoward familiarity show through. Graduation was less than six weeks away, and she was counting on recommendations from him and the others with him. "It's an honor, sir," she said.

Dean Washington smiled again, though this time the expression struck her as sincere. He looked from side to side, giving both professors and Miss Temple a look that seemed to tell them that they could relax, that there would be no trouble here. He leaned back in his large leather wingback chair, turning a bit to the side, and folded his hands on his round stomach. "I have been looking over your records, Miss Wills, and I have to tell you that I am impressed." He spun the chair back to the center, not taking his eyes from her or his hands off his gut. "Your achievements here have indeed been outstanding."

He stared at her, his face beaming with benevolence, and rocked in his chair, seeming to await a response. "Thank you, sir," she said a moment after the silence began to feel heavy.

No longer rocking, he leaned forward and planted his hand on his desk, his stomach reaching out to touch its drawer. "Such a fine young lady," he said, looking first at Charles and then at Ward.

Professor Charles must have read the comment as an invitation to speak. "One of the finest students I have ever had the pleasure to teach."

Somehow his words affected her more than the dean's compliment. Winning this man's approval meant a lot to her. Jilo blushed and lowered her head.

"Don't you agree, Lionel?" Dean Washington asked.

Lionel—Professor Ward's lips curled into a smooth smile. "Unequaled." Jilo glanced over at him, wishing that he still looked at her in private the way he regarded her now. Although their affair had continued, he no longer volunteered the words, "I love you." When pressed, he would offer her, "You should know that I do," but he grew cooler with each passing day. He cited pressures from work—although Jilo had begun to write and grade the exams for his courses over a year and a half ago, long before the physical aspect of their love had begun to be expressed. He blamed his wife's continued declining health, although Mrs. Ward had begun to spend more time at her sister's home than her own. He spoke with resentment of Jilo's "clinginess"—explaining her own insecurities as the reason he had begun to pull away.

Last week Jilo had spotted Jeannette Walker, a freshman, a pretty girl with an hourglass shape and a secondhand intellect, carrying Professor Ward's copy of *Leaves of Grass*. With a singular lack of care, she had left it deserted on a picnic table outside the auditorium with heavy clouds building overhead. Jilo had rescued it . . . and then watched later as the panicked girl returned, frantically seeking to retrieve that which she had so callously abandoned. It wasn't stealing. This book belonged to Jilo now. She'd earned it.

Lionel had used this book as a tool to seduce her, and she had paid for it with her flesh. With her heart. The words "*the embrace of love and resistance,*" haunted her now, for they seemed to have divined the course of the affair, understanding it in a way Jilo herself only did now that she'd witnessed its full fruition. "*I sing the body electric,*" Ward had quoted, "*The armies of those I love engirth me, and I engirth them,*" he'd continued, pressing her back into the wall as he leaned one arm forward to brace himself and wrapped a leg around hers. He'd held them locked together like that, his lips hovering a mere hairsbreadth from her own, as he spoke in a soft whisper the remainder of the stanza. That moment. Yes, it was precisely then that she had fallen in love with him. "*You are the gates of the body, and you are the gates of the soul.*" A gate he now shunned in favor of a new portal.

"Unequaled," she heard her own voice repeat Professor Ward's appraisal of her, using the word as an agreement, a pledge, a threat, and a promise all rolled into one. A worry line creased his forehead, but other than that he remained cool. Perhaps for the first time, she saw him completely—not as her love, not as the mate who completed her, but as a vain and aging man. A seaman whose sextant had enabled him to navigate this course many times before; an actor who'd returned again and again to the same role, employing the same props for each performance. "You're far too kind. I'm sure you've known many like me before."

"Oh, no, Miss Wills. You are special," the dean continued, oblivious to everything save his own agenda. "Unless you face a spectacular reversal of fortune during your final examinations, Miss Temple assures us you are certain to graduate as your class's valedictorian." He raised his hand and pointed at her. "So you make sure to stay on course. Don't go letting spring fever or the sight of some young buck turn your head."

"No, sir," Jilo responded.

"Fine," the dean said, shifting his weight and pushing a bit back. "You have given this institution your best work, and we four have spoken. We all agree that we would be remiss if we didn't band together and address the issue of what should come next for you." He looked from her to his colleagues. Taking their silence as assent, he continued, "With that in view, we've invited you here to discuss your future." He nodded toward Professor Ward. "I understand from Lionel that you have ambitions in the field of medicine."

"Yes, sir, I do." Jilo shifted forward on her seat, sitting up straight. "I believe more opportunities are available to me today than any of my sister graduates since the inception of this institution." Enthusiasm overtook her, causing her to slide out of her seat and stand. "As you may know, three years ago the American College of Surgeons admitted its first Negro female into its ranks. My dream, no, my intent is to follow in her footsteps. I hope that you—"

"Miss Wills," the dean said, holding up his hands in a gesture of surrender, "I have been apprised of your goals." One hand waved her back into her chair. He waited for her to slip onto the seat, wiping his hand across his mouth as he seemed to consider how to proceed. "I do so admire your youthful passion." His lips puckered, then bunched up into a reassuring smile. "But I worry that your youth and your passion may in fact work against you. Here, at this institution," he raised his hands palms up and gestured widely around as if to take in the entire campus, "we seek to ingrain confidence in our girls. However, we must also educate them in regard to the greater world in which we find ourselves. Inject a bit of reality into their dreams." Nodding, as if in agreement with himself, he tilted his head to the side. "It is true that a few women have succeeded in obtaining medical degrees. Some have even begun to practice medicine. But they are curiosities, the bearded ladies, if you will, of the medical profession. Medicine is, after all, a man's profession."

"Any man would refuse treatment from a woman doctor," Professor Charles broke in.

"Then I will treat women . . . and children."

A look that straddled the line between amusement and irritation rose up on the dean's face.

"Miss Wills," the registrar spoke for the first time. "I assure you," she said, pushing her thick spectacles back up the bridge of her nose, "women would be no more inclined to seek out care from a female doctor than would a man. Important issues such as a person's health shouldn't be left to a woman's discernment."

The dean nodded approvingly.

She and Lionel had spent hours together, speaking of her dreams, discussing the changes that were coming about in the world. He had supported her. Encouraged her. In spite of her feelings for him in this present moment, she turned to him for support.

He shifted uncomfortably under the weight of her pleading eyes. "You must understand, Miss Wills"—she felt a chill creep across her heart at the sound of her lover's voice speaking her name in such a formal, removed tone—"medical schools have a limited numbers of seats available for incoming students. Only a fraction of those seats are open to Negro students. You have to place your community's needs before your own unrealistic dreams. Even if you could make it into medical school, even if we supported you in this effort, you have to understand that you would be stealing that seat from a deserving male student, a student who could actually help the Negro community." His hand reached up to straighten the knot of his tie. "Besides, you're a young woman. You will undoubtedly choose to marry, and children will follow. You'll have to stop working at that point. So your entire career would last how long? Two years? Perhaps five? This type of education is a waste on a woman."

She stared at him. Frozen. Knowing without a doubt that these were his true thoughts, and before, he had only spoken the words she'd wanted to hear. She turned back to the dean, "But I could help—"

"Miss Wills," the dean said, his tone harsh now. As if realizing he'd gone off message, he drew a deep breath. "Jilo," he said more kindly. "We seek to help you reach a more realistic goal. Miss Temple has kindly looked over your transcript and compared your course of studies with the requirements of our nursing program. Miss Temple?"

The registrar cleared her throat. "Yes, that is correct. With a little creative interpretation on the part of Professors Ward and Charles of the coursework you've completed, we are delighted to offer you a degree in nursing." She paused. "Of course, you'll have to be tutored on certain practical aspects of patient care, dressing and cleaning wounds and the like, but your friend Mary has volunteered to get you caught up by graduation," she said, tugging on the white gloves she was wearing, as puffed out and pleased as a preening chicken. "I hope you are aware that we would not go to this trouble for just any student."

"But I don't want to be a nurse." Jilo said, and the room fell silent as Miss Temple's face formed a sour pucker.

"The French have a saying," Ward broke the silence, leaning forward and turning toward her, "roughly translated, it states that one must learn to put a little water in his wine, meaning one must ground his ambitions in reality."

"And if I choose not to accept this nursing degree?"

"Well, young lady, that would be a mistake . . ."

"It will be my mistake to make," she interrupted the dean, no longer caring if she lost his goodwill.

"In that unfortunate occurrence, we will, of course, issue you the bachelor of science you have earned, but it is our opinion that you will find it to be of very little practical use in the real world."

What she wanted was to tell them all to go to hell. But she held her tongue and began to calculate the odds of this game. The nursing degree would get her into the medical field. Perhaps she could find a true mentor once she was in a hospital setting, someone who would see her value and help her to achieve her dreams. It wouldn't be a direct route, but without this institution's support, it might be the only one available to her.

"All right," she said. "I will accept the nursing degree you offer."

The dean slapped his palms happily down on his desk and pushed himself up. "I told you all she was a smart girl, that she'd see the reason." He beamed at her as he held out his hand in an apparent offer to shake hers.

She wrapped her arms around herself. "May I be excused?"

- — -

As she made her way back to the boarding house, Jilo began to regret her capitulation, very nearly turning back and forcing her way into the dean's office to make one more attempt to reason with him. Or maybe she should circle back to Lionel's house later. She could throw herself at his feet, prostrate herself before him, beg him to step up to the promises he'd made in the past.

But that son of a bitch had betrayed her, and not just by making her a link in what she now guessed was a career-long chain of girls. He had manipulated her into thinking he believed in her. In her dreams. In her capabilities.

When she arrived home, Jilo eased the door open and closed it quietly behind her. Not wanting to talk to anyone, she did her best to creep past the pastor and his wife, who were deep in a discussion about the house's finances, and flitted past the archway that opened onto the sitting room. She found the stairs and mounted them, carefully avoiding the steps that squeaked.

As she made her escape, it occurred to her that she wasn't taking these precautions because she wasn't in the mood to see a single living person. The truth, it pained her to realize, was that she felt ashamed. After years of hard work, all her dreams had been dashed in a single afternoon. And she felt like it was her own fault. If she hadn't let Lionel touch her, if she hadn't given into her own need to believe he saw her as special, would he have respected her more? Would he have viewed her as being a serious enough woman to become a lady doctor? Had giving in to him cheapened her in his eyes?

Hot tears began to flow down her cheeks, but they stopped cold when she opened the door to her room and caught sight of Mary sitting at her desk. Mary, who turned to face her with a smile on her lips and a look of excitement in her eyes. Both of which faded as soon as Mary's eyes took in Jilo's face. "Why, Jilo," she said, "what's wrong? Why are you crying?"

"What," Jilo began, her voice breaking, "is wrong?" She swallowed hard to force the frog down. "You lying, conniving Judas Iscariot."

Mary pushed back from her desk, rising and drawing near Jilo, her arms held wide for an embrace.

"Don't you"—Jilo held up a hand in warning—"don't you dare come near me."

Mary froze as tears of her own began to brim in her eyes. "I don't understand. Why are you angry? What have I done?"

"You knew. You knew and you didn't tell me."

Jilo didn't expect Mary to out-and-out lie; Mary was not a liar. But she did expect her at least to feign ignorance of what she meant. Instead, Mary tilted her head, looking more confused than guilty. "But the dean told me not to say a thing till he could talk to you. He said they were going to look out for you, keep you from making a big mistake, and they needed my help." For a moment her smile threatened to return. "I get to help catch you up on all the practical things you missed out on. Dressing wounds, rolling bandages . . ."

"I do not want your blessed help," Jilo cut her off. "You knew this isn't what I wanted. My sister is a nurse. I know what it is to be a nurse, and it was never my dream." She clenched her fists in frustration. "You know that. I can do more. I can do better."

Mary stumbled back a step, her shoulders slumping forward like Jilo had just knocked the wind clean out of her. She raised her wide-open eyes to meet Jilo's gaze. "Well I am sorry," she said, straightening as she did. "I am sorry if nursing isn't good enough for you. If it isn't your dream. 'Cause it *is* my dream. It always has been, since I was a little girl. And it was my mama's dream for me, too. She saved every penny she could after feeding my brother and me to make it possible for me to come here. After daddy died in the war, she started working nights and weekends, scrubbing floors and taking in laundry. And you know what? After I finished my schoolwork, I would be right there with her, down on my knees, scrubbing at her side. So I am sorry, Miss Jilo Wills, who has plenty of money in her pockets and all the pretty dresses in the world, if my dream isn't good enough for you . . ."

"Now, Mary," Jilo found herself shift to the defensive, "you know I didn't mean it quite like that."

"Oh, yes, you did mean it. *Quite* like that." Mary raised her chin and pulled her arms up around herself. "And fool that I am, I was happy to have the opportunity to help out my best friend. When I learned what the dean intended, I marched right out and got you a job. With me. At a fine hospital right here in Atlanta. The Greelies." Mary said the name of the hospital with such obvious pride, and despite Jilo's bitter disappointment over this turn of events, she felt like an absolute ass. Jilo took a step forward, but it was Mary's turn to pull away. "I went to the hiring supervisor at the Greelies. Told him that if he thought I was good enough to bring on, he would be over the moon to have you on duty there."

Her forehead bunched up into angry folds, and her eyes narrowed the way they always did when she remonstrated with Jilo. "I told him that, even though I knew I'd be the one who would need to catch you up and cover for you until you actually learned how to handle a patient." Her features smoothed, but her lower lip pushed forward. "I was so looking forward to telling you." And with those words, the tears started in earnest. "I thought the two of us could stay on here at the pastor's. Together."

"Well," Jilo said, daring to draw near, "I don't see why we can't do just that." She slipped an arm over Mary's shoulders and pulled her into an embrace.

SIX

June 1953

It was a busy night at the Kingfisher Club. The music was fine, and everywhere around Jilo couples danced.

Classes were over. Jilo had her diploma in hand, a hell of a lot of good it looked like it was going to do her. Still, she wanted to celebrate. Kick up her heels a bit. She'd even managed to coax Mary out to the club by loaning her an orchid-colored rayon-satin dress Mary had been admiring for two years. The two had arrived together, but they were barely across the threshold before the men descended on sweet, demure Mary like ants on a church picnic.

Jilo sat alone nursing a bourbon.

Every so often, Jilo caught sight of her friend. Each time Mary flitted by, she seemed to be in the arms of another fellow. Jilo was glad Mary was enjoying herself, but *damn*.

Wasn't she pretty enough? Jilo cast an eye around the teeming room. She wasn't vain, but she knew she looked as good as many, if not most, of the other women in the club. Mary had done a fine job on the McCall's pattern dress Jilo had paid her to sew. Ice-blue chiffon, a respectable scoop V-neck with beaded lining, the shape echoed by the darting around her tiny waist. She'd done spins before the mirror, loving how the skirt flared up. She wanted to take it out on the floor and show it off. But here she sat without a single taker.

Dammit, she felt pretty, but she couldn't get more than a smile and a nod from any of the passing men. The next time Mary swung by with her umpteenth gentleman, Jilo couldn't help but feel a little bitter.

A tall fellow in a well-cut suit drew close to Jilo's table. She raised her chin and pulled back her shoulders. She smiled at him and—God help her—batted her eyelashes. For a moment it seemed he would say hello, but then he froze in his tracks, gave her a quick nod, and turned sharply away. Her eyes fixed on his shoulders as he bounded off like some kind of scared jackrabbit.

"Oh, you're a pretty one all right," a man said from behind her, seeming to read her thoughts. His voice was deep and rich. The speed with which the other fellow had taken off suggested this newcomer might be a bit dangerous. "That isn't the problem. I'd even say you're beautiful when you aren't scowling at the whole damned room." The way he spoke, slow, the vowels a bit too long, gave his words an exotic flavor. A picture of the speaker rose in her mind's eye, a picture that unleashed a swarm of butterflies in her stomach, and equally ticklish sensations in lower regions.

She kept her eyes on the receding back of the last man to reject her. She wanted to turn and look at her new companion, but she feared that her Cupid would be the Kingfisher Club's equivalent of a winged serpent. She felt a little ashamed of herself. She'd been sitting here for an hour hoping and praying a man would approach her. Maybe she was being shallow? No, she realized, she wanted a taste of magic, just once in her life, and she knew it was pretty damn unlikely that the man speaking to her was some kind of prince. She just wanted to stretch the mystery out for as long as she could.

"No, the problem is that you scare half these fellows to death. That's why you aren't dancing." She sensed his approach. A finger traced along her forearm, sending a tingling sensation through her.

She felt her heart thud in her chest, and in spite of herself, she turned to face him. The image she had held in her mind was put to shame.

Smiling down at her was the most beautiful man she'd ever laid eyes on. His hair was trimmed close to his skull, not all slicked back like most of the men here wore theirs. The light in the club was dim, so she couldn't quite make out the color of his eyes, but she thought they were a clear brown, maybe hazel. His nose was straight. His lips full, the lower one a tad more so than the upper one that curled a bit beneath a well-defined philtrum. His chin strong and with a cleft. "And the other half?" she asked, though her mouth had gone dry.

His nose crinkled up, followed by a raise of his eyebrows. "They just know they're not man enough to handle a woman like you."

Feeling herself flush, Jilo lowered her eyes and took a sip of her sour mash, her lips puckering at the taste. She only looked up after she had set the glass back on the table. "So who the hell are you?" she asked.

His eyes lit up, and he leaned in like he was about to confess the darkest of secrets. "I'm the man who's going to ask you to dance." He pulled back and lowered his eyelids. "When I'm good and ready to, that is." He placed his hand on the chair she'd been saving for Mary. "May I?" he asked. But he pulled the seat out and joined her before she could say no.

As if she would say no.

"Aren't you scared of me, too?" she asked, looking directly into his eyes.

"A little, but I kind of like that." He slid his hand over toward hers, the space between them not even wide enough to accommodate a sheet of parchment.

Jilo burst out laughing. At him. At herself. "Shit." She swiped up her whiskey and downed what was left.

"That's no way for a lady to speak," he said.

Jilo returned the glass to the table and cast an eye over her shoulder in each direction. "I don't see any ladies here."

His hand shot out and caught hers. "I do. Right here." He turned her hand over, tracing his finger along her palm like he was some kind of sideshow fortune-teller. "You can try to pretend otherwise, but you're a good girl." He released her and leaned back, eyeing her like he was surveying her. "I might even go so far as to say 'respectable' if you weren't sitting here by yourself sucking on that swill."

"I'm not as respectable as you might think." Her mind flashed to how it had felt to have Lionel on top of her, inside her, rutting for his pleasure alone. The way sex with him had always left her feeling disconnected from her own body. On the outside, watching from a corner of the room. An unloved convenience. A hole where he could spill his seed. The thought of Lionel cut through this new man's glamour. "Did you borrow that tie?" she asked, the devil in her trying to drive this man away before he could drive her out of herself, too. Suddenly she wanted nothing more than to be gone from this place. Pushing away from the table, she reached out for her purse.

"Stay," he said, "I'm sorry. I'm not sure what I've done to upset you, but that wasn't my intention." If he'd so much as blinked, she would have given in to the urge to flee, but he sat perfectly still, watching as she decided. She let her bag slip back down to the table.

He waited for her to relax in her chair before he spoke. "Maybe it wasn't something I've done. Maybe it's what the fellow before me did." He raised his eyebrows. "Hmmm? You should tell me, 'cause I'd hate to chase you off before I get that dance."

"Then you better get to asking," she said, but her urge to flee had already dissipated.

The band wrapped up the fast swing it had been playing, and began another, a sentimental one that drew the couples closer. He stood and held out his hand to her. "I was only waiting for a slow dance." A naughty smile curled his lips, and she felt a matching expression form on her own face.

The band played "The Very Thought of You," though their version featured a few improvisations she'd never heard on the radio. The handsome stranger held her close and swayed to the music.

"I don't even know your name," she said, nearly ready to kick herself for ruining the moment.

He leaned in. His breath felt warm on the sensitive skin on her neck. He whispered into her ear. "Guy," he answered, though the way he said the name, it rhymed with "bee."

"Guy," she said, leaning back. "What the hell kind of name is Guy?"

At that very moment Mary swung by them with another beau. At least this one was a repeat. "Jilo," Mary called out while passing, "this place is wonderful." She laughed. "And I don't even know how to dance!"

Guy and Jilo came to a dead stop on the dance floor. "What the hell kind of name is Jilo?" he demanded, though she could see a spark of laughter in his eyes.

"Oh, shut up," she said and laughed, expecting him to start dancing again. But he didn't. No. He leaned down and pressed his lips to hers, and her knees gave way beneath her. It didn't matter though, he held her tight. She closed her eyes, and reached up to link her fingers behind his neck. Fire passed down her spine, returning the strength to her legs. Then she felt his body begin to sway again, her own slipping easily into his rhythm.

SEVEN

April 1954

Jilo leaned across the table, her breasts exposed and hanging down over it. They had filled out some since Guy first started the portrait, but he hadn't seemed to notice.

She wore a tatty shawl tied around her waist. It wasn't hers, just one Guy had borrowed for the painting. From whom, she didn't know. Guy was real good at talking women into—and out of—things. She didn't look at him; he'd told her not to. It was easier not to. She kept her gaze fixed on the dark bands in the grain of the tabletop. In her peripheral vision, she could see the bottom of a vase Guy had filled with flowers. Not a gift, just part of the scenery.

She was tired—he wanted her tired, said the painting needed it. Her feet cramped, but he insisted that she balance on the balls of her feet for reasons of light and composition. Again, the painting needed it.

"Jilo," he said, her name a rebuke on his lips. "Stop fidgeting."

"I'm sorry," she mumbled. She'd just come off of a twelve-hour shift at the hospital, where she worked in the colored wing. The Greelie Hospital was really a single building, but still most folk referred to it in the plural, as "the Greelies," since the white and colored wings were separated by a corridor. She'd walked that corridor at least a hundred times in her shift, so her feet already felt like they'd been beaten with a board.

Mary had found Jilo the job at the Greelies, but Mary herself had been forced to return home to Missouri not more than a week after graduation. Her mother had suffered a heart attack that had rendered her incapable of seeing to herself and Mary's younger brother. Jilo had been left on her own to catch up on the procedures and practices the hospital's hiring manager already thought she knew. On parting, Mary and she had promised to stay in touch, but no more than a handful of letters had passed between them through the post. Mary, Jilo knew, had her hands full. Jilo, well, she didn't have much she felt she could share without shame.

"I'm worn out, Guy. I just need to rest a bit," she said. "Can't we do this another time?"

He sighed. "I'm not sure you appreciate what I'm attempting here. I'm not sure you appreciate my work."

Jilo bit her tongue, but she felt her expression harden, a layer of anger varnishing the exhaustion.

"There," he said, "that's better. Concentrate."

He thought she didn't appreciate *his* work. Hell, it was Guy who didn't give a lick about all the work *she* did. She spent six days a week emptying bedpans, cleaning bedsores, and lifting patients who couldn't manage to shift themselves. This man didn't even understand the concept of real work. And he didn't know what it meant to pay a bill either. It was her work that paid their rent for this rat-ridden hovel. It was her work that fed them. It was her work that paid for the damned paints and canvas he was using now.

There was a quick rap on the door, and it opened before either of them could respond. "It came. The letter came," Guy's friend Charles said, storming into the room, waving a white envelope around.

"Please," Jilo said, straightening up and turning her back to the men.

"Come on, girl," Guy said, "you don't have anything Charles hasn't seen before."

"Maybe not, but he hasn't seen it on me." She unknotted the shawl and whipped it around her body. After grabbing her nurse's uniform off the bed, she slipped behind the changing screen she had insisted on procuring, even though Guy had made fun of her modesty. Lately he found a lot of things about her worthy of contempt. "You still got too much girl in you," he'd taken to saying, "not enough woman." It was true that she wasn't as experienced or worldly as he was. She hadn't realized it at first, but Guy was a good decade older than her, and though that didn't matter to her, lately it seemed to matter to him. Every time she spoke up—about anything, from the weather to where he'd spent the night—he would remind her of her immaturity.

Guy and Charles had been friends since the war. They'd met in the army, and it was Charles's presence in Atlanta that had prompted Guy to come for an extended visit. A visit that had culminated in her leaving the Joneses' boarding home going on a year ago and moving into this tenement with Guy. The building was filled with musicians and artists. And whores. Nobody cared that she and Guy weren't married. The building's owner didn't ask too many questions as long as you didn't get too far behind on the rent.

She had thought their love would be enough. In those first few months, she would press her body closer to his whenever she heard the rodents moving in the walls. Then came the nights when she'd come home from the hospital to find their room dark, when she would flip on the overhead light and stand in the doorway as the last of the cockroaches scurried for cover. Until then, she had never thought she could miss the Joneses' house. But it wasn't only the boarding house she missed. She missed the pastor and his wife as well. Yes, she missed them. She would like to go pay them a visit, but shame held her back. They'd ask too many questions that would require too many lies.

She flung the shawl up over the top of the screen.

"What does it say?" Guy asked. She had no idea who this letter was from, but she could hear the tension in his voice. This was something that mattered to him. Really mattered to him.

"They want us," Charles said. "They want both of us." The word "both" was spoken with great emphasis.

She buttoned the uniform and stuck her head out around the screen. "Who wants you? For what?" she asked as she stepped up behind Guy, who was now holding the letter at arm's length, looking at it like he couldn't quite believe what was written there. Charles's eyes rose as she spoke, but then passed over her. She glanced over her shoulder to realize he was focused on the shawl she'd been wearing. There was a sly smile on his lips. Evidently he knew who owned it. Jilo asked herself if she cared to learn that woman's identity. No, she decided, but she did want to know what was in the letter Guy still held. She reached for it, but he snatched it back.

He held it to his chest, as jealously and as guiltily as if it were a love letter. She slid her hands down to her hips and tilted her head. "Who," she said, angry and tired of his games, "wants you?"

He slipped the letter back into its envelope and handed it to Charles. "A gallery," Guy said, squatting down and opening his arms like he expected her to come running into them. She held her place. "A real one where they appreciate real art. Not like the little crap holes in this town."

"So," she said, determined to draw the whole story out of him with as few equivocations as possible, "I take it this gallery is not in Atlanta."

"No," he said, shifting from one foot to the other. "It isn't. It's in New York."

"Ah," she said, nodding. "Well, of course you'll be going."

A look of relief flooded his face. His shoulders relaxed, letting his arms fall to his sides. "This is big, Jilo. I've been working for this all my life."

"I understand," she said. "How long will you be up north?"

He focused on the floor by her feet. "If things go well, I won't be coming back."

"Then I'll go with you," she said, though the look on his face told her all she needed to know.

His head jerked as he cast a glance at the silent Charles. An embarrassed smile curved his lips when he looked back at her. "I can't ask that of you, sweetheart. It's a different world up there. You're a small-town girl at heart, and New York, well, I'm afraid you won't take to the big city. Besides, you have a job. Your whole life is here."

Jilo flung her arms into the air and spun around. "Yes. How could I possibly give this up?" She noticed Charles slinking backward toward the door. "That's right. You go on. You get the hell out of here." He slipped through the door, and she rushed over and flung her full weight at it to make sure it slammed behind him.

She turned on Guy. "When?" she demanded. "When are you leaving me?"

He lowered his face, trying not to look at her. "Couple of days, I reckon."

She nodded, more to herself than to him. "You reckon." She knelt by the side of the bed and tugged out her suitcase, the one she'd brought from Savannah to Atlanta, the one she'd carried from the Joneses' boarding house here. She set it on the bed and undid its straps, pausing for only a moment after she opened it. "If I told you I was pregnant, would you stay?" She looked toward him, heavy tears brimming her eyes. "Would you take me with you?"

He turned his back toward her. "You wouldn't lie to me just to hold on to me. You wouldn't do that."

She sighed and realized she was trembling. Forcing herself to regain composure, she wiped the tears from her cheeks. "No, I guess I wouldn't." She opened the battered chifferobe that had come with the apartment and scooped out the dresses she rarely wore now that she spent most days in her nurse's uniform. She didn't bother to fold them neatly; she just dropped them into the case. Next went the jewelry box that held the few pieces that hadn't disappeared over the past months. She'd pretended not to notice as one after the other went missing. It didn't really matter whether he'd given her purloined baubles to his other women or hocked them for money. Either way they were lost to her. She tossed the box on top of the dresses and closed and secured the suitcase's lid.

She reached under the table to pull out the shoes she'd kicked off beneath it, then sat on the edge of the bed to put them back on. She stood and tugged the case from the bed. It was heavy, but not nearly as heavy as her heart. "The rent is covered till the end of the week. You need to clear out by Friday, unless you're prepared to pay for another." She lifted the case and walked to the door, praying with each step he'd call out to stop her. But he didn't. She reached out and turned the brass doorknob. She opened the door, but she paused for a moment at the threshold, staring at his broad shoulders.

He turned. "You take care of yourself," he said.

She nodded and stepped into the hall. The damnedest thing, she realized, was that even after this, after everything he'd done, she'd go to her grave loving the man. She pulled the door closed behind her. "I'll do that," she said quietly. Her free hand slipped to her stomach. "I'll take care of both of us."

EIGHT

Jilo stood at the bus stop, forcing herself not to sob and make a scene like one of the fool women who used to wash up at her nana's door—screaming, crying, begging Nana to help bring back the wrong man or make the right one love them. Nana would always try to talk the women out of going after a man whose heart lay elsewhere. The smart ones would return home with a bit of wisdom and with fuller pockets than the fools.

There had been two men in Jilo's life now, and for a brief period of time with each of them, she had allowed herself to believe she was loved. Maybe they even had loved her in their own way, but they had only turned her away from her dreams and ambitions. They had only held her down. She could feel bitterness creep into her heart. What would it take to find a partner who would support her rather than belittle her and drag her down? Just once, she would like to find such a man. She shook her head. Frankly, she didn't believe such an animal existed.

An electric sign on the storefront behind her short-circuited with a loud pop. She jumped and nearly dropped her suitcase as a spray of turquoise sparks showered down on her. She moved a couple of yards farther down the sidewalk, but she could see the bus drawing near the stop, so after casting a wary look at the now burned-out sign, she moved back to where she'd been.

She tried to shake it off, but something wasn't right. The bus rolled to a far-too-slow stop before her, like the air around it had congealed, hindering its progress. Her own movements seemed impeded, like she was swimming in molasses. She heard another pop, but this one seemed to sound in her own head. The world returned to normal the next moment, and she found herself boarding the bus.

Jilo struggled down the bus's narrow aisle, grasping the handle of her heavy suitcase in both hands, making sure that despite the movement of the bus, she wouldn't jostle any of the other riders, especially the white folk near the front. A pleasant-looking man in army khakis hopped up from his seat and approached her. "Allow me to help you, ma'am."

A part of Jilo wanted to take his head off for showing her kindness. She felt like her heart had been hollowed out with a wire brush. She was nauseated. She wanted to be left alone, and there wasn't any place in her world for helpful hands and gracious smiles. The soldier beamed down at her as he placed one hand beneath the case, slipping the other over the hand that still clutched the handle. He tilted his head, a curious look coming to his eyes, when she didn't release her grip.

"Thank you, I can manage." The words came out with a sharper edge than she'd intended. At that very moment, the bus swung wide to avoid a careless pedestrian, and Jilo and her case toppled forward. The man caught hold of her shoulders and steadied her. She felt her jaw tighten and her tongue ready itself to lash out. Then she looked up into his warm eyes, so full of kindness. Unable to bear the sight of them, she looked away. "Thank you," she said again, blunting her ingratitude.

Though she did not release her hold on the case, he helped her into a seat. She set the case on the seat next to her, then—still feeling the weight of the man's stare on her—glanced back up at him. "Thank you," she said once again, doing her best to add a tone of finality to her words.

"My pleasure, ma'am," he said, plopping down across the aisle from her. "I'm just here in Atlanta for the day," he said, turning sideways to face her. "Just got decommissioned last week. Wanted to get out a bit while I was here to see your fair city," he added. She stared straight forward, but it didn't stop him from talking. "Took the train all the way from San Francisco. Got to see pretty near the whole country through the window." He stretched the words "all the way" out. At first she thought it was an act to try and impress her, but then she cast a sideways glance at him. There was true wonder in his eyes; he wasn't trying to impress her at all. "I thought for sure when they sent me overseas I'd end up in Korea, but one of the officers in Tokyo took a liking to me, kept me on there." His voice lowered a bit. "Came back to the states by carrier. Not much to see between Tokyo and San Francisco, other than a bunch of water." He leaned in toward her. "The rest, though, well, that was something to see." His shoulders relaxed as he sat back. "This here's the last leg of the trip. Grew up just a bit outside Darien. Catching the Greyhound home from the terminal in town tonight."

She turned in her seat so that she could get a good look at him, and scanned his shirt for the name she knew she would find embroidered on his uniform. "Listen," she said, "PFC Poole . . ."

"No. Not Private First Class anymore, just a regular old civilian now."

"Mister," her voice rose loud enough for the two elderly women sitting on the seat in front of her to turn and stare. She dropped it to a near whisper. "Poole. I do appreciate the assistance you were so kind to offer me, but I wish you would just let me finish my trip in peace."

His face fell, and the light went out of his eyes. She felt as if she'd just kicked a puppy. "I'm sorry," she said. "I don't mean to be short with you, but I'm not having a very good day."

"No," he said, lowering his chin and his voice in the same moment. "I'm the one who's sorry, ma'am. It's only with your suitcase, I thought you might be heading to the bus station yourself. I'd only meant to say that I could help you there with your case if you'd like, but then my fool mouth got started going and . . ." A shy smile came to his lips. "Well, there I go again. I'll just shut up and leave you be." He underscored his promise by turning forward on his seat, then turning his head away and facing left out the side window.

Jilo stared at the back of his head, and while she knew she should just keep her trap shut if she wanted peace and quiet, there was something so kind and gentle about this fellow. And he'd just arrived home, maybe not from the front, but her nana would skin her alive if she knew she'd given a friendly veteran a bad time. She rolled her eyes. "The bus station is in the opposite direction. If you're looking for the station, you're heading the wrong way. And stop calling me ma'am."

He turned back to look at her, his expression cautious at first, his lips pulled tight together. Then that spark returned to his eyes. "Yes, ma—" His smiled widened. *"Miss."*

"And I know where Darien is. I grew up in Savannah myself." In spite of her decision to remain aloof, she felt herself relaxing into her seat. "Came here for school," she said, "and stayed on . . ." Her attention was drawn away as Five Points Baptist came up on the right. She turned and bent over the case that sat between her and the window. From a block away she could see that the side windows had been boarded over.

Behind her PFC—no, Mister—Poole had begun going on about something, but she held her palm out behind her to quiet him. As the bus pulled before Five Points Baptist, her heart sunk in her chest. The doors had been secured with a heavy chain and lock. She sensed someone hovering over her and glanced back to see Poole standing in the aisle, craning his neck to see what had so distracted her.

"I'm sorry," she said, turning back to the window. "But that's my church." She felt a bit like she was lying. "Well it was."

"Why they got it all shut up like that?" he asked.

"I don't know, but I'm on my way to the pastor's house now." She continued to turn in her seat so she could keep her eye on the house of worship's receding steeple.

"You family?" Poole asked.

Jilo turned away from the window. "Family?"

"Yes, you and your pastor."

Jilo shook her head. "No, nothing like that." The site of the seemingly abandoned church worried her, leaving her in even less of a mood for conversation. "He and his wife rent out rooms." She turned to face Poole. "Listen. You seem like a real nice fellow . . ." Poole straightened in his seat and smiled at her. "But I'm not in the mood to talk right now. I don't mean to hurt your feelings. I appreciate your kindness, and I do hope you have a good visit to Atlanta and a pleasant trip home, but . . ."

Without forcing her to finish, he nodded at her and stood. He hesitated an instant, his black eyes so full of empathy that for a mad moment Jilo felt that this total stranger *did* care about her church, about her pastor, about the things that mattered to her, and about her. As deeply as she did. A small rueful smile quivered on his lips, then faded. He moved a couple of seats back.

She stared out the window at the familiar landmarks that filled the mile and half between the church and the Joneses' boarding house. When they got within a few blocks of the cross street that led to the house, she stood and tugged the case from the seat. Before she realized what was happening, Poole had grabbed ahold of the case and was maneuvering it with great care toward the exit.

The bus halted at the stop, and Poole hurried out to set the case on the ground. Jilo approached warily, hoping he hadn't decided to accompany her to the boarding house. She already had enough to explain without arriving at the pastor's door with a strange man. To her relief, he bounded back onto the bus after she passed him.

She gave him one quick and cautious look, not daring to smile for fear she might encourage him.

"Joseph," he called out just before the doors closed behind her. "My name's Joseph." The doors muffled his voice. "But my friends all call me Tink . . ." His voice was drowned out by the bus's engine as it pulled away.

She lifted the case and trudged down the road. The boarding house lay six blocks south and a block east from this point. Only now did she realize she should not have come here. She'd left the pastor's house against his wishes, claiming she wanted to live closer to the hospital. But when she refused to allow Pastor Jones to check up on the apartment house for young single women where she was supposedly moving—a place she had visited only to provide a cover for her actual plan—he'd expressed both disappointment and dismay. She had promised him that she would continue as a member of his congregation, but she had never made it to a single service. At first it had been unintentional; she'd been asked to work a few Sundays, and she and Guy often stayed out late on Saturday nights, leading to late wake ups the next morning. After a while, it seemed as though she'd been too long gone to just show up with no kind of good explanation for her absence. If the pastor had ever discussed her lapse in attendance with her grandmother, Nana had never mentioned it, even though she insisted Jilo call her collect each Saturday afternoon.

None of that mattered now. She needed a place to spend the night, maybe a couple of days, while she figured out just what the hell she was going to do. No, she realized, she was lying to herself. She needed a couple of days to screw up her courage. She was seven weeks along. It was the last time they'd gone out for an evening together, the last time Guy had touched her. He had gotten drunk enough to believe he still loved her, and she'd been drunk enough to believe it was true.

At best, she might hide the pregnancy for a couple of months longer, but she'd lose her job as soon as anyone remarked on her condition. There was nothing left for her to do but go home to her grandmother's place in Savannah, if Nana would still have her. *What's Nana gonna think of her smart girl now?* The thought stopped her in her tracks. She drew a breath and walked on. She'd probably think Jilo hadn't turned out so different from her mama, Betty, after all.

It surprised her how happy the sight of the wide front step leading up to the porch made her. Still, she took her time climbing those stairs, unsure of the reception she would receive. Even though the day was cool, she was sweating, somewhat from lugging the case, which she set at her feet, and somewhat from the changes going on in her body.

She smoothed down her skirt, managing to dry her palms with the same effort, and adjusted her blouse, making sure it was well buttoned. She curled her hand into a fist and rapped on the door. There didn't seem to be any movement within, so she knocked again, louder. She leaned over to her right to try to catch a glimpse of any life showing through the lace curtain. A shadow moved in the hall.

"Jilo," Mrs. Jones said as she swung the door open. "My dear girl, how I have missed you."

Jilo was both taken aback and shamed by the sincerity in the woman's voice. "I . . . I've missed you, you and the pastor, as well." Mrs. Jones's eyes drifted down to the case by her side. "It's only, I'm hoping that you and the pastor might allow me to come back. Not permanently. Just for a day or so." She lowered her eyes, not wanting to see the woman's reaction. An eternity of awkward silence passed between them. "I know," Jilo began, "I know I disappointed the pastor . . ."

"Of course you can stay," Mrs. Jones interrupted her. "As long as you want"—then, seeming to read something in Jilo's expression, she added—"or need." She stepped back, making room for both Jilo and her case. Jilo moved quickly over the threshold, almost as if she feared the pastor's wife might change her mind. "You can have your old room back, if you'd like," Mrs. Jones said. "It's empty." To Jilo's surprise, tears brimmed in the woman's eyes. "They all are. The girls, their parents took them out of here."

Jilo stopped, confused. She realized quickly that the house was far more quiet than she'd ever experienced during her years there. Even though late afternoon was giving way to dusk, not a single light was burning. There were no smells of cooking from the kitchen. She reached out and grasped Mrs. Jones's hand. "What's wrong? What's happened here?" She thought again of the boarded-up windows and padlock at Five Points Baptist. "And why is the church all locked up?"

"The church is closed," Mrs. Jones said, her voice quavering as she spoke. "When Robert" —Jilo had never heard anyone refer to the pastor by his Christian name before—"began speaking publicly about the angels, the congregation turned against him. Some thought he'd gone mad. Others thought the devil had gotten in him. But they all thought he was blaspheming." She wrapped her arms around herself. "I know you know about the angels. He told me he shared his experiences with you . . ."

"Well, no, ma'am," Jilo began, "not really. He said he'd been 'taken up' by them when he was a child, and maybe . . ."

"It wasn't only as a child." Mrs. Jones cut her off. "They've been visiting him all his life. *All his life*," she said with emphasis. "He shielded me from the truth, but I knew I had married a special man. A holy man." She raised her chin, and Jilo could see the pride glowing in her eyes. "It was right after you left. He started seeing them all over. All the time. He couldn't protect me from the truth any longer."

"Where is the pastor?" Jilo asked.

Mrs. Jones didn't reply, she simply tightened her grasp on Jilo's hand and led her deeper into the house and down the hall leading to the pastor's study. When they reached the room, Mrs. Jones released her and crossed to the pastor's desk, where she turned on the green-shaded brass lamp that sat there. The older woman stood there trembling as she stared down at her husband's desk. She stifled a sob, raising her right hand to her mouth, then pointed at the wall. Stepping around the desk, she walked toward the defaced wall.

Jilo saw that "GEN 5:24" was scratched into the wall's plaster in characters five or six inches long.

"He took a knife from the kitchen. Cut this into the plaster." Mrs. Jones traced her finger along the jagged grooves. "The next day," she said, turning back to Jilo, "he was gone. Just gone." She crossed back to the desk and turned the opened Bible there around so that Jilo could read its words. "And Enoch walked with God: and he was not; for God took him."

NINE

Savannah, Georgia—May 1954

"I want you to understand there are good men in this world, Jilo," Nana said. "My Reuben, your grum'pa, he was a right good man. He took good care of me and his family. He bought your nana this here house. Your daddy, my Jesse, he was a good man, too." A bright smile broke out on her aged face. "He sure loved his girls, he did," she said and stroked the back of Jilo's hand. "All three of you. He'd be proud of all his girls, he would." She nodded. "Especially you."

Jilo had to wonder if that were true, if her father would be proud of her now, with her dress tight around her breasts and middle. And without a man to claim the baby that was making it so.

Nana's chair made a scuffing nose as she pushed it back. The table squeaked a bit as she leaned into it to help push herself up. "Pastor Jones, I think he's a good man, too. Made a mistake here and there, and I sure got no idea what he's gotten himself up to now, but at his root, I believe he is an honorable man." She walked across the room, the floor creaking with each heavy step. Jilo noticed she was moving slower than she used to, her right hip seeming to catch every other step or so.

Jilo wasn't sure where this conversation was heading, so she sat in silence as her grandmother crossed the room to the pantry. The old woman disappeared into the pantry for a few moments and emerged with three bottles, a cobalt-blue one like you might see hanging on a spirit tree, tucked beneath her left arm, and one small clear bottle in each gnarled hand. She crossed to the sink with no sign of hurry, then set the bottles down on the counter.

"Your nana's afraid," she said, reaching into a cabinet to retrieve a drinking glass, "that you done figured out all on your own that not all men are good." She set the glass down beside the bottles and reached for one of the clear ones. She unscrewed its cap, then raised the bottle and the glass up to her eye level, and measured out a dram or so of dark brown liquid by sight. Jilo could tell by its scent that it contained creosote, but there were higher notes to it, too, one of them a bitter smell that reminded her of unripe tomatoes on the vine. Nana returned both to the counter, and though her joints seemed to protest the movement, screwed the cap back on the bottle. "Good men," she said, turning her attention to the second clear bottle, this one with a ceramic stopper held in place by a metal bracket, "they deserve a loving woman, and children, if God sees fit to send them." She flipped the metal lever that held the stopper in place, then took a spoon from a drawer and used it to measure out some of the clear orange liquid. Jilo rose and came to look over her grandmother's shoulder. Her nana set the still-open bottle down on the counter. Jilo lifted it to her nose. The orange liquid, Jilo decided from the peppery scent that nearly brought tears to her eyes, was capsicum oil.

Her nana looked back at her, and seeing what she was doing, said "Careful now. Don't get that in your eyes." She took the bottle from Jilo's hand and closed the stopper before setting it next to the other clear bottle. Jilo noticed the old woman's hand trembled a bit as she reached for the neck of the tall blue bottle. Her nana took the bottle in her right hand, and used her left to twist on its cork stopper until it came out with a pop.

She turned her attention back to Jilo. "Not all men are good, but someday you're gonna meet one of the good ones. You're gonna want to have his babies because of who he is, not just 'cause it's something that happened to you." She tilted the bottle up, and Jilo watched as a liquid unlike any she'd come across—even in her advanced chemistry classes— flowed out of it. A fluid somewhat resembling mercury spilled into the cup, but this substance glowed with a phosphorescence unlike any of the normal properties of the liquid metal. Rather than blending with the other two ingredients, it seemed to come alive, like a tiny serpent in a brackish sea. Her nana stopped the bottle up, then handed the concoction to her.

"That there gonna burn a bit going down, and it's gonna make you sleep for maybe a day, but when you wake up, your situation'll be cleared up for you. If that's what you want."

Jilo stared into the glass, watching as the band of glowing silver swirled around, connecting head to tail into a figure eight, then break-ing apart again. Her nana always swore to her that her "magic" wasn't real, but the behavior of the unidentified quicksilver-like substance made her wonder, if only for a moment.

"What is in this?" Jilo swiveled the glass in her hand, growing even more curious as the substance refused to dissolve into the rest of the mixture.

"It's safe. For you," Nana said, not really answering the question. "You ain't the first girl Nana's done this for, so you don't need to worry." Nana's features softened. "You *ain't*"—she emphasized the word—"the first girl Nana's done this for, so no need to feel like you doing something wrong." She reached out and took Jilo's free hand. The old woman's touch felt cool, dry, papery. "Men, they'll tell you that you shouldn't have a choice in the matter, but Nana figures until those men step up and help raise what's in you, it ain't none of they business anyway. You, girl, Nana wants you to know you have a choice."

She released Jilo and collected her bottles, then walked off stiffly to return them to where they'd come from.

Jilo weighed two possible futures. Perhaps there was still time. She could write the women doctors whose achievements she wanted so badly to emulate. Take a job. Maybe even save up enough money to go visit them in person.

If she had this child, she'd be branded a fallen woman. She'd have a hard time finding any kind of employment, and she'd certainly never see the inside of a medical school. Her life would be hard. Probably lonely, too. Not many men—even the good ones—would willingly raise another man's child. Her nana was right, there was no shame in making the decision to return to the path she'd envisioned for her life. But up until this moment, she hadn't thought she would have a choice, and she'd begun to imagine other things. What it would be like to have someone of her very own, someone so completely connected to her that they were a part of each other.

"Nana," she said as the old woman returned from the pantry.

"Yes, baby?"

"If you were me, what would you do?"

The old woman's eyes brightened and a smile stole over her face. "Nana, she'd do the same thing she reckons you about to do." She reached up and pulled Jilo's forehead down to her lips and planted a kiss on her brow. Releasing Jilo, she stepped back. "Nana be out in the garden for a while, if you need her." She turned and shuffled toward the door that opened to the outside. The room grew brighter as she opened the door, then dimmed again as she pulled it closed.

Jilo looked down at the glass in her trembling hand. She closed her eyes and raised it to her lips. The liquid's fiery, bitter smell promised her freedom, a chance to start over. There was no shame in letting go of this child. But her heart was not willing to do it.

Jilo opened her eyes and emptied the glass's contents into the sink. No matter what folk thought, there was no shame in having this baby either. She turned on the faucet to wash the silvery band down the drain.

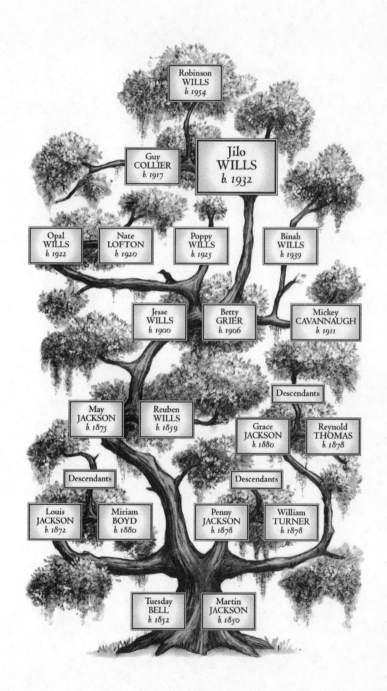

BOOK THREE: MOTHER JILO

ONE

Savannah, Georgia—July 1954

May sat at her kitchen table, unmoving, her cup of chicory long since cooled.

Lately, May had been dreaming of days long since past, days that, this morning, seemed strangely closer and more real than the world around her. Some of the dreams were about cleaning the house of her first employer, and though she was sitting at her own table now, she felt certain that if she closed her eyes, she would see every nook and cranny of a house that she hadn't set foot in going on sixty years.

May had begun working as the Farleys' maid just after her thirteenth birthday. Right from the get-go, the lady of the house, known by one and all as "Miss Rose" despite being married to Mr. Andrew Farley, struck May as an anxious, nervous child, even though Miss Rose was a good ten or fifteen years older than May herself.

"Mr. Farley likes an orderly kitchen," Miss Rose said, opening the pantry door and stepping just over the threshold. "He likes to see all labels facing forward, and they should be in alphabetical order." She paused and gave May a nervous glance. "You do know how to read, don't you, dear? You understand what alphabetical order means?"

"Yes, ma'am," May nodded. She was so young. She still cared about making a good impression on this weak and spineless woman.

Miss Rose led her past her husband's study. "If the door is closed, you may not enter." She wagged her finger in May's face. "Mr. Farley likes a clean, orderly space, and you will be expected to keep his office in good order, but"—she stopped and set a grave expression on her face to underline the seriousness of the knowledge she was about to impart—"you must never touch the papers on Mr. Farley's desk." And May never did.

May got on fine at the Farleys', right up until Miss Rose died during labor. When Mr. Farley married again soon after, his new wife brought servants with her from her family home in Augusta. Though she felt at ease with the servants she'd grown up amongst, she simply couldn't bear the thought of an unfamiliar colored poking around in her private belongings. It was nothing personal, the new Mrs. Farley wanted May to understand, but she had such pretty things, and well, an ounce of prevention and all that. It was really in May's best interest to seek out alternative employment.

And so May did. She found work cleaning house for old Mr. Whitcomb, with his shock of snow-white hair, and his spotted hands that would run over a body, if that body didn't move quickly enough away. He lived all alone, his wife gone and his children distant, emotionally if not physically, in a grand house on Calhoun Square.

At their first meeting, the old man had presented her with a box, wrapped with brown paper and string. "Take it home with you. Keep it there, but don't open it until I tell you that you may. Don't go opening this until it's time, or things won't go well for you," he warned, a gleam in his eye telling her that in fact he would like nothing better than for her to go poking around in his squalid business, and he believed her incapable of leaving well enough alone. Only a wealthy white man like him, a man who had never felt powerless or threatened, would think that way.

He couldn't imagine finding himself in a position where folk could treat you however they wanted, saying or doing anything and feeling more than justified, making up lies for themselves so they could paint you as the threat and themselves the innocent, the defenders of good. He couldn't fathom the possibility of ever finding himself incapable of even saying a word in his own defense, just having to take it from those who are waiting with angry, jealous hearts for you to step out of line so they have an excuse to beat you down. But May didn't have to imagine it; she'd lived her life there.

No, leaving things unsaid, undone, this was how May survived back in those days. Averting her eyes, turning a deaf ear, hiding any tone of hurt or defiance. The buckra told you to leave something alone, you damn well left it be. The old fellow gave up the ghost about a year after she began working for him. The next day she returned the package, still as tightly wrapped as the day she'd taken possession of it, to his house.

She met and married Reuben around that time, and she spent nearly two decades taking care of him, eventually giving birth to her sweet Jesse.

Jesse who'd died twenty years ago today.

She could hear Binah's bell-like laughter streaming in through the open window. She knew the girls were out there tending the garden, pulling weeds. She could hear their voices, snatches of their conversation, carrying into the kitchen. They were discussing names for Jilo's baby. Binah had her opinions, but Jilo would only entertain girl names. Seems that if it were a boy, she planned to name him after two of her heroes: Jackie Robinson and her "father," Jesse Wills.

Funny how May's heart had claimed both of these girls as her natural granddaughters, given that neither of them truly belonged to her boy. Of course, Jesse himself had claimed Jilo, but would he have found it in his heart to claim the younger one? Binah was a rare beauty, no denying that, though her beauty was not of the kind many folk around here would appreciate, at least not openly.

Binah had gotten her features, and her sweet voice, from her mama. Would that be enough to bend Jesse's heart to the girl? But that red-tinted hair—auburn, folk called it—and those bright blues eyes of hers, those came from a father who'd probably never even bothered to set eyes on her. Would Jesse have found enough love in his heart to take the girl on as his own? May would like to think so, but Jesse was still a man, after all, and a man's pride could prove a fearsome barrier. Didn't really matter though. Her Jesse was gone, and May had fallen completely in love with yet another of Betty's cast-off children. Didn't matter whose blood ran through either of those girls' veins. They both belonged to May now.

May heard another voice. Still high, but breaking every so often as it began to slide down into the speaker's chest. Binah's friend, that young boy Willy, was out there, probably helping them with the watering. Despite the delicate way he carried himself, he was good at hauling the heavy bucket from the spigot to the garden. Seemed he was always underfoot, but May didn't have the heart to chase him away. Binah had been born straddling two worlds, marked as she was by her parents' different traits. May figured it was her granddaughter's firsthand knowledge of what it was like to be not quite the one and not quite the other that drew her to Willy. Some might protest having the kid shadow their girl at every turn, but May had seen this gentle, delicate kind of boy before. Binah, and her honor, were safe as could be in his presence. The world didn't cotton to boys like him, and soon he was gonna have to learn how to hide his softness or have it beaten out of him. But that day didn't have to be today, and that beating certainly wasn't gonna happen here.

May rose and emptied her cup, then rinsed it and set it on the counter. She gripped the porcelain lip of the kitchen sink and leaned forward.

"Your nana," she called out to the girls, "she's gonna go lie down for a spell."

Jilo's head shot up at her words. "You feeling okay, Nana?"

May knew she was fading, and she knew Jilo could see it. "Fine. I'm fine," May said, surprised by the annoyance she heard in her own voice. "I'm just old and worn out." She forced herself to smile. "Don't you worry about your nana. She just needs a little rest." May wondered what was going to become of these children once she was gone, though rightly, neither one could be called a child anymore. Jilo was full-grown, with a baby of her own coming, and Binah was fourteen, not really that much younger than May herself had been when she married.

Jilo nodded, but said, "I'll come check in on you shortly."

May felt another flush of irritation, but refused to let herself show it. "All right."

Backing away from the window, she headed down the hall to the room that once again served as her bedroom. Instead of meeting customers in the house, she now held audience with them in the old cemetery in the center of town, where any and all could see. Cut down on the folk who weren't serious enough about their troubles to need her help. Before, when she let people sneak into her house, she found most of the problems she addressed could've rightly been handled with a little more common sense and a little less laziness. The folk who were desperate enough to set aside their fear and pride and walk right into Colonial Cemetery, they were more likely to have problems that merited her help, and the courage to face whatever solution her magic would provide.

Of course, she made a lot less money that way. She'd questioned more than once if she should open up her home once again, especially now that Jilo was home and expecting. But in truth she no longer had the energy for the midnight knocks at the door. No, best to keep business and home separate. Still, May wished she'd managed to set more aside, but she'd paid for Jilo's and Opal's schooling, hoping they'd manage to take care of themselves afterward. Although Opal had done well in school, she no longer worked as a nurse. She'd married Nate, her soldier, years ago, and the two of them had three children of their own now. Children May had never laid eyes on in person. Nate had stayed on in the service, and Opal always said she couldn't visit because they were stationed in places like Japan and Germany. But May didn't believe it. She knew it was the magic that kept her eldest grandbaby away as sure as it did sweet Poppy.

May had wanted to cut all ties with magic that winter day Poppy had taken off for Charlotte, swearing on the Lord's holy name never to set foot there again. But life hadn't left her much of a choice. Maguire had long ago seen to it that she'd never find another respectable job again. Besides, even though she wished it were otherwise, she knew she'd grown too frail to do the hard physical work she'd once done at the Pinnacle. It struck her that the hotel was no longer there, anyway. Destroyed by fire caused by faulty wiring, they said, though May had her doubts. She'd seen something else in the paper, too—Sterling Maguire had welcomed his third son into the world. If May failed, as her mama, too, had failed, to take Maguire out, the old man would probably find a way to continue jumping from body to body to continue poisoning the world centuries after May had been forgotten. May knew that any attack against Maguire would most likely culminate in her own death. That's why she'd put it off as long as she had. But she was running out of time. She'd sure like to help see Jilo's baby into the world first, but maybe it'd be better to make sure that babe could be born into a world without Maguire.

She entered her bedroom, trying not to see the haint blue that still dominated there, floor to ceiling. A part of her would love nothing better than to do away with it, paint it over with good white lead paint. Leave nothing but plain white walls to shelter her, a plain white ceiling to shield her from the heavens. No magic, just a fresh start. She could have the floor sanded down to the grain, or maybe have it ripped out and replaced with new strips of oak. But the haint blue still served its purpose. Forces, not quite so friendly, still wandered nearby, attracted by the power they sensed residing in this house. If anything, she should give it a fresh coat, as well as the outside of the house, the overhang of the porch, and the shutters and doors.

She kicked off her shoes and sat on the bed, staring at the door to her closet, almost expecting it to open and reveal the Beekeeper's grand chamber. But it didn't, and she very nearly regretted that. The magic had left May so alone in the world, exploiting it for those who feared her, trying to shield those she loved from it. The Beekeeper was the source of this divisive magic, but devil or no, at least with the Beekeeper, May had someone who could accept her exactly as she was.

She well remembered the night she'd ordered the creature away from her home, but the truth was, May had never really expected the creature to honor her wishes. Even today, she kept a bottle of the spirits in the pantry, just on the odd chance the Beekeeper might return.

But it had been years now. The war had come and gone since her last visit from the Beekeeper herself, though the cry of a rooster at odd hours seemed an assurance that, even unseen, the Beekeeper was still keeping an eye on things. Her magic had never deserted May. If anything, it had grown stronger, and might be, it struck May, the only thing that was keeping her going.

Her heart jumped as she heard a door creak open, but it settled when she realized it wasn't the door to her lost friend's world, just her granddaughter checking in on her.

Jilo poked her head in. "You're awake now?"

"Of course, I haven't even lied down yet."

Jilo's brow lowered, and she turned her head a touch to the side. "You just been sitting here staring at the wall all this time?"

"What do you mean 'all this time'? Can't a body have a minute to collect her thoughts?"

Jilo smiled and came into the room. May noticed that she held something clutched against her bosom. "Of course, Nana. Just want to be sure you're doing okay."

The girl sounded worried. May stopped and studied Jilo's face for a moment, registering the concern in the girl's eyes. "How long have I been in here?"

"It's a little over two hours now."

May startled at Jilo's words. "It's all right, Nana. There's nothing wrong with you," Jilo said, rushing over to sit next to her on the bed, placing her free hand over May's own cold one. "I know what today is," Jilo said, and shifted so that May could see the old cigar box she'd brought in with her. "I know Daddy died twenty years ago today. And I know you're hurting over it today even more than usual." Jilo tilted the box up so its illustration caught the light streaming in through the window. "I was thinking about him, too, and I remembered this here old thing, so I went and dug it out. Don't really know what it's supposed to be. Some kind of good luck juju or something." Jilo placed it on May's lap. "Opal told me that your mama made it for Daddy, and he passed it on to her. When Opal left for California, she gave it to me."

May lifted the box in both hands, surprised by its heft. She held it up to her ear and gave it a shake, then another, like it was a gift she was anxious to open.

"Don't bother trying to open it," Jilo said, placing her finger on the seam of the lid. The top didn't so much as wiggle. "It's cemented shut somehow. Tough enough to keep Opal, Poppy, and me from getting it open. Heck, I think even Binah had a go at it once. I guess your mama didn't want the good juju to spill out." Jilo tapped the face of the dark-skinned fellow above whose picture the name "John" had been written in large block letters. "Whatever's in the box is supposed to keep you safe from that fellow. The Red King, I think Opal said Daddy called him." The girl laughed. May had done a good job of convincing Jilo that the monsters weren't real and all such charms were nonsense. "Opal told me Daddy said never to let you see it, 'cause you'd toss it out, but . . . it's all I have of Daddy to share with you."

As May stared at the box's illustration, a sick feeling settled in her soul. The man's top hat. The dandy red scarf.

May positioned her fingers along the seam of the lid. The top flipped open in an instant.

Jilo gasped. "How on earth did you do that?" She reached out for the box, but May pushed her away with a trembling hand. In spite of the box's weight, it was empty inside, save for one shiny black feather from a rooster's tail.

"I have been so blind," May said. The chill that ran through her bones was so acute, she knew she'd never feel warm again. "They were in it together. The two of them. They tricked me."

Jilo sprang to her feet, grasping May's forearm and feeling, May realized, for her pulse. "Don't you be silly, Nana. Daddy and your mama loved you. They'd never trick you." May felt she should explain, but the door of her closet began creaking open, and a dark mist Jilo didn't seem to notice came spilling out from the space.

The box fell from May's grasp, and she pointed to the closet door, trying to form the words to warn Jilo, but they wouldn't come. May watched paralyzed as the mist flooded the room, dampening the light. May's lungs began to burn, and she couldn't catch her breath. It came as no small relief that Jilo seemed unaffected—unaware, even. But, of course, the Beekeeper had finished with May. She hadn't, May realized with a breaking heart, finished with Jilo.

May reached out and caught ahold of her granddaughter's arm. She had to warn her. May had to explain so Jilo wouldn't ever make the same mistake that she and her mother had made. But she couldn't speak. She couldn't breathe. And even if she could, would Jilo listen? Would Jilo even believe her, or would she assume May's mind had gone soft? Jilo's entire life, May had been lying to her. Wanting to free her girls of the temptations of magic, she had pretended to make her living off mundane tricks played on those with more cash than common sense.

In truth, the ruse was mostly for Jilo. The girl was just so clever. So curious. So full of her own power. An aptitude for magic that the Beekeeper herself hadn't seemed to understand. She squeezed Jilo's arm as tight as she could, willing her granddaughter to somehow understand.

"Nana," Jilo said, then called out, "Binah!"

May could hear the anguish in Jilo's voice. As Jilo's image faded, May grasped that she herself had never been the one the Beekeeper wanted. It had been Jilo all along. May's last wish was that she could do something, anything to protect the girl. Her last thought was the realization it was too late.

TWO

December 1954

Robinson Jesse Wills stared at his mother's breast with solemn fascination. Jilo reached back to adjust the bed pillow, then laughed as she shifted her boy, slipping a hand behind his head. Robinson grasped the sides of her breast in his tiny, damp hands and clamped down on her nipple. A smile crept onto Jilo's lips as she watched his mouth tug away at her flesh. He was hers. All hers. The men in her life, even the ones she'd respected and loved, like her father and Pastor Jones, hadn't stuck around for long.

But this one here, he was hers. No one would ever take this boy away. She forced away thoughts of Guy, even though this child in her arms was the spitting image of him. Yes, Robinson looked like his father, but she was his mother. She'd be the one who would help determine what kind of man he became.

Rain hammered on the roof above, so loud it sounded like hail had entered the mix. Her eyes drifted up, settling on the eternal summer-sky blue her Nana had chosen for the room that had once been hers, and was now Jilo and Robinson's. During Nana's time, the walls had gone unadorned, giving the monochrome chamber a sense of expanse, making a body feel like she could be flying, or maybe falling, depending on the longings or fears in her heart.

Jilo had chosen to break this illusion by hanging photos along the wall, each spaced an equal distance apart: one of her father; one of a much younger, and oh, so pretty, Nana; one from Opal and Nate, showing their ever-expanding family; and a recent one of Poppy and her new husband, Isaiah Davis. Shame Nana hadn't lived long enough to hear the news—for Jilo knew Nana would have been thrilled. In spite of the rupture between the two stubborn women, Nana had always hovered over Jilo's shoulder whenever a letter from Poppy came, eager to read her news.

They'd all pretty much given up on Poppy ever finding herself a man. She was a pretty, tiny, little thing, so she had never lacked for suitors, but she'd put off marrying, focusing instead on the garment business she'd built up all on her own. As of her last letter, Poppy employed a dozen other women up in Charlotte.

It struck Jilo that she was the last of the Wills girls; Poppy was now Mrs. Davis, and Opal had long since taken the name of Mrs. Lofton. Certainly, Binah, too, shared the Wills name, but it was a secret to no one, especially Binah herself, that this name was a mere matter of convenience. After Nana's passing, the two sisters had even managed to laugh about it. "Mama must've kept her legs closed real tight to hold on to me so long," Binah had joked, once Nana was no longer there to get angry over such talk. Jilo knew that in Nana's mind, Nana was every bit as much Binah's grandmother as she was the other three's. That meant Jesse Wills was Binah's father, mathematics and biology be damned.

Jilo found herself staring at the photo of Nana's sweet, young face. Oh, how she missed her nana.

Though May Wills had always been an old woman in her eyes, she'd come to believe, as irrational as the thought may have been, that her nana was somehow eternal, that each wispy gray hair on the woman's head was a testament to her ability to withstand anything, even time.

Jilo felt her eyes tearing up, so she looked away, and her gaze was once again caught by the turquoise-blue of the walls, ceiling, and floor. Even faded, it was the color of the heavens. A memento of a July sky on this darkening winter day.

The thought of summer used to bring her happiness, but as she sat on her nana's old bed, rocking to the rhythm of Robinson's nursing, she wondered how they'd manage to hold on until summer. If Jilo had the slightest idea of how to sew, she'd call Poppy to see if her sister might take her on at her factory. But Jilo couldn't even thread a needle. And Poppy had been so distant over the years, staying up in Charlotte, always finding one reason or another not to come back to Savannah, even for a short visit. She'd written a lovely letter after Nana's passing, but she still hadn't bothered to come down for the funeral, even though Opal had made it all the way from West Texas, where Nate was now stationed.

Jilo had often wondered what had happened between Nana and Poppy the last time she'd come around to visit. It had been back before the war, fourteen or so years ago now. Maybe Jilo should call and ask Poppy to come home for a visit.

Then again, what would they do if she accepted? Once Poppy arrived and saw how close to the bone they were cutting things, she would be bound to view the invitation as a petition of charity. Jilo did not want charity from anyone, especially family, but she knew she was going to have to come up with a way to earn a living quick. She and Binah had torn the house apart to look for stashes of cash Nana might have left behind. Her nana's closet yielded no cash, just her clothes, a few hats, and—much to Jilo's surprise—her old doll, the red-haired one that had gone missing years earlier. The doll's pretty face had been smashed, though whether by accident or design, Jilo would never know. For years she had thought it was lost forever, but now it seemed as if Nana had kept it stashed in her closet all along. Perhaps out of guilt for having caused the damage, certainly with the intent of having it repaired. The doll was clean, but its dress carried a musty scent, almost like it had been buried in earth.

They did uncover forty-two dollars in a mason jar, in the pantry, shoved in behind a row of bread-and-butter pickles, but that was about the only windfall they'd discovered. The search also unearthed a scrapbook beneath Nana's mattress, filled with clippings and notes made in her nana's hand about a family by the name of Maguire. Jilo had barely even scanned its contents; she was looking for cash, and the clippings seemed worthless. Still the scrapbook held some value to her nana, so rather than toss it, she put it on the closet's top shelf, next to her father's old cigar treasure box containing the cock feather. Neither was going to put food on the table.

The rain made another assault on the roof, coming down so hard that it sounded like a frantic banging of a lost soul seeking refuge. An angry flash of lightning, unexpected from a storm on a day nearly cold enough to snow, lit up her window, just before the electric light of the lamp on her nightstand flickered. The wind picked up, giving the old house a couple of good shakes. The closet door creaked slowly open. A trick of the flickering light made her, for the shortest of moments, think she saw the fingers of a lace-gloved hand reach around the closet door. An involuntary yelp escaped her, causing Robinson to pull back and look up at her, his tiny eyes widening in surprise, his face quivering, trying to decide if he should cry. Jilo blinked, and the illusion was gone. She patted Robinson's back and turned him so that he could feed from her right breast.

An easily distinguishable chain of natural events, but the illusion still sent a cold bead of sweat down between her shoulder blades. She made herself chuckle at her own nerves, but she still held Robinson in a tighter grip. A rap on her door made her jump.

The doorknob jiggled, and the door began to open before she could invite her visitor in. "Jilo," Binah called in a hushed voice through the enlarging crack. "There's some white woman out front, banging on the door." For a moment Jilo had a sense of déjà vu—an old memory very nearly surfaced before slipping back beneath the waves of the past.

"Well, go see what she wants," Jilo said, her tone meant to convey that this was the obvious action. She tugged Robinson off her tit and settled him down next to her on the bed. He began to fuss. "Shh. Shh," she repeated, trying to comfort him as she tugged her nursing bra—a gift from Poppy—into place, and pulled the top of her dress back up.

"I don't want to. You come with me," Binah said, casting a nervous glance back over her shoulder as a more insistent knocking sounded on the door.

Jilo quickly hooked the buttons of her dress through their loops. "She's probably had trouble with her car. Maybe an accident out there in the storm." After placing a cloth over her shoulder, she hefted up her growing boy and rubbed gently between his tiny shoulders. "She may be hurt," Jilo said in a firm tone, hoping to spur her sister into action, but Binah just stood there shaking her head.

"Oh, for pity's sake, girl. How much trouble do you think one woman, even a white one, is gonna cause you?" The baby gave out a loud and liquid burp. Rising to her feet, Jilo wadded up the cloth with one hand and handed it to Binah. "Here, you might as well be of some use around here."

Another series of loud bangs sounded on the front door. "Yes, ma'am," she called out. "I hear you. I'm coming."

Jilo padded down the hall and through the front room, then thought twice before opening the door. She turned back to find Binah creeping along at her heels. She held the baby out to her. "Take Robinson to your room. I'll see what the lady wants." Jilo was amazed by her sister's trepidation at meeting the strange woman. Binah snatched the baby from her and took off like a shot. Another knock wrested Jilo's attention back to the door.

Jilo switched on the porch light, then opened the door just enough to get a good look at the woman—and to make certain that she was alone. The woman was older than Jilo. Certainly thirty, probably forty. She was well dressed, in a gray box jacket suit with trim in a darker shade of gray. A red pillbox hat topped with a pearl stickpin and a black bird-cage veil. Her lips were painted a red that mirrored the shade of her hat. She stood there drenched and trembling in the cold, mascara running down her cheeks. But still she held her chin high, looking down at Jilo over the bridge of her nose. Her eyebrows were raised as if in expectation that Jilo would pay her obeisance. As Jilo took her in, it struck her to see how such vulnerability could be paired with such a look of haughtiness.

"May I help you?" Jilo asked, adding as an afterthought, "Ma'am?"

"I need to speak to the old Negress," she said, yanking on the screeching screen door with such vehemence, Jilo feared this cry might be its last. "Oh, do let me pass," she said, pushing past Jilo, her tone impatient and irritated.

Jilo faced the intruder, amazed to see this buckra woman standing there before her, steam starting to rise up from her damp garments.

"Well, where is she? The woman"—she seemed to be searching her memory—"May. Yes, Mother May. She helped me before. Years ago now. I need her help again. I went to the cemetery three days in a row now, and she hasn't shown up like usual. I know this is where she lives."

"She did live here, ma'am . . ."

"Did?" the woman interrupted her.

"Yes, my grandmother passed some months back."

The visitor's face hardened. "This is very inconvenient. I am in great need of her services."

Jilo had to swallow back a laugh. "I apologize for the inconvenience my grandmother's death has caused you," she said, a good dose of sarcasm creeping into her words, though she had done her best to modulate her tone.

The woman didn't seem to notice. Instead, her gaze narrowed on Jilo. "Wait, you say she was your grandmother?"

Jilo nodded. "Yes, ma'am, she was indeed."

"Then you can help me, can't you?" The woman grasped Jilo's forearms in her small, pale hands, made to look even paler by the scarlet nail polish she wore. "That's how it works with your kind and this Negro magic isn't it? It gets passed on through the blood. Right?" The woman shook Jilo's arms, tugging hard enough to make Jilo take a step closer. "You can help me." The words sounded more like a statement of fact than a question.

Jilo smiled and began shaking her head. "No, ma'am, I can't . . ."

"I'll pay you." To Jilo's surprise, the woman fell to her knees sobbing, pressing Jilo's hand to her tearstained cheek before pulling back to kiss it.

Jilo jerked her hand free. "I don't know," she said, the wheels in her mind spinning fast. "The work is dangerous. And I'm not as practiced at it as my grandmother was."

"I will pay you well."

Jilo took a couple of steps back and placed her hands on her hips, giving the fine lady the very same stink eye she'd given Binah only minutes before. "You tell me what Nana—I mean, Mother May—did for you, and I'll see if I can help. No promises, though. And it's cash up front."

The woman's hand flew up to her breast and she froze in place, suddenly, it seemed, cognizant of her humble position. "There's a woman. An ungodly and lascivious woman. A rival for my husband's affections." She rose, turning her back to Jilo, undid a button on her suit, and tugged a stash of bills from her brassiere. "Again. Last time, she tried to turn my husband's affections from me. This time, she's determined to take my life so that she can have him. She's put a fix on me." She carefully peeled off two five-dollar bills, which she held out to Jilo. "I need you to remove it." Jilo stepped forward, amazed at her own temerity, and took the rest of the bills from the woman's other hand, leaving the woman clutching the two fives.

"But that's so much more than your grandmother would have ever charged," the woman protested.

Jilo tilted her head and rested her left hand on her hip. "My grand-mother's just a bit up the road at Laurel Grove. You think you can get a better deal from her, you're more than welcome to try." She wanted to sound confident, and to her own ears she did, but she held that wad of cash in a death grip.

The woman relented, lowering her head. "All right. But this had better work."

Jilo stuffed the bills into her own bra. "Like I told you, there are no guarantees. Don't try my patience. The spirits," she said, stretching the word out, giving it a sense of fearsomeness, "are taxing enough." She secured another button on her dress, just to help make the money harder for the woman to retrieve. Jilo would never have treated a buckra woman with such audacity outside her home, but this woman seemed torn between her belief in her own superiority and her fear of Jilo's mysterious Negro powers. It was as clear as water that the story of what happened here tonight would never be shared with a single soul. Still, it wouldn't hurt to threaten the buckra with unpleasant repercussions if she were to speak of the secrets she saw here.

"Come through to the kitchen. We can talk better in there."

She rapped on Binah's door as she passed by. "Get on out here," she commanded. "We're calling on the spirits." Binah opened the door a crack, her eyes wide and brows arched in a mixture of worry and con-fusion. Jilo gave her a wink. "The missus here has paid us to approach the spirits on her behalf."

Binah's face froze in disbelief, but she quickly recovered. She opened the door fully. "Then I should bring the baby, too. His innocence will protect us from any unclean ones."

Jilo smiled and nodded. "You are a wise child."

After leading the way to the kitchen, Jilo pulled a chair—one that faced away from the pantry—back from the table. "Sit here," she said. The woman stepped into the kitchen, looking around it with wide eyes, filled with a mixture of expectation and fear, as if she might bolt at any moment. Jilo stepped back, giving the woman a clear and unhindered path to the seat. There was a moment's hesitation, but the woman made the decision to do as she was told. She slid the seat an inch or so farther back from where Jilo had left it, then sat down, tugging on the hem of her skirt as she did.

Jilo decided to move slowly. She wanted the woman spooked, but not spooked enough to flee without feeling she'd gotten her money's worth. Even if the woman never spoke of this night to a soul, a poor outcome could still lead to some very unpleasant repercussions for Jilo herself. A rich buckra like this could find other ways to strike back.

The woman looked around, taking in the exotic setting in which she'd found herself. "Should we dim the lights? Light some candles?"

"No," Binah said, entering the room with Robinson in her arms. "Dim lights, dark spirits," she said. Though she managed not to laugh, there was a twinkle in her eye.

"She's right," Jilo said. "The good spirits aren't afraid of the light." She nodded at the table, signaling for Binah to join their guest. "But they will only come to us if we provide them with an offering." She paused. "I'll only be a moment."

She took her time crossing to the pantry, but once inside, she attacked the shelves, searching for ingredients she remembered from her first days of her Chemistry I class. On the lower shelf, not far from the front, sat the yellow box that held powdered sugar. The sugar was left over from frosting Nana had made for the cake she baked for Cousin Barney's funeral, only a couple of months before her own. Jilo shook the box, disappointed that it felt so light, but relief swept over her when she opened it. There were about six teaspoons of the powder left, which should be plenty for her needs.

One shelf up sat another box, also yellow, but with a blue circle circumscribing a hand wielding a hammer. Baking soda. Plenty heavy, nearly a full box.

"Don't let me down, now, Nana," Jilo mumbled under her breath. On the top shelf should be a bottle that Nana had forbidden the girls ever to touch. She went up on her tiptoes, her heart falling when she didn't see the bottle of clear rum she would certainly have sampled if she hadn't forgotten it until now. She strained, stretching up even farther, and ran her hand along the shelf. There. She nearly cheered as her fingertips found the round glass container. She grasped the body of the bottle, sliding it forward a few inches, and then snatched it by the neck.

After tucking the two boxes under her arms and grasping the bottle, she left the pantry and crossed to the table, assuming an air of solemnity as she placed the ingredients on the table before the woman, whose expression showed marks of skepticism as she stared at the elements of Jilo's purported offering to the spirits.

Jilo acted quickly to circumvent any questions. "A simple offering for pure spirits. The dark ones, they demand blood," she drawled out the last word, then flashed a sharp look at Binah, hoping her little sister wouldn't forget herself and laugh.

But there was no need for worry; her sister proved quite the worthy actress. "No blood, Lord. No blood," she said, shaking her head as she clutched Robinson close. "Don't want any evil ones coming in here to lap it up."

Her manufactured fear served to engender true terror in their visitor. "No," the woman echoed Binah. "I don't want to enlist any dark spirits . . ." She hesitated. "Unless it proves absolutely necessary."

"Won't be necessary," Jilo said in a steady, reassuring tone. "We're taking the fix off you. That's white magic. Good magic. The dark spirits can't help us with that." She turned away and grabbed a spoon, a small mixing bowl, and a thick ceramic meat plate, arranging them next to the boxes and rum bottle. Then she lifted the rum bottle and unscrewed the lid. After pausing to nod at their guest, she lifted the rum to her lips and knocked back a shot. She wiped her lips with the back of her hand. "Helps me get in tune with the spirits." A shot's worth of rum went into the bowl, too, and then she set the bottle aside. "The fiery water that separates our world from that of the spirits." She grabbed the spoon and measured out four rounded spoonfuls of the sugar into the rum. "To remind them of the sweetness of the lives they led here on earth. Makes sure we only attract the happy, helpful spirits. Not the angry ones." She set the nearly empty sugar box aside and clutched the baking soda. "To assure we get only the purest of spirits." She added one rounded teaspoon of the soda to the bowl and stirred the mixture into a thick paste, which she then scooped into a ball and dropped on to the meat platter.

Jilo laid the spoon on the table and closed her eyes, holding her hands out over the ball of paste. "We call upon you, our guiding spirits. This fine lady has had the fix settled on her by an impure woman, a woman so covetous she wants to take this innocent's very life." She paused, pretending to listen to voices from beyond. "Yes. Yes. You must be her judge, but I come to you on her behalf. I do believe her to be worthy." Jilo opened up her eyes, forcing them wide, and held her right hand out toward the woman. "Do not move. Not an inch. They are here. They have heard us. They must determine if you are indeed worthy of their help." The woman blanched, but held still. Jilo allowed her hand to tremble and her eyes to roll upward. Slowly she let a smile form on her lips. "Yes. Yes." She closed her eyes, then opened them again, focusing on the woman. She nodded. "They have deemed you worthy."

Praying that the box of safety matches in the drawer by the sink wouldn't be empty, she crossed the room, speaking as she did. "They have agreed to accept our gift to them, and in return, they *will*"—she emphasized the word—"remove the black fix that has been set on you by your rival." She tugged open the drawer, pleased to see that a red box emblazoned with a blue tiger was tucked in next to a box of fuses. She retrieved the matches and returned to the table. Once there, she pulled out one of the matches, but before she struck it, she pulled the bottle of rum over to her and took another sip. "You must concentrate. Open yourself up to the spirits. Give them your permission to remove this curse."

"I do," the woman said, leaning forward. "I do give them permission to cleanse me."

Jilo flashed the woman her most reassuring smile, then doused the ball of paste with a bit more rum. She struck the match, not hesitating this time, and touched the flame to the white paste.

The woman's eyes widened as the ball of paste caught flame and then began to darken, expanding, lengthening, and growing into what resembled a small black snake wriggling along.

"There it is," Jilo said. "That's the fix. Right there. The spirits done drew it out of you."

The woman wobbled in her seat, nearly swooning, but caught hold of the edge of the table and steadied herself. Her eyes filled with tears. "You have the gift," she said, a tone of gratitude overriding her earlier haughtiness. She raised her hand like she wanted to reach out for Jilo, but instead she stood and rushed out of the house, to all appearances a terrified but happy customer.

Jilo and Binah squealed in simultaneous delight, shocking the drowsy Robinson awake. He began to wail in displeasure, but Jilo swept him into her arms and spun him around and around, planting one kiss after another on his face. As his cries lessened, she looked up at Binah. "We're gonna get by just fine." She looked down at Robinson and planted another kiss on his cheek.

THREE

April 1955

"You? You the one claiming to be able to work the root?" The woman had only been in Jilo's house a matter of minutes, but she was already struggling to pull her heavy frame up out of Nana's haint-blue chair so she could leave. "I ain't got time for none of your nonsense."

"I wish you would give me the chance to assist you with your difficulties," Jilo said.

The woman snorted. "You ain't got none of the Hoodoo in you, girlie," she said, laughing, her fat cheeks, mottled with rosacea, rising as her jowls jiggled. "Anybody with eyes can see that." She huffed and puffed, but couldn't wrest herself out of the chair on her own.

Jilo's early optimism about resurrecting her grandmother's business had faltered quickly. It wasn't easy finding folk who would place their faith in her particular brand of Hoodoo. She'd done her best to imitate her grandmother, but truth was, she didn't know the first thing about working the magic tricks that fueled her nana's act.

Though Jilo sometimes felt remorseful that she was perpetrating out-and-out trickery, not even backed by the belief of those who practiced genuine Hoodoo, Nana had taught her that sometimes a little deception was the best way to free people of the fears and beliefs preventing them from leading happy lives. Jilo had read in magazines about people spending hundreds, even thousands, of dollars to undergo years of psychoanalysis, just to work through childhood traumas that might not—in reality—have ever happened to them. No, she wasn't claiming to be able to cure disease or help people strike it rich; she was just putting names to their fears, setting up boogeymen only to knock them down.

After her first go at "magic," Jilo had called upon her nana's faithful clients to tell them she was taking up the mantle. Word began to spread, especially after she cleared herself and Robinson out of Nana's old room and returned it to the calling room it had been in the heyday of Nana's business. But after a handful of visits, the trickle of callers had dried up. Nana had a touch that Jilo did not seem to have inherited.

So desperate was she for customers, Jilo had actually been happy to welcome this vile woman into her home. It was midday, so she had turned Robinson over to Willy's care before leading the visitor into the haint-blue room. Though Willy was a few years younger than Binah, he'd left school long ago. He could read. Some. He could write. A little. It had been almost a year since the government had proclaimed white schools had to be open to black children, but Savannah was having none of it. And with only a handful of schools in the city open to black students, no truant officer would ever come looking for Willy. Jilo wasn't his mama, even though it was sure starting to feel like it, so she didn't force him to go.

"Don't just stand there like a natural-born fool, girl." Her visitor's forehead had bunched into a concertina of angry wrinkles. She was holding out an arm for help out of the chair, probably had been for some time. Jilo hated the thought of touching the woman's pasty, sweaty flesh, but she realized that helping the rotund old woman rise would be the only way to get her out of the house. Besides, she'd faced plenty worse in her nursing days. Bracing herself, she wrapped her fingers around the woman's clammy wrist and pulled until the woman managed to shift her heft from her haunches to her feet.

"Naw, girl. You ain't got none of the root in you. Just look at you."

"I'll have you know my grandmother was Mother Wills, and her mother was Mother Tuesday Jackson . . ."

" 'I'll have you know . . .' " The woman parroted the words back to her and cackled, her small gray eyes peeping out through curtains of flesh. "Listen to you. I don't give a damn who whelped you. You walk around here puttin' on airs like you somebody. But you don't know nothin' about the root, you just another uppity Negro, done got yo'self a bit of learnin' on how to talk fancy. Think you smart enough to pull the wool over folks' eyes, but I done seen through you, girlie." The woman ambled toward the door, then turned back. "I don't fault you none. I saw those diapers out there drying on the line. I know you ain't got it easy."

Something about the woman's sympathy angered Jilo more than her insults ever could. She didn't want this woman's compassion. "I think perhaps you should leave."

A yellow, snaggletoothed smile broke out on the woman's face, and the red patches on her sallow jowls seemed to catch fire. "I'm already on my way, girlie."

Jilo turned away, lunging toward the window she had painted over in a color similar to, but not quite the match of, her grandmother's haint blue. She opened the window, wanting to banish the woman's scent, then turned and followed her out of the house. Standing on the porch, she watched the woman's back as she trod away, her steps leaving heavy impressions in the sandy soil.

When the woman was far enough away that Jilo felt sure she wouldn't turn back, Jilo went and sat on the porch swing, giving herself the gift of listening to the silence. The quiet felt peaceful for a moment, then due to what she could only guess was her burgeoning maternal intuition, it struck her as worrisome. In an instant, all thoughts of her disgruntled visitor faded. She pushed up from the swing, feeling it slip back away from her, and pushed her way around the argumentative screen door. The house was utterly silent, which only alarmed Jilo further. Willy wasn't prone to silence.

She almost called out, but instinct told her not to. She passed through the front room, then crept down the hallway, ears straining for the slightest sound. Perhaps both Willy and Robinson were sleeping? She slid up to the bedroom door and wrapped her hand around the doorknob, which she turned ever so carefully. The mechanism still clicked, but it was a soft, nearly unnoticeable sound. She eased the door open, relieved to see the baby sleeping on the bed, surrounded by pillows to prevent him from rolling off. She craned her head around the door, where, unaware of her presence, Willy stood before the mirror, admiring himself in the dress she'd once worn to the Kingfisher Club. The night she'd met Guy, her mind reminded her, though she was quick to alert the part of her mind that considered that an important fact to shut the hell up.

"Willy," she said, stepping into the room. "What in the world are you getting up to in here?" she asked as if she didn't already know the answer to her question. As if she hadn't always known the answer.

Shock turned Willy's face into a nearly comical mask—his eyes wide, his mouth open and working like a fish trapped on dry land. "I didn't mean no harm. I didn't."

Jilo felt herself flash hot and then cold. She bit her lower lip as she considered the situation. "You get out of that dress," she said, each word a command in itself, the path she was going to take becoming clearer as she stepped onto it. "Then you get your clothes on, and get out of this house."

"But I got nowhere to go. My pa. He said he'd kill me if he ever laid eyes on me again."

She hated it. She had known. She had always known. But seeing it with her own eyes had made it more real. She cast a glance at her still-drowsing son. "I'm sorry, I can't have you around Robinson." She started to turn away.

"I love him. I wouldn't hurt him. I wouldn't."

She stopped and turned back. "I'm not saying you'd hurt him." She felt her heart reach up into her throat. "I know you'd never hurt him. But I can't have you around him. I can't have him learning"—she waved her hand in wide circles in his direction—"this."

"But I didn't learn this. Ain't nobody taught me." Fat tears burst from his eyes. "If it was something I had learned, don't you think I would've done all I could to unlearn it?"

Damn. Jilo wanted to turn her heart to stone as she watched Willy's head fall forward, his body, still dressed in her old blue cocktail dress, racked with sobs. She fought her own instinct to step forward and put her arms around the sobbing boy, who had lived under her roof for months now. His words and his sincerity touched her, and besides, what exactly was she so worried about? Messed up as Willy must be, she knew he would give his life to protect her son.

Maybe if Robinson had a father, a strong, male figure around to keep him in line? Then a question rose in her mind, one she didn't like very much. This child before her. With his big heart. When it came down to it, would she rather have Robinson grow up like him or like Guy?

No. It was impossible. She couldn't have Robinson growing up around a boy like Willy. She couldn't take that chance.

No, a very different part of herself spoke up: What was impossible was to send Willy away, especially since he didn't have anywhere to go. She loved the child too much. Was she hypocrite enough to punish him for this confirmation of what she had always felt to be true?

She took a deep breath and closed her eyes, wishing she believed in God, so she could ask for guidance. Instead, she asked her own troubled heart what to do, but to her disappointment, it couldn't supply her with a definitive answer. The path that had for one moment seemed so clear grew hazy. She crossed the room to Willy and lifted his chin up. His eyes were red, and full of fear.

Why would you want this, boy? she wanted to ask, but didn't. It seemed to Jilo there was only one thing in this world treated with less fairness and respect than a black man, and that was a black woman. "You take that dress off. Put on your own clothes." She paused suddenly, wondering why it should matter so much anyway, but a fearful part of her own heart felt that it must. If it didn't, why would folk make so much of a fuss over it?

"I haven't made up my mind," she said. "I'm not saying you can stay on. Not permanently. But you don't have to leave today." He fell into her, wrapping his arms so tightly around her she had to fight to catch her breath. She managed to free one arm, which she wrapped around his back, pulling his sobbing head into her bosom. "Shhh . . ." She comforted him just as she might Robinson. "Shhh . . ."

- — -

Jilo laid the hen down on the wide, bloodstained tree trunk they'd been using as a chopping block, her subconscious saying a prayer her conscious mind would rebel against, for the beast about to die at her own hand. She held the bird tight and swung the hatchet hard, doing her best to make sure the hen didn't suffer. The body kicked a few times, but did not, much to her relief, find its feet and take off running. She'd seen that happen once when she was girl, and it had put her off chicken for nearly a year.

"Willy," she called out. He came out the back door and down the steps, carrying a pitcher of water and a kitchen towel. Without being prompted, he poured water over her outstretched hands till they were as clean as hands that had just taken a life—of any kind—ever could be. He handed her the towel, and she wiped her hands dry. "You finish plucking her, then singe off the fuzz." He nodded. "There're matches and some newsprint in the drawer in the kitchen. You know which one?" He nodded again. Of course he knew. He'd lived with them for nearly a year now. This, she realized, was his home. "You be careful. Don't burn yourself. And make sure you keep the fire good and far from the house. You hear me?" He nodded a third time. She realized he was afraid to speak lest he say something that would change her mind. She reached out, letting her fingers brush his cheek, and said, "When you're done, bring it in. I'll cut it up and get it ready for frying."

She heard the cry of the front screen door, announcing Binah's return. Oiling the door never worked, and it occurred to her for the umpteenth time that she ought to have the thing replaced, but at this point it would almost be like losing an old, if annoying, friend. She went in through the kitchen, where Robinson seemed content enough sitting in his high chair and banging a wooden spoon against its tray, and headed down the hall. She stopped before the open bedroom door. Binah sat on her bed, the contents of her book bag spilled out around her. Jilo entered the room and closed the door behind her.

"Please tell me you aren't in love with that boy."

"In love with what boy?" Binah looked up at her, one arched eyebrow and a confused smile on her face. Her eyes widened as meaning of Jilo's question seemed to dawn on her. "Willy?" She began laughing, then her laughter stopped abruptly, and any signs of amusement fell from her face.

Jilo folded her arms across her chest and nodded at the chifferobe where she kept her clothes. "You know about him, don't you?"

Binah's look of concern faded, her mouth pursing and her brows edging downward. She pushed herself up from the bed and stood directly before Jilo. "Yes," she said, and paused. "I know. And if you're telling me you didn't, at least deep down, then you're lying to both of us."

Jilo looked away, casting her gaze at the floor near Binah's feet. She took a step back, reaching behind her, and opened the door. "Willy," she called loud enough to make sure the boy would hear her out in the yard, even though she suspected that he was lurking nearby, straining his ears to hear what they were saying, rather than cleaning the bird like she'd asked. "Bring Robinson and get in here."

"What are you doing?" Binah asked, a fierce, protective tone in her voice.

Jilo felt a tiny bit proud of her baby sister, who seemed to have transformed into a fierce mama lion ready to defend her cub. She didn't say a word till Willy appeared in the doorway, Robinson in his arms.

Willy's face looked ashen. His lips were trembling, and his eyes looked like the dam was going to burst at any moment. Jilo pulled Robinson into her own arms. "You can stop with all that. I'm not," she said, then paused. "*We're* not sending you away." The boy looked up, his expression brightening, but still cautious. "Now get in here." Willy stepped across the threshold, his shoulders slumped forward, still expecting the other falling foot to crush him.

Jilo shifted Robinson onto her hip, then lugged the ever-growing boy over to the chifferobe. After tugging open both doors, she turned back to face Binah and Willy. "I still don't understand this. Any of this," she said, "but then again, there're a whole hell of a lot of things in this world I don't understand." She cast a quick glance down at her own boy, hoping that she was doing right by him, then returned her gaze to Willy. "Out there"—she nodded toward the door—"you won't be safe if folk were to learn about this. There are a lot of people who'd want to kill you. You understand me?"

"Yes ma'am," Willy said.

If his expression weren't so grave, Jilo might have snorted over his calling her ma'am. But it was, so she didn't. Instead, she swallowed, forcing herself to soften her tone. "Maybe someday, some place, things will be different. For your sake, I hope so. But for now, that's what we can expect. In here, though, with that door closed, you're safe. You do what you need to do." She crossed back to the chifferobe. "These things on the left side." She made a show of running her hand down the garments.

"You can have them. They don't fit me anymore anyway. The things on the right, though? Those are mine. Do not touch them." She paused, casting a glance down at the boy's feet. "And Willy?"

"Yes," he said, his eyes welling up again, from relief, she hoped, or maybe even happiness.

"You scuff up or stretch my shoes, and everything I just said about you being safe is off. I will kill you myself." His face froze. "Just so we're clear." She closed the chifferobe's doors and headed back into the hall. She gave Robinson a slight bounce, then looked back over her shoulder. "Now get out here and help me finish making dinner while Binah does her schoolwork."

- — -

The three of them sat on the wide front porch, beneath the artificial haint-blue sky. Beyond the porch's overhang, night was fast approaching, replacing the blue with brilliant roses and oranges. Before today, Jilo would never have dreamed of nursing in front of Willy, who was sitting on the porch with his back to the front wall, but tonight they all felt like family. So while she rocked on the swing next to Binah, Jilo undid the buttons of her blouse and shifted her fussing baby to her exposed breast.

As Robinson nursed, Willy and Binah chattered on. Mostly about how bad they needed to buy themselves a television, so they could watch *I Love Lucy* along with the rest of the country.

Jilo used the ball of her foot to rock the swing back and forth. She looked down at Willy. "You already spend half your life listening to that damned radio." Jilo was both annoyed and pleased that he'd forgotten how tenuous his living situation had been only hours ago. "Besides, if we don't find a way to start getting some money in around here," she said, giving voice to her own more pressing worry, "we may not have anywhere to put a television set."

Binah locked eyes with her. "What do you mean?"

"I mean we have to pay taxes on this place. We don't pay taxes, they'll come and take the house away from us."

"Who are 'they'?" A vertical line formed between Binah's brow, and her eyes narrowed. "This was Nana's house. Now it's ours. Nobody has the right to try and steal it from us."

"The law. That's who 'they' are. The law. And 'they' say we're stealing from them if we don't pay taxes. They take from us, and then they tell us we're the thieves. That's how it works, my sister," Jilo said, regretting that she had brought the subject up. A tumultuous day had led into a pleasant—happy, even—evening. She should have held her tongue. It was just that she had begun to feel mighty alone when it came to dealing with the problems that life kept bringing.

"What about that fat woman? The one who smelled?" Willy asked.

Jilo pursed her lips, her nose wrinkling as she remembered the woman's sharp onion scent. "She didn't believe that I have any of the 'root' in me." Jilo said, shifting Robinson to her other breast. He fussed a little as she did, but he settled down as soon as he realized dinner wasn't over.

"But nobody does," Binah said, her eyes bright with humor. "There's no such thing as magic."

"Yeah, well, you know that, and I know that, but if we're lucky, the rest of the world isn't going to figure that bit out." She pushed the swing back again, then let go. "She said she could see I didn't have the Hoodoo because of the way I look. The way I talk." Jilo felt the woman's words grate at her once again. "She said I was just 'another uppity Negro.'"

"She didn't believe in you . . ." Willy said in a hushed voice. Jilo twisted to get a better view of him. "She couldn't believe in you, 'cause you didn't match what she was expecting to see." He stared forward into the deepening twilight. "Sometimes you just gotta show folk what they want to see."

"Tell her," Binah said. "Tell Jilo about Audrey."

Jilo had believed she knew every person in these two children's worlds, so the unfamiliar name surprised her. She was intrigued, but Willy fell silent.

"Go on, I'm listening," Jilo said. "Tell me about this Audrey." Willy shook his head, drawing his knees up into his chest.

"Go on, Willy," Binah coaxed him.

Jilo glanced at her sister before returning her attention to the boy. "Go on. Tell me. Who the hell is this Audrey friend of yours?"

"She isn't a friend," Willy said, then his mouth clamped shut.

"Go on, Willy," Jilo said, softening her voice. "I want to hear about her. I do."

Willy raised his eyes to meet hers. "You saw her. You saw her today." He pushed himself up. "I know you think this is me," he tugged on the tail of his shirt. "This boy you looking at, but he ain't me. Not really. Willy isn't the real me. He's just someone I pretend to be. He's a shell I wear. Audrey," he said the name with reverence, "that's who I really am. On the inside at least. To get by in this world, I make believe I'm Willy. But when I'm alone. When I'm really me . . ."

Jilo tugged her nipple from Robinson's lips, surprised to find he was already sleeping. She handed the baby to her sister and buttoned her blouse, not quite sure how to react to the boy's admission. Should she get on her knees and take Willy into her arms? Or should she pretend she'd never heard any of it?

Willy looked up at her. "You need to make yourself a shell. One you can wear when you dealing with people looking for Hoodoo. You need to give them what they're looking for. When you dealing with them, you can't just be Jilo. You gotta be Mother Jilo."

Jilo froze. His words chafed her, but they struck her as the absolute truth. She'd been trying to sell candy in a box marked "soap," and there weren't many folk willing to believe it was candy on the inside. She needed to create a package that matched what she was selling. Jilo stood, pushing the swing back as she did. "So who is she then, this Mother Jilo?"

FOUR

June 1956

"It's you. It is." Jilo heard a voice call out from a shop she'd passed on West Broad. It didn't even occur to her that the words might be intended for her. After finishing up a round of errands in town, she was focused on getting home to Binah and her boy.

She'd had to wait at the bank, so she'd been gone longer than expected. The colored service window had opened up an hour later than usual. No explanations. No apologies. Just a command for them not to lurk about before the bank was ready to receive them. Still, Jilo had been too happy about the fresh packet of cash she had ready to deposit to let herself focus on why she couldn't just use the manned window where not even a single white person was waiting. No, she wasn't going to let herself be bothered by that today. Things had started looking up for her, and she was going to hold on tight to each and every victory.

She struggled beneath the weight of her new nylon shopping bag, but she found she didn't mind the effort. This bag wasn't just full of needed groceries; no, there were a few things in there that her family simply *wanted*. Luxuries, which would have seemed like an impossible dream even a year ago. She wasn't sure whose eyes she was more excited to see: Robinson's at the sight of his new windup clockwork robot or Willy's when he unwrapped the coral chiffon head scarf that she herself planned to borrow from time to time. For Binah, she had bought a book, featuring a red sun with gold and silver coronas on an otherwise black cover. Something dreadful about people blowing up the whole damned world, but Jilo felt certain Binah would like it.

Romance wasn't her girl's thing—Binah's interests ran in just about every other direction. Jilo was proud that her girl seemed more interested in books than she was in men.

"It is!" The voice grew closer, accompanied by the clapping of leather-soled shoes along the tabby sidewalk. Jilo nearly dropped her bag when a strange man grabbed ahold of her arm, but the man reached forward to keep the sack from falling. "It's you."

She looked up into the stranger's gleaming eyes.

He smiled. "I mean, you look different. You're dressed different." He leaned back as if to take her in from head to toe. "Real pretty, though." She'd taken to wearing her Mother Jilo costume—kaftans in bright, eye-catching shades, mostly blues and purples, with wide-brimmed sunhats or turbans in opposite and equally blinding colors. After a lifetime of trying to blend in, her income had become contingent upon her ability to stand out. Whenever she walked down West Broad, voices would drop, and crowds would part before her as the name "Mother Jilo" trailed behind her like a wake on the water. It had taken a while to build Mother Jilo's reputation, but now every outing was an opportunity to advertise.

Still, this man was a complete stranger to her.

"Mother Jilo, she sorry," Jilo said. "But you wrong. Mother Jilo, she don't know you." She tried to make her tone sound final, if not severe. She was still in too good of a mood to want to scare the poor fellow. Shrugging him off, she began to walk away, but he circled around her, his movements so full of joy it resembled dancing.

"Why are you talking that way?" he asked, his face scrunching up with confusion.

So much for her good mood. She shook her head and glared at him. "Mother Jilo done say she don't know you. Now scat."

"No, you know me. Well, you met me once. On the bus." He stopped directly in front of her, looking down at her as if he were sure she'd recognize him and fling her arms around him like a long-lost friend. She tried to squeeze past him, but he blocked her escape. "You know. In Atlanta. The bus. You had a suitcase. I talked too much." His shoulders slumped forward. "I'm talking too much now. I'm sorry. You don't remember me. Why should you? A beautiful woman like you must always have one fellow or another trying to catch her eye."

Most days, she would have snapped the head off anyone who dared to say such a foolish thing, but it had been a long time since any man had paid her any attention, let alone called her beautiful. The compliment near took the wind out of her. Jilo stopped and gave the man a good once over, and to her surprise, an encounter she'd all but forgotten surfaced in her mind. An encounter that had evidently left its mark on this poor jabbering fellow.

"Poole," she said, "Private First Class Poole."

A wide smile set up camp on his beaming face. "Yes. That's right. Poole. But just regular old Tinker Poole these days."

"Tinker . . ." Jilo said, the name almost coming out as a question.

"Well, yeah, my real name's Joseph, but everybody calls me Tinker, 'cause I'm always taking things apart that don't work right and putting them back together again so that they do. That's what I do. For money, that is." He pointed to an open doorway. "That's my shop. Right there."

She glanced over her shoulder in the direction he was pointing. When she turned back, it struck her that he had leaned in, just a tad. Not enough to be threatening. Not enough to assume an intimacy between them. Still, it felt as if the air that surrounded him was caressing the air that enveloped her.

He bowed his head, the lids of his happy eyes lowering, lending his gaze a more serious look. "I'm real good at it," he said, "fixing things what've been broken." For a moment she was captivated by his tender black eyes, so dark that she couldn't be sure where the pupil and iris met. For a moment, she felt as if he had plumbed the depths of her soul, uncovering every hurt, every loss, every crack in her foundation. Without laying a finger on her, he had touched her, brushing up against an old wound. This was much like her first meeting with Tinker Poole, the one she'd almost managed to forget, or at least convince herself that she'd forgotten.

She stepped back, angered, clutching her shopping to her chest. He looked at her with such familiarity, spoke to her as if they'd known each other all their lives. How dare he?

He read the language of her body. "Please," he said. "I'm sorry. I've said something . . ." He took two steps back. "Done something to offend you." Shaking his head, he continued, "I sure didn't mean to upset you."

His voice soothed her. She felt her shoulders relax. "It's nothing. It's fine." She remembered herself, that she was out here in the guise of Mother Jilo. It wouldn't be suitable for folk to see her crumbling before this ridiculous—no, that wasn't fair—this unusual man, this kind man. This inconvenient man. She raised her chin and pulled back her shoulders. "Mother Jilo, she gotta be getting on now." She paused, for a moment letting her act fall away. "I wish you well with your business."

She stepped around him, feeling his eyes on her shoulders, willing her back.

"You got far to go?" He came jogging up along her side. "I'm just asking, 'cause I got my truck out behind the shop. Be glad to run you home. That sack looks might heavy and all."

"Thank you," Jilo said, still moving. "Mother Jilo, she fine. She don't need your help."

"Listen," he said, reaching out for her, but pulling back before he could lay hands on her. "I'm doing this all wrong. I know I'm doing this all wrong. And I'm sorry. I don't do this all the time. Chase after women, I mean. Especially a woman who's looking at me like she just wants me to go away." He shifted from foot to foot, nervous, maybe embarrassed, too. "Do you want me to? Just go away?"

Jilo looked the poor man over. Her head said she should tell him to take off. But she hesitated, and in so doing, the moment for her to make a quick, decisive break slipped past her. Even if she told him to go away now, he'd know, deep down, just as she knew, deep down, that a part of her wanted him to stay right where he was. She held the bag out to him. "Don't think this is more than a ride home," she said as he pulled himself taller, tilting his head to the side and smiling. Jilo liked his smile. He took the bag from her. "Where's that truck of yours?"

- — -

"So what is this 'Mother Jilo' bit?" Tinker asked, casting a cautious look her way as they drove south.

"Business," Jilo said, not willing to offer more.

"Business," Tinker echoed her. "All right, I respect that," he said, his tone telling her he knew better than to push for more. His truck, an ancient Ford held together by not much more than baling wire and a good man's faith, lumbered down West Broad toward West Gaston. Jilo kept her eyes fixed forward, but in truth her peripheral vision was focused on Tinker. The truck lurched forward and jerked, coughing out—Jilo felt certain without looking back—a plume of black smoke.

"She a good truck," Tinker said, his tone wavering between pride and apology. "Took a bit to fix her up, but I picked her up for almost nothing from my friend Henry."

Jilo couldn't resist turning toward him as she made the connection between the name and the jalopy. "Henry Cook?"

.D. Horn

Tinker looked at her, then let out a surprised laugh. "Yes," he said, turning back to the road, "Henry Cook. You know him?"

" 'Course. He used to court my sister Poppy. Years ago. Back when I was little girl." She turned her focus to the storefronts they were lumbering past. "Didn't end well, I reckon. Don't know why. I was too young at the time, and well, it doesn't seem worthwhile digging up old bones to ask."

"Old Henry's married now anyway."

"So's Poppy," she said, happy to be able to say so, although she had never yet met her brother-in-law, Isaiah.

"Of course she is," Tinker said, sounding so sure of himself Jilo turned back. He was looking at her rather than the road. "She's a beautiful woman."

"You've never seen her."

"No, ma'am, I have not, but I've seen her sister." He flashed her a big smile, and Jilo was surprised to feel the blood rush to her cheeks. Though she tried to fight the impulse, she found herself returning his smile.

She forced herself to look away. She was making a fool out of herself. She should just tell him to pull over. Let her out. She could walk the rest of the way home.

"I got a bit of a confession to make," he said, interrupting her attempt to decide whether to give him the shove off now or in a location a bit closer to home. Folding her arms over her chest, she refused to look at him. She did not care to hear any revelations. "That night, after I saw you on the bus. I was supposed to go home, but I didn't. I stayed on for a week, riding that darned bus back and forth every day, just hoping you'd get back on it. I talked to everyone who'd answer me, asking if any of them recognized you from my description. But no one did. So, I went on home. Tried to get settled. Tried to forget I'd ever laid eyes on you."

He reached over and placed his hand near hers. They didn't touch, but she still felt his energy once more. She turned toward him, transfixed

255

by the slim space between them. "Oh, I know how it sounds. I sound like some crazy man." She let her gaze drift up to his face, surprised to see his eyes fixed on the road before them. "But tell me. Do you believe in love at first sight?"

"Turn here," Jilo said, pointing west as they approached West Anderson. "Then go south on Ogeechee."

He did as he was told, but remained silent, evidently waiting for a response. She wasn't sure she had a response to give, so she said nothing at first. She felt disappointment descend on him like a dark cloud. "Look," she said, her tone heated, impatient. She took a breath and began. "What I believe is that it's easy to imagine things about someone you don't know. And what I know is you don't know me."

"You're right. I don't know you. I . . ." He paused, shaking his head a little side to side. "This is not how I planned this . . ."

"Planned?"

"Well, imagined. This isn't how I meant it to happen. When I imagined getting a chance to see you. To talk to you."

"And that's the problem. You're in love with your own imagination. Life just doesn't work the way you'd like to believe," she said, her voice nearly breaking. "There's no magic in this world." She coughed to clear the frog from her throat. "I'm not some angel like you've obviously imagined me to be."

Tinker laughed, but it wasn't a happy sound. "Oh, no, ma'am. I never imagined you to be any kind of angel. Remember, I've been on the receiving end of that temper of yours."

"All the same. I've got a son. I've got family to look after."

"You say you have a son, but I don't hear anything about you having a man."

"Doesn't having a son imply there's a man in my life?" She wished the old truck would move more quickly. Still, she felt a touch of sorrow when she looked over to see that in spite of the way the beast was crawling along, Tinker had pressed the pedal all the way down. Looked like she'd nearly succeeded in pushing him away after all.

"Ah, now, we both know that ain't true." The truck jolted, then relented by putting on some speed. It sputtered and shuddered as they traveled south, giving up the ghost right where Kollock and Ogeechee intersected at the tip of the cemetery.

Tinker looked over at her, then leaned in toward her, his brow low, his eyes full of embarrassed anguish. "Just give me a second to look at her. I'll get her up and running again right quick."

Jilo shook her head and reached for the door handle, surprised to see it had been replaced with a homemade rope pulley. She tugged on it, and the door opened. "I'm almost home anyway." She climbed out of the truck, nearly jumping as a large black bantam rooster perched on the cemetery fence cried out like he was greeting the last dawn the world would ever meet.

She turned back to the truck and retrieved her shopping bag from where it had been sitting by her feet. After the brief rest, the sack felt heavier. Just like her heart did after imagining—even for a moment— that this Tinker Poole might somehow know how to fix what had been broken in her. Tinker hopped out and ran around the front of the truck. Jilo felt certain he was about to offer to come along with her on foot, shouldering her burden as his own. She clutched the sack in both arms and shook her head. "There is no magic in this world," she said again. "No magic whatsoever."

She trudged down Ogeechee, making a turn onto the gravel road that would, after a long bend, lead to her own sandy drive. As she neared that drive, she looked up, and from across the field, she could see a sleek and shiny red convertible sitting in front of her house. She knew Binah would be doing her best to entertain this new, and obviously rich, client long enough for her to make it home. She picked up her pace, hoping to arrive before he, or possibly she, lost patience and sped away in that little red number.

She was sweating profusely, her turban growing damp and limp, as she made it around the bend and approached the front of the house. From a distance, she could make out Binah offering what looked like lemonade to a young man with a complexion as pink and as fresh as bubblegum, his hair almost as red as the car he drove. A wealthy buckra boy. What on earth could a fellow like that be wanting from Mother Jilo? What else, she answered her own question, than the key to some wealthy buckra girl's heart?

As she drew a step nearer, Binah handed a glass to another man who leaned forward to accept it. Jilo stopped dead in her tracks. This man, with his dark complexion and wavy hair, she recognized instantly. "Guy," she said his name, feeling the earth beneath her feet tremble, just like the world was ready to open up and swallow her whole.

FIVE

Her feet felt like they'd been replaced with anvils, each step requiring every shred of determination she could muster. "Binah," she called out, holding the shopping out to her sister. Binah looked up, then ran down the steps and relieved her of the sack's weight.

"He doesn't know. He hasn't seen him," Binah whispered in her ear.

Jilo placed a hand on Binah's shoulder and gave her a gentle push. "Take those inside," she said, relying on Binah's momentum to set her own feet back into motion.

"There she is, the muse," the redheaded young man said, standing as she approached. Jilo had been so overwhelmed by the sight of Guy, she'd all but forgotten the white boy was there.

"Muse?" she said, incapable of either looking fully at or fully away from Guy.

"Yes," he said, drawing closer to the edge of the porch. "You must know that you're hanging, well, your image is hanging in galleries all over New York."

"Well, the better galleries, at least." Jilo froze at the sound of Guy's voice. He kept his seat in the swing, not rising as the buckra had. She raised her eyes to take him in. Hoping she would hate him, certain that she would. But oh, how she had to fight not to run right up those front steps. Struggle not to throw herself in his arms. "The last one. The large painting I was completing when . . . well, the day . . ." His voice trailed off. "It sold to a private collector. For quite a nice sum."

"Yes, but it isn't about the money . . ." the redhead began.

"Spoken like someone who's always had it," Jilo found her tongue. "For the rest of us, it's always about the money."

The young man looked at Guy, and they both burst out laughing. "You're right about this one, Guy," the young man said, surprising Jilo by how he pronounced the name to rhyme with "my" rather than "me."

"Listen," Guy said, standing and coming forward, wrapping his arm around the young fellow's broad shoulders. "Jilo, this is my friend, Edwin Taylor." He nodded toward her. "Edwin, this is my 'muse'—" He hesitated, almost like he was looking for a more precise word to describe her. "—Jilo." Guy released Edwin, then padded forward to the head of the steps and held his hand out to her. "Or as I understand it is now, 'Mother Jilo.' "

Jilo felt a wave of embarrassment wash over her.

"Yes, indeed," Edwin said. "I was surprised enough to learn the vison in Guy's paintings lived in my own hometown. Imagine my astonishment when I found she was also the rising star of Savannah's magical community."

"It's just an act. To help make ends meet." Jilo forced herself to look him in the eye. "There's no such thing as magic," she said, the well-rehearsed words shooting out like shrapnel.

Edwin, ignoring the rising bile in her tone, smiled and tilted his head to the side. "Is there not?"

"I met Edwin in the city," Guy said, coming down the steps, taking her hand in his own. The sparks she felt at his touch nearly made her question her own disavowal of sorcery. "The other night we got to talking about my art. About you."

"Of course, I'd heard of you," Edwin said, slipping back into the porch swing. "All of Savannah knows about the amazing Mother Jilo Wills."

"When we made the connection, we realized we had to see you . . . I," Guy said, tipping her chin up so her gaze met his, "had to see you." For a moment, Jilo felt the world around her fall away, leaving nothing beyond the feel of Guy's gentle touch and the glimmer in his eyes. The old feelings, the good ones, rushed up, like a wave intent on carrying her out to sea.

"So," Edwin spoke, stifling the inchoate spell that had only just begun to build. She turned to face Guy's new friend. "We hopped into my car and drove pretty much straight through. It's a long drive, but then again, I know a few shortcuts." The way he spoke that last word made Jilo feel it held a different, or maybe enhanced, meaning to him that other people didn't share. There was something odd about this boy; he struck her as being somehow strange and familiar at the same time.

"I've missed you, you know," Guy said, putting his arms around her. Pulling her close. Pushing away her concerns about the Taylor boy. "I can't get you out of my mind. I've drawn you from memory, painted you, every day. Carried on full conversations with your likeness."

Jilo felt her heart weakening, but then her mind registered the gist of his last few words. She put both hands on Guy's chest and pushed him away. "Yeah, 'cause the Jilo in your pretty pictures never talks back, does she?" A hell of a world she was living in, with one man, a stranger, imagining her as his ideal, borrowing her likeness to build his fantasy, and another, the man who'd held her heart, redacting her memory, tracing, erasing, and redrawing the lines until nothing was left of the real her. "Those weren't conversations, Guy. You weren't talking to me. You were masturbating." She pushed around him and mounted the steps to the porch.

"When do you plan on telling me about that baby I heard crying in there?" Guy called after her, causing Jilo to spin on her heel to face him. "The one Binah and whoever the hell else that is in your house are hiding." He drew near the porch, resting one foot on the steps, and leaned in toward her. "Is it yours?" he asked, watching her. She folded her arms over her chest, trying to look calm, unaffected. She held her tongue. "More importantly," he said, shifting his weight and mounting the steps to stand before her, "is it mine?"

She tilted her head back, defiant, as if that might stop the tears brimming in her eyes from falling. "I don't know," she said. "Is he yours? Have you fed him? Have you clothed him? Made sure he had a roof over his head? Or did you just skedaddle off to the big city so you could play the big man?"

"Perhaps I should be going," the redhead said.

"Yes, Mr. Taylor," Jilo said, each syllable coming out barbed, "perhaps you should. And perhaps"—she nodded toward Guy—"you should take this one with you. Get him out of here before he gets pressed into anything so conventional as raising his own child."

"That isn't fair. You never told me. You didn't give me a chance. I didn't know." He stood before her, his shoulders slumped, his hands extended palm up toward her, the look on his face wounded enough to convince anyone else in the world that he had been the injured party.

His words made her face flush. For a moment she stood there stammering, unable to find the right words to answer his complaint, but then the right words finally came.

"Bullshit," she said, two years of anger and fear and hurt pride, yes, pride, boiled up, boiled over. "Bullshit," she said again, backing away from him, till her backside bumped up against the house's siding, sure that if she didn't put some distance between them, she would slap the pained, innocent look right off his face. "You saw me, Guy, you saw me. You saw me grow, swell, and fatten as you painted your damned picture. You saw me sick in the morning. Sick at night. You saw me. You just didn't want to see me. You didn't want to know. You wanted New York, and you weren't going to let anything get in your way."

"That isn't quite true." His face flushed. He puffed up. Stretching to his full height, he leaned in over her, reminding Jilo of her own slight size, her own vulnerability. He reached out both arms and pinned her to the wall. The anger she felt shifted to fear. He seemed to realize he was frightening her, and when he spoke again, it was in a softer tone. "Maybe you're right. Maybe I should've seen." He stepped back, lowering his arms to his sides. "Hell, maybe a part of me did see. But still. You should've contacted me. At least to tell me the child had been born."

"Contact you?" Jilo felt the fire inside her rekindle. "How the hell was I supposed to do that? Write you general delivery?"

"It's a boy, isn't it? I have a son?" he said, ignoring her frustrated jibe, and glanced over at the Taylor fellow like he intended to start handing out cigars.

Jilo saw his vanity shine through. He would never see their child as anything more than an extension of himself. A boy to carry on his name. Ensure his immortality. She hated herself for loving this man. Yes, even now. Even in this light, she still loved him. But her feelings for the father came second to her love for her son. "Yes, Guy, *my* child," she said, pausing to make sure he registered her claim, "is a boy. His name is Robinson. Robinson Wills."

Guy pulled back his shoulders and tossed out a laugh, one intended to save face in front of his rich buckra buddy. "But he can't be a Wills. He's my boy. He's a Collier," he pronounced the name like they would in New Orleans, bringing it out through his nose, the final "R" sound getting lost somewhere in the process.

"He," Jilo spat out the word, "was born a Wills. He will live as a Wills. And in the long and distant future, Wills is the name they are going to chip into his tombstone."

"Jilo," Guy said, his shoulders slumping as he shook his head. "I'm the boy's father. You have to let me be a father to him."

"You haven't been here."

He took a step toward her. She held up her hand and pointed at him. "You have not," she wagged her finger with each word, "been here." Her face felt hot. Her hand felt cold. Her body trembled.

He took another step closer and reached out to grasp her hand. Gently bending the accusing finger toward her palm, he raised her hand to his lips and kissed it. "I am here now," he said. She tried to pull away, but her back was still against the wall. "I am"—the words came out slow, measured—"here now." He leaned in and pulled her into his arms. "And I'm not leaving again."

SIX

"Really, Guy," Jilo said as she joined him in the front room, "it's close enough to walk from here. No need for your fancy friends to drive us." Edwin Taylor had pretty much become a fixture around her home ever since Guy had moved in with her. Jilo didn't much cotton to the idea of having to make nice with Edwin's sister Ginny now, too.

Guy sat in the haint-blue chair that had once again made its way from the haint-blue room into the main room. Guy felt it was the most comfortable seat in the house, so the day after moving in, he had dragged it to its current position and claimed it as his own. He waved his hand, making a signal to stand clear of his fan, but Jilo didn't budge. "It's hot out there, woman," Guy said, his voice languid and nearly drowned out by the drone of the oscillating fan positioned so that its sweep would cover him with each pivot. "In case you didn't notice. Besides, it isn't about the getting there, it's about the impression we'll make arriving."

Jilo grunted. Guy had been going on for weeks about that Taylor girl's shiny new Continental Mark II. "There is nobody at the Boxcar Club I need to impress."

"And it isn't about us making a good impression, either. It's about the Taylors, the impression Edwin and his sister want to make when they pull up with us riding in the backseat. We are their entrée into what for them is an exotic world . . . the Negro nightclub. Now scoot." He waved again, and she obliged him by stepping aside. As the full breeze hit him, he stretched out his legs, leaning back and laying his head against the ancient tatted doily her nana had always cherished. She hoped his hair oil wouldn't stain it, but held her tongue. It wasn't worth the fight that would ensue. "The Taylors, they're important people," he continued. "Especially around these parts." Guy spoke to her like she hadn't grown up in Savannah, as if she could have possibly escaped knowledge of one of the wealthiest buckra families in her own hometown. Guy was right that they were an important family. What he didn't know was that the gossip shared by maids who worked in Savannah's finer homes made it clear that, though wealthy, the Taylors were always kept at arm's length by Savannah's other leading families. Everyone, regardless of their position in society, agreed that there was just something not quite right about the family. Perhaps if Guy's infatuation with their wealth ever faded, he'd begin to sense it, too.

She stepped between Guy and the fan again, surprised by the sensation of the breeze blowing up against the trickle of cold sweat tracing its way down her spine. Now that the breeze of the fan couldn't carry away his scent, she could smell the alcohol on him. She stared down at him, trying to see even a glimmer of the man she'd fallen in love with. When they first met, hell, even when he was making his plans to leave her, he'd been so filled with drive, with passion for his work. That passion seemed to have dissipated the second he began spending time with Edwin Taylor.

Guy had made a big show of bringing home fresh canvasses. And he must have spent a small fortune on fresh oils. But so far he hadn't made a single brushstroke. No, he spent most of his days sprawled out right here, in front of the fan, lulled into a near torpor by its incessant drone and the Taylors' cast-off bourbon. He rose at dusk, the sound of Edwin's approaching convertible his reveille, and then the two would be off until the small hours. Some nights, Guy would return, all sweat and spirits, and clamber on top of her; other nights, he would pass out at her side.

Until his nightly return, Jilo would lie alone in the haint-blue room that she'd once again taken over as her, *their*, bedroom. Robinson continued to share a room with Binah. At first Willy had carried on sleeping on a cot in the front room, but lately he'd taken to staying in the back yard in an army surplus tent. He'd be okay out there for now, but she had to get things sorted out before winter.

She wore no ring on her finger; Guy was beyond such "bourgeois" conventions, and took every opportunity he could find, especially when Edwin was in earshot, to pontificate against society's small minds. Still, these two freethinkers had driven Willy from the house, mocking him for his effeminate gestures and the way he carried himself. They insulted him with cruel names, half of which Jilo had never heard before, though "catamite" was the one that seemed to bring them the most mirth, eliciting peals of raucous laughter. Edwin got himself so liquored up one night that he grabbed Willy, spun him around in a rough dance, and forced a contemptuous kiss on the boy's lips.

That night, there had been no choice but to intervene. Jilo had pulled the bruised and frightened Willy from Edwin's grasp, and then, to her astonishment, Binah had dived forward and slapped the white man's face, leaving a dark red mark on his rosy cheek. Jilo had expected trouble after that, but Edwin just flushed red and stumbled out the door. When she turned around to look for Guy, he was already passed out in her nana's old chair.

"How could a woman fall in love with such a man?" Binah asked from behind her.

She couldn't bring herself to turn to face her sister. "I saw a spark in him . . . once." *At least I thought I did*, she said to herself. "And he is Robinson's father. A boy needs his father." She allowed herself a quick glance over her shoulder. Binah had a lost, faraway look on her face; her gaze was cast downward, and she was biting her lower lip. "Go on," Jilo said. "Go see to Willy."

Edwin had returned the very next night, and whether it was true or merely pretense, he seemed to have no memory of his actions the previous evening. A part of Jilo wanted to take him to task for his behavior, but she suspected that it would do no good. A man like that always sees himself as the hero. He'd find some way or other to excuse himself, and without a doubt, Guy would take his drinking buddy's side. She had to get these Taylors out of their lives. They were a bad, disruptive influence. With Edwin out of the picture, Jilo would find a way to get Guy working. A way to get Willy back into his own house.

Jilo felt goose bumps crawl up her arm. "I don't know, Guy," she said, crossing her arms and trying to rub the gooseflesh away. "I know you like this Taylor fellow, but there is something off about him. I can't put my finger on it, but I feel uneasy around him. And I'm not the only one. Ask anyone about the Taylors, and they'll tell you there's something odd . . ."

"And just who have you been asking about the Taylors?" Guy slid to the edge of the chair, suddenly alert. "Edwin. He's my friend. How's he going to feel if he finds out you been out shopping for gossip about his family?"

"I haven't been gossiping. And I haven't been asking anyone about the Taylors either. Not really. I've just been listening, whenever their name comes up. And their name comes up in casual conversation a whole lot more than any honest family's name ought to." Guy gave her a hard, long look before dropping his gaze down to the side, turning his head and lowering his chin, telling her without saying a word that he wasn't interested in what she had to tell him. "People talk about the Taylors all the time. Most of it isn't pretty."

"Enough." He met her gaze again, a hard look in his eyes. "They're my friends. I can't believe your lack of gratitude."

"Gratitude?"

"If not for Edwin," Guy said, slipping back into a more relaxed position, "we'd still be apart. It's almost like he was sent to New York to bring us back together." And there it was, the source of the uneasy feeling that had been lurking in her subconscious mind. *Could their meeting have been arranged?* The question had nearly risen up above the waters many times, only to be submerged anew as her conscious mind objected that the thought was utterly ridiculous. "It's like it was fate. Meant to be."

What if Guy and Edwin had never met?

"The least you could do is show him a little kindness. Unless Mother Jilo," he said her working name in a contemptuous tone, "is above such niceties."

"You've been drinking," she said. Her words came out sounding like an accusation, though she'd intended them as an excuse for his harshness. "Quite a bit, by the smell of you."

"And the night is young," he said, leaning his head back and closing his eyes. "I got a lot more drinking to do. Now go get yourself prettied up, girl. Got a big surprise coming for you."

- — -

"Bourbon. Ice," Ginny called over her shoulder to her brother, two years her junior, according to Ginny. Then she turned back to Jilo, leaning in so that she would be heard over the music. "So nice to let the men fetch for us for a change, isn't it?"

Jilo smiled, but didn't respond verbally. She doubted this Taylor girl with her blonde brushed-under pageboy and soft hands ever did much of her own fetching anyway.

Jilo felt embarrassed by her own appearance. Her hair was a bit of a mess. She'd been wearing it covered in her Mother Jilo guise for so long now she'd stopped paying much attention to it. Binah had been encouraging her to try some of the new hair relaxers, but until Guy's return, she hadn't cared to put much thought into her appearance. After Guy's return, she'd been faced with much bigger problems. Earlier, as she was dressing before her mirror, she had considered commandeering the wig Willy kept hidden in his small steamer trunk of belongings, but the day was too hot and sticky for a wig. She reached up, without realizing what she was doing, and patted the back of her head, like her subconscious mind felt a simple pat or two could fix the frizz.

"Your hair is lovely," Ginny said, picking up on the gesture, if not her very thoughts. "So untamed and earthy. You blacks are just so much more in touch with nature than we whites are." Jilo wondered for a moment if this coiffed and pampered young woman could be serious. The thought brought an actual smile to Jilo's lips. Yes, she realized in flabbergasted amusement, the girl truly believed she had just paid Jilo a compliment.

Jilo felt her mouth gearing up, readying itself to tell this cotton-candy-pink confection of a woman just what she thought of her praise, but then she noticed Guy and Edwin pressing through the crowd, drawing near the table. Guy had two whole bottles of bourbon in his hands. Jilo prayed that Guy had swallowed his pride and allowed the young man with the deep pockets to pay for the liquor. Edwin followed on Guy's heels, carrying a tray over his head like one of the fancy waiters Jilo had seen in the movies. On the tray sat an ice bucket and glasses.

"Your dress is beautiful," Jilo said, offering a compliment of her own rather than the barb she'd nearly launched. What she said was true, if not entirely heartfelt. Jilo had made her best effort, managing to squeeze into one of her old Kingfisher Club favorites, a pale yellow, hammered-satin peg-top dress that, in spite of having been aired outside all day, still held a faint scent of naphthalene. She had no doubt that this was the first time Ginny's dress had been worn. Its boatneck cut was demure, but it was sleeveless, so it displayed the young woman's athletic yet feminine arms to their best advantage. The fabric was a pale blue satin with a pattern in a soft gold of what appeared to be leaves and vines looped through other less familiar shapes.

"Balenciaga," Ginny said as if the word should hold some meaning for Jilo. She shifted as Edwin leaned over to place the tray on the table. "Father says it's a shame to waste such a pretty dress on such a plain girl." She reached over to grab one of the glasses. "But I say fuck him."

Jilo's mouth fell wide open, incapable of believing such language could come from such a pretty, young society lady.

Edwin laughed and clanked a still-empty glass against his sister's equally empty tumbler. "Fuck the old man," he called out, as if it were a toast. "C'mon, Guy." He grabbed two cubes of ice from the bucket, using his fingers rather than the tongs provided for that purpose. "Get to pouring."

"I'm sorry," Ginny said looking at Jilo, shoving her own glass toward Guy. "I know with all the real problems in this world, such slights shouldn't matter . . ."

"But you are a very pretty woman," Jilo said, surprised to feel any level of sympathy for this debutante.

"And I thank you for saying that," Ginny said, grasping her now-full tumbler and taking a good swig. "It's only Father prefers a more delicate type, like our mother. When Father is feeling generous, he refers to me as 'handsome.' "

"Poor mother," Edwin said, rolling his eyes, then knocking back his tumbler of whiskey as if it had only contained a shot rather than three fingers. He didn't offer any further context for his comment.

"Yes, poor mother," she said, her tone so dispirited that Jilo nearly began to feel sympathy for the line of Taylor women in general. Ginny took another drink, her voice rising, sounding more gay. "I keep telling Father that if he wants to savor a delicate beauty, he need look no further than his son Edwin here." She threw her head back, laughing.

"Hey-oh," Edwin said, patting his hand on the table, either protesting her comment or urging Guy to refill his glass. Jilo remained uncertain of which. Edwin turned toward her. "The old man would positively blow a gasket if he knew we were here." He turned and flashed a gleeful look at his sister. "Couldn't you just see the old boy?"

"What, he doesn't approve of dancing?" Jilo said, the words powering their way out before she could throw the brake on her tongue. She felt the tip of Guy's shoe tap roughly against her calf. His lips were puckered, and a line ran down the center of his forehead.

"Well, no, he's quite fond of dancing . . ." Edwin began, his voice trailing off as he recognized the sarcasm in her voice. "Jilo, you have to understand, my father, he thinks along the old lines." He leaned back and waved his hand back and forth between Ginny and himself. "We certainly don't share his opinions."

"Of course not," Ginny said, relaxing into her chair.

"You wouldn't be here," Guy said, raising his own full glass in salute, "if you did, now would you?" He clinked glasses with Edwin, then knocked back a gulp. Even in the low light, Jilo could see that his eyes had already gone glassy with drink. Without a doubt, Guy and the Taylor boy had sampled a few shots before choosing the bottles they had brought back to the table with them.

"No . . . we . . . would . . . not," Edwin shouted over the swelling music, each word coming out as if it were its own separate and complete thought. He flashed a drunken smile at Jilo, looking for all the world like an imbecile rather than the scion of Savannah's wealthiest family. While trying to make small talk, Jilo had once asked the boy about the nature of his family's business. He'd only mumbled about being involved in a bit of this and a bit of that before deflecting the topic entirely. "I'd so much rather talk about your family's business," he'd said. "Imagine, a line of witches, going back how many generations now?" Jilo had told the fool boy till she was blue in the face that there was no real magic to it, but he kept worrying the subject like he believed there might truly be something to it, turning it over again and again like a dog gnawing the meat from a shank bone.

"We have to find a way," Ginny said, leaning forward, running her right hand over her left shoulder and then down her left arm, "to begin to welcome you all into the white world, just as easily as you have accepted Edwin and me into yours." She motioned around the club, evidently feeling they'd been welcomed with open arms, oblivious to the uneasy stares and nervous whispers Jilo'd witnessed all evening. "Anyone with half a brain can see that Jim Crow is an abomination. Even if separate but equal were truly equal, it would still be wrong. The racial minorities must be integrated into the white world."

"To making room in the white world," Edwin said, raising his glass.

Jilo felt torn by Ginny's seemingly sincere words and her brother's obvious enthusiasm. Part of her felt that she should be glad these young, wealthy buckra seemed to want the same damned thing she wanted—a legal and enforceable acknowledgement of the equality of every human being, regardless of their color. Still, something was missing. "Thank you kindly for the sentiment," Jilo said, "but I do wish you'd realize the world isn't white. You might be in the majority here, but if you take into account the racial makeup of most of the world, whites are the minority."

Edwin's face froze, a look of annoyance rising to his eyes, and Ginny startled. The white woman's gaze lost its focus for a moment, and she seemed to be partaking in an inner dialogue. Guy's hand darted out, pulling hers beneath the table and giving it a hard squeeze, with the full intention of hurting her. She tugged it free, feeling a fire explode in her. *Oh, hell no.* Drunk or not, she thought, he was not going to start that kind of nonsense with her. She was just about to tell him so when Ginny interrupted her thoughts.

"You're right," Ginny said, holding her glass up to Jilo, smiling and shaking her head. "You are right. I've got to start looking at things through different eyes. I try to reach out. I try to do right in this world. But I sometimes get trapped within my own tiny perspective." She lowered her glass to the table, and reached out to lay her hand over Jilo's. "If

I can count on friends like you to call me out on it when I do"—a wry smile formed on her lips—"I might grow into a woman of substance rather than a mere confection." Jilo was so shocked by her choice of words, one that seemed to have been gleaned from her own thoughts, she tried to pull back her hand, but she found herself incapable of doing so. The look in Ginny's eyes spoke to her of an honest and loving, if clumsy, soul. "I do hope someday you might think of me as a friend."

Jilo surprised herself by laying her free hand on top of Ginny's. "I think we might just be friends at that," she said.

"Ah, it's time, Guy," Edwin said.

"Time for what?" Jilo said, a sense of caution overriding any feeling of new warmth. That these two men were in cahoots over anything left her feeling anxious. Both were already pushing back from the table, clearly not intending to answer her.

"To prepare for your surprise," Guy said, adding, "not that you've earned it the way you've been speaking to our guests."

"Don't be ridiculous, Guy," Ginny said.

"Wait," Jilo called out as the men stepped away. "What's the surprise?"

"Aha," Edwin said, wagging a finger at her. "You just hold on and you're gonna see."

"And hear," Guy added, clasping his arm around Edwin's shoulders and leading him over to the bandstand.

Jilo turned a worried glance to Ginny, who just smiled and shrugged. "I haven't a clue." She turned in her seat to keep an eye on the men.

The lights dimmed, plunging the room into utter darkness for a few moments. The band began to play as the lights came back up, and a bright spotlight shone down on the girl singer who had taken her place by the conductor, setting fire to the royal-blue sequin gown she wore. The men in the room went wild at the sight of the exotic beauty. *No.* Jilo stood and took a few shaky steps toward the bandstand. The singer turned to face the audience, her warm auburn hair newly coiffed to better frame her lovely face. *It can't be.* The band began to play, but the catcalls threatened to drown them out. The conductor stopped the music, signaling for the hecklers to quiet themselves. Once they'd settled down, he turned back to the band. Jilo recognized the tune, "I've Got It Bad, and That Ain't Good." She felt her heart fall to the pit of her stomach. Standing there, in a low-cut flashy grown-woman evening gown, offering up her own sweet voice to the swine in this room, was Jilo's own little Binah.

Ginny came and stood beside her, taking her hand. The moment they touched, a shriek of feedback on the mic caused many in the audience to throw their hands over their ears. Jilo pulled free of Ginny's hold. She pushed her way through the crowd that had gathered around the stage, shrugging off Guy's grasp as she passed, stopping Edwin's advance with a single look. Sparks shot throughout the room as the overhead spotlight exploded. Shouts and shocked cries filled the space. The conductor turned. "Just an electrical surge, everyone. Nothing to get excited about."

Paying no attention to anyone, Jilo mounted the steps to the bandstand and laid her hands on her sister's shoulders. "No," she said, sliding her hands down to catch hold of Binah's, "this is not the life for you." Binah tried to pull back, her pleading eyes not focused on Jilo, but—Jilo felt her blood go cold as she followed Binah's gaze—on the Taylor boy. Binah opened her mouth to protest, but Jilo dragged the girl down the steps and out of the club.

- — -

When a car pulled up to the house, Jilo was almost relieved to hear something other than the sound of Binah's weeping and Robinson's howls, which had begun the second Binah slammed into the house. Jilo had never seen her act that way before. It broke her heart to think her little sister, like Guy, had fallen under the Taylors' sway.

Jilo had sent Willy and Robinson to her room. There was no way Guy was going to be sleeping in there tonight anyway.

She made her way to the window, tugging the curtain just far enough to the side to peek out. It was the Taylor girl's black Mark II rather than her brother's flashy red Corvette. Letting the curtain fall back into place, she waited for Guy to come bursting through the door. Well fine. They would have it out tonight. She could put up with a lot, but the sight of her sweet baby sister dressed and painted up like a whore, this she would not, could not bear. Guy was too lazy. Too self-centered to come up with such a scheme. No, it had to be that Taylor boy who'd tempted Binah with music and sparkle, a weakness for which she'd inherited from their mama. Binah was a good girl. She did not belong with these dirty musicians. Dressed up like that, they wouldn't see her as a girl. They'd see her as woman. And they'd get ideas.

Jilo stood directly before the door, her stance wide and her hands on her hips. She was surprised by a light knock on the door. Then another. She crossed to the door and cracked it open. She hadn't thought to turn on the porch light earlier, so her visitor stood in shadows, only a thin bar of light landing on her. Ginny stood there alone. Jilo opened the door wide.

"I know what you're thinking. I do," Ginny said, "but I don't plan on forcing my way in, and I'm not here to convince you you've overreacted." It surprised Jilo to realize that these were her actual thoughts, though they hadn't yet surfaced in her conscious mind. "But I'm here to do neither." Her voice dropped. "I've come to warn you."

"Warn me about what?"

Ginny lowered her eyes, looking ashamed. "About my brother, for one thing. He's my brother, and I love him." Her gaze rose back to meet Jilo's. "I hope he will grow into a good man, but he isn't quite that man yet." She reached through the door and took Jilo's hand. "Your sister, she's lovely. She has a light that shines from within. She's precious, and you need to protect her from . . ."

"From your brother," Jilo said, and Ginny nodded.

"Edwin, he's fascinated by her. Infatuated with her. He won't intend to, but he will take her and destroy the light that's in her. You can't let him."

Jilo grasped Ginny's hand tighter. "Can't you do anything to discourage him?"

Ginny shook her head. "Not my brother. Once he's set his heart on possessing . . ." She paused. "And yes, it shames me, but that is the right word, he won't give up. What I can do is try to find someone shinier, someone less innocent, to draw away his attention. But it's up to you to show your sister that a man like Edwin is not the man for her. That's not the only reason I'm here, though. Your sister, she isn't my main concern. You are."

Jilo shook her head. "I don't understand."

"Don't you?" Ginny said, looking her up and down. "I felt you draw on my power."

"What are you talking about?"

"I felt you access my magic."

"Your magic . . . ?" Jilo said, flabbergasted. A wave of panic washed over her as a memory began to surface. The sight of Poppy, hunched over, her eyes red as hell's most precious rubies, murderous. Jilo herself rising. Lifting off the ground. She pressed her hands to her temples, refusing to let the memory claim its rightful place in her personal history. "You've had too much to drink. You need to get on home now." She moved to shut the door, but Ginny held up her hand. Visible ripples, like heat coming from hot asphalt, shimmered off it. The woman didn't lay a finger on the door, but it felt like a strong man was pushing it open. Jilo slid back into the room as the weight of the door pressed into her.

"Stealing magic comes with a price," Ginny said. "I don't know how you managed it." She stopped, seeming to search Jilo's eyes. It was the oddest sensation she'd ever experienced, but for a moment, Jilo felt something akin to a tickle inside her mind. She shook her head, trying to put an end to the prickling. "Maybe you don't either," Ginny said, "but somehow you did, and it's a dangerous game to be playing."

"I'm not playing any games." Jilo's unease flared into anger.

"No, perhaps you aren't, but we need to examine what happened tonight. If the wrong people learn of your abilities, if they learn this 'Mother Jilo' character you've created has real juice behind her, you'll find yourself in over your head in no time."

"I want you to leave." Jilo put all her weight into the door, but it still wouldn't budge.

"Of course," Ginny said. Jilo was surprised to recognize a look of hurt in her eyes. "I'm sorry. Perhaps I've handled this badly. I was just so taken aback." She lowered her hand. "I do still hope we can be friends."

Jilo laughed. "I don't see how that can possibly happen." She slammed the door shut, the bang reverberating through the house. In her room, Robinson began to wail.

SEVEN

November 16, 1957

My dearest Jilo,

By the time you read this, Edwin and I will be gone. I wish I could have found the courage to speak my heart to you face-to-face, but I was afraid you'd try to stop us. I love him more than I could have ever believed possible. And he loves me, too. He swears his feelings are even stronger, but I cannot conceive how any heart could be fuller than my own.

Edwin isn't the man you think he is. He really isn't. He regrets how he treated Willy. And he regrets that he ever came between you and Guy even more. He hopes that without his being a distraction, Guy will get back to painting. Please tell Willy that Edwin is sorry for everything.

Edwin says that in Paris it will be possible for us to marry. To live as man and wife. That's what he wants of me, to be his wife, and I can't imagine living life without him.

Of course, Edwin's parents would never approve of our marriage. He's turning his back on them so that we can be together. I know, my sweet sister, that you, too, will not approve, at least not at first, not because you feel it is wrong for us to be together, but because you fear I might be hurt. I hope seeing how far Edwin is willing to go to make me his wife will convince you that he will never, ever hurt me. I hope that you will someday see that Edwin and I were meant to be united as husband and wife, and grant us your blessing.

I will write again, once we are settled, and let you know how to reach me, should you wish to write. I do hope you will, and that you know how much I love and will miss you.

Your sister,
Binah

January 8, 1958

My sweet Binah,

I received your letter from Paris this morning. I have read your words now several times over, and have done my best to understand what you have done.

Know that I, too, love you. I hate that you're so far away, that I can no longer see your beautiful, shining face each morning. It pains me deeply that you felt you had no choice but to leave home without saying good-bye. I would have so dearly loved to hold you once more, to wish you well. But maybe you were right after all. If you had given me that chance, I might never have let you go.

Edwin is not the man I would have chosen for you, but then again, we both know I'm not that skilled when it comes to picking men. We Wills girls always listen to our hearts. I hope yours has served you better than mine appears to have done me. Still, we have made the choices we needed to make, and with those choices we must live.

If Edwin brings you happiness, if he watches over you and cherishes you the way you deserve to be cherished, then I give my blessing and my love to both of you.

Just imagine, my baby sister in Paris! Yes, my Binah is in Paris, but you'll always be in my heart. Please write often, and share your life there with me.

With all my love,
Your Jilo

EIGHT

April 1958

Jilo had hoped she could help Guy get back on an even keel, once he was out from under Edwin's influence, but the opposite had proven true. Edwin's departure had signaled Guy's collapse. Guy took to bed for days after Edwin and Binah ran off together, just lying there as still as the dead, refusing to speak, facing the wall, like he'd lost his life, a limb, or a love. It was a relief when he rose and returned to drinking. At least for a few days, it was.

Now he sat in her nana's old chair, his "throne," he'd come to call it. Red-eyed and simmering, the king was waiting for any excuse, any perceived slight to use as an excuse for another bender. Only two days ago, he'd come back from one that had begun three days before that. He'd stumbled in stinking of whiskey and another woman. Ignoring both scents, Jilo had covered him with a light blanket and left him to sleep himself sober.

Watching now from the corner of her eye, she wondered again, "What is wrong with me?" She loved this man. Loved him. Shouldn't a good woman's devotion be enough? Still she couldn't manage to pull him out of the ditch where he seemed determined to lie. Maybe she wasn't good enough. Maybe she wasn't woman enough. Because she sure seemed to lack the ability to help Guy become a better man.

The sofa stuck out farther into the room than in the past; the canvasses Guy had purchased when he first came around remained propped up behind it, blank. The tubes of oil paint remained unopened, buried at the back of their tiny shared closet, in an old tackle box he'd adapted to hold them. "Maybe later, you could set up your easel, paint me like you used to do back in Atlanta," she said, thinking that her participation might again inspire him. *Or New York*, she thought, fearing that only in some state of perfected absentia could she still act as his muse. Perhaps not even then.

"No," Guy said, kicking out his feet, reclining deeper into the chair. "I'm not up for it right now. I'm having a dry spell. Just need to rest a bit. Need to recharge. Besides, the light's all wrong in here." The light was plenty clear for her to see the truth. He didn't need any more rest. And he sure didn't need any more drink. A day or two of honest work would be plenty to put an end to this dry spell of his.

She sat on the sofa, placing her hands on her lap, preparing herself to walk through a minefield. "You know, I heard they're hiring over at that new hotel they built where the Pinnacle burned down."

"Naw, I don't want you leaving Robinson with that . . ."

"No," she stopped him before he could insult poor Willy once more. "I didn't mean me, Guy. I was just thinking that it might do you good to get out of the house a bit until you feel up to painting again. Have something to occupy your time . . ."

He pressed his fingers against his temples, and looked at her through slitted eyes, his jaw jutting forward into a snarl. "Nothing would make you happier, now would it? You'd love to see me out there, nothing but a common laborer. You don't understand my work," he said, laying the needle back on a record he'd played a thousand times. "You've never appreciated my work."

"That's not true," she began to protest. But just then Robinson came tearing into the room, all dressed up in his new Easter outfit.

"What the hell is all this then?" Guy said, dropping his hands from his temples and gawking at their son. "Where'd you find the money for that getup?"

Same place I find all the money around here. Mother Jilo, she earned it, Jilo thought, then pushed the notion away before it had time to register on her face, where Guy might see it lurking deep in her eyes.

"You come here and let Mama get a good look at you." Jilo knelt before Robinson, placing her hands on his tiny shoulders. He looked for all the world like a little man, dressed up as he was in his new black suit and red tie. "You are the handsomest young man your mama has ever laid eyes on, you know that?" Robinson nodded yes, and Jilo laughed and tugged him into a tight embrace.

"Why do you got him dressed up like that?"

"It's Easter." The words came out almost like a defense, or maybe even an apology.

"You taking him to church?" His expression changed in an instant, and the look on his face was wide-eyed and smirking now, as if he would've been less surprised to hear she was planning to send Robinson to the moon. "Mother Jilo, she don't go to no church," he said, mimicking her in her professional guise, "won't do to have them good Christian folk see Mother here poking around. Might scare them near to death." He tilted his head to the side, dropping his imitation, and continued, "Or maybe Mother Jilo's the one who's afraid. Afraid the church is gonna fall on her if she tries to step in."

Jilo knew he was only joking, but his words still made her cringe; there was a patina of truth to them. Before the Taylors, before she'd learned that magic might be real, it had all felt like playacting. A bit deceitful perhaps, but not dirty, not damning. She had come to know she'd been wrong about magic. She had to wonder if she could be wrong about other things as well. "More like sending him," she said, "but yes. Willy's going to take him into town."

"Well, I don't know how I feel about that. I don't like having that pansy hanging around here, and I sure don't like my boy spending time with him. Not one little bit," Guy said, then, "Get over here, boy. Let me see what your mama has put you in."

Robinson hesitated, but Jilo gave him a gentle nudge. "Go on, let Daddy see how nice you look." She tried to sound confident. Reassuring. "They aren't going alone," she said, this time addressing Guy. "Mr. Poole, that nice fellow from the new church over on West Broad, he's coming to pick them up. Any moment now."

"That fool Tinker?" Guy asked, never taking his eyes off Robinson.

"He's a good man, Guy," Jilo said, an odd flutter in her heart as the truth of what she said hit her. Everybody around knew they weren't churchgoing people, but two weeks back Tinker had sent one of his employees by with a note for her, asking if she'd agree to let him take her boys to services for the holiday. She couldn't find the heart to turn him down. "He's no fool. Just kind." Jilo stood and smoothed down her dress, trying to make the movement seem natural, unhurried, but still wanting to be ready to put herself between Guy and their son if need be. It only amounted to horseplay, what she'd witnessed so far, but Guy had started getting a little too rough with Robinson. Guy said it'd toughen the boy up, but Jilo had drawn a line, and she, by God, was going to see to it that Guy stayed on the safe side of it.

Guy leaned forward, turning Robinson in a circle, then flopped back against the chair. "Done been Easter three times since he was born. You've never worried about getting him religion before. At least not since I've been around."

"This is the first year he's old enough to understand. To remember." Jilo stepped forward and took Robinson's hand, pulling them both beyond striking distance. "I just want him to learn a bit of what's decent," she said. *He's seen enough of our kind of living.* These last words went unspoken.

Robinson began tugging on her hand, trying to get her attention. When she looked down, he held up his arms to her. "Naw, baby, you're getting too big for Mama to carry around." He wasn't. Not yet. Not really. But that's what Guy had decided. He didn't want her coddling Robinson. Turning him soft. "And I don't want to wrinkle your nice suit."

She looked out the door at Willy, dressed very much the same as Robinson, hovering near the end of the hall, doing his best to remain out of Guy's line of sight. The older boy looked handsome, too, but it seemed odd to see him done up in a coat and tie. Like he was some kind of actor in costume, preparing to play a role for which he was ill-suited. With a nod, she signaled Willy to turn back and head to the kitchen. She looked at Guy. "I'm going to take him to the kitchen for a glass of milk before Mr. Poole arrives for the boys." Guy didn't seem to care. He didn't respond. He just closed his eyes and leaned his head back against the chair.

Robinson began jabbering about one thing or another, so she led him quickly down the hall before he managed to irritate his father. The second they were far enough for Guy not to witness the act, she swept her boy into her arms.

"You're gonna be a good boy today for Uncle Tinker aren't you?" she asked.

Robinson clasped his hands together and nodded, a big smile on his face. "I like Tinker." Jilo knew Tinker was in the habit of treating the boys to candy or ice cream whenever he saw them together on West Broad Street, a habit that encouraged Willy to walk Robinson by Tinker's business more often than he otherwise would.

A part of her felt she should set a clear boundary with Tinker, but she wanted both boys to see that there were kind, decent men out there. For Robinson to emulate, and Willy, well, she was beyond lying to herself anymore about that one, for Willy to love. She didn't want either of them to leave her home thinking all men were like the ones she'd brought into their lives. Besides, treats had grown scarce around here now that she was supporting Guy's habits—and those of his friends—with Mother Jilo's earnings. And all this without a proper place to meet folk, now that she could no longer welcome them into the privacy of the haint-blue room. Deciding it was better to keep work and family apart, she'd followed in her nana's footsteps, meeting folk in Colonial Cemetery rather than at home. She'd begun to understand what would have led her nana to setting up shop there toward the end of her life. She got fewer clients than she did before, but those willing to meet right where God and all the world could see tended also to be willing to pay a heck of a lot more for her services.

Yes, Mother Jilo earned plenty for the family. Plenty more than they should've needed. But Guy drank away a lot of it. And he spent a lot of it "entertaining." She wondered how much of Mother Jilo's hard-earned cash went up Guy's nose, or into some whore's veins.

"I like Tinker," her boy repeated himself when she didn't respond. Robinson was getting to be old enough that they could hold real conversations. Jilo felt proud to see him growing, but it worried her that he'd be able to pick up on the sharp words that passed between his father's lips.

"I like him, too," she said, whisking him into the kitchen. "But you need to show respect to your elders. You should call him Mr. Poole."

"And that goes for you, too," she said to Willy as she entered the kitchen.

Willy stood leaning against the counter, his neck craned toward the window, searching, Jilo surmised, for the first sign of Tinker's arrival. "But," Willy said, "he told us we should call him Tinker."

"Mr. Poole is a kind and generous man. He may have said to call him Tinker, but I don't care. You call him Mr. Poole."

She pulled out a chair from the table and deposited Robinson into it. She took the pitcher of milk from the refrigerator and crossed to the cupboard to find a glass. "You want some?" she asked Willy, but he didn't answer, even though she could feel the weight of his eyes on her. She turned back to see his lips all puckered tight like he'd tasted something sour. "And just what's wrong with you? We made a deal, you wear that suit to church today, and I'll . . ."

"How come you do it?" he said, his voice coming out hushed, his eyes darting toward the hallway.

"How come I do what?" She made her way to the table and began filling the single glass for her son.

"How come you let that man stay on here?" Willy's words caused her to stop cold and set the pitcher down. "How come you let him treat us like he does?" His voice grew louder, almost like his courage was growing with each word spoken. "You ain't stupid. You must know by now you can't change him." She raised her hands, a signal for Willy to keep quiet lest Guy overhear what he was saying, but the boy wouldn't be hushed. "I don't care if he hears me," Willy said, standing tall. "I ain't afraid of him. You shouldn't be either," he said, though his gaze was fixed on the kitchen's entrance, telling her that his words were only so much bravado. "Not if there are two of us and only one of him," he quickly added. "We can make him leave. We can go back to like it was before. Back when it was good."

She stood there for a moment, at a loss for words. Her heart pounded with the expectation that Guy's heavy boots would come stomping down the hall. Much to her relief, the only sound was that of Guy snoring in his throne.

"Sit," she commanded, watching as Willy dragged out a chair, turned it around, and then slumped over its top rail. She placed her hand on the back of Robinson's head to reassure him, then realized she was actually doing it to comfort herself. "I'm not afraid of him," she said. She only realized it was a lie when the last word left her lips. "I love him," she said by rote, wondering if there were still even a shade of truth to that statement. Then finally she said the one thing she knew to be true. "Remember," she said pulling Robinson's cheek against her

J.D. Horn

hip, "he's my son's father. I won't have you showing disrespect for him in front of my boy."

Willy forced his way up from the table, leaning over it toward her. "He done disrespects himself enough in front of him. Won't look after him. Won't work a lick. Won't even get up out of that old chair 'cept to grab another bottle. He ain't the kind of man a woman like you could love. No," Willy said, his tone softening as his eyes lowered to Robinson's face. "I don't believe you do. Love him, that is. You want to love him. But I don't know why. What has he ever done for you, really?"

The young man's words knocked the wind out of her. She reached out to brace herself against the table, nearly upsetting the half-full glass of milk that her wide-eyed Robinson hadn't yet touched. Her lips began working long before she found the words. "He came back . . ." she said, for the first time letting herself hear the truth of her heart. "The men in my life," she said as the image of a photo of her father, Jesse, passed before her mind's eye, giving way to the memory of Lionel's golden glasses glinting in the overhead light as he held her pinned to his desk. The haunted expression on Pastor Jones's face as he confessed his delusions to her. The look in Guy's eyes as he read the letter inviting him to leave her behind. "All of them. They've all let me down somehow and left me. Even the good ones who never intended to." She raised her gaze to meet Willy's. "Guy, he's the only one who ever came back."

"We'd all been better off if he hadn't," Willy said, and she had to wonder if he was right. His head made a quick jerk, and he hastened to the window. "Here comes Mr. Poole now." Willy's voice grew excited. "He's driving his new Impala."

Jilo went to the window and leaned to the side so that she could see the bend of the road. A shiny new Chevrolet, a metallic shade of aqua not so very different from the familiar haint blue. She knew Tinker was doing real well for himself. He'd grown his business from the one shop on West Broad to include a small grocery over on Whitaker, some blocks

289

south of his original shop, and a gas station in Garden City. These days everything the man touched seemed to turn to gold. And every black mother with a daughter anywhere near marrying age had taken to asking him over for Sunday dinner. Certainly on Easter, he'd be able to pick and choose from a wealth of invitations, but still it was *her* children he had wanted to spend it with.

Excited by Willy's enthusiasm, Robinson slid off his seat and scampered to her side. She lifted him and placed a kiss on his forehead. She shifted Robinson into Willy's embrace, then herded the two over to the back door. "Now get out there where he can see you, before he comes knocking and bothering Guy. And you treat his new car real gentle. You hear?" She pointed at Willy. "You make sure Robinson keeps his feet off the seats." She opened the door for them and hurried them out. "You make sure to tell Mr. Poole I thank him for his kindness," she said, but her words might have been lost on Willy's ears, scurrying as he was to head off Tinker.

She thought of Tinker's warm black eyes. The desperation in them the day she'd accepted that ride from him, then deserted him by the cemetery. The day she'd arrived home to find Guy and Edwin waiting on her front porch. It had all just seemed too foolish to consider. She didn't even know the man, and he certainly didn't know her. With Guy she had a history. She had a child. And though she knew the kind of man Guy was, she still believed in the kind of man she knew he might one day become, if he'd get out of his own way. Yes, a part of her still loved him. A part of her always would.

Still, she now found herself wondering how things would have turned out if Tinker's old truck had held up long enough to get her home, or if Guy hadn't been waiting just outside her door.

- — -

She turned to see Guy standing in the doorway that separated the kitchen from the hall. He was watching her with a dead look in his eyes, propping himself up with one hand against the wall. "What is there to eat around here?"

He hadn't shown much interest in eating for quite a while. "Come sit down," she replied. "I'll fry you up some eggs. Got a bit of salt bacon, too." He nodded and crossed to the table, pulling back a chair and collapsing into it. "You want coffee?" He despised the chicory she'd grown up drinking, so she'd taken to buying the more expensive beans to please him. Bought a new percolator and a hand grinder, too, as he liked his coffee better freshly ground.

"Yes. But the food first." He put his elbows on the table, rested his head between his hands.

She nodded, realizing even as she did that he wouldn't see her doing so. She turned and crossed to the stove, igniting all four of the electric eyes, hoping that one of them would begin to glow. The old stove was failing. It had been new when she was a girl, purchased by her nana right after she got the house hooked up to the power lines. But now the burners took a lot longer than they should to glow red, sometimes not heating up at all. They needed a new stove, but she felt it best to hold off on a purchase that would anger Guy. He had firm opinions about how "their" money should be spent. Maybe after he went a few days without a hot supper, he'd realize the wisdom of replacing it, or maybe he wouldn't even care. Regardless, until it was good and dead, she'd force it to limp through.

She pulled out a heavy iron skillet from the drawer where she kept the pans. She set it on the stove, happy to see the back right burner had begun to heat. Once the pan was on the active burner, she switched off the others and went to the refrigerator to fetch the bacon and eggs. She watched, silent, as the white fat of the bacon began to liquefy, a memory from a chemistry class—how many years ago now?—of an experiment to determine the viscosity of some solution rising up in her mind. It fell away at the sound of Guy's voice. "You got that coffee yet?"

She turned. "Not yet. I was getting your food ready first."

"I said I wanted the coffee first." He looked up at her, clenching his fists.

She didn't contradict him. It wasn't worth it. "I'm sorry. I'll get it started." She'd get some food in him. Some coffee. Maybe then he'd be sober enough to talk some sense.

"No, you might as well finish with the food since you got it started." He lowered his head back into his hands. "It would just be nice if a man would be listened to every once in a while around here."

She said nothing. Just grabbed a fork and turned the meat. She went to the cupboard and pulled down a plate, which she brought over to the stove. She fished the bacon from the pan before it cooked too crisp—Guy liked it tender—and cracked two eggs into the hot fat. Sunnyside up. Mustn't crack the yolks. Guy wouldn't touch them if the yolks got cracked. As soon as the food was ready to his liking, she carried the plate and fork to the table and set it down beside his elbow. When he didn't look up, she placed her hand on his shoulder. "Here you go," she said. "I'll get your coffee."

He grunted, but didn't otherwise react.

She crossed to the counter to retrieve the coffee mill and the canister that held the beans. As she began to crank the mill, she looked over at Guy. He hadn't budged an inch, hadn't even made a start on his breakfast. She realized that he was killing himself, slowly, right before her eyes. She had to break him out of this mood, get him up and going again. Or failing that, she finally acknowledged, she would have to get him out of here. Yes, he was Robinson's father, but she couldn't have her boy growing up around a man like this.

"I've been thinking," he said, the sound of his voice startling her, even though it came out quiet, his words, mumbled through his hands, nearly indiscernible. "You may be right." She deserted the coffee mill on the counter and drew near to hear him better.

She waited a few moments, but he didn't continue. "Right about what?" she asked, pulling out a chair and joining him at the table.

He looked up at her, his eyes red, still dazed from drink. "About this damned dry spell of mine. I can't just sit around waiting for it to pass."

She nodded, feeling hopeful for the first time in a long time. "Anything, Guy. Anything you got to do. You just tell me." She said it, and she meant it, too. She wanted him to find his way back to himself. Still, she braced herself for whatever might come next.

He leaned back in his chair, pushing away his plate and fixing her with his gaze. "I've been thinking it's this place—Savannah. It's this town that's the problem. If I could just get out of here . . ." His eyes lowered, a flash of guilt showing in them. "If *we* could get out of here. Get back to New York. I'm sure I'll be able to work again." As he spoke, he leaned forward, a fire building in him, the likes of which she hadn't seen since the old days, back in Atlanta. "We could even take Willy if you want. There are others there like him. He'd be happier there, too. The change would be good for us all."

For a brief and bright shining moment, she let herself be infected by his zeal. Maybe it was, after all, Savannah's fault. It was true, before Edwin had found Guy and brought him south, Guy seemed to have been making something of himself. She imagined her small family living happily in that great northern city, far from old memories, far from Jim Crow. Then reality set back in. "It'd take money to get us set up in New York. We don't have that kind of money, Guy."

His eyes opened wide and he pointed toward the ceiling. "I already got that figured out; Binah's done married herself one of the richest fellows in creation. You write your sister. You write Binah. You ask her to arrange for Edwin to make you a loan. He got me down here. He can help get me the hell back out of here."

She shook her head. She hadn't shared any news of Edwin with Guy. She'd figured it best not to bring up her brother-in-law. "No, he isn't rich anymore," she said, steeling herself to weather his disappointment. "Binah wrote me to say that his parents have cut him off. Edwin is in no position to help us."

A small smile curved his lips, and a light ignited in his eyes. He laughed. "Good ole Edwin's gonna learn what being a working man is like now." It surprised her to see Guy so callous about his supposedly dear friend's misfortune—especially since Guy himself had been counting on that fortune. Worse, it infuriated her that he would take any satisfaction in the thought of her little sister doing without. But before she could speak, he continued. "No problem, we'll sell the house. That'll give us something to get started with."

Jilo pulled back. "We can't do that, Guy."

His face darkened. "And why the hell can't we? A second and a half ago, you were saying you'd do 'anything.' "

"Well, 'cause Nana left this place to me, Opal, Poppy, and Binah. Even if they agreed to sell it, we'd have to split it all four ways." She wondered if they might. Based on their history of not visiting, Poppy and Opal didn't give a damn about the place, and Binah might just be happy for the cash.

"And where the hell are they? If it weren't for the two of us, this place would've been a deserted ramshackle long ago. No, this here place belongs to us. No need to share anything."

She cast her eyes around the kitchen of the house that had been in her family now for three generations. It was true, this place belonged to her, and she belonged to this place. She realized that even if her sisters would be willing, she wasn't. This was her home. And she knew, as badly as she wanted to believe in Guy, he'd blow through the windfall, and she and the boys might end up homeless in that great northern city. "No, Guy, that isn't going to happen."

Guy reached out with a wide sweep of the arm and sent his plate flying. It crashed against the wall, taking a divot of plaster out before falling and shattering on the floor. Jilo pushed back from the table, ready to flee, ready to fight, but Guy was already up and stomping down the hall. She followed him out through the living room, catching hold of the front door as he passed through it. She held up her left hand to fend off the protesting screen. "No more, Guy," she called out after him. "No more. We can't go on living like this. I'm not gonna go on living like this."

He didn't stop. He didn't turn around. She waited there in the doorway and watched as he marched down the sandy drive, around the bend, and out of sight.

She turned, pushing the door closed behind her as she did.

When she looked up, her heart jumped to her throat. "Good Lord," she exclaimed as she realized she was not alone. Another man sat in the partial shadow that fell on her nana's old chair, her lover's "throne." Her pulse beat in her neck, even after she recognized the face, even after all sense of danger had passed. "Pastor Jones," she said, relieved, confused, taking a few steps closer to the man she hadn't seen in years. "You frightened me." She smiled, pressing her hand over her heart. "I didn't hear you come in." She flushed with embarrassment, wondering just how much he had witnessed of her argument with Guy.

"I was called here," he said, the words coming out quiet and flat. His voice sounded odd, like it was reaching to her from a great distance.

"Called?" she said, but he gave no further explanation. She took a closer look at him.

At first glance, he seemed to be in good shape. His clothes appeared clean and neatly pressed, his well-blocked hat rested on his knee. Still she could see there was something wrong with the man. Too quiet. Too still. Shell-shocked, that was the term that came to mind—his gaze was both blank and fixed at the same time, like he'd seen horrors he couldn't look away from, even though they were no longer before him. He looked up at her through wide and haunted eyes. "They aren't angels," he said. "They never were."

NINE

"They aren't angels," the pastor repeated himself.

Jilo crossed and knelt before him. "Are you all right? Can I get you something? Some water?" He didn't respond. He just sat there staring straight ahead. "Does Mrs. Jones know you're here? Does she know you're all right?" Jilo tried to remember the boarding house's phone number. Would it still ring? Had Mrs. Jones managed to hold on, or had she lost everything, going to drift in the wind? Jilo felt guilt flood her. She should've done a better job of keeping in touch.

" 'For we wrestle not against flesh and blood, but against principalities, against powers, against the rulers of the darkness of this world, against spiritual wickedness in high places.' " It unnerved her to look at him, his words were spoken with such intensity, but his body remained still, unmoving, other than an occasional dart of his gaze. "They aren't angels. Not at all. They're devils. That's what they are. They killed me, my girl. Took me, then broke me apart piece by piece, looking to see what made me tick."

"No, no," Jilo tried to comfort him. "You're all right. You're fine. You're right here with me." The light in the room began to dim. At first she was so fixated on the pastor, she didn't notice, but soon it was impossible to ignore. The room had darkened from full daylight to an unnatural twilight within a matter of seconds. She cast an eye at the window, afraid that they might be in the path of a sudden oncoming storm.

The window was black. Not like the weather had turned. Like it had been painted over. Jilo rose and crossed the room, approaching the window with caution. As she drew near, the entire wall began to darken, a stain spreading out in all directions from the window, like a bruise, changing the wall's color from its customary lead white to a deep indigo, from indigo to a midnight blue.

The darkness began to sweat through the plaster of the wall, beading up and dripping down the windowpane. Jilo stumbled back, her heart once again pounding to escape her chest. She turned to the pastor. "We have to get out of here. I don't know what this is, but we need to move." It struck her that she'd just told a lie. She knew what this was. Magic.

He didn't stir, but remained staring at some invisible point six feet or so before him. "I didn't know you were mine. I don't think Betty knew it either."

Jilo had no idea what he meant, but there wasn't time to listen. She lunged forward to grab his hand, to tug him out of the chair and away from whatever was happening there. Her fingers bent to scoop up his hand in hers, but they passed right through him. A cry escaped her lips, and she jumped back from him, uncertain of which way to turn. He seemed to take no notice of her panic. She spun and ran toward the door, only to find that it, and the wall surrounding it, had also begun to change color. The darkness was bleeding through the wall, bubbling up through its surface like drops of ink. She stepped back in horror.

"It wasn't like with me." The pastor's voice caused her to turn back. "They only took her the one time." She slid around him, keeping her back against the unsullied side wall. "I never lay with her. I never touched her. But somehow they created you. From the two of us. Betty must have thought it was only a dream." A bead of darkness broke free from the wall, taking flight on buzzing iridescent wings. Then another, and another. The wall appeared to bow in as the droplets took life and broke free. A swarm of insects, the likes of which Jilo had never seen before, neither bee nor wasp nor dragonfly, but some unholy combination of all three, spiraled around her. She began swatting at the winged intruders in wild panic, but every time her hands came into contact with one, a sharp pop, like a burst of static electricity, shocked her.

"They'll want you now, if they see you have magic," the pastor's voice cut through the swarm's buzz, capturing their attention as it did. The creatures seemed to lose all interest in her, coalescing instead around the pastor, drowning out what remained of his nonsense words, forming a spinning and ever-constricting cloud around him.

The cloud settled on him, concealing him, consuming him, then one by one the insects began to break away from the mass, each creature snatching away a bit of gauzelike substance as it disengaged from its mates. Bright pinpoints of light broke through the remaining swarm as its individual members took flight, like they were peeling away the pastor's exterior and exposing the spirit that lay beneath.

A part of Jilo's brain ordered her to move. To flee the front room, run down the hall, and make her way through the kitchen and out the back door, but she remained frozen in place until a light flared up from the center of where the pastor had been, a spark of white light that rose from the swarm and shot straight up through the ceiling. In that same instant, the light in the room returned. The swarm was gone.

The door began shaking as if someone were trying to force an entry. Jilo bolted down the hall, intent on making it out the back way, only to freeze in the entryway to the kitchen. She wasn't alone. There were four others sitting at her table. A man wearing a top hat decorated with a bright red satin band was facing her. Something about him seemed familiar, but she couldn't place what it was. "Little sister," he called, "come join us." He raised a glass in salute.

To this man's right sat another with jaundiced white skin so thin the light seemed to pass right through it, giving him the look of a skeleton wrapped in fine vellum.

In spite of her earlier impression that there were four at the table, Jilo realized that the chair to the right of the fellow in the top hat sat empty. Then her eyes spied the flicker of a shadow, and that flicker solidified for an instant into the figure of a man so dark, so lusterless, that it was impossible to discern any features. In the next moment, the figure was again gone, replaced by a flat shadow that draped itself over the chair.

The fourth figure was facing away from Jilo. From the back, she had the succinct impression of maleness, but when the visitor turned, his wide shoulders seemed to narrow and soften. His skin darkened, and his bald pate covered over with dark hair. "Yes, little sister," his baritone voice rose with each syllable, ending in a high alto, "come." Jilo found herself looking into her own face. The room seemed to sway around her as memories—no, these were more than memories, it was as if she were reliving each experience, fresh, present, and real—of her every sadness, failure, and defeat weighed down on her. It seemed as if all hope had drained from her soul in an instant.

"Stop it, Brother," said the man in the top hat—she still thought of this creature as a man, though only due to his appearance, which was more normal than that of his peers—causing her imitator to turn. The visitor shifted in appearance as it looked away from her, gaining in both height and girth, its skin lessening in pigment, its hair retracting inward, leaving nothing but a snowy bald pate. "This one is not for you," the man in the hat continued. "At least not until she has accomplished what we need of her."

"What you need . . . ?" The words squeaked out from her, but she had no sooner begun to speak them than the world around her began to change. Before her very eyes, the walls of the kitchen unfolded, peeling down and away, exposing the world around them. Soon the kitchen had disappeared, and the entire house seemed to dissolve and retract, sinking beneath the earth. Without moving an inch, Jilo found herself beneath the wide sky, looking out on her backyard. Only the table and chairs with their weird occupants remained—any other evidence of the house that had sheltered her family for decades had been erased, and although her feet told her that a solid floor remained beneath them, her eyes swore to her that she and her visitors floated at least a yard above the earth.

Jilo noticed a movement, just at the edge of the tree line. A figure stepped out from the grove of live oaks, her movements as graceful as the steps of a dance. Covered head to toe in lace, this odd woman—Jilo thought of the creature as female because of its dress and sashaying movements—began drawing near, holding her gloved hands overhead and slightly behind her. Her fingers wiggled, like she meant to tickle the sky. The sun followed her as she crossed the dry, gray field, so as she came closer, morning passed to high noon, and noon passed to dusk, the sun scraping the sky red as the figure in lace teased it along behind her. *This can't be real. This can't be the real world. Dreaming. I must be dreaming.* The sight of twilight approaching on the horizon caused Jilo's thoughts to turn to Robinson. In the real world, was the sun also setting? Would her boy be crying? Was he worried about his mama? For the first time, Jilo wondered if the everyday world was permanently lost to her. Had she somehow died and found her way, if not to hell itself, at least to some kind of purgatory? Were these creatures the same ones Pastor Jones had believed to be angels?

The veiled creature stopped mere feet from her and howled with laughter. "No, child, we're not angels. I've never even seen one of those things." She did a final twirl, the lace of her veil and of her skirt flitting up as she did. "What do you think?" she said, though now she seemed to be addressing the man in the top hat. Without waiting for him to answer, she extended a hand toward him, not in greeting, but as an impatient signal for him to hand her the bottle he held. He rose and offered it to her. Only then did Jilo realize the creature most resembling a normal man was the only one of the four remaining; the other three had disappeared from their chairs with no notice, as if they had been unwilling, or perhaps unable, to remain in the presence of the veiled one.

"You ever see one?" The woman whisked back the veil, revealing an even more absolute void than Jilo's soul could have ever imagined. Not even a spark of light lived there. She swiped the bottle away, tilting it back to where Jilo reasoned her lips would be, were she not an abyss bound up in lace.

"No, can't say that I have," the man said, "though maybe they exist in the hidden places in between."

For a moment, absolute silence fell all around them. Then the female lowered the bottle, hissing like an angry cat as she let her veil fall back over the emptiness. "Do not speak to me of the hidden places." She hurled the bottle at the man with such force that it shattered against him. "My piss fills your hidden places." The man stepped back, trembling, and the veiled one spun back toward Jilo. "These bastards. It pleases them to know there are things that remain hidden, even to me. But those things are few"—she stopped and turned again on her companion—"and oh, so very far between." The man stood frozen in place, seeming to be too terrified to move, until the creature once again turned her attention from him to Jilo.

She drew closer, the shape of a head bobbing up and down beneath the lace. She circled Jilo, as if she were examining her, then came to a stop in front of her and leaned in, making a sound like she was sniffing. "And no," she raised her head, stepping back as she did, "you don't smell dead, though you would be if I hadn't been keeping an eye on you." Another burst of raucous laughter rose and fell away.

"I don't understand," Jilo said. "Who are you? Why are you here?"

"Oh, dearie," the woman said, her veil sucking in and puffing out, as if a heavy breath were causing the movement, "I can tell you what they've called me, but I could never tell you who I am. Your grand-mother May called me 'the Beekeeper,' as did her mother, Tuesday, before her. I reckon you might as well do the same. You humans are, after all, so dependent on labels."

"You knew Nana?"

This Beekeeper took a few sashaying steps away, then turned back. "We were dear friends, these women and I. Long ago, I saw that I would find you through them, though I never guessed you wouldn't share their blood. Not till the outsiders took your mama. Swept her up into the skies. Impregnated her with you. You," she said, anger returning to her voice, "were one of those tiny mysteries, emanating from those damned spaces in between." She turned again toward her companion, her rage emanating from her as a visible wave in this otherworldly ether. "Long ago, I sensed your coming." She turned back toward Jilo. "I saw your destination. But I didn't understand your essence. I do understand you now. I can see your path, even if the fools around you do not.

"But as for why we are here, it was *you* who summoned us. Why else would you have made the offerings?" The woman gestured at the table with a wide wave, and once again, all four chairs were occupied.

A cry escaped Jilo's lips at the sight of the four corpses bound to the table. The chair over which the shadowy figure had draped itself now supported an elderly black man. She recognized his face. She hadn't known him by name, but she had often seen him playing checkers with his friends outside on West Broad Street. His figure had been secured with a strap of leather, a belt, she realized, as her eyes narrowed in on him. He looked peaceful, as if he were sleeping.

The chair where the man with the parchment-like skin had sat was now occupied by the remains of a painfully thin white woman with graying black hair. Her hands were bound together behind the back of the chair, but she had slid a bit forward and her head was tilted to the side. Her sallow complexion suggested a long-term illness. Jilo had seen patients at the hospital with that same complexion, which usually spoke of some kind of renal failure. A look of quiet acceptance, relief after a long period of suffering, showed on her features.

Jilo remained perfectly still, but the table and seats rotated, like some kind of lazy Susan, revealing a middle-aged white man where her double had been. The man's white shirt was drenched from the collar down. His hand, seemingly frozen by rigor mortis, still clutched the straight razor Jilo surmised he'd used to slice open his own throat. This one sat rigid in his seat, seemingly of his own accord, no sign of a binding to secure him.

The man in the top hat, too, had now disappeared, but in his chair sat a man with a wide bullet hole blown through his chest. His head was thrown back. Jilo felt herself compelled to draw near to him. His eyes bulged open, wide with fear and disbelief. This man's death had come as a terrible surprise to him, Jilo felt certain, at the hands of someone he'd trusted. As Jilo raised her eyes, her kitchen began to fade back in around her. Her attention was drawn to the blood and splatter covering the wall behind where this man sat. This killing, for there was no mistaking it for anything other than murder, had somehow happened here, in her own home. Right in this very room.

"Yes, the offering," the Beekeeper's voice broke through Jilo's shock. "A tribute to each king, and a restless spirit for me. You summoned me, dearie, though for you, I would have come without all this formality."

Jilo heard a pounding sound, distant at first, but closer and louder with each knock. She turned to look for the source of the noise, only to find herself standing in her darkened kitchen, the house once again solid around her. When she glanced back, the Beekeeper was gone, though the four bodies remained gathered together around her table. The hammering on the door continued, a thundering boom, as if the devil himself were trying to gain entry. She glanced around the room once more, trying to decide if it would be best to go forward and see to the noise at the front of the house or to slip out the back. It suddenly dawned on her that though she had watched the night descend in her vision, the light that was now filtering through the windows indicated it was still midmorning. She cast her eyes up at the clock on the wall. It showed that only an hour or so had passed since Guy's departure. Her heart leaped in hope. The boys were safe. Out there with Tinker, probably praying the sermon would finish soon so they could get on with the church's Easter potluck that followed the service. She took a breath, ready to sigh it out.

"Jilo Wills," a man's voice called her name, stopping her breath as his fist pounded against the kitchen window. "I see you in there. Don't you try to hide." He disappeared from the window, and within seconds the back door burst open. "You can't hide from me," he said. It was a buckra man with curly corn-silk blond hair and sharp blue eyes. She had never met him, but somehow she knew his face. "You've never been able to hide from me." As she backed away from him, the reason she recognized him dawned on her. It was from her nana's strange collection of newspaper clippings, culled from front pages, business sections, and society pages, though his name failed to come to her distraught and tangled mind. She couldn't begin to comprehend why this man was here, what he could possibly want from her, but the entire day had followed a dream's logic. None of this made any sense, but she somehow knew it was all real, all happening. She turned and ran to the drawer where she kept her knives, drawing out a long carving blade. Weapon in hand, she turned back to face the man, and in that same moment, his name came to her. Maguire. Sterling Maguire.

He raised his nose to the air, sniffing around. "It worked." He cast a glance at the four dead bodies at the table. "She's here. I can feel her. I can smell her."

He stopped his advance, even backed up a few feet. He held up his hands in mock surrender and laughed, seeming to delight in her trembling. "No need for any of that," he said. "I'm just here to make a delivery. Come on outside." He turned, without any apparent concern about showing his back to a woman holding a knife, and walked out the door. Still clutching the handle of the knife, Jilo took a few cautious steps toward the doorway. The man turned back after he made his way down the steps, signaling with a beckoning wave that she should continue. "Come on, my girl, keep coming. Don't you want to see what I have waiting for you?"

No. The answer to his question was a decisive no. She did not want to see what this man had in mind to spring on her. She'd seen enough horrors today, four of them right there with her, growing more rank by the moment. She froze.

Maguire's face flushed red when she didn't obey him. "I said move it, girl, or I will come and take that knife from you and use it to carve up that nappy-headed boy of yours." He nodded. "Yeah, that's right. I got him. Right out front. With his daddy and that little frill boy of yours. So you'd better come. Fast."

The knife dropped from her hand, and she took quick, stomping strides past her ruined table, out the door, down the steps. Maguire was already disappearing around the side of her house, moving toward its front. Picking up her heavy feet, she hurried to catch up to the man.

"Toss him down," she heard Maguire's voice call, "then get the hell out of here." She came around the side in time to see two men clambering into the back of a green-and-white pickup truck. They bent over and hoisted up another man. They flung him over the side, and the man rolled to the ground, coming to a rest on his back. Jilo dashed to his side, looking down in horror and disbelief. His clothes were ripped and bloody. His face beaten beyond recognition. Still she knew him. She would know him, if by nothing else, by his fine artist's hands.

"Guy," she screamed, and fell to her knees by his side.

TEN

Guy's nose was crushed. His eyes purple and swollen shut. His mouth gaped open, his chest heaving and rattling as he struggled for breath. "I have to get him to the hospital," Jilo cried out, though her rational mind had already examined him in minute detail, had already done the calculations. Guy, this part of her mind stated plainly, was in his death throes. It was too late for hospitals. His lungs were filling with fluid. His abdomen had swollen, and he was most likely bleeding internally.

"He don't need no hospital, girl," Maguire said as the truck that had brought Guy tore off, spraying sandy soil over Guy's supine form. "What he needs is what your friend the Beekeeper has to share with him. You take her magic into you, girl. She'll give you what you need to fix that boy up."

"Magic?" she felt the word roll off her tongue, a bitter pill she could neither spit out nor bring herself to swallow. "Are you mad? Why have you done this?" Another thought hit her, causing her heart to feel like it would explode from her chest. "Where is my son? You haven't hurt him." Her last words came out as a statement, a warning. No matter who this man was in the world, no matter what he owned or how much influence he held, she would take him apart, bit by bit, with her bare hands if he'd hurt her baby.

Maguire strode toward her, grinning down at her. He stuck out a foot and rested it against Guy's side, using it to roll his battered body back and forth. "Not yet," he said, then pulled back his leg and delivered a hard kick to Guy's ribs. Jilo heard something snap. She leaped on top of Guy, using her own body to shield him from further harm. "But," he continued, "if this fellow don't mean enough to you for you to welcome the Beekeeper, we'll start in on that little pansy friend of yours next. And if that don't work, I'll go fetch that knife of yours and start carving me up some of your little one's tender dark meat." Cupping his hand around his mouth, he looked up and called. "Bring 'em around, Thomas, so she can get a good look at them."

Willy came around from the far side of the house, clutching Robinson for dear life. A young fellow, a near carbon copy of Maguire, followed behind them, training a revolver on Willy's back.

"Jilo," Willy cried. "Those men ran Mr. Poole's car off the road. Mr. Poole, I think he's dead. His head was bleeding, and he wouldn't move. Not even when I shook him."

The terror in the child's eyes crushed her. Robinson began wailing, reaching out for her. She wanted to cry out, too. Howl. Tinker dead. Guy as good as. What chance did she and her boys have?

"Shut that thing up," Maguire shouted, and the younger man reached forward and gave Willy a rough shove between the shoulder blades, causing him to lunge forward and almost stumble. "And while you're at it, shut your own trap, too, boy."

"It's gonna be okay, baby," Jilo called out, though she wasn't sure if she meant the words for Robinson or Willy. Both of them, she realized. No help was coming. Jilo would have to do whatever it took to protect those she loved. "What do you want from me?" She looked up at Maguire, shaken to the core. "I'll do anything. Just tell me what you want. I'll do it. Please just leave us be."

"I done told you what I want," he squatted down next to her. "I've even gone to the trouble of summoning her. Now all you got to do is take her in."

"I don't understand what that means," Jilo shook her head.

Maguire lifted up from his haunches and bent over her. Grabbing her wrist, he yanked her off Guy, the force of his effort lifting her several inches off the ground. He dropped her down onto her own two feet. "It's always the same with you Wills women. Your grandmother. Her mother. Even her mother before that. The Beekeeper, she follows you around, attaching herself to you, though I'll be damned if I can figure out why. She pours her magic out at your feet, and all you do is turn your noses up at it. You, my girl, you're gonna accept her gift, and then you're going to do me a little service."

He spat on the ground, right next to Jilo's foot. "I need her help. This body, should've known it was a weak one. Forty-two years old, and already it's failing. Cancer." He said the word as though it were an insult to his stature, to his manhood, even, as if it were a disease meant for those who were weaker, perhaps even less well-placed in society. "You and my son Thomas, here. You two are going to stop it from eating me alive. You two are going to help heal me. And as an incentive, if you move fast enough, you might just have enough time to fix what's ailing him"—he nodded over at Guy—"too."

After crossing the yard to his son, Maguire relieved the boy of the pistol. "Go on, you know what to do. Get started, and be quick about it." As Thomas took off around the side of the house, Maguire wagged the pistol at Willy. "Come on, boy," he said, "you look like you might be pretty fast. Why don't you drop that little ape you're holding and see if you can sprint out of here? I'll even make it sporting. I'll count to ten." Willy looked first at him, then at Jilo, his eyes round with horror. He clutched Robinson even tighter, placing one hand behind the little one's head, doing his best to shelter the boy from all that was going on around them. Jilo blessed the day Willy had followed Binah to her door. She was going to take care of him, take care of them both. She cast a glance in Guy's direction. The truth was finally clear to her now, in this horrible moment—she would never share a life with this man, but she couldn't let him die. Not like this. Not if she could help it. Especially since for once it looked like Guy was blameless; this mad buckra had only used him to get at her. If it were true this Beekeeper could heal Guy, Jilo would take care of him, too. She didn't care what it might cost her.

The younger Maguire returned, holding a sword, one of those Confederate officer's sabers she'd often seen carried by men dressed in Confederate gray and Kelly green as they marched in the Saint Patrick's Day parade. He stripped down to the waist, then stabbed the sharp point of the saber's slightly curved blade into the earth. He began cutting lines in the soil, his movements quick and practiced. Jilo knelt beside Guy, first tracing her hand along his brutalized cheek, then placing a hand on his still-rasping chest. "I'll fix this," she whispered into his ear. "I'll make it right."

She rose and began to cross to Willy and Robinson. "Uh-uh," Maguire said, shaking his head. "No sweet reunions till we're done here." He took aim at Willy's head. Jilo nearly jumped away from the boys. "You had your chance," he said, addressing Willy. "Don't go getting any ideas now."

Maguire's gaze softened. "Ironic really"—with those two words his tone changed from threatening to wistful—"that I'm reduced to using this popgun to keep you in line." He sighed. "There was a time when I could have set loose the very hounds of hell on you, or at least a reasonable facsimile thereof. But what can I tell you? I cut the wrong ties. Backed the wrong side leading up to the war. A man lives. He learns. And now, well, you're the first step toward helping me regain all I've lost." Only then did Maguire lower the pistol, though Jilo figured the gesture was more for his own comfort than for any other reason.

She couldn't bear to see the tears running down Willy's cheeks, so she looked away. Her eyes fell on Thomas's handiwork, all the while thinking how his movements as he carved up the earth reminded her of the Beekeeper's dancelike stroll. She stepped far enough back to take in the larger picture. The young man had cut the symbol for infinity into the earth. Each of the two loops was around three, maybe three and a half feet in diameter. He drew a circular band around it, then began making long strokes, slices that came together to form an eight-pointed star.

When the final point had been joined, Thomas stopped and looked up at his father with an expression that seemed to combine great pride and expectation. His efforts had left his broad shoulders and taut chest glistening with sweat.

"Good boy," Maguire said, then pointed with his free hand at the young man. "That," he said, addressing Jilo, "is a good, strong body. I saw to it this time. Made sure the boy was disciplined, not soft and coddled like this body was raised to be." He spoke as if he thought any of his rantings should make any sense to her. "And he's going to share some of that strength with his father," Maguire said, though his intonation told Jilo the words were meant as encouragement for his son, rather than for her own ears. "He's going to share some of that glowing health, and once he's got his old man set right, the two of us are going to go out and take over the world, aren't we, my boy?"

"Yes, sir," Thomas replied. "The whole damned world."

Jilo remained silent, not daring to open her lips lest she begin screaming at Willy to run, to hold Robinson tight and run as swiftly as his long, strong legs could carry them.

"That's my boy," Maguire said, holding his free hand out to Thomas. "Bring me the saber, then take your place. Let's get this finished."

Thomas jogged to his father's side, holding the sword out so that the elder Maguire could grasp its hilt. For a moment, Thomas turned his gaze on Jilo. The boy seemed so full of pride, so certain that this world was his birthright, his to carve and his to wound, his to rule or destroy, depending on his whim. He turned and strode into the inner circle, stationing himself in the left loop of the lopsided figure eight.

To Jilo's surprise, Maguire held the saber out to her. "You'll need this." When she didn't move, he shook the blade, angling its hilt toward her. "Good God, girl, come take it."

She approached him with great care, fearful that at any moment he might swing the blade around and cut her down. Seeming to read her fears, he laid it down on the ground by his feet, then strode into the sign Thomas had cut into the wounded earth, entering the right loop of infinity. "Here, take this," he said, holding the revolver out to Thomas. Once they had traded off the gun, Maguire reached out with his right hand and grasped his son's left.

Jilo went to where the sword lay, looking down at its glinting blade. "What do I do with it?"

"Pick it up," Maguire said, "and bring it to the edge of the sigil." She hesitated. "The picture," he gestured with his free hand to the design surrounding him.

A bit of anger broke through her wall of caution. "I know what a sigil is."

"Then pick it up and get on with it. Come on, it's a saber, not a rattlesnake."

She bent over and grasped the hilt, lifted the sword from the ground. It was heavier than she'd imagined it would be, but she could still raise it high enough to cut this monster down, to put an end to both him and his seed. She wondered if she could find it in herself to drive it through his heart, and she decided that yes, to protect her own, she could. She could do it without a qualm. And if even the slightest of opportunity arose, she would. A wave of sadness descended on her—because of this man, she now had murder in her heart, something she'd never expected to find there.

"That's it," Maguire said, his voice rising, waxing eager. "Bring it over."

Jilo glanced at the boys and tried to give them a calm, reassuring smile. Willy's face showed he didn't buy the story she was trying to sell. He stood there, nearly vibrating with the urge to flee. To save himself. To save Robinson. But Jilo knew that if he gave into that urge, his heart would cause him to remember her and hesitate. Then he would be lost, and probably her Robinson, too. She shook her head, signaling for him to hold on for just a bit longer. To have faith in her, even if in this moment, she, herself, was without faith.

She carried the sword to what she assumed was the base of the sigil.

"Stop," Maguire said. "That's far enough. Whatever you do, do not enter the circle drawn around us."

"All right," Jilo responded. "What now?"

"We're almost there," Maguire said, "almost done. All you have to do is say that you accept the Beekeeper's magic."

"That's it?"

"Yes, then take the blade and run it across each of your palms. Gently. It's very sharp, and we won't need too much blood. Just a few drops. The cut is the opening through which her magic is gonna come into you. And the blood will seal the deal. You just make sure some of it gets on the lowest point of the star, there. Yep," he said as her eyes fell to the ground, "that one there, right next to your foot. One hand on those two points where the lines intersect. That's all I need from you. That's it. You do that, and you can get on with patching up that fellow of yours. My son and I will get on out of here. You'll never see hide nor hair of either of us again."

In the distance she heard Guy cry out in agony, warning her that if she wanted to save her son's father, the time for hesitation was over. She traced the blade across her left palm, wincing as the slightest pressure did indeed open a deep gash. Trembling, she repeated the action again with her right palm. *I accept the power*, she thought as she dropped the sword to the ground and knelt beside it. "I accept the power," she spoke the same words aloud again, unsure whether she actually had to say them, or if thinking them was enough. She felt no change. No change at all.

"It has to come from your heart, girl," Maguire called to her. "You have to want this in your heart. And you should, 'cause I promise you, if you don't make this work, none of you are gonna walk away from this. I will take that sword and hack that boy of yours in half myself."

I accept the power, Jilo thought, but this time the words were neither a statement of fact, nor a simple affirmation. They were a plea. A prayer to any force that could come and help her save the children, heal Guy, and free them all from these monsters. A sound like the buzzing of a thousand bees rose up around her.

An electromagnetic surge slammed her upper body to the ground. It took a few moments, but she managed to push up to her hands, gasping as she caught sight of them. A blue fire, like the hottest gas flame, covered them, yet she felt no pain. The fire, she realized, was not consuming her as she feared it might, but instead was emanating from her, racing out and tracing along the design carved into the earth, setting the whole thing alight. It spilled out from her, shooting out in both directions, clockwise and counterclockwise, traveling along the intersecting lines that made up the star, then setting fire to the circle at its center. As the liquid flames traced through the earth, she was filled with an odd sense that somehow she'd experienced this before. But no, she realized, she had never witnessed such an event. The energy flowing through her had given her that sense. The power. It remembered.

She felt the power's memory of her nana, and her nana's mama, too. And a terrified girl, much younger even than herself, cringing and crying as the power took her over, just as it was now filling Jilo. Through this girl's eyes, she looked up at a face very much like Maguire's. This girl, she realized, was her nana's own grandmother. And then the image faded. Jilo wondered just how many more generations this nightmare might reach back.

The energy rose up and spilled into the infinity sign that both linked and separated the men. Then, without warning, Thomas began screaming, a tortured, agonized cry. Jilo looked up to see his twisted face—mouth open wide, eyes round and full of fear. He was shaking wildly, steadied only by his father's hand. Jilo looked on, unable to break free of the energy that held her. "Run, Willy, run," she began screaming. She hoped that he heard her, that he obeyed, but she couldn't even turn her head, frozen in place by the power linking her to these two men.

The shaking that seemed ready to rip Thomas apart lessened, but then transmitted itself from son into father. Now Maguire was the one who was screaming, with even greater volume and at a higher pitch than the son had done. Thomas now nearly glowed with a look of satisfaction, seeming to take no small pleasure in his father's agony. Jilo watched in amazement as Thomas raised the pistol his father had handed him and put a bullet between his father's eyes.

The fire fell away, draining from the earth, releasing Jilo with such force, it knocked her backward. "That's my girl," Thomas said, but somehow Jilo knew the man addressing her was not the son, but the father, looking out through the son's eyes. Her eyes jumped to the gun, but he dropped the revolver onto the ground. He drew near, reaching out to offer a hand to help her stand.

She shook her head and crawled backward to get away from him, stopping only when she realized that she did, in fact, need his help. "What do I do?" She pushed herself up and ran to where Guy lay. "What do I do?" she asked, kneeling beside him.

"Just lay your hands on him. Will the magic into him. Will the Beekeeper to heal him. Her magic is now a part of you."

She fell to her knees, positioning both hands on Guy's chest, calling to the Beekeeper, praying to God. She had moved beyond any certainty about how this world worked. If there was a chance there was a God, she sure as hell wasn't too proud to plead for mercy—at least not on Guy's behalf. She looked down at Guy, but his chest was no longer moving. She placed her finger against his neck. There was no pulse. "You help me," she screamed, calling out to the power she felt flowing through her. The same strange blue fire flooded out from her, enveloping Guy, lifting him several inches off the ground. But he remained still, unbreathing.

Feeling a hand on her shoulder, she looked back to see the veiled one, the Beekeeper, standing behind her. "It's too late for that one. He belongs to my boy now," the Beekeeper said. "You want this one back, you're gonna have to make a deal with the Red King."

"Yes. Yes," she cried without giving the consequences a single thought. "Anything. I agree. What do I do? Just tell me."

"You'll have to take his mark."

"Okay, I agree. I'll take his mark."

"But it's not as easy as all that," a deeper voice spoke. The odd man wearing the top hat appeared before her. "I don't give up those I've won without a substitute."

"A life for a life, dearie," the Beekeeper said. "A life for a life."

Jilo's eyes shot up to where Maguire—now in Thomas's body—stood before her. "Yes," she said, "I can honor that deal." Maguire began backing away, shock and terror filling his eyes as it dawned on him for the first time how quickly, after hundreds of years, the balance of power could shift.

Jilo released Guy from the web of energy she had woven around him, his body drifting to the ground like a descending leaf. She raised her hands toward Maguire. The flames, a beautiful cerulean, began to change, purplish and indigo bruises rising up in them. As their color shifted to the deep blue of midnight, they grew sharp, forming themselves into tiny daggers, barbed candles that seemed to swallow the light around them rather than add to it. She was ready to strike, ready to consume this foolish monster with the fire, but a shot rang out. Maguire's hand went up to his chest, then he slumped over onto the ground.

Her head jerked to the side. She was astounded to see Tinker standing there, Maguire's own revolver in his hand. Tinker's temple was bruised and swollen, but he was alive. And Maguire lay dead, the thirsty gray soil swallowing his life's blood. "I heard what you said about that mark," Tinker said, dropping the gun and drawing near the Red King. "I think it should be mine."

"And so it is," the Red King grasped Tinker's wrist, encircling it with his thumb and middle finger. Jilo could smell the charring of flesh as the Red King burned his mark into Tinker's skin, but Tinker didn't flinch. He just stood there, focused on her, as if the mere sight of her was all he needed to carry him through the pain. She knew in that moment that it was not some silly infatuation this man held for her. He loved her. Plain and simple.

The Red King released Tinker, and Tinker crossed to where Guy's body lay.

"How do I do this?" he asked the Red King.

"You only have to want it. Are you sure you do?"

"She wants it," Tinker replied. "That's enough."

"Then it is done."

The ground beneath their feet trembled. A flash of lightning fell from the sky, striking Guy's body right in his solar plexus. Guy began coughing, moaning.

"Hurry, my daughter," the Beekeeper's voice sang out. "Repair the damage before he slips away again." Jilo returned to Guy's side, once again willing the cocoon of healing aqua light to form around him. "I will see you again. Soon," the Beekeeper called, causing Jilo's gaze to rise to the veiled face. Her image vibrated, blinking in and out, then in the next instant, both the Beekeeper and the Red King faded away.

"Thank you. Thank you. Thank you," she said, not to these unworldly creatures, but to Tinker, the words repeating themselves as she knelt beside Guy and laid her hands on him. This time the magic took hold, healing his ravaged features and realigning them into their usual handsome configuration. His eyes opened. Jilo leaned in and placed a kiss on his brow.

"I'll get started on burying the bodies," Tinker said, his voice flat, exhausted.

At the sound of Tinker's words, Jilo looked up at him, for a moment forgetting the miracle happening before her. "There are four more in the kitchen."

He nodded, drawing near, looking down at Guy. "See," he said, his voice full of sadness. "There is magic in this world."

ELEVEN

The Savannah Morning Star
April 9, 1958
Page D12

NEGRO COUPLE DEAD IN CAR CRASH

A single vehicle crash south of Hardeeville has claimed the lives of a local Negro man, identified as Guy Collier, 41, of the Ogeecheeton area, and his companion, Reena Jewel Lovett, 19, of Limehouse. Both were found dead at the site of the incident. Alcohol and evidence of illegal intoxicants found in the vehicle have led the Jasper County Sheriff's Office to determine impaired judgment and excessive speed were factors in the accident.

Jilo sat in her nana's chair, Guy's throne, unwilling, unable to move. As best she could remember, the sun had peeked in through the windows on the east, then through those situated to the west twice, maybe three times now, since the call came, telling her that despite her best efforts, Guy was no more.

The second Guy was able to rise to his feet, he had stormed through the house, turning out every spot where she'd managed to tuck away any cash. Not enough to get him far from Savannah, but enough for a decent bender. He packed her suitcase, the one she'd carried with her to Atlanta so many years ago now. Back when she had thought she understood how the world worked. Back when she had known beyond the shadow of any doubt that there was no such thing as magic. She didn't raise a finger to stop him, figuring it would be better for him to be far from her. He'd almost been killed because of her, and she'd already managed to drag Tinker down with her. Poor Tinker, covered head to toe in blood and dirt, had stood between them as Guy screamed insults at her. Raged at her till he saw the haint-blue sparks building on the tips of her fingers and then ran off like a scared jackrabbit. That was the last she'd seen him. The last she'd ever see of him.

She understood now why Opal had never visited, why Poppy had never set foot in this house after that long-ago Christmas. She remembered it all now. Waking to the sound of Henry Cook's cries. Stepping out into the shadows to see her big sister standing over Henry, that fire poker in her hand, raised and ready to end him.

That demon in Poppy. She had no idea how it had found them, or how it had managed to possess her sister's body. She still didn't understand how she did it, but she now could remember peeling away the spirit's own energy—taking it into herself, then turning it back against him. Her very next memory was of Nana coming home, pulling her into her arms and lying to her, over and over. Just a bad dream.

A bad dream. That's what all of this felt like. Too much loss, too many lies. Her whole damned life had been a lie. Hell, she wasn't even a Wills. Not really, at least not by blood.

She was broken, and she knew it.

Perhaps if Jilo hadn't been able to count on Willy, as faithful as ever, to see to Robinson's needs, she might have found the strength to move. But she knew Willy would take care of her boy. Now and again, he would come and set Robinson on her lap in an attempt to rouse her, to pull her back. She barely noticed. It was all she could do to dig her hands into the chair's padded armrests and try to make the world stop swirling around her.

The sun circled around the room once more. She'd sensed no movement, no one approaching, but then out of nowhere, another person's hands had grasped her own. She felt the weight of eyes on her. Her gaze rose up to meet Tinker's. "You're not going like this," he said, taking care as he worked to loosen her grasp on the chair. "I'm gonna fix this. You'll see. They don't call me Tinker for nothing."

TWELVE

"Thank you for coming," Jilo said, opening the door to Ginny Taylor. Less than a year had passed since she had shooed Ginny away from this very door, but Jilo found it hard to believe she was looking at the same woman. Any sign of Ginny's feisty gaiety, of her sensuality, had been erased.

"I'm so pleased you've reached out to me." The stylish dress Ginny had worn that night at the club had been replaced by a dark and sensible skirt that fell well beneath the knee, paired with a long-sleeved gray silk blouse. And pearls, each an identical match to the others in size, luster, and whiteness. Ginny's hair had grown out, and she wore it pulled up in a twist.

Jilo wondered if Ginny, too, was appraising her appearance. She'd lost weight. Too much weight. She couldn't bring herself to don one of Mother Jilo's fandango costumes, so she had dressed herself instead in a drab and shapeless dress her nana had picked out for her to wear in Atlanta a million years ago. Jilo had assumed she'd given the thing away, left it in a church charity box, but it had been lying there, all this time, folded in a drawer, just waiting for Jilo to fall far enough to find it.

"Of course," she said as Jilo stepped aside to allow her entry, "we're family now. Practically sisters."

Jilo's nerves betrayed her, causing her to titter at Ginny's words. What dim light had remained in Ginny's eyes froze and faded.

"I'm sorry," Jilo said. "I didn't mean to be rude. It's only the whole world has gone sideways lately." Her agitated laughter turned as quick as a breath to an unwanted spray of tears. Ginny dug into her purse, then offered Jilo a crisp white handkerchief. Jilo noticed the monogram, VKT, embroidered on its exposed corner.

"Katherine," Ginny said as she forced the linen into Jilo's hand, somehow picking up on Jilo's dim curiosity. "Virginia Katherine Taylor," she said, closing the door behind her. Placing a hand on Jilo's shoulder, she guided her into her own front room. "I'm sorry for your loss," Ginny said, adding, "Guy," as if by some slim chance Jilo would not have understood. What this decorous woman didn't understand was that it wasn't just Guy that Jilo had lost. She had lost herself, too, and she was only now finding the misplaced pieces. "He was a great talent, a loss not only to you, but also to the art world." Ginny stopped talking and bit her lip, evidently realizing that Jilo couldn't give a damn about the art world. At least not today. Someday, maybe, someday the old news articles, the ones Guy had kept in a beat-up leather scrapbook, the cuttings that spoke of his genius, of his sense of composition and his use of color, perhaps she would be able to present these to Robinson, engender a sense of pride in her son. That kind of thing was important for a boy.

"I would have come sooner," Ginny continued, bringing Jilo back to the current moment, "but my own life has undergone great changes since Uncle Finnian died." Her gaze grew soft, falling away from Jilo. "I've inherited certain familial duties that once belonged to him." She glanced back at Jilo. "Edwin felt quite fortunate to have dodged my fate," she said, for a moment a bit of her old self shining through.

"You've spoken to Edwin?" Jilo asked. From what she'd gleaned from Binah's letters, Edwin had been out of touch with all of the Taylors.

"Of course," she said, "he was here in February, for the drawing of lots. He didn't have a choice. Family schism or no, the line won't be denied. Of course," she continued, as if Jilo had the slightest clue what she meant, "he didn't remain for the investment ceremony." Again she turned inward, "I wish he would have. I could have used his support."

"And Binah?" Jilo couldn't believe her brother-in-law could have come and gone without even a word. And Binah hadn't mentioned Edwin's visit in any of her letters. It was almost like she had been ignorant of her husband's travels.

Jilo didn't care whether it was fair or not. She let herself wonder if a visit from Edwin might have somehow changed the course of events. Maybe her son wouldn't have been left without a father if Edwin had popped by, even for an hour, to spend time with his great friend, Guy. Maybe he could have somehow anticipated that fool Maguire's machinations.

Ginny seemed almost surprised at the mention of Binah's name. "Oh, no, she remained abroad. It wouldn't have been appropriate for her to come," she said, not bothering to justify the claim. Binah was Edwin's wife. How could her presence at this gathering be inappropriate? *Inconvenient*, that was more like it, Jilo reckoned. "Besides, Edwin was only here for the day, and he didn't travel by . . ." She paused, seeming to search for the right word. ". . . *conventional* means. I'm sorry"—her tone suggested she wanted to change topics—"but I can't stay long, and I do want to answer your questions, as best I can. May we sit?"

Jilo cast an eye to the sofa covered with the toys Tinker had insisted on bringing for Robinson, and the battered chair whose gravity she'd barely escaped. "Of course," she said, "come through to the kitchen. I'll make coffee . . ." She choked on the word. She hadn't even considered brewing a pot since Guy's passing. "If you'd like."

"Yes," Ginny said. "Let's settle wherever you're most comfortable. But no need to play hostess. Lead the way." There wasn't much way to lead, but Jilo directed Ginny down the hall to her kitchen. "Truth is," Ginny said as they entered the room, "I've never been much of one for coffee. Always preferred chicory myself."

For a moment, Jilo felt an odd and unexpected sense of comradery with this woman. "I could—" she began, but Ginny held up a hand.

"No, please, I don't want to be a bother. And our time is short."

Jilo motioned to a chair at the table. "Have a seat." Tinker had offered to replace the furniture, but these battered pieces had once belonged to her nana, and Jilo found it too difficult to part with them, even though she was tormented by the knowledge of her nana's deceptions. Willy had cleaned the soiled table set, scrubbing it with bleach water and a wire brush before painting it with a fresh coat of lime-green enamel. Jilo had told him he could choose the color. He'd been so proud of his efforts, Jilo found herself proud of them, too.

Ginny placed her hand on the back of a chair and froze. "I'm sorry." She jerked her hand away. "I can't." She traced a finger along the top of the backrest. "I can still sense them." She looked up. "Yes, the bodies, but the forces that were connected to them, too. I can't risk letting myself come under their influence."

Jilo nodded. Perhaps she should let go of the pieces. Commit them to flames.

"I've asked about these entities," Ginny said, "at least as freely as I can without arousing the suspicion of the others. All I've learned is that there isn't much to learn. They've been around seemingly forever, lurking in the periphery. The one thing every source and contact I've found agrees upon is that they are tricksters, and tricksters are always dangerous, regardless of what their intentions might be." Her tone turned sharp. "You do not want . . . *we* do not want anyone to learn you have been in contact with them, let alone that they have taken an interest in you. The Red King, your fellow in the top hat, is the most notorious of the quartet. He draws his energies from all—animal and human—who die through mishap or murder. He's been giving his mark to those who kill for him as far back as anyone remembers. I wouldn't be surprised if the story of Cain and the mark placed on him was a remembrance of an early pact between this king and a man seeking magic.

"This one. The one who sat here," Ginny focused on an invisible point inches from her nose. "He calls himself the White King. He feeds from the leftover energies of those who take their own lives. He is the youngest. And the most loathsome."

"He made himself look like me."

"Of course, he would. The better to distort your true self." Ginny's eyes traced a path around the table. "The others. They, too, call themselves kings. The Yellow King, he was your fellow with the paper-thin skin, the Black King, your shadow. Like their brothers, they feed from the residual energy we leave behind when we die. It's a bit like Jack Spratt, though; each can reputedly only digest the energies left by a particular type of death. Our 'friend' the White King would choke on the leftovers of a murder victim."

"The bastard should choke." Jilo felt her bile rise at the memory of his presence.

"Indeed," Ginny said. "But as real as they may have seemed to you, they're only doorways, portals to your Beekeeper, the source of this world's first magic. Now, the Beekeeper, she is the stuff of legends among my kind."

"Your kind?"

Ginny's head tilted to the side. "Oh really, Jilo, by now you must have guessed. We're witches, my brother and I, though your understanding of the word is without a doubt vastly different from its true meaning. I don't mean to sound condescending when I say that. There are only a handful of those not of our kind who even know we exist. Even fewer know of our influence. The knowledge of how we came to be, well, that information is jealously guarded, even among witches.

As a matter of fact, it was a bit above my own pay grade until Uncle Finnian's passing."

"Edwin is a witch?" This was the one point that stuck with Jilo.

"Yes, though Father has seen to it that his power has been greatly curtailed since he took off with Binah. My little brother has given up much more than you can guess for love." She smiled. "But I suspect your sister's love is worth any cost." The smile drained away as quickly as it had arisen. "Listen, I need to be sure you have understood me regarding the Beekeeper. No one"—she pointed to Jilo as if she were reprimanding a child—"no one can learn of your connection to this force." She lowered her hand, nearly placing it on the top rail of the chair before snatching it back. Stepping away from the table, she crossed her arms over her chest. "There are those who won't judge you in terms of innocence and guilt. They'll only see you as harmless or a threat. And you've been touched by a force we witches don't understand. Witches are, in spite of our powers, still human, and humans tend to fear what we don't understand."

"But you don't understand, and you don't fear me."

"No, I don't fear you, but I fear for you. For a multitude of reasons." She lowered her arms. "Now, I've answered your questions. I have one of my own for you."

Jilo bit her lip, waiting to see where this was heading.

"The man, the one you're trying not to think of, the one you don't want me to know about," she reached out and took Jilo's hand. "Who was he?"

Jilo yanked back her hand and lowered her eyes.

"I know who he was already. Perhaps even better than you do. I just want to hear it from your own lips."

Too much. Too much. Jilo began trembling.

Ginny drew her into her arms. "Tell me."

"His name was Robert Jones," she said, whispering the words in Ginny's ear. "He used to be a pastor. I lived with him and his wife in

Atlanta while I went to school. And I think . . . I think . . ." She swallowed hard. "I think he may have been my father." She pushed back, freeing herself from Ginny's embrace, astounded to hear herself give voice to those words. "He talked such nonsense. About being taken up by angels. Being showed visions of the disasters about to befall us. He disappeared. And then just before the Beekeeper came to me, he appeared here in my house. In the front room. He told me he'd been wrong all along—they weren't angels who took him. They were devils. And he told me these devils took my mama, too, and used the two of them to make me. It's nonsense. It has to be."

"I wish it were, but I'm afraid it isn't. That night at the club, I sensed there was something different about you. Your ability to tap into my magic makes sense to me now. It seems you weren't so much born, as engineered. You were created as a weapon."

"I'm no kind of weapon," Jilo said, sure that at least one of them had lost her sense of reason. "I'm only a woman. A mother." Her voice nearly broke, but she forced herself to remain strong.

"Oh, you are indeed a weapon, even more potent than that H-bomb these mad scientists have blown out their balls. But you are also a woman. And I believe you are an honorable woman," Ginny said. "A trustworthy woman. That's why I'm about to bet my life on my faith in you. If the others even dreamed that I might share this with you, they would kill me. No, worse than kill me, they would bind me, leave me in a permanent coma, no more than a seat for the power that has joined itself to me." Her face hardened. She lifted her chin and pierced Jilo with a sharp gaze. "I once said to you that I hoped someday we'd be friends. I meant it then. I mean it now. I trust you, Jilo Wills, I trust you with my very life. Will you trust me?"

Jilo stared into the eyes of this woman, so complex in the way she seamlessly combined admirable attributes and detestable ones. Still, when Jilo delved to the root of her soul, asking if she could trust Ginny Taylor, her heart said yes.

Jilo nodded, and Ginny reached out and placed her fingertips on Jilo's temples.

Images rose before Jilo's eyes. Places, structures, some seeming to reach back in antiquity, others gleaming towers of polished glass. She saw them laid out together on a single plane, like the time separating them meant nothing at all. "We witches"—Jilo heard Ginny's voice sound all around her, as if she had fallen deep into a well—"we built the machine, like the outsiders commanded." Jilo could see strands of light, the exact shade of haint blue she'd grown up around, surge up from the different points of the field. They rose up, converging on a single point. She'd seen this point in many pictures. It was the Great Pyramid.

"But we were clever, rebellious monkeys, we witches. We made a plan. A plan to chase away the outsiders."

"But what was this machine meant to do?"

"It was meant to strip this world of all life, of all magic, to beam its energy across the stars, through the dimensions, leaving Earth nothing more than a dead rock. And once we'd delivered them this planet's very life force, we were to spread out among the stars, like some kind of virus, to find other worlds to devour. But we tricked them. Took advantage of their own technology to cast them out. We shifted our world, our whole reality, to a slightly different frequency, then wove a net of magic—what we call the line—to keep them out."

Jilo looked on as the collected energies joined together in a large pool arranged before a large and monstrous statue. It was familiar to her, yet she couldn't place it. After a moment, it dawned on her that this was the Sphinx, though its head was a jackal's head rather than that of a man in headdress. This head, Jilo suspected the original, was much larger than the one she'd seen in pictures. It seemed to suit the body much better, both in size and in composition. Jilo realized the familiar human face must have been hewn from this canine head.

"I suspect that you," Ginny said as Jilo watched the energy drain from the pool and coil up through the Great Pyramid, "are part of a planned assault against the safety net of magic we've woven. You have been created as part of the outsiders' attempt to collapse the line." The power shot up through the pyramid's golden apex, but then turned, spinning in on itself, weaving a net of energy that stretched out in less than a blink of an eye to surround the entire globe. Then the light faded from sight.

"Not all were shut out by the barrier we raised. There were a few outsiders, functionaries and bureaucrats, here to see to the final stages of the operation. They were trapped within the boundary of the line. Most were captured. Executed. But a few escaped, and those few began working to create a new kind of witch, one to whom they could give magic—or take it away—however it suited their cause. I fear you might be one of their creations, no more to them than an appliance waiting to be connected to the power supply of their choice. Within each race, on each corner of the globe, throughout time, they have placed a weapon such as yourself in preparation to put their plan in motion. They intend to turn you all on when it suits them, cause the line to falter, and finish the job they set out to do when the witches first rebelled. I have no idea how this might connect to the Beekeeper, but I'm sure it's why you caught her attention. It would seem that even among your peers, there's something special about you. That you might have a pivotal role to play."

"But that's ridiculous. I wouldn't help them. And if you witches still exist, certainly you must be capable of maintaining the protections you created."

"Not all the witches want to keep the line. They resent that we're not so special anymore, that we're no longer the masters of this world the way we were when we served the outsiders. Some witches want to bring the line down, strip this world, and flee into the sky to join their masters. Help them spread the contamination of colonialism from world to world, star to star."

"Well, they can't make me help them. I won't help them."

"You must never practice magic," Ginny said, her words a warning, "not even the charlatan tricks Mother Jilo has been peddling. Now that you're connected to the Beekeeper, you'll find her magic may just rise up in you even if you're only attempting a ruse. And if that happens, you'll begin to draw attention, unfriendly attention, to yourself."

"Or maybe," Jilo said, her ire stirring at being told what she was and was not to do, "if this Beekeeper is on my side, I should start practicing magic in a grand way. If you witches are so afraid of her, sounds to me like I can handle any 'attention' you all care to throw my way."

Ginny stiffened. "Of course, that would be your choice. But it might cause far more harm than you could even guess."

"I," Jilo straightened her spine, "will worry about the harm I do after I know my own family is safe." She raised her hand, shaking it in anger. "You're telling me to hide. To keep my head low. To pray that no one takes notice. Well, I've had enough of living that way, Miss Almighty Taylor. Maybe you should try it for a change." The two women stood facing each other for several moments, their eyes locked together.

Ginny flinched first. "Don't ever let me off easy," she said, and Jilo was surprised to see a smile building on her face. "Stand up to me. I'll need that more from you now than ever." Her smile pulled into a tight, straight line, and her gaze sharpened. "There's one more thing, though. Something I think you should know about your Beekeeper. Then, if you choose to use the magic she's offering, so be it."

Jilo nodded. "All right, I'm listening."

Ginny's gaze fell to the floor, giving Jilo the impression that the other woman felt ashamed by what she was about to relate. "The Maguire family has been influential in this state for generations now, and my family has long been aware of Maguire and his activities." She paused, her gaze drifting up to meet Jilo's, an unspoken request for forgiveness. "But we did nothing, as . . ."

"As his crimes didn't touch you."

Ginny didn't try to defend herself or her family. She nodded. "But that isn't all. You see, after the war, we thought he'd lost all access to magic, but up until just before the war, Maguire was a collector, a practitioner of blood magic." She paused. "A servant of the Red King, and by extension, of the Beekeeper herself." She gave Jilo a moment to drink in her words. "Your magic," she continued, "his magic, are of the same source."

Jilo's mind flashed to the wreck that had taken Guy's life only days after she and Tinker had made a deal with the Red King to save him. She had no doubt the report had it right when it said drugs and alcohol had played a role in the crash. But the paper got it wrong when they called the wreck an accident. Jilo felt certain that in some fiery hell, the Red King and his mother were laughing at her gullibility. Laughing at the bargain price she'd placed not only on her own soul, but on Tinker's as well.

"My nana," Jilo said, growing ice-cold in an instant, "kept a scrapbook on Maguire."

"That doesn't surprise me," Ginny said, again casting her glance downward. "It seems Maguire's relationship with your family goes back several generations." She halted, seeming to feel it was unnecessary to say more, but Jilo needed to hear the whole story. She needed to hear it spoken aloud.

"Go on."

"Maguire. He got his start in blood magic by willingly letting himself be possessed by a demon, a nasty piece of work called Barron. Maguire was the vessel by which the demon was brought from the old world to the new. And," she bit her lower lip, seeming to weigh her words, "the vessel that carried Maguire was his own ship. A ship he customarily used to transport human cargo."

"Damn him." The words came out as a reflex, without premeditation. But they felt so right, so good on the tip of her tongue. "Damn him," she said again, this time letting it take on the full weight of a curse.

"Yes," Ginny said, her voice tight, quiet, "damn him, indeed." She crossed the room to the kitchen's entrance. "I'll see myself out." She took a step, then turned back. "If you make a choice that puts the line in danger, I'll have no alternative but to act against you. But I promise to respect you. I'll never ask you to hide again."

"And I promise to never let you off easy," Jilo said, wishing there would come a day when she would truly be able to call this woman a friend.

"I've seen to it that the disappearance of the Maguires won't be traced back to you. Now I'm going to head out back and set a concealment spell on that little graveyard you've got hidden in the trees behind the house." Jilo gasped at her words. "You know, the one you've been trying not to think about," Ginny said, apparently by way of explanation. "Even if someone sees those dips forming in the ground, they'll take no notice." A smile twisted her lips. "I'm helping you hide the bodies, Jilo. If that doesn't make me a friend, I don't know what does."

THIRTEEN

My dearest Jilo,

I do so wish I could have been there to attend your wedding. This Tinker of yours sounds like a wonderful man, the kind of husband I'd always dreamed we'd both find. I can see from the snapshot you sent how deeply he loves you.

I understand your decision to retire Mother Jilo. It's for the best, I'm sure, what with Tinker being such a successful entrepreneur. Mother Jilo's activities might reflect poorly on his reputation with other businessmen. Still, a part of me will miss the old girl. The good Lord knows she took care of us when no one else would. Funny, isn't it, that I still think of her as being somehow separate from you, a distinct person in her own right. May the dear lady rest in peace.

You look so beautiful in the snapshot, and I'm going to risk that you will scowl at this page by saying you even look happy. You. Willy, too. He has found a home with you, and I thank you for caring for him. He's a special soul, our Willy.

And Robinson! He has grown so, since I last saw him. I'm happy he'll have Tinker as a father. Tinker seems like the kind of man who'll stay around, unlike Guy. I'm sorry. I shouldn't have written that. I should tear this page up and start over, but, well, perhaps it's better you know how I felt about Guy. It may help you to understand how I've come to feel about my own husband.

Edwin's changed since Juliette was born. He's so distant. Resentful is the word that comes to mind. Always finding excuses to be out, away. He tells me he's looking for work, but I know he spends his days in bars and most nights in the *boîtes de nuit*, as they call the clubs here. As you know, Edwin's father has cut him off from the family trust and other sources that might have helped make our existence easier. I swear, we would starve if it weren't for his sister Ginny's kindness. I'm sorry. I meant this to be a congratulatory letter, not one for a newspaper's agony aunt.

No more words, only my love.

Your sister, Binah

May 4, 1959

My dearest Jilo,

The cord has been pulled tight, past the breaking point. I'm laughing and crying as I write you. It's all such a sad and embarrassing cliché. Edwin has been gone a week now. Gone without warning, having told me he was going out for cigarettes—yes, cigarettes.

He evidently prefers a brand sold only in America, for that is where he's gone. It's far too comical, really. A night and a day passed without word from him, then a strange man, a man with a briefcase full of documents for my signature, knocked at our door.

Edwin has returned to Savannah, and is, as I write this, probably readjusting to the luxuries he so sorely missed during our time together. He can salve whatever conscience he may still possess with the knowledge that his family has agreed to support us financially—I'll never have to worry about money again, and though I know you have Tinker to help provide for you, neither will you. I can see to that.

In exchange for their largesse, the Taylors demand that I never reveal my marriage to Edwin to anyone. There will be no divorce. It seems a divorce decree would just be another piece of evidence that could one day be used to sully the prodigal son's soon-to-be-rehabilitated reputation.

Nor can I identify Edwin as Juliette's father. They insist we no longer use the Taylor name, so from now on we will live as Binah and Juliette Wills. (I hope your father will look kindly down upon us.) I assume this same prohibition will extend to our unborn child, too—yes, I'm sorry to bury this news in with the rest, I am pregnant again—once they learn of his or her existence. If it is a boy, I'll name him Jude. I hope it's a boy, though I don't know why, growing up as he will, without his father. I hadn't even found a way to tell Edwin I'm pregnant again, but if he could leave his firstborn, a second child probably wouldn't have swayed his decision.

I know you're hoping that I'll come home now, but they won't allow that. I must never set foot again in the state of Georgia, let alone Savannah. But that's all right. I'm going to head north, and I hope, in time, I can convince you and Tinker to join me. Paris is a museum, and Savannah is a graveyard, but things are happening in Detroit. That place is alive. I'm going to take this fortune of blood money I'm receiving from the Taylors, and though I'll never see Savannah again, I will use it to see to it that Edwin will never be able to forget me or his children.

They want to hide me and my children from the world, but I will see to it that we're hidden in plain sight. And Jilo, my dearest sister, don't worry about me, as I am going to make this world mine. I love you.

Your sister, Binah

May 1959

Jilo stood before the Taylors' enormous house, a well-maintained Victorian that took up the better part of the city block, by far the largest house in the immediate area. The house struck Jilo like an oversized and overly adorned princess surrounded by crumbling ladies-in-waiting. Jilo clutched her sister's letter to her breast, waiting to confront Edwin with it. She'd read the letter over and over, unfolded and folded it so many times that the creases had cut through the words, angry tears, and the sweat from her hand causing Binah's careful script to blur and run. She had stood before the house for an hour now, determined to catch that son of a bitch Taylor boy either coming or going, hoping he wouldn't be coward enough to slip out through the back.

But he may have done just that. Weak and soft, he'd make a tasty morsel for the Red King, one she'd gladly offer up without asking for anything in return. She felt the Beekeeper's untapped magic rising up in her like sap, begging her to release it on the residents of this turreted monstrosity.

There hadn't been a single sign of movement the entire time she'd stood there, but finally she saw the edge of a curtain pull back. A few moments later, the front door eased open a crack, then closed tight. Perhaps another five minutes or so passed before the door opened again, emitting a sturdy woman with red hair and freckles. Her gray uniform and apron revealed her as the Taylors' domestic. The woman cast a cautious eye down each side of the street, then closed the door behind her and scurried across the street to Jilo's side.

"May I help you?" the maid asked.

Jilo never took her eye off the house. She saw the curtain move once again, and a lovely face peered out. Sun lit up the blonde hair framing the face, then the curtain winked closed.

"I'd like to speak to Mr. Taylor. Mr. Edwin Taylor, please." She nearly choked as she used a title of respect for the boy.

The maid flushed red. "I'm sorry," she said, "but I don't see how that is appropriate." Jilo finally turned to face the maid. She came close to explaining to this blotchy creature just how appropriate her request was, but the fear in the woman's eyes stopped her. She wasn't a Taylor, she merely worked for them, her experience probably not so different from what Jilo's nana's had been when she worked at the old Pinnacle. "Mr. Edwin doesn't make decisions about hiring for the household, and I can assure you we're fully staffed. There are no openings."

"I'm not looking for employment," Jilo said, and the woman relaxed a bit. Perhaps she was only worried about a perceived threat to her position. "Please, if you will just tell Mr. Taylor that Jilo is here. He'll know me. He"—she prepared herself to lie—"will want to speak with me."

The maid hesitated for just long enough to arouse the curiosity of the woman who was still peeking out from behind the drapery. The door opened, and the woman whose lovely face Jilo had seen shining from behind the pane stepped out. "Is there a problem, Coleen?" she called out, her voice pristine, sweet. The perfect voice to sing lullabies.

The maid—Jilo surmised named Coleen—sprinted back to her mistress. Jilo watched the maid's animated gestures, obviously intended to persuade the young miss to go back inside. To Jilo's surprise, it was the maid who found herself shooed away. The young blonde stood on the doorstep for a moment, seeming to consider Jilo. Jilo felt a sensation almost like a tickle as the beautiful blonde witch—yes, witch, the magic in Jilo sensed the magic in her—with the long neck and clear eyes took Jilo's measure from a distance. What she read, how much she understood, Jilo didn't know, but the odd prickling stopped, and the beauty strode with a practiced grace down the steps and across the street to Jilo.

"What business do you have with my fiancé?"

Her question struck Jilo as hard as a slap. She staggered back a few steps and placed her hand, still holding Binah's letter, against her temple.

"Are you quite all right? Do you need to sit down?" The young woman grasped Jilo's free hand, wrapping an arm beneath hers to support her. "Would you like some water?" Jilo wondered that this usurper should seem so kind, so gentle, so honestly concerned about Jilo's well-being. Jilo froze and turned to look into the woman's sweet eyes. Could she be as innocent as Binah had been? Was she unaware of the situation she was walking into? Jilo fingered the letter in her hand, wondering if she should simply hand it over to the young woman and walk away. Let Binah's words save this girl from making a huge mistake.

"Come into the kitchen," the woman said, guiding Jilo across the street toward the Taylors' house. They got as far as the lowest step, but then the woman stopped, seeming to remember herself. "Well, of course, you'll have to go in the back way," she said, releasing Jilo's arm and motioning toward a stone pathway that led around the house. "I'll go tell Coleen to see to your needs."

"No," Jilo said, causing Edwin's new woman to startle. *Let this buckra woman sleep in the bed she'd made for herself.* "No," she said again, this time her voice coming out softer. "I'm fine now. I apologize for being a nuisance." She spun on her heel and began walking away, moving as fast as her feet could carry her.

"Wait," the woman called. "You wanted to speak to Edwin. It seemed like it might be an important matter." Jilo felt the tingling sensation begin again, this time around her temples. She knew the witch was making a weak and clumsy attempt to see her thoughts. Somehow, without fully understanding how she'd known to do it, Jilo slammed a heavy curtain down between them. The young witch stammered. "He isn't here right now, but I'll pass on a message if you'd like."

Jilo turned back. "No, ma'am. That isn't necessary. But your kindness is much appreciated."

"Are you sure?" the woman said, her tone growing anxious.

"All right then, ma'am. Please tell him Juliette asked me to say hello to him when I passed by." Jilo headed west, determined never to lay eyes on this house again.

FOURTEEN

"Who is she?" Jilo asked as Ginny came down the sidewalk toward her. Jilo had been waiting on a porch swing outside of a strange house a bit south of Forsyth Park for a good hour, right out there for God and anyone else to see. Damn the Taylors. Damn their secrets. And damn any buckra fool who'd complain about her sitting there.

Ginny stopped before mounting the steps, casting Jilo a look of disappointment. "You used your magic to find me." Jilo didn't deny it. She'd known Ginny was away from the big house. That part wasn't magic—deep down, she didn't think Ginny would have left her standing out there like that. Jilo had to believe that despite her brother's actions, Ginny herself had a shred of decency in her. So, yes, she'd used her magic, as much out of rebellion against these damned witches as from a desire to learn what had happened, and what was going to happen, from Ginny.

"I asked you who she was," Jilo said, keeping her voice firm.

Ginny climbed the steps and stood before her. Holding a hand out in front of her, she announced in a stentorian voice, "Mr. and Mrs. Oliver Taylor of Savannah"—Ginny was being so loud that, in spite of her earlier resolve, Jilo glanced around her shoulders to see if anyone was near—"are pleased to announce the engagement of their son Edwin to Miss Adeline Rose Connelly. Miss Connelly, a graduate of the internationally renowned Institut Alpin finishing school, is the daughter of Riley and Marguerite Connelly of Richmond, Virginia. A date has not yet been set." She lowered her hand and turned toward the house's door. "There, satisfied?"

She opened the door and stepped through. Jilo expected Ginny to slam the door behind herself, but instead she called out, "Are you coming in or not?"

Jilo rose and took a few cautious steps toward the opening. Ginny stood in the hall with her hands on her hips. As Jilo stepped over the threshold, Ginny raised her hands and motioned around the space. "Like it? It's mine. All mine. Not my daddy's, not my mama's. Mine. Close the door behind you, please." Jilo did as she was asked, and Ginny flipped on an overhead light.

Seemingly intent on providing Jilo with a tour of the place, Ginny raised her hands and turned a full circle. "The foyer," Ginny said, referring to a wide, but altogether ordinary, hallway. Ginny pointed toward the entrance, and Jilo followed Ginny's gesture to an old-style chair that sat right inside the door. "It's a Savery." Ginny nodded at the blank wall facing the chair. "Of course it's posing me a bit of a problem as I have a smaller work on paper by Rothko I'd intended for that very spot, but then I found the chair and began questioning . . ."

"I don't mean to be rude, but I didn't come here to discuss decorating."

Ginny shook her head. "No, I know you didn't. It's only I was thinking how much you and I are like that chair and the painting. Both," she said, brushing past Jilo and placing a hand on the back of the chair, "of the highest quality." She turned back to Jilo. "But so very different in our design." She held a hand out to Jilo, but Jilo couldn't bring herself to take it. Ginny let it fall back to her side. "I wasn't allowed to hang the painting in my father's house, but this house belongs to me. There's room, and respect, for both Savery and Rothko in this house." She cast a glance back up to the wall. "Oh dear," she said, "would I be ruining my metaphor if I said I just decided that is entirely the wrong place for the Rothko?" She pursed her lips for a moment, then turned back to Jilo. "I'll just leave that spot open for now, till the right work comes along." She did an about-face and led the way into a sitting room on the left side of the hall.

Jilo stepped into the room, taking in the unexpected juxtaposition of antique furniture and cubist art. A sound caught her attention, and she turned to face a clock on the mantle that struck off each second, loud enough to wake the dead. Ginny motioned toward the sofa. As Jilo obeyed her unspoken request, Ginny crossed the room and retrieved a bottle of amber liquid from an unlocked tantalus. "Do you like scotch?"

Jilo shrugged. "Never tasted it."

"Then you don't like scotch," Ginny said, pulling out the stopper and filling two tumblers almost to the rim. "But you're going to learn to." She crossed the room to Jilo and held one of the glasses out to her. Jilo took the drink, watching as Ginny swept her skirt to the side, bent her knees in a smooth, though Jilo reckoned practiced, motion, and sat down next to her on the sofa. "Until then, at least it'll dull the pain." She tipped the tumbler to her lips, downing a third in one draft. "So, how is Binah? Are she and Juliette settled?"

Jilo brought the tumbler up to her nose, uncertain she wanted to taste the witch's brew it contained, uncertain she wanted to discuss Binah and her daughter with the sister of the man who'd wronged them. She took a taste of the scotch, almost coughing it back up. "That is vile."

Ginny nodded and clinked her glass against Jilo's. "Finish it. Doctor's orders."

Jilo took another sip. Prepared, this time, she managed to choke it down, appreciating the pleasant warmth flowing through her. "She's got some crazy idea, Binah. Gonna take up singing. Like our mama did."

"Doesn't sound so crazy to me. Binah's got a beautiful voice. And she's a beautiful woman."

"A beautiful woman who's also a mother."

"Oh," Ginny said with a laugh. "She can afford help to watch over Juliette." She took another deep gulp, grimacing and closing her eyes. When she reopened them, they were filled with fire. "I saw to that. I'll be damned if our niece doesn't get the best of everything."

"Our niece," Jilo said, taking a quick and pleasant sip of her drink, "and the one who's on the way." Ginny's eyes flashed in surprise. Jilo nodded, pleased that she had managed to withhold a secret from this woman who seemed to read her every thought—until she was ready for that secret to be revealed.

"You've learned how to block me out, haven't you?" Ginny raised her glass in salute. "I should be worried, but truth is, I'm a bit proud." Her brow furrowed. "So my brother is to be a father again," she said. Jilo nodded again. "God, I already regret the devil's bargain I made with my kith and kin."

"Bargain?" Jilo felt her spine stiffening.

"Yes, my silence in exchange for the fortune paid to your sister." She gave Jilo a sideways glance. "Notice the word 'small' wasn't part of that sentence." She tilted her tumbler to her lips, draining the rest of her drink. "Now I just wish I'd pushed for double." She rose and reached out for Jilo's glass. "Let me top that off for you."

- — -

Over the last year, Jilo had gotten into the habit of avoiding the stretch of Ogeechee Road that passed by the cemetery, even though it often meant adding a mile or more to her journey. Each time she passed the cemetery, her mind's eye would envision the family she'd been led to believe were her flesh and blood, sitting there side-by-side in lacquered white rocking chairs. Together they would rock, taking their ease in the shade of the large oaks, shaking their heads as one at the mess she'd made of things. Maybe it was only the Dutch courage of Ginny's scotch, but today, she finally felt ready to face them.

She paused, but only for a moment, as she passed beneath the gate. It felt foolish. Coming here to confront people who were dead and buried. Just a couple of years ago, she would've considered it a mad waste of time. The dead were dead, she'd thought, not listening, and certainly not capable of talking back. She knew better now. Sometimes dead didn't mean gone. Perhaps it was this knowledge that kept her feet on the marked path, following the circuitous route rather than cutting straight over strangers' graves to where her nana and the man she still thought of as her father lay buried.

Soon she stood before their graves. There were no rockers. No disapproving stares. There were only four stones in a row. The leftmost was her nana's, and next to it was the oldest of the four, honoring Reuben Wills, the averred grandfather she'd never met. To Jilo's right lay Jesse Wills, a man she only remembered from photographs, gone as he was before she could walk, and beside him, Tuesday Jackson, her nana's mother, related to her, Jilo sensed, through inherited magic, if not by blood. She let her gaze return, right to left, over their stones before coming to rest on the newest of the granite quartet.

She walked up to the foot of the grave. "You could've warned me of what I'd be up against, old woman." The words came out angry, sharp. Instantly she felt a pang of regret. "I'm sorry. I know you were only trying to protect me. I just wish you'd let me know what you were protecting me from."

"Not to worry, dearie," a voice came from beside her.

Jilo startled. A moment before, she'd been alone. Now a veiled form swayed next to her.

"She can't hear you. None of them can. They're all at rest. You can thank me for that, you know." The black lace shroud billowed up around the specter even though the wind was still. "You took long enough to come find me."

"I didn't come for you . . ." Her first impulse was to flee, but she felt caught in the Beekeeper's gravity.

"And yet you knew you'd find me here. I waited for you to come. Willingly. I did not search you out or force my presence on you." She took a few sashaying steps back, then spun around and reached out to caress Jilo's cheek before dancing away again. "No matter what lie you've been telling yourself, I was the one you were avoiding. And I am the one you've come to see."

Jilo shook herself. She ran her hand over her cheek to wipe away the sensation of the Beekeeper's touch. "No. You're the liar. You're a trickster. You and your 'sons.' You deceived me. Tricked me into letting you have influence over me. And Tinker." Guilt nearly knocked the wind out of her. She struggled to catch her breath. "God, Tinker. I helped you tarnish one of the purest souls ever to walk this earth."

"My, my, listen to you now, you ungrateful child. *God. Souls.* You are indeed a preacher's daughter." She paused, as if to make sure Jilo had felt the sting. "Perhaps," her tone changed, sounding of regret now rather than venom, "I am a liar, but when all is illusion, only the trickster speaks the truth." A gloved hand extended toward her. It held a bottle. A conciliatory gesture. "Rum?" she offered. Jilo didn't budge. She could feel the creature's disappointment at her refusal turn to anger. "Unless, of course"—the sharpness returned to her speech—"you've already had too much of that prig of a witch's brew." She lowered the bottle. "Shame, she has to die as she does, our poor Ginny. I've grown rather fond of her, now that we've gotten to know her."

"You won't harm her." Without thinking, Jilo advanced on the Beekeeper, only then realizing that a ball of blue lightning, unbidden magic, had formed in her hands, ready to shoot out and destroy the interloper. "You won't harm anyone I love ever again."

"Very good. Very good, dearie. You were indeed made for magic." She leaned back as if she were admiring a work of art. "But can you really believe that little spark is going to do you any good against me?" The Beekeeper waved her free hand in a circular motion and laughed as Jilo's magic took the shape of a hummingbird and flitted away. "You are but the lightning, dearie. I am the storm." She swept away her veil, and Jilo stood there staring into the face of the void.

For a moment Jilo felt like she was lost in that unending emptiness. No, not lost. Searching. Searching for something important. *Someone* important. A girl. *A girl who could never exist.*

"Yes, you're the one, all right."

Jilo found herself at the foot of her nana's grave again as the Beekeeper tilted the bottle high. When she pulled the bottle away, the veil fell back into place, once again creating the illusion of features behind it. "The girl in the darkness. You two are so damned linked together, I don't think the one of you could exist without the other."

"I have no idea . . ." Jilo began, but the creature rushed up to her. Her veil puffed out, as if she'd just exhaled a heavy breath. The creature began sashaying, rum sloshing from the bottle she held at a careless angle. "She's awakening. She's awakening," she said, at first chanting the word, then nearly singing it. The creature reached out with her free hand and lifted the skirt of her garment. She began swinging in mad and widening circles, singing out the word "awakening" over and over again till it lost all meaning, till it became nothing more than the drone of a thousand wings.

Jilo couldn't bear another moment of this madness. "What do you want with me?" she screamed, causing the weird woman to stop short.

"I want you to join in the dance, dearie. That's all I've ever wanted." She sent the bottle crashing against Tuesday's stone, and though the shards of glass remained to bear witness of her presence, the Beekeeper herself was gone.

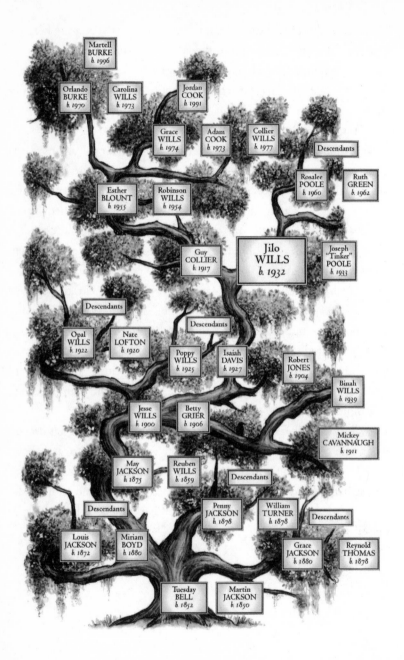

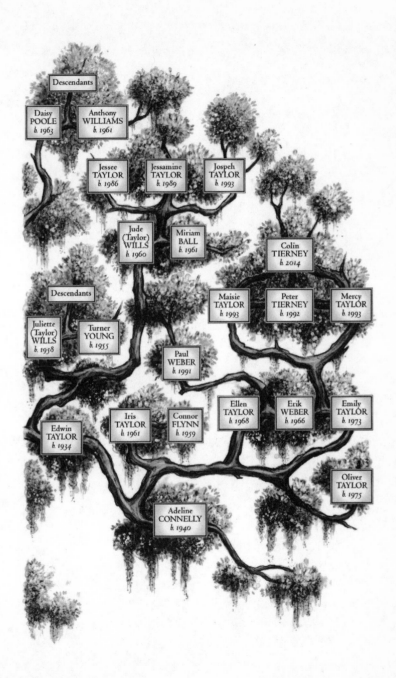

Descendants

Daisy
POOLE
b. 1963

Anthony
WILLIAMS
b. 1961

Jessee
TAYLOR
b. 1986

Jessamine
TAYLOR
b. 1989

Jospeh
TAYLOR
b. 1993

Jude
(Taylor)
WILLS
b. 1960

Miriam
BALL
b. 1961

Colin
TIERNEY
b. 2014

Descendants

Maisie
TAYLOR
b. 1993

Peter
TIERNEY
b. 1992

Mercy
TAYLOR
b. 1993

Juliette
(Taylor)
WILLS
b. 1958

Turner
YOUNG
b. 1955

Paul
WEBER
b. 1991

Iris
TAYLOR
b. 1961

Connor
FLYNN
b. 1959

Ellen
TAYLOR
b. 1968

Erik
WEBER
b. 1966

Emily
TAYLOR
b. 1973

Edwin
TAYLOR
b. 1934

Oliver
TAYLOR
b. 1975

Adeline
CONNELLY
b. 1940

EPILOGUE

The Savannah Morning Star
January 1, 1960
Page B1

Connelly, Taylor Wed at Midnight Service

As church bells and fireworks announced the dawn of a new decade in Savannah, Edwin Taylor and Adeline Connelly were married at the stroke of midnight in an opulent ceremony attended by many of our fair city's premier citizens. The bride eschewed the recently popular tea-length dress for a Paris original (see photos above and Page B5) featuring a flaring, ankle-length skirt. When asked about the unusual timing of her nuptials, the bride commented . . . (Story continues Page B5.)

JILO

Sapelo Island—March 1960

Tinker didn't need to open his eyes to know his wife had already risen. Their bed was too narrow for two bodies to sleep without touching, especially now that Jilo's belly hung low and hard and round. The baby was taking its own good time to come into the world. Way things were going lately, Tinker couldn't say he blamed her . . . or possibly him. The women all had their opinions on the sex of the child. Baby hanging low, said some, gonna be a boy. Others insisted it was a girl because when a needle was hung suspended over Jilo's stomach, it always swung left.

Tinker had learned to listen to his wife's intuition. She didn't share her private thoughts often, so when she did, he paid attention. Jilo said it would be a girl. Said the little one had told her so herself. Wanted them to name her Rosalee. They'd both already started referring to the little one by that name. As for Tinker himself, well, he didn't give a damn. Boy, girl, didn't matter. He was gonna love that child no matter what. Loved its mama too much to feel otherwise.

Tinker let one eye pop open, only to discover the room was still full dark. He let the other eye open to serve as a second witness. He pushed himself up on his elbows and listened, hoping to hear any signs of movement, but the only sound that met his ears was Robinson's steady breathing. A pang of worry struck him, and he swung his legs out of bed, resting his feet on the cool wood floor. He found his way to the window and pulled the curtain to the side. Still full dark out there, too.

Feral hogs wandered the island. Poisonous snakes were plentiful. It seemed that nothing on God's green earth frightened that woman, which made Tinker proud, anxious, and angry all in the same instant. He'd fought too hard to find her, to turn her heart toward his own. He was not gonna lose her to some preventable tragedy. It was one thing for Jilo to wander off by herself during the day, but heading out before the sunrise? That he truly wished she wouldn't do. He'd talk to her once again of his worries, founded or not, and hope that this time her stubborn streak would let her hear how afraid he was for her.

Most men would have simply put their foot down, forbid their wives to go off wandering in the wee hours, but he knew better than to try that with Jilo. Heck, Tinker wouldn't want a woman who'd let him boss her around. Not Tinker. He liked his women with a bit of spine, and the woman he'd found had plenty of it. Stubborn, proud, on her worst day twice as smart as he was on his best. The very things that caused him to worry over her were some of the same characteristics that made him love her so. She combined all these impossible traits with being strong, brave, and having the kindest heart he'd ever known.

He had brought her down to the island to get her out of Savannah during that Taylor fool's wedding. It had been a feat to drag her here, kicking and screaming, to this small house his family owned on the island, but as soon as they began to cross the sound, a change had come over her. He'd watched as the tension fell from her shoulders, listened as her laughter came, and came easily. This small stretch of land, barely a stone's throw from the mainland, seemed to bring her a sense of peace. What had been intended as a week's vacation had turned to two, then three. Jilo seemed so happy here, he kept finding excuses to put off their return to Savannah. Her lack of objection told him it was right.

Every three or four days, he'd cross back over to the mainland, use the telephone in Meridian to check in with the men he'd left in charge of his stores, handle any odds and ends that came up, then he'd get right back into his borrowed bateau and go home to his wife and children, born and unborn, adopted and natural. They were his. All three of them.

He was taking advantage of the free time this long stay had given him to take Willy in hand. Tinker had known boys like him before. He wasn't fool enough to think he could change Willy, and besides, he loved the boy exactly as he was, but he would be good and goddamned if he didn't teach Willy how to fight. The day those sons of bitches forced his car off the road, he'd stayed conscious only long enough to watch as Willy was dragged, defenseless, from the car. Nope. Never again. He was Willy's papa now—he didn't care if he was only a dozen or so years older than him—and that boy was gonna be nobody's victim. He felt the anger steal over him again, and the Red King's mark twitched, prodding him, encouraging him to commit violence. He drew a breath, then shrugged his shoulders to make them relax. The mark was fading, had been since the day the Red King placed it there. In time, with enough prayer and good works, Tinker hoped the good Lord would take it from him. For now, he'd make sure he did nothing else to help it sink its roots deeper into his soul.

He lit the kerosene lamp and cast a glance at Robinson, still dead to the world, his peaceful expression helping to calm Tinker's spirit. He rose and dressed, then carefully carried the sleeping Robinson under one arm into the kitchen where they'd set up a cot for Willy. He set the lamp on the table and then nudged the cot with his knee. "Here," he said, "take care of your brother." A groggy Willy reached up and pulled the boy into his embrace.

Tinker passed by the table and blew out the lamp's flame. His eyes struggled to readjust to the dark. Life was kind of like that—it was a constant back-and-forth between moments where everything seemed so clear, so perfect, and those in which a man was left to grope around in the dark, nothing to guide him but the few familiar objects found by his own fumbling hands.

He found his way out to the house's main room, then crept out the door. When they'd arrived here, the small front porch had been sagging, but he'd spent two afternoons replacing the rotting boards and bad brace. Now the porch was set to face another decade or so of whatever Mother Nature had to throw at it. He chuckled to himself. Might even outlast the rest of the house.

He stepped off the porch and turned to the east. The sky overhead was changing. The deep black-blue of nighttime was giving way to the color of fresh plums. Though the tall pines blocked his view, he knew a strip of red would soon form on the horizon, and the entire sky would catch fire. He passed around the side of the house, heading south to find the thin stretch of land that cut across the marshes and led to the beach.

As he made his way along the trail, the bushes began to shake. Two whitetail deer burst out of the growth and turned to run on ahead of him. As they faded into the distance, he found himself humming Binah's song, "Come Some Sunny Day." Binah was living the life of a queen up there in Detroit. He'd meant to tell Jilo he'd heard it on the radio again, playing in the store in Meridian when he went to call Savannah, but the song's hit status had come to seem like old news now that radio stations, white and black, all around the country had begun to play it.

"*Beneath your feet and always faithful, like your shadow on the floor . . .*" he sang the song's opening lyrics, though not loudly. It was the crack of dawn, and no one was in sight, but he still didn't want to risk being heard. He wasn't a singer, not like his sister-in-law. That girl had a voice. She'd cut her record soon after landing in the Motor City. She'd written Jilo to say she'd recorded the whole song barefoot, her feet swollen from pregnancy. Jude Wills had been born soon after. When she performed for folks now, Binah always kicked off her shoes before singing "Come Some Sunny Day," because it just didn't feel the same if she tried to sing it with her feet bound.

"She's a star!" Willy had exclaimed the first time the family listened to the song together.

"She always was," Jilo responded. Tinker knew his wife took great pleasure in the knowledge that everywhere that Taylor boy went, Binah's voice was there to remind him of his foolishness. She took a bit less pleasure in knowing Binah had gone to the trouble of tracking down their mama Betty. Even though Binah hadn't laid eyes on the woman since she was an infant, she'd taken Betty in and showered her with every luxury. Their mama, Jilo sometimes groused, had found a way to live her dreams through her abandoned daughter. Still, with each letter, each phone call from Binah, he could see Jilo was softening. Someday she might actually take hold of the receiver when it was Betty on the other end of the line.

As he drew near the beach, the sound of the crashing surf inspired him to sing out louder, but the sight of his beautiful wife, all done up like a morning glory in hues of purple and blue, the sweet darkness of her features set aglow by the red-and-orange dawn, made him fall silent.

Jilo wandered along the white sand, dyed rosy by the first light of day, both hands over her round stomach. Another conversation, he reckoned, with Miss Rosalee.

For a moment, he felt like he was intruding. He was about to turn now that he knew she was safe, head home and leave her to her private thoughts, but she stopped and turned to look at him, like something had alerted her to his presence. She raised both hands and waved him forward, welcoming him to join her.

His heart filled with so much love, he wasn't sure he'd be able to take a single step, but still he felt his body begin to jog along, his shoes, meant for city streets, digging down into the loose sand, grains of it kicking up and grinding into his socks. He didn't care. He kept trotting along, and soon, the wet, compacted sand helped carry him to her side.

The wind was whipping so, he worried she'd catch her death. He shrugged off his coat and wrapped it around her, then draped his arm over her shoulders and pulled her to him. When he leaned over to place a kiss on the top of her head, she raised her face to him, offering him her lips. He smiled and kissed that beautiful, smart mouth. A little fire lit in her eyes—passion, love, and her own brand of sauciness.

He could have held her there forever, but all too soon she slipped from his embrace, leaving him to trudge behind her as she continued north along the glistening sand, not stopping till she reached the beached remains of a fallen oak, its branches missing, its tangle of roots bleached bone white by sea and sun. He held back, watching, positioning himself just far enough away that he could take the whole of her in.

She traced her finger along a blanched root, then turned to face the sea.

"Thank you for this," she said, without ever taking her eyes from the whitecaps breaking on the surf. Her words were nearly lost in the roar of the wind.

He drew nearer to her. "For what, my love?" He wanted to know the specifics of what pleased her, 'cause he wanted to make sure he kept on giving it to her.

"This place. Our time here." He began that instant to calculate what it would take for him to move here and make this place that pleased Jilo her permanent home, when she spoke again. "I've been thinking about the students they arrested in Savannah."

Tinker was taken aback. "I didn't realize you were paying attention to the goings-on there." A couple of days earlier black students had been arrested for demanding service at downtown Savannah lunch counters, but he hadn't realized his wife knew. He hadn't said anything, not wanting to upset her this close to Rosalee's delivery.

Jilo glanced over her shoulder at him, a smile on her lips. "I'm always paying attention." She turned back to the sight of seagulls soaring above and swooping down into the sea. She stretched out her hands, like she was trying to catch the rising sun, then wrapped her arms around herself. "The baby's not coming yet. Rosalee says she won't be ready for a week or two." She paused and looked back at him. "It's time we got back, Tinker. It's taken its own sweet time, but the world's getting ready to change. I can feel it, as sure as I feel that sun on my skin and the wind on my face."

Tinker could resist no longer. He reached out and pulled her into a tight embrace, her back pressing up against him. "It isn't gonna happen overnight," he said, "and it isn't going to happen easy. There are too many people out there who like things just fine as they have been." He let his voice drop. "Too many people out there who'd even like to turn back to the way it was before."

She pulled free of his grasp and turned to face him. "And that's why we have to go back." He could see the fire building in her eyes. "I'm no fool. I know the kind of evil we're facing won't disappear overnight. Hell, it may never die away at all. At least not completely." Her sweet face hardened, a tiny line forming between her brows, and her eyes narrowed. "I'm not saying we're going back so we can deliver the children into a land of milk and honey. I'm saying it's time we take them back to the real world, so they can learn how to fight."

Damn, how he loved this woman. He pulled her close and nuzzled his wind-chilled nose against her ear. "Are you ready, then? Ready to go back to Savannah?" He leaned back and craned his neck, so that he could better see her face.

Jilo glanced up at him, her eyes warm, full of confidence, full of love. She nodded. "Yes," she said, her voice soft in the rasping wind, "I believe I am."

A seagull screeched and barreled down to touch the sea, pulling up as it brushed the crest of a wave. Jilo patted his forearms, signaling him to release her. He did so, even though he sure hated letting go. She stepped out of his embrace and walked a few paces away before turning back and extending her hand to him. He trotted to her side and took her hand in his.

"Hell," she said as she turned inland, leading him home, "I know I am."

Afterword

Even though some portions of this book were inspired by the customs and history of the Gullah/Geechee people, this book remains a work of fiction. The Gullah/Geechee Sea Island Coalition is an organization that not only serves as a reference for an accurate history of the Gullah/Geechee people, but also fights to keep Gullah/Geechee historic traditions alive. To learn more about the Gullah/Geechee culture—and what you can do to help preserve it—please contact the Gullah/Geechee Sea Island Coalition.

Gullah/Geechee Sea Island Coalition
Post Office Box 1207
St. Helena Island SC 29920

www.gullahgeechee.net
Email: GullGeeCo@aol.com

ACKNOWLEDGMENTS

This book was a team effort, and I have so many people to thank: Kristen Weber for her early comments. Jason Kirk for his guidance, patience, kindness, and commitment. (I should probably mention his patience twice.) Angela Polidoro for her insight and mad editing skills. Sybil Ward, Sarah Ham, and eagle-eyed Pat Allen Werths, three of the best beta readers an author could ever hope for. James Caskey, for his willingness time and again to help track down increasingly recondite facts about Savannah. (James writes great true ghost stories. Trust me. Check out his books.) Of course my furry coauthors, Duke and Sugar, for the cuddles. And again, Rich Weissman for playing Willy to my Colette on this one. It would've never come together without his unwavering belief in this book and its author.

Finally, I would like to thank Queen Quet of the Gullah/Geechee Nation for her kind guidance on how to become a contributor rather than an exploiter.

ABOUT THE AUTHOR

J.D. Horn was raised in rural Tennessee and has carried a bit of its red clay with him while traveling the world, from Hollywood to Paris to Tokyo. He studied comparative literature as an undergrad, focusing on French and Russian in particular. He also holds an MBA in international business and worked as a financial analyst before becoming a novelist. Along with his spouse, Rich, and his furry coauthors, Duke and Sugar, he divides his time between Black Butte Ranch, Oregon, and San Francisco, California.